Opening Day

A novel by Ernie Koepf

ISBN: 978-1-09833-691-2 (print)
ISBN: 978-1-09833-692-9 (eBook)

BookBaby Publishing

Photo credit:
Front cover: Mike Koepf
Back cover: Samantha Suda

It was the times; things were slow, and people accepted it. They slept good at night, they had their doors open, nobody broke into your house, the milkman came and delivered his milk, the bread was delivered; it was a different world.

We might think, "Hey, we got it made now", but- you gotta talk to those people, those people are all buried in Colma now-they're gone.

Those people had a way of life that was enjoyable. They had an association over there; they had something going like when you cut a pie at home on the table. Everybody was sure they got the same piece-nobody got the bigger one and nobody got the smaller one. Everybody was doing their thing and they were happy.

All they had to do was make 5-15 dollars every day and that was more than enough for them. And, they brought up 5-7 kids apiece! They were all dressed fine and fed well and everything was cool. Now, if you got three or four children, you might as well go sign up at the bank and say, 'Hey look, you gotta' do somethin', I'm not gonna make it'.

Today, if a guy starts out with a couple of hairs on his head, after he's 35, after what they gotta' go through now, they're wiped out! They're either bald or they're ready to drop.

Gimme my old way, I'm out of the business now. I'm happy, I take care of the boat- she took care of me.

—*Frank D'Amato, aka 'Green Crab', 2007*

Dedicated to all the men and women who love their boats and fish.

Life can only be understood backwards; but must be lived forward.

—*Soren Kierkegaard*

Opening Day

Opening Day

The year was 1961; the place was the West Coast. The tumult of the decade was not yet felt in the communities that listened to Frank Sinatra and had given their hearts and minds to the newly elected president, John F Kennedy. It could be said that one era was ending, and a new era was beginning. Most on the West Coast enjoyed a life of prosperity, or at least entertained a notion that their life would become prosperous eventually. But there were problems stewing in the nation that would soon come to define the decade. 400 US military personnel arrived in South Vietnam. Black activists and white students were beaten with axe handles by the white residents of Alabama. These events were the harbingers of much to follow in the ensuing years, but life was good now for the Skarsen family along the West Coast.

The well published space race was the most prominent event (besides girls) for 11-year-old Alex Skarsen. The pilots of Russia and the United States were blasting off their launching pads and headed for orbit in space. In April it was Yuri Gagarin of the USSR, claiming the title of the first man in space, closely followed a month later by Gus Grissom in a US spaceship. Alex had always assumed that it was a world of unlimited adventure and possibility and the reality of spaceships flying overhead monthly now confirmed it. On this early morning in 1961, Alex stood before the bathroom mirror and scrutinized his face. Pimples on his face were the only thing that was being confirmed daily on his personal planet. No evidence yet of facial hair, cruel puberty, not even evidence of a light mustache! Alex was more than ready to shed this boyhood skin and become a young man.

He was not going to school today and he was up early this morning with his dad. Born into a family of commercial fishermen, the boys of the family could join the world of boats and men when they approached maturity, and he was at that age when boys turn from their mothers to fathers for an example. It was 4 AM and today they were going to bring the boat from the mooring to the dock and load it with crab gear. The season opener would be in two days and today was the final day of preparation. Alex had been helping the crew after school to get the crab traps ready and it was the first time that he was a part of the crab season opener. His father made coffee in the kitchen this morning as Alex closed the light in the bathroom and walked into the hallway. He thought he might try some coffee today. He approached his father and uncle at the little table, both of whom sat staring at their mugs in silence. He was greeted by his father with a nod. His father, Arne, was not prone to excitement ever, especially at 4 AM.

Arne Skarsen was of wiry athletic build, not a physically big man, but he was a big man around town, respected. He had a calm demeanor and didn't waste words as some men do. When he spoke, those around made a point to listen because they respected him, and he usually had something to say they wanted to hear. After college he served in World War II and then he worked in Canada on the highway to Alaska. His relatives had made good money with shark fishing during the war and after Canada, commercial fishing looked like a smart career move to make, and the life appealed to him, so he took his Canada money and bought his own boat. In short order he rose within the community of commercial fishing as a man of ability and good judgment. That was twenty-five years and two sons ago. Alex had an older brother, Leif, and he was going with him today. Arne's brother Sig Skarsen was present also. He had big shoulders and a big frame. Uncle Sig favored young Alex and it was he who spoke first as the boy entered the brightly light room.

"Vell, vee gotta big day today, Alex. I got something for you." Uncle Sig said in his laconic Scandinavian drawl. He sometimes pronouncing his W's as V's. He handed Alex a box.

Alex took the box and removed the lid to reveal a rigger's knife, marlin spike and all. The handle was fancy and made of bone. It had Alex's name on it below a carved image of a fishing boat that was sailing out under the rays of a rising sun. It had a lanyard and a snap, and you could put it on your raingear or snap it on your jeans.

"Thanks Uncle Sig." Alex's' eyes brightened, his spirit awakening. Alex snapped the lanyard on his belt loop and dropped the knife in his pocket.

Uncle Sig rose about six foot-four inches from the floor to the top of his squared off head, matching the square jaw and shoulders below. His size had guided him in his life toward certain jobs and situations that others were not suited for. He could handle the heavy work and do so with a natural ease. He was known for his ability to weld and fabricate with metal; he had been a pipe fitter in the shipyards during the war. For him, it was steel that was emerging as the new material for fishboats, replacing the iconic wooden beauties that had been the industry standard for decades. He had built his own boat, the *Valkyrie*, of steel and he had cut, burned and packed a lot of metal and his physical brawn spoke to it. He had little use for books and what he did know he had come by through personal experience, mostly boats and fishing. People respected Sig just like they respected his brother Arne. Both men had not fallen far from the tree, but Sig was more like his father than Arne.

"Don't go waving that knife around in front of your mother," spoke Arne to his son and continued, turning to his brother. "That's a real nice gift, Sig." Arne looked back toward his boy. "Is it sharp Alex?" Arne inquired, seeking assurance. Alex pulled the knife out of his pocket and unfolded the big broad blade of the riggers knife. He ran his thumb crosswise and felt it scrape across the very thin edge of the blade. He knew it was sharp, knew it would cut him if he ran his thumb horizontal across the blade. Uncle Sig had warned him

that a dull knife was more dangerous than a sharp one and you didn't have
to press hard on the work.

"Yeah, it's real sharp, Dad." Alex closed the blade carefully and dropped
it back in his pocket. It would cut through crab rope with the first pass, Sig
had personally seen to that.

"You be careful, yeah?" Arne asked.

"I will," Alex replied and turned for the refrigerator.

Arne was a family man as most fishermen were. He married Olivia
Lundeberg 25 years ago and they had two boys. They lived a pleasant life of
routine and habit, socialized at the Sons of Norway Hall and enjoyed their
home. Easily identified, he was bespectacled and narrow of face under an old
gray Stetson hat and always dressed in his blue denim overalls. It was a contrast that made you think him to be blue-collar on the one hand and
white-collar on the other. Arne had graduated from college before the war.
He was savvy and the other fishermen watched what gear he was buying so
that they may profit as he did. At home, he talked matters over with Olivia
and she was his close companion since high school. She worked at the library
and was active in the community. She was no stranger to waterfront activities,
being her husband's confidant. Arne and Olivia worked hard, raised their
family and payed the mortgage, this was their definition of how to be in the
world. Early in his fishing career, Arne had been in on a couple of fisheries
that paid off and he owned a few properties in town owing to Olivia's judgment with money. She was sharp and savvy and they were both quick off the
blocks upon sensing an opportunity. This was the basic model for financial
success in ethnic communities; work hard, acquire property.

Alex's brother Leif entered the room. Leif went straight for the coffee pot
without a word. He was a little red-eyed. Leif was twenty-two years of age
and he didn't have much time for sleeping on most nights.

"Morning Leif-y," Arne spoke.

"Morning dad, I need some coffee." Leif replied briefly as he steered his over-filled cup toward a seat. Uncle Sig was alongside him at the little yellow and chrome table and looked him over with a dramatized regard and stare. He seemed to be measuring his words, not taking his gaze off of the young man but remaining silent.

"Is it too early now? Or is it still late, Leif-me-boy?" A little smile formed at the corners of Uncle Sig's mouth. Alex watched Leif with interest from across the table, quietly drinking the warm brown substance that tasted of nuts and looked like mud puddle water.

"I got some sleep; don't you worry Uncle Sig. I'm ready." Leif reassured his smiling uncle across the table. He continued.

"I'll meet up with Cal and load the truck. We should be at the dock a little after daybreak. We'll be in good shape, don't worry. I tell you true." Leif replied with his usual air of self-confidence. Everyone was used to self-assuredness from Leif; whether he got any sleep or not he was always ready - according to him anyway. Like most twenty-two-year old's he considered himself to be bulletproof. He was heavily armored mentally against any doubts regarding his ability.

Arne walked over to Leif and put his hand affectionately on his shoulder and asked, "Late night?"

"Not too bad." Leif replied honestly. Leif's reply had no bravado, just a son's reply to his dad and as a crewman.

"Your brother, Uncle Sig and I will bring the boat in and get the hatch ready for the first two loads. I gotta tighten up the stuffing box and clean out the sump in the shaft alley first. Now that I think of it," he said turning to Alex, "maybe we'll let Alex do the sump, eh?" Arne smiled at Alex who nodded back in the affirmative. The other men smiled for a reason. Little did Alex know that cleaning out the shaft alley sump was the dirtiest and smelliest job. Arne continued, "Make sure the extra shots of rope are on that first truck 'cause they're going in the lazarette before we load the deck."

"How 'bout I bring 'em on the second load?" Leif asked, starting to wake up and think now.

"No. I want to get them below and out of the way. Let's not forget and remember them too late." Arne had lived through this mistake before.

"Better you put the ropes *and* the spare block on the first truck, get 'em aboard, then it's done." Uncle Sig offered.

"Okay, sounds good. I'll have that stuff on the first truck." Leif replied, just wishing to end the conversation and wake up with his coffee.

Alex had been listening quietly all the while. He was absorbing this dialogue and the behaviors, noticing how men talked to each other. This was a world apart from school chums, birthday parties and mom. Just yesterday, she had taken him and his friends to the amusement park for his birthday. He could still see the fun house with that life-sized laughing doll in the window: scary, sexy and ugly all at the same time, she was not a funny addition to a supposedly fun house. That birthday party child belonged to yesterday, now gone today.

Alex's summer had been good, and school was now two months underway. In this past summer he had learned how to row a boat. He jumped in the skiff whenever possible. All through the months of June and July he rowed the little skiff that had heretofore been on sawhorses in the yard. He and his father had patched and painted it and it was his for the using. He would pretend that he was a coastal pirate and glide stealthily about the harbor. He would skillfully pilot the little boat through imagined rocky passages and skirt the tiny hazards in the harbor, pretending there was treacherous surf to overcome. All day long his imagination sparkled as he played in the little wooden skiff that his father had built. It was his father's voice that now brought Alex's attention back to the kitchen.

"Well, shall we go, Sig?" Arne announced.

"Yeah, we'll eat in town after we load. Sound OK, boys?" Uncle Sig looked over toward Leif and Alex.

"Sounds good to me," Leif replied and rose from the table.

They all filed out from the kitchen into the mud room and pulled on jackets and hats. Leif was the first to leave in his cherry Ford pick-up and Alex watched the taillights grow smaller as he went past the front gate and out to the highway. Alex squeezed in between his dad and uncle in the front seat of Sig's truck, the gear shift between his knees. It was a 37 Chevy truck. It was in immaculate condition; Alex liked the front window because you could roll it up and open it. It was forest green and it had oiled wood chaffing gear on the bed rails and chrome baby moon hubcaps. It was Uncle Sig's first truck that he had bought brand new out of the showroom in 1937. He kept it clean. The engine purred to life immediately after the starter button was depressed to the floor and they bumped along out the yard to the gate and onto the road. Alex was pretty excited; this was high adventure in a real-life way, not kid-fun, not that birthday-fun-house fun, some kind of adventure.

They drove through town to the dock and Uncle Sig parked the truck. They walked out on the dock and then over to the hoist where Arne's big skiff was set on its cart. Sig wheeled it under the hoist and readied to lower it away into the darkness below where the water of the still harbor rhythmically surged against the pilings of the dock. Arne stood at the hoist with the control buttons in one hand, ready to lift the skiff and lower away, his other hand rested upon the overhead stanchion of the hoist. He spoke now to Alex.

"You go on down the ladder and then unhook the skiff from the hoist. Then, pick me and your uncle Sig up off the ladder. We'll wait and come down after you get squared away and we'll give you plenty of time, so don't hurry. Be sure to step into the center off the boat, now, she'll tip over if you don't." Alex was anxious to row the skiff out the 200 yards to the mooring where the boat waited at anchor. It was his first turn at the oars with his dad and uncle. He knew he was up to the task, considering himself to be the best oarsman in town after spending the summer behind oars.

"Right." Alex replied to his father's instructions.

There is a special stillness in harbors in the small hours of the morning before daylight, when the world is still asleep. On this morning, as always, there was the regular and prominent report of the electric horn on the jetty at one-minute intervals. There also could be heard the random sigh of the whistle buoy, mournful and lonesome in the distance as it rose and descended on the swells beneath it, driving the air through its bellows. When the swell increased in the winter, the sound from the buoy could change to an urgent and plaintive sound, wet and airy in its trenchant report, but this morning it was casual, signaling fair weather. From the front of the skiff bubbled the very small and delicate sound of the bow parting the water as it moved out into the dark harbor. As Alex rowed the skiff, he watched the water trail away in diminishing ripples, triangulating away from the stern quarters of the sturdy little boat. He seemed to move effortlessly over the glassy surface of the dark harbor, digging deeper into the water with his oars to accommodate the extra weight of the occupants. Long and ghostly images of the receding harbor lights fluttered in the wake as the skiff slid quietly out to the mooring. The sounds and dancing images in the mirrored water added to his sense of adventure. Alex was now pulling hard and setting the oars deep and the boat did energetically glide. Pull and glide, pull and glide. It felt graceful like a bird flying low on the water in the night. Alex would occasionally feather an oar on the surface to alter the course, delicately and with precision.

"You're getting pretty good at this," spoke his father approvingly.

"It's not that hard." Alex replied nonchalantly, giving his best imitation of understatement and modesty that he had learned from his dad and uncle. He was learning how to act, how to be in the world from these men, he knew this to be the proper modest response. Any enthusiastic form of bragging was always considered poor form in this family. Inwardly, however, Alex was bursting with pride and joy.

"I see you out here in your boat all summer, you been practicing. You wore out the leathers." Sig referred to the leather wrapped on the oars where they rested in the oarlocks "Quite the boatman, aren't 'ya?"

"They call it a coxswain; the man that drives the boat." Arne said.

"Yeah well, I only got one use for a word that sounds like that. Sounds like a word you wouldn't say in front of your mother, cock-son." Sig answered, slightly amused.

"Don't listen to your uncle Sig." Arne chuckled. "That is the correct word all right."

They reached the mooring to which the fishing boat was attached by a sturdy chain. Alex approached the stern and the name of the vessel loomed in big letters just inches from his face as he tied the skiff to the stern, "*Valkyrie*" it read. After making the skiff fast, the men climbed up and over the rail. Alex remained seated and holding on to the main guard rail of the steel boat. Uncle Sig took the painter and Alex clambered aboard. Arne led the skiff up to the mooring chain on the bow to tie it off and while he did, the diesel engine kicked into life with a flood of white smoke out the stack, immediately followed by lights in the wheelhouse and then on deck. Well-rehearsed activity was quickly underway, and the *Valkyrie* was quite suddenly transformed from the quiet, dark and sleeping vessel to a little entity bristling with kinetic energy. The deck pump went on and a flood formed on the deck before it found the scuppers. The clank of the cast iron lid of the diesel stove could be heard coming from the galley, followed by the whir of an electric pump filling fresh water into a teapot. Arne emerged from around the corner of the pilot house and hollered into the back door.

"We're tied off Sig, ready."

"Go ahead, let 'er go." Sig said. Arne immediately returned to the bow, slipped the mooring chain off the cleat and instructed his brother.

"All clear, you're loose." Arne tapped on the window and did not wait for a reply as he moved to the stern and made ready the tie up lines. The clunk of the reverse gear was all the reply that was necessary to let them know they were off the mooring and headed for the dock.

Alex watched in silence as his Uncle reversed the vessel at an idle from the mooring and skiff before he throttled up, shifting ahead. Alex took his station at the bow and made ready the fat dock line, wet from the morning dew and foretelling wind. It was heavy and wet in his hands and it wasn't like the ropes he handled in the skiff all summer or like crab rope. He stood like a statue, but he was ready- reviewing what he was supposed to do when they got to the dock. Alex felt important. He felt like he was part of the operation as much as any of them. His dad would handle the stern line and he would handle the bowline, simple. From behind the glass he could see the image of his uncle's face looking past him and out into the harbor darkness toward the dock. Alex remained motionless and anticipated the next thing to happen on this part of the adventure. He was not an observer, this time it was different. The men talked to him differently, not like a little boy but as part of the crew, expecting and trusting his abilities. The *Valkyrie* approached the long wooden pier and gently touched the pilings. Alex summoned all the strength he possessed and successfully flung the heavy line up to the waiting hands of his brother up on the dock. Never thinking past the next moment, he had no idea of the dimensions that this adventure would grow to. This was only the beginning and the events were about to be upon them.

*   *   *

Calvin Harris worked for the Skarsen family. He was just waking up and all the muscles in his body remained motionless while his eyelids opened, and his eyes scanned the ceiling. He lay perfectly still and listened to his new clock radio and the crooning pipes of Frank Sinatra,whose voice didn't seem appropriate at 3AM, but not much besides the upcoming cup of coffee did. He didn't care for Johnny Mathis or some of the others, but Frank was okay, he was tough. A lot of other singers sounded like they were crying when they sang. He thought they should be more of a man- they just didn't have the right attitude somehow. Sinatra was different, he was a man of the world. He could take it and he knew about women, he called them 'broads'. Calvin Harris could relate to Sinatra.

Everybody in town called him Cal. He had been in grade school with Arne but behind him a few years. Cal was different than Arne. He was a jock in school and a committed bachelor now. Arne got good grades and Calvin didn't care for classes and books. For him it was sports, cars and girls in that order. There was also a class difference; the Harris family was poor. Although Calvin's father was a fisherman also, he had had a string of unfortunate events that set the family back. His first boat broke up on the beach during a storm and then the shark liver fishery collapsed shortly after he geared up for it. Calvin's mother found it necessary to start work as a bookkeeper and that became the economic glue that held the family's finances together. Her widowed mother moved in to help raise the kids while she was away at work. Mom was devoted to her first-born son, Cal; she wanted him to have all the advantages. Despite the money-or lack thereof- they sent him to a Catholic high school. He wished he was rich like some of his classmates, but he adapted to the culture of the rich and middle-class kids from the suburbs at that school, returning to the rural poverty at the end of each day. Cal was a scrappy kid with a charming side to his personality and his athleticism won him friends. But all his friends secretly knew he was different. He was marked as a poor kid. If any were stupid enough to cross him at school, he pounded their asses into the pavement and did so with a relish. Cal's anger at any taunting tapped into a reserve of anger that years of resentment and envy at school had inculcated within. He could summon this anger forth, resulting in not the typical playground fight of pushing and wrestling, but he could administer a real beating. Charm and the threat of brutality worked well for him in school. After high school he joined the army and when Cal came home, he rejoined Arne as crew. He was deck boss, friend and right-hand man to the best fishing operation in town.

And Cal hadn't changed much in the ensuing years. He did lose his immature envy and was satisfied with his adulthood. He was still trim and fit but no longer sported a flat top with wings on the side of his head. Now, he resembled an older James Dean and the local divorcees gave his trim and fit frame a second glance when he walked by. He would flirt and date but remained a confirmed bachelor; that's the way he liked it and that's the way it was likely to stay. He now spent Saturday nights at home reading Popular Mechanics or Popular Science, watching TV or going to a movie with his old friend Sally. She would spend the night and leave the next day, which was just about the way it should be the way Cal saw it. He had tried going steady and had tried living with women and those attempts all ended with different versions of a familiar theme that he didn't care for because in the end, the woman always thought that he was fucked up. That didn't bother him though, that just made it even; he thought they were fucked up too. He was much happier with this settled single version of his life and it was not likely to change. He liked his job and he was like a partner with Arne. He had a house and a nice car and he had a lot of friends on the waterfront. The way Cal saw it, what more could you want?

On this morning, as Sinatra explained just why the lady is a tramp, he swung his feet out from under the covers to the cold linoleum floor and sat there scratching his head. He walked to the kitchen, filled the little round coffee tray in the percolator, plugged in the shiny chrome pot and then shuffled to the bathroom in his bare feet. He came out of the bathroom and reentered the kitchen for coffee. To his annoyance, he could hear Johnny Mathis on his new clock radio. It was too early for that, Johnny Mathis crying *Chances Are* in Cal's house at 3 AM was definitely unacceptable. He poured coffee and sat at his kitchen table sipping, waiting for Leif to arrive and to begin the long day.

*   *   *

It was now 4:30 AM and Leif Skarsen was walking out the back door of the family house with his little brother, dad and uncle. As he walked past the side of his Chevy, he stood there a moment looking at the reflection of the yard lights in the shiny-red, buffed-out paint job. He ran one hand through his hair and the other across the left rear fender thinking, "the truck is cool". He opened the door and slid across the new seat covers, red and black diamond shapes with the vinyl coverings. In his faded blue Levi's and white tee shirt, he was a younger, blonder version of Calvin Harris. Not entirely coincidental.

But Leif was different than Calvin in a significant way; Leif had no anger; life had been rather normal and with a minimum of conflict. He had stepped into crewing with his dad right after high school and that was going well, he figured to have his own fishing boat someday soon. He was easy-going, good looking, popular and the hard guys in school never dared mess with him. He still wore his high school letter jacket over a tee shirt, as much as an acknowledgement of fealty to a school and a community as to his past athletic merits he had achieved. Leif had come to look like Cal lately because of the same haircut they wore, one of the 10 styles offered by barber shops everywhere. It wasn't surprising to see people looking the same. No one questioned the need for more choices than ten different styles (that all looked the same), because, who, in their right mind, needed more choices than ten hair styles? Leif chose number seven because it was similar to number eight. Cal chose number eight nowadays because it looked most like number 9. James Dean in East of Eden (who was also named Cal) had a number 9 haircut.

Leif turned the key on the ignition of his Chevy and the engine caught on the first crank and came to a high idle. He sat there thinking about the day ahead as the engine warmed up, then he slipped it into first gear and rolled out the yard, going smoothly through the gears as he left the dirt road behind. Leif shifted into fourth gear when he reached the straight blacktop road and took a moment to adjust the heater and punched a chrome pre-set button on the radio in the darkness of his cool truck. The new black, white and red seat covers had a pleasing vanilla-smell and the vinyl had a crispy feel. He extended his hand down to the floor in the general area where he had placed his coffee cup, found it and his pinky finger dipped up to the knuckle in the cup as he found the handle loop. He took a drink, set it back and wiped his hand off on his pants. He arrived at Cal's orderly front yard and steered the Chevy over by the shed and parked. In the house, the lights were on in the kitchen and Leif walked up the wooden stairs of the back porch.

"Hey Killer." Cal head-faked and threw short right-left jabs Leif's way. "You ready for this shit?" Cal asked.

"Born ready. You?" Leif replied.

"You bet. Let's go." Calvin's matter-of-fact words trailed behind him as he exited toward the yard ahead of the young man. Leif knew he was in for a work-out; keeping up with Cal throwing the heavy crab traps around guaranteed a sweat. Cal never let on to getting tired even if he was and he was always showing off strength to Leif. The job always went on without relent until it was done when Cal was involved.

Cal walked straight to the shed, turned on the yard lights and then jumped on the platform of the fourteen-foot stake bed truck. He hitched up his pants and rubbed his hands and spoke to Leif who was still crossing the yard.

"I'll be up, you be down. Hand 'em to me the same every time, lid bales facing me. I'll go six high with two lockers." Cal was ready

"Oh-kee doh-kee. "Leif answered and started in.

He pulled the first trap off the top and walked it over to the truck a few feet away. The traps were stacked eight high on the ground, side by each in the yard. They would make two truck trips to the dock before it was all over and have the *Valkyrie* loaded with gear before calling it done. Sig and Arne were partnered up again this winter, crabbing off the *Valkyrie*. Arne's boat, the Fin, was laid up with plank work. Between them they had more than enough traps to get the job done and besides, it felt right to be partners as well as brothers. The crab traps were round, 38 inches in diameter and a little over a hundred pounds with rope and buoys. They were a little cumbersome to handle and they required an arched posture and strength while walking around the yard with them against the hips. Leif had a special belt buckle that he liked to wear that helped support the weight of the trap as he walked.

That little buckle came in handy as the stack wore down and the traps felt heavier. He set the first trap down on the bed and Cal picked it up and walked it to the cab-end of the bed and then came right back for another, making a show of it for Leif's benefit. The stack on the ground slowly diminished as they worked back and forth from the stacks to the truck until eighty almost a hundred traps were gone from the yard and the first truckload was ready for transport. They tied down the stacks on the truck with rope, only conversing briefly and only about the task at hand. They had their thoughts and quiet interior conversations, but it was much too early for chatting. Their energy was concentrated on the work and their brows were beaded with sweat in the cold pre-dawn air. The sky was only just now beginning to show a little blue and gold in the east. It had been a 45-minute workout.

"Well, that's about it for the first load, huh?" Leif peeled off his tee shirt and wiped his brow with it and put it back on.

"You wipe your face with your shirt and put it back on? What kinda animal are you?" Cal asked.

"What's the difference, it's all sweat, it's all my own?"

"The difference is you wiped sweat *on* your face, Einstein. Do you wipe your ass and then blow your nose too? Or is it the other way around?"

"Up yours. I hardly even broke a sweat anyway."

"If you say so stud," Cal conceded unconvincingly. "What about those shots of rope in the shed. Are they going in the lazarette, or what?" Cal asked.

"Oh shit. I almost forgot."

"Well get that truck of yours over here then. We'll throw them in the back, you can follow me."

"I'm not putting those fuck'in ropes in my truck!" They'll scratch the fenders all to shit!" Leif protested. His truck was not to be used for transporting anything related to crab gear. He explained further, "I never put gear in this truck."

"Well we can just pop that cherry. Or you tell me *what* then, Hot Rod?"

Leif looked around the yard and shook his head and spit on the ground. He walked over to the gleaming red Chevy and looked at it. He shook his head again; he was not putting ropes in his truck.

Cal was silent but kept his eyes on him the whole time. Leif wheeled away from the truck toward Cal and kept on walking right past him. Leif climbed into the cab of the stake bed, fired it up and put in reverse. He backed it up to the bundles of rope and shut it off, climbed back out of the cab, climbed onto the tops of the stacks on the truck and instructed Cal.

"I'll yard those sons' bitches up here. Hand 'em to me." Leif stood on the top of the wobbly stacks, ten feet up from the ground.

"We'll see about that." This was Cal's kind of fun; tests of strength. He threaded a piece of line through a bundle of twenty ten fathom shots. "Just one bundle or two?" He asked.

"Two bundles are fine," Leif said and waited for Cal. Leif no sooner got the line than he jerked the two bundles of rope ten feet up to rest on the top of the traps under his feet. "Keep 'em comin." Leif said.

"You're the one stud, the son of a gun."

Truck loaded, ropes secured, stacks tied down, they were now off to the dock. They were in good spirits after the morning workout, riding in the comfortable old bench seats of the flatbed, window down and arm out in the morning air. They talked about baseball, Leif's truck and the price of crabs. They drove through town and the little harbor appeared below the hill as Leif slowly turned the burdened vehicle down the grade, mindful of the load.

"Let's not handle these traps again *unnecessarily*, Sport." Cal warned in a sarcastic tone as they went around the turn and the stacks shifted slightly to one side threatening to tip over in the street.

"Relax: It's under control." Leif replied.

They could see the Valkyrie at the dock as they got close to the harbor. There was a lot of activity already underway in the morning light. The flat parking lot of the dock had become a staging area for the loading of the boats with the heavy metal traps wrapped in rubber and knitted with stainless wire. The stacks of traps completely covered the spacious paved lot. The traps were orderly in their groupings and distinguished from the neighboring stacks by the buoy colors of the owners. They were stacked very high to conserve space in the lot and before this day was over there would be more, stacked ten high with hardly room to get another load off the truck to the pavement. The sight of this created an atmosphere of competition and anticipation. It also served as a gauge of the magnitude of how much gear would be fielded this year. It was going to be a high-water mark for traps hitting the water from what Cal and Leif could see stacked here in the lot. There were going to be a lot of out-of-town boats.

"Holy shit; look at this." Cal lifted a finger towards the stacks of traps and let out an airy low whistle.

"There's more and more traps every year. Where'd all these traps come from?" Leif remarked.

"They come from up above; Eureka, Crescent City, Oregon, Washington, who knows where all else. From the looks of it, everyone from everywhere is going fishing this year," Cal answered.

"Don't they have their own season opener in two weeks?"

"Yes, they do." Cal answered and continued." They figure to come down here and get the gravy, then pack up and leave for the north country and get the gravy again in their own back yard."

"Greedy bastards."

"Some call it that, I'm sure they don't. They got this figured out by now. A few boats showed them how to travel and make it pay- now it looks like they all want to be in on it. It doesn't take a lot of brains to catch these things." Cal said.

"Just doesn't seem right somehow. We don't go up there and get their crabs."

"Well we could if we took a notion to, it's happened before, and it'll happen again. And you better believe we would feel within our God damn rights to do so if *we* did. We fish anywhere on the God damn ocean we like, and everybody sees it the same. Time was, your father and I went up there on a regular basis and we got *their* crabs, you will too if you fish long enough. There was a time when you could hardly get 2 crates on opening day down here, let alone a tank load. It was bad and it was bad for a long time. That's all changed now looks like." Cal explained.

"Just seems like it's gonna be a gang bang. Quick and dirty." Leif mused as he passed the stacks on the way out to the dock.

"Leif-y, it always *has* been a gang bang when there's a few crabs around. It just is. Difference now, it's happening in your back yard and not theirs. Now me, I like it when there aren't lotsa crabs around everywhere. That may sound funny and even stupid, but I tell you this; there sure as shit aren't too many boats, the price is always good and there ain't no God damn pressure to go out and kill yourself in bad weather for a few bugs. Scratch fishing around here? If you shuffle the gear around and find your own spot, maybe you can get a few. Your Uncle's really good at that kind of fishing." Cal said.

"Lotta our guys will be at a disadvantage." Leif observed with no small hint of resentment.

"Yes, they will." Cal paused before he continued, this time a little more upbeat. "Don't worry-your old man and uncle know what to do and the *Valkyrie* is every bit of a boat as what might come down from up above. Nobody's gonna get the ups on them in their own backyard."

It was clear that young Leif was feeling the pressure from the sight of the stacks of traps, more than he had ever seen in his harbor parking lot. From these stacks, vessels would take their second and third loads after the initial salvo hit the water. And rapid deployment of the gear was crucial, this was a race to get the most gear in the water first. Everyone was all about being first under the hoist, first to get a forklift, first to get a flatbed, first to get the fresh hanging bait, first to get the gear in the water and first to get on the right spot, the spot with the most pounds per trap. 'First with the most', was the operative phrase of the opening week and there was very little that got in the way of the task at hand-short of death. Opening day was guaranteed to be the best pull of the season and 90% of the entire 6-month season's harvest would occur in the first week. Time was money and money was the prize; that and the glory of a big season. Money and poundage were the measure of the boats and the man at the wheel. Nice guys finished somewhere in the middle of the pack or dead last. Those who had the best season were remembered for their prowess and poundage. Everyone who had ever fished a crab season a time or two knew that when crab season started, goodwill and friendship was replaced by a foremost instinct to kill crabs. It did something to men, but all participants would transform back into normalcy again when the season was over.

Cal and Leif drove past the stacks and out onto the dock. The week before the opener was charged with emotion, anticipation, rumor and gossip. Questions took on oversized proportions; 'How many boats would show up? What would the price be? Who had what in the test pots? "Were they in the deeps or in the shallows?" The inevitable question in the final moments of the week was, "Would there be a tie-up, would there be a strike? Drama and dread hovered around *that* issue because strikes were a force to contend with.

Talk of a strike was troubling; veterans never spoke of it unless given good reason. It was unwise and it was possible to speak it into existence. The old hands would be dismissive at the first word of a strike. The young guys were more apt to talk of fairness and rebellion; they had not been through strikes for a nickel or a dime that lasted weeks on end. This they did not know. They did not know that once started, a strike could begin to take on a life of its own and become a thing to be served. The uninitiated did not know that right and wrong weren't actually the thing after a length of time during a strike. They did not know that threatening empty words did not help matters. Old hands knew that right and wrong changed according to who was talking and the money lost in a tie-up would never be regained. Strikes tested wills on both sides of right and wrong. They would find that arguments pro and con could split lifelong friends into warring camps. An underlying current of tension took the place of good-natured banter in the coffee shop whenever they were on strike and some very hard opinions formed and once formed, they were very slow to soften. Those who lined up on the wrong side of popular positions did so at their own risk. Talk of wildcatting was followed by talk of retribution and nothing was ever forgotten. Tempers were easily ignited as time went by in a strike.

*   *   *

Arne climbed up the ladder from *Valkyrie* and stood on top of the dock. Down below, Sig and Alex remained, getting things ready in the hatch. Arne could hear his youngster protesting that the shaft alley was too stinky, and he couldn't fish around in the black water with his hands, grasping chunks of unknown ugliness that might clog the pump intake. This amused uncle Sig, chuckling on deck and watching over him.

"What is this stuff? It stinks!" Alex hollered in his high voice to his Uncle Sig.

"It's bilge water. Part water, part diesel and part rot. It'll go away, just wash your hands really good. It won't hurt ya" said Sig reassuringly.

"It smells like rotten eggs!" Alex whined and protested.

On the dock the smell was quite different. Arne could smell the resins vaporizing from the creosoted pilings capped with tar. It was going to be a warm day and Indian summer was extending into November. There hadn't been a rain yet, not even a southerly air. The planked dock was crowded with traps waiting to be loaded and their freshly painted and multicolor buoys made them pleasing to look at. A man with a camera was taking pictures in the morning light. Each boat had his own color scheme and the brighter the better. Arne walked over to a small group of men congregating by the hoist.

"Morning boys." Arne addressed the group on the dock. "Cal's backing the truck out now and we'll start loading. Waiting on me, Jack, are you?" Arne motioned to the other boat tied to the dock. It was the *Warlord*, owned by Jack Dewey.

The men in the group grew quiet and turned their heads toward Arne and Jack Dewey. Jack Dewey: his behavior and reputation attracted nicknames and he was reviled and admired simultaneously by many. The men grew quiet because they were interested in what these two men had to say.

"That's right, Arne, I'm next." Jack replied. "We got truckloads to get aboard." Jack scanned the faces of the men before his eyes rested on Arne for his reply.

"Well, we won't be too long. I think that's Cal and Leif I see coming now." Arne motioned to the approaching truck, "We got our usual load if it's good weather like this, we'll see ," Arne explained and continued, "We got an association meeting this afternoon, Jack, if you care to sit in."

"I don't think so. And I tell you this Arne; I respect you more than any man in this town and we go back a long way. But I don't wanna' strike for no nickel or dime just to delay the opener. I don't think a man should try and sabotage another man for his own gain. I run a business here, Arne, and right is right. I'm not about to play fucky-fuck." Jack said. He had spent a few seasons here, been through strikes. He knew this port operated by the book, not so sure about the other ports. He wasn't about to tolerate any manipulation from any local association to stop his operation.

"Well, you know how I feel Jack. The fellas don't want no strike either. But we talk it over and vote, just like always. It's an open meeting Jack and you could come over and give voice to not strike if you like." A little smile accompanied Arne's reply. Arne was president of the association and he believed in its purpose. "If you change your mind, we're up at the Grange at 3 o'clock."

"Arne, I just run a business here, that's all. And I know how this works and it's not always right." Jack stated flatly. He always expected the worst in people and he always kept his anger at his side like a pet on a leash.

"We *all* run businesses here, Jack, you know that. You know how we do things and its better we do those things together, with a market order signed in all three ports. We all gotta live here; this isn't just about getting as much as you can, that's the easy part." Arne concluded congenially and with a small chuckle, the men quiet as they looked on.

Jack just shook his head and tightened his lip as he walked away. "We'll see about that." he spoke. He had his doubts and made it obvious.

Jack Dewey had made his own way since early on in life. Associations and community just did not fit his idea of self-sufficiency. The way he saw things, the most you could trust was yourself and even that had exceptions. He was not born into a fishing family or community and he was not amongst fishing relatives. Whatever he got, he got on his own. His parents lived on a houseboat when he was born, the houseboat chosen for economy and convenience and they worked odd jobs on the waterfront. There was always plenty of work for them if they wanted it, but that wasn't a high priority. They were drinkers. Jack's father fell in the water drunk and drowned one night when Jack was twelve years old and after that his mom wasn't around on a regular basis. And neither was Jack; adulthood arrived early and that was simply fine by him. He caught pile perch from the dock and sold them in Chinatown. Then he got a skiff and went out and got halibut and stripers. He sold everything he caught, legal or not. Jack figured out early on that there was money just waiting to be pulled from the water and hauled off to market. He bought a fishing boat at seventeen and a whole new life started to open up for him, beginning what would be a career which gained him something heretofore unknown, respect and money. He got his first big check from fishing when he was 19 years old and by the time he was twenty one, he had accumulated a reputation in the coastal fishing communities, delivering big fishing trips to the dock. The notoriety and money became seductive to young Jack. From here on out, Jack Dewey always did well. He never talked about his childhood and never had one more thought about it.

* * *

Leif and Cal arrived at the foot of the dock in the truck and they began backing it out toward the waiting boat under the hoist. Arne parted company with the group of men on the dock and said, "See you at the Hall," in parting. Some of the men nodded recognition and all the men talked about the conversation they had just witnessed with Jack and Arne, gossip being one of their specialties during this time of year, that and talk about the price to be asked.

The Skarsens loaded the boat in the warm morning, never stopping between loads. Alex opened cupboards in the galley and found open packages of bread, cookies, raisins and whatever else had been put away and forgotten. He ate the things that weren't scary looking and looked on out the cabin door as stack after stack came down to the deck via the hoist. He was ready to make himself handy, but the four men worked seamlessly and efficiently and had no need of his help. Alex found a job in handing the men the tie-down ropes as the stacks filled a completed row across the deck of the *Valkyrie*. While he waited for the row to fill, he leafed through a copy of a Playboy magazine on the galley table. The finding of this magazine lying about was worth getting up early for. He studied the glorious and wonderful women spread across the glossy pages. The pictures of the naked women answered questions he had been tossing about in his head, the mysteries of the female anatomy. The diesel engine rumbled quietly far below, and the stacks rose on the deck. Alex leaned in the door jambs and could feel the gentle vibration of the idling machinery down below and the warmth rising from the stack pipe that rose through the galley. His uncle and brother continued to stack the lowered traps on the deck of the boat. His attention was diverted only when it was time for him to hand them a rope. Alex watched his brother walk with a trap to the back and then pump it up to the top of the stack at the stern. He adjusted its position for stability and uniformity before returning to get another, repeating that over and over inthe warming day. He perspired in the morning heat in his sleeveless tee-shirt, keeping up with the pace being set by his dad and Cal up on the dock. Alex looked out the back door with envy at the well-defined muscles of Leif's arms and chest when he grabbed a trap and walked it to the back. Alex figured his brother was about the strongest guy he knew. His uncle Sig was right beside Leif in his plaid shirt, keeping up with the pace as well, not making it look like an effort as his big hands and arms engulfed the trap and flung it onto the stack.

"Hey kiddo, how about a couple of Cokes?" asked his brother Leif of Alex.

"Ok." Alex replied, and went to the galley refrigerator and returned with the cardboard carrying carton that held six bottles shaped like little rocket ships. He shouted up to the dock, "How 'bout you guys, Dad?" holding up the Cokes.

"Send 'em up with the hooks." his father replied.

Alex took three Cokes from the carton and set them on the hatch. He put the rest in a bucket and attached it to the hoist hooks. His father raised the hoist and the operation paused for a break halfway through the truckload. It was only 9AM, they were making good time.

You're loading light, Arne?" asked an onlooker.

"Well, I guess so, 250 is comfortable on the *Valkyrie*. We'll take more with us on the first pull."

"Might be a smart move for sure-at least you'll have some in the right spot by the end of the day," observed the onlooker.

"Well that's true too. There better not be any blanks on opening day." Arne conceded.

Down below on the boat Sig turned to Leif, sitting on the hatch and drinking his Coke. "You gettin' tired Stud, eh?" Sig said half-jokingly.

"Tired of what old timer?" Leif smiled and cocked his head quizzically at Sig's joke.

"Oh, you're the tough one for sure." Sig remarked and then added, "Not too smart, but plenty tough."

"Smart enough for this job." Leif said smiling.

"OK Leif-y, let's go." Sig declared, "Send 'em down Cal." He hollered up at the dock, signifying that break time was over. By noon they got the last load aboard and they were soon untying the lines from the dock, done with the loading of the gear on *Valkyrie.*

The three Skarsens that brought the empty *Valkyrie* to the dock in darkness now returned to the mooring fully loaded with gear and attached the heavily burdened vessel to the mooring chain. They rowed into the dock and there was just enough time to eat before going on to the meeting at the Hall. They entered the café at the foot of the pier. It was the Snug Harbor Café and the name was appropriate; boat people of all type congregated there. There was a big horseshoe shaped counter in the café and the men there talked across the opening to each other. Several red vinyl booths completed the room. Cal and the Skarsen family took one of these. Plaid shirts and baseball caps, along with striped Big Ben work shirts with the iconic red and black gorilla logo; these were the uniforms of the day here. Coffee was consumed here just about any time of the day and the coffee wasn't particularly good, just strong. The seated men greeted Arne and Alex as they sat in the enclave. Pictures of local boats were on the walls.

"Hi Arne. See you got your helper today," remarked a crusty-looking person.

"Oh yeah, Alex is on the crew list this year. He's a helluva hand for sure, rowed us out this morning and back again." Arne offered.

"You don't say," asked a big man with a leathery face who paused to cross examine the youth, turning toward Alex before he continued, "Did you ask the old man about your cut, what your share would be?" The man's name was William X-Ray.

William X-Ray was big with a big voice to match. His outlook on society and the world had been firmly cemented in his head during WWII in the 1940's and hadn't changed much since. He was possibly the last man alive to use the phrase "pogey bait" in a sentence, let alone know what it meant. His name had originally stemmed from his FCC license number, WX 5327, which he would recite phonetically over the two-way radio; "William X-ray 5-3-2-7". His voice would boom out, pushed by 200 watts of transmitting power, sounding much like the voice of God, rattling the little speakers in the listening AM sets. X-Ray often spoke in riddles and he liked to follow one of his riddles saying, "here's the punchline," exhibiting a philosophical bend that often left you scratching your head and wondering what the heck he was talking about. He featured himself a blue-collar dockside guru and he would often say in reply to many things, "No, no. You don't see what I already know", which was just what you would suppose an x-ray would say if one could talk. Problem was, everyone *did* see what he already knew, and they also knew a lot that he *didn't see,* or they saw it differently than he. He was good-natured and an entertaining character to talk to even though the conversation could be frustrating or confusing. But occasionally he would utter a few pearls of wisdom when you least expected it.

"I don't need a crew share; I just like going out on the boat." Alex answered meekly and innocently. He hadn't ever thought of getting paid to play hooky on a school-day down at the boat.

The whole table erupted, "No, no, no." they laughed, "That's not how it works," said X-Ray through the talk. "You get a share, it's the rule."

"He gets a share-minus the cost of the groceries he eats-and he eats a lot," Arne answered.

X-Ray continued, "Workin' for nothing is for the birds kiddo. Jailbirds work for nothing; a crewman gets a share"

The waitress arrived. Alex looked at the menu and wondered what all he could have, he was starving.

"Have anything you like, son." said dad.

Alex ordered a waffle, a side of raisin toast, bacon and a milkshake to wash it down. He took pleasure in eating.

There was a cast of regulars at the counter, open to all who wished to park themselves there for a helping of caffeine, gossip and humor. The regulars attended the morning session for hours, the old timers had history stories, the young hot shots excitedly described some new gear. Some offered advice on equipment, locating parts, services or how to repair faulty machinery. Machinery was always a popular topic. It was a close-knit group and the morning coffee session served as a sounding board, a system of checks and balances on values generated by gossip and opinion. Values in the community occasionally needed updating or confirmation and there was no lack of judgments in this group. They always managed to dish it out with a degree of lightheartedness, as if everyone was in on the joke and conscious of the fact that the fickle finger of fate eventually touched everyone.

After lunch, Arne rose from the table, picked up the check and went to the register. Alex made a final sweep across the pool of syrup and floating waffle bits with his fork. After he got the last of the soggy chunks, he followed his father towards the door. Arne turned back towards the table and spoke, "See you over there, Tom, Bill, X-Ray. It's an open meeting George, so no treasurer report. Put out the word that out of town boats are welcome." Out the door they went.

*   *   *

Back out on the dock, the *Warlord* was getting another truckload aboard. Jack climbed down the ladder to his boat. After talking to Arne and the group, he had been about half pissed-off in anticipation of what he feared. The more he thought about it and how it might play against him, the more pissed-off he got at Arne and his god-damned association. He wasn't in the mood for it and he said so aloud to his crew,

"They better not play fucky-fuck with these market orders. I'm going fishing on opening day and I know others that feel the same god-damned way. There are chicken-shits at that coffee shop that won't say it, but I know what every God-damned one of 'em is thinking and they better not be think'in they can run *me* out of town. That's not gonna happen- they don't tell me how to run my operation," Dewey groused to his crew. The smaller of the two crewmen spoke.

"You got that right, boss. We ain't been work'in on gear all month just to *sit* around another month on strike or go home empty. Sheee-it, no!" The crewman was Wilbur Jenkins and he spat through a gap in his front teeth. Saying 'sheee-it' exposed the little dark hole in the middle of his front teeth, which allowed him to spit over the rail and into the water for accentuation.

The taller crewman was called Duster and now it was his turn to weigh in on the subject. "Let the dumb sons a' bitches tie up. We'll go out and get all the more, boss. I'm in on that, fuck. We'll spin 'round that gear like a top, heh, heh, heh." Duster ended his statement with his customary laugh.

"Welllll, we'll see what goes on at this meeting. I'll know just by how they're talk'in what is gonna happen and it didn't take 20 years to figure that out; it's the same shit every year as soon as ten out-of-town boats show up." he reached for a beer in the cooler and punched it with his church key.

"Tell you what else," he continued, "I even know who is going to be saying what by now. Arne's fair and runs a good meeting, but some of those other fuckers got cards they ain't showin'," Jack Dewey said aloud.

"They just want more for themselves after we go home with nuthin'" Dewey exclaimed, and Duster and Wilbur nodded in agreement. Duster piped in, "And this time we ain't going to hold no candle while they pork us where the sun don't shine! That's for damn sure!" Duster was all puffed up now in his usual way, his bravado making him step slightly from side to side as he hitched up his pants.

Jack growled in his whiskey voice and walked off into the wheelhouse and took a heart pill. He was forty years old and looked to be around fifty. Most of those years had been on the water and he had done it all. If he wasn't fishing, he was getting ready to go fishing. If he wasn't getting ready to go fishing, he was thinking about getting ready. He didn't know much else and he didn't want to know much else. He was not a conflicted individual, it was simple; catch, unload, go back out for more. Jack Dewey wasn't a lot of things to be sure and one of them was being stupid. Matters of fairness didn't concern him much. He was familiar with the concept and knew that fairness was a subject that was conveniently changed, depending. The way he saw it, much that could be considered *unfair* had come his way. But that didn't bother him; he had found a way to deal with that and looking out for Number One was the surest way. He knew how to play ball and he knew what everyone recognized as fair. He also knew that there was a reoccurring problem with this so-called fairness: it always caused him some kind of loss when some prick decided he wasn't going to play by the rules.

*   *   *

A group of men stood around outside the hall before the Association meeting. As Arne approached one stepped forward and spoke,

"Whattya think Arne, trouble?" Henry was the local high liner and he was an old hand at this. He had headed up the Association himself in the past and found that he would rather fish than talk in meetings. People looked up to him for leadership mostly because he caught the most fish, but also because he had a solid sense of right and wrong and was the first man to buy a round at the bar.

"Don't think so, Henry. The guys wanna go. The City isn't making a lot of noise. Have you heard from anybody up there, JT or anybody?" Arne asked.

"Nothin. They'll probably call us- as they go out the Gate to set!" Henry laughed at the thought. It had happened before.

"They better not, better to play it straight. Let's go in and get this under way. The sooner we start the sooner we're done." Arne walked up the steps.

"Amen to that, but I'll tell ya, there's not a lot of votes for a strike Arne." Henry followed up the steps.

Arne stopped at the top of the staircase and turned toward Henry. "I know. The new guys want to go, market order or not, open ticket. Is that how we do things now? I sure hope not, I seen *every man for himself* and it doesn't hold up too good in the long run."

"That may be so Arne, but nobody's thinkin' about the *long run* today, the thinking is about what happens *now*." Henry replied.

Soon after, the Grange Hall filled with the members of the Association and non-members as well. There was a buzz and a charge in the hall as little groups of 5 and 6 fishermen stood in circles discussing the opener.

There was a lot of history to trade associations negotiating for price. Unions and collective bargaining were still alive and well on the waterfront here, but waning nationwide, where it once claimed most laborers. Fishermen Marketing Associations up and down the coast arose out of a need to bargain for a price on their crabs and fish. But the labor movement was fading. There were those committed to it and those who were not too sure of its value, but each port still had one just the same. But resentment was growing against cents per pound deducts out of the fishermen's pocket and into the association kitty. As a result of these mixed feelings, some ports were strong Association ports and others were weaker in membership.

There was a time when there was no mechanism to bargain collectively at all; prices fluctuated and usually, they were on the low side. Eventually fishermen decided it was better to leave the dock in the morning knowing what the price would be when they came in to unload fish and to feel that the price they got was a fair price. This was the era in which the Associations and Unions flourished. Strikes and tie-ups would occur when a bargain could not be struck with the buyers. But those strikes were losing popularity among an ever-growing number of men. Strikes tested the ability to place principle above dollars and that often proved to be a difficult or foolhardy choice. Also, the strikes seemed to take on a life of their own and once they started it was hard to stop them and get back to work. The unsuccessful strikes were always remembered and talked about and that worked against the staging of another, the bad memories malingered. The argument that always won the day was that fishing time lost never added up to the gains of a strike. The longer a strike lasted, sooner or later, all men began to question the wisdom of having it in the first place.

The old-old timers recalled when the fishermen first got organized in the 1920's. Time was that the Marine Transport Workers Union was the outfit to be in. The Union was strong in San Francisco and the idea of collective bargaining was taking hold among many workers across the land during this era. Commercial fishermen were no exception. During the 1920's, the Marine Transport Workers Union, comprised of longshoremen, sailors and fishermen, would place member fishermen in dock worker positions in the off-season and the fishermen had work on the docks if they wanted it. But the sardines were plentiful during these times and most found work there. Demand and markets expanded accordingly as canned sardines were shipped domestically and abroad. Seiners from Seattle to San Pedro participated in the harvest and San Francisco had numerous canneries to handle the production of canned sardines. It was said that you could travel from the Golden Gate to the Farallon Islands and never once be out of the sardine schools breezing on the surface, flashing phosphorescent fire in the night as they danced in the bow wake. Seiners would set several miles outside the Golden Gate, capture 250 tons in the net and begin to brail the load to numerous other boats from the burgeoning net. Men would hold the boats away from each other at sea with long wooden poles while a brail net worked to share sardines from the heavy net that held enough sardines for numerous boats. Loaded boats would travel into the Bay with their share and unload at the canneries and no boat needed to go in empty. Men would pour wine and break bread and go out the next day and do it again, day after day. Year after year this scene was repeated in Monterey and San Francisco until one season the fishermen found themselves looking farther and farther south for the fish; from San Francisco and Monterey to Morro Bay, to Pt. Concepcion, to Santa Barbara, to San Pedro and then there was none. Just like that in one season's time the fish were gone. The big sardine boats lay idle, boats were sold, canneries closed. The sardine fishery that so many had depended upon had failed. As always, the little boats that fished locally for crab, salmon and the long line fish continued and prospered in their modest way. Without the sardines though, the game had changed dramatically.

The Marine Transport Workers Union, now affiliated with the Industrial Workers of the World in the 1930's, came under attack and events began to conspire against the labor movement. Organized labor became viewed as the first cousin to the mafia or communism, later demonized in the infamous McCarthy hearings. Labor organizations became suspected as being 'red' and this suspicion found a willing companion in business interests wishing to weaken the labor movement. Within the unions there was racketeering. Corruption and large sums of money generated by union dues attracted organized crime involvement. This further eroded the public image of the unions. The Korean War came, and the red scare became real when American men died fighting the Red Chinese communist troops that backed the North Korean incursion into South Korea. Now, not every fisherman wanted to be a member of an association. There were incidents between members and non-members. The tempers of striking crabbers in San Francisco were inflamed one pre-dawn morning when a truckload of crabs arrived from northern California to satisfy the markets of San Francisco, markets which were deprived of crab by the local strike ongoing in the port. The San Francisco guys were tipped off by the truck driver of the scab crabs and they met the truck with Gerry cans of diesel. They dumped the diesel over the neatly stacked boxes of crab in the truck parked in the alley, waiting to be unloaded to their markets. Northern fishermen were not going to break the strike on this day in the port of San Francisco. The buyer was forced to dump the entire load and the Alioto fish company suffered the loss of 12,000 pounds of crab. In-fighting and squabbling amongst the different ports grew steadily worse as the days of the strike added up. Challenges to their solidarity mounted. But the independent nature of fishermen proved to be the real enemy in the demise of the labor movement of fishermen. Fish companies who purchased the catches of the fish profited from the disunity of the fishermen and a young antitrust lawyer from a prominent family of fish buyers pointed out that the striking groups of fishermen colluded with each other to fix prices: it was legal for association members to talk amongst brother members but they could not collude with other ports.

Now, Marketing Associations once again attempted to bring collective bargaining to fishermen within their homeports. It was just more complicated now as some were for it and some were against it. There were membership agreements and market orders, all legal and proper, but there were more and more 'free riders', those that benefitted without paying assessments. Although talking to other ports about price was the thing that was illegal under antitrust, ways were found to accommodate that need with a wink and a nod.

*   *   *

Most in the hall today were association men, working class people dressed in blue chambray, plaid shirts and Big Bens. The men were a good-natured lot and laughter occasionally erupted in the din of the conversations. They had all known hard times, worry, and success; this was accepted and expected as part of the deal of being a fisherman and it was a component of their life that William X-ray summed up pretty well: "Hell, the Depression could come and go again and Patsy and I wouldn't even know the difference!" A pearl of perspective from X-Ray. Occasionally a raised voice would erupt in the hall from one group or another as someone gesticulated with arm movements in an argument. It was not long thereafter that Arne called the meeting to order.

"OK, let's get started." Arne clapped twice and then repeated himself. He got help from some members in quieting the group, though most talked on until they concluded their private conversations.

"We got one order of business today and that's the market orders. I think we got a chance to get signed up with the buyers before opening day, maybe. Cal Shell isn't talking, but that's okay, that's normal for them. Now you know I have no idea what the City and Bodega are doing," Arne paused, and laughter broke out because they knew *he knew* but couldn't say, "but my guess is its pretty much the same up there as it is here. A few of the fellas up there aren't ready to go and would rather sit out awhile, but that's not right, we're lookin' for a fair price here." Arne stopped and a voice from the crowd stated flatly but clearly like a bullfrog croaking from the pond.

"Well they never are ready. They like to wait around for a week on strike and keep the out of town boats away," spoke the Lump in his matter of fact baritone voice. His statement was commonly held knowledge. "Not such a bad idea when you think of it." he stated as an afterthought and a chuckle.

Shouting erupted.

"Well that's not right; we don't tie up for that!" A voice spoke like a shot from a barrel. Thereafter, an avalanche of opinions followed:

"We all go together or we all tie-up together, otherwise it's every man for himself!"

"We can't let them tell us what to do down here, we can't let them play our hand for us and make us go, that ain't right either!"

"If we get signed, we should go fishing, right is right; support the local buyers who support us!"

"Wait a minute, Wait a minute. Hold it there! This isn't the way to start out! Everybody settle down a gall-darned minute!" Arne waved his hands as he spoke. He continued after the mob quieted a bit.

"Let me tell you what I know for sure. I talked to the City *and* Bodega a few days ago-not about price-but on another matter..." Arne waited a few beats for it to quiet down; it didn't, so he started back in, "The guys up at Bodega feel they can get signed up with Harbor Joe and Meredith. They figure that's enough to get going and the other buyers in the port will fall right in line. Now, listen to me." Arne spoke over a few loud voices still chattering in the back of the hall. "Harbor Joe already said he'd sign and United is ready to sign in the City. If United signs, the rest of the buyers in the City will sign."

"What about Cal Shell?" Someone shouted from the back of the room.

"No word yet." Arne said in brief reply. This question was the elephant in the room and was on everyone's mind, at least anyone who was familiar with the way the markets worked. Cal Shell was the largest buyer on the coast, and they set the price and most knew it. Everybody wanted to know what Cal Shell was going to do, especially the other buyers. It was risky for a competitor to buck Cal Shell and the man in charge, Big Bob Bogota, had a long memory when it came to adversaries.

"They gotta sign if everybody else does, don't they? They can't *not buy* when everybody else is buying?" There came the shouted question from the crowd.

This set the meeting off like a firecracker, some men shouting, some agreeing and some disagreeing. The little groups now realigned themselves and the room took on a heightened emotional charge.

"Hold it, hold it!" Arne yelled, "We're all off course now, let's start over. We gotta decide what we think is a fair price amongst ourselves in this port and submit market orders *here* to see if we can get 'em *signed here*. That's the first step and we're not going to get anywhere by talking about what other ports are doing or what the smart thing to do is up and down the whole darned coast! You know how I feel about that but the way you and I feel about what other ports are doing is not the thing here today. We can talk about that later after we vote on a port price *here*. We can take it from there but we gotta have a market order price here *first*." Arne tried to speak some sense to the gathering momentum of chaos. There were some real hard-heads in the meeting that weren't afraid to speak stupid-talk or throw a punch.

Young Alex had been in the back of the hall all the while, listening to every word. He was a bit intimidated by the emotional pitch and tempo that the meeting had reached, expressed in loud voices by large men, the very same men that he was otherwise used to seeing as friendly and jokey in the coffee shop. Now in the hall, these men were shouting at each other. His Dad was no different; he had been transformed into a ringleader. Alex felt small and invisible now and in unfamiliar territory, territory that was increasingly turning hostile.

The meeting continued and it began to narrow its focus to just what the asking price for crabs in the port should be. Arne used all his efforts to keep the meeting from straying into chaos, lest all be lost to the loudest voices in the room. Cal and Leif walked in late and stood next to Alex, listening to the discussion from the back by the door. Sig had been mostly silent from the beginning of the meeting, differing to Arne as the voice for *Valkyrie*. Other stragglers and late comers filtered in, including the deckhands from the *Warlord*, Wilbur and Duster. They didn't like what they were hearing, it wasn't long before they started running a critical dialogue amongst themselves in low conspiratorial tones, sniping as they listened to the meeting. Other people spoke in low tones and grumbles as well.

Arne attempted to bring discussions on the floor to a halt. Things were getting out of hand.

"Hold it, hold it. Let's have a motion on a particular price and discuss that, otherwise we'll never get anywhere." He said.

"I make a motion that we submit for sixty-five cents," a voice rang out and an avalanche returned various replies, issued like rifle shots.

"Why not submit for six bits? Seventy-five cents! I say."

"Submit for seventy-five, then you can negotiate from there!"

"They're worth six bits if they're worth anything at all, hell. Ask for what they're worth!"

"If you do that, I guarantee you won't be setting gear on opening day, mark my words. You better go for what you know you can get signed and not screw around!"

"You never know what it is you *can* get until you ask! You better not start low and negotiate down from there!? Shit."

A phone call came into the hall office. It rang from a little room behind the back wall which separated it from the larger interior of the Grange hall.

The little room didn't get much use and the calendar on the wall hadn't had the month changed and was exactly a year behind. There was a small window with a spring-loaded pull-down blind, sun bleached at the half-open mark. It was big enough for a desk, two file cabinets and two other chairs besides the bigger one behind the desk. Everything looked old-fashioned-from the phone taking up space on the desk to the off-kilter picture on the wall, everything was out of date. The telephone was a blocky, black device that took up a chunk of desk space, a desk adorned with a ratty old green and leather blotter with phone numbers written all over it. Arne turned away from the rising conversations in the roomful of agitated men to answer the ringing phone. He was getting weary of being the crowd monitor and cooperation was swiftly giving way into disorder. It was with some relief that he turned away. He had a pretty good idea who was on the other end of the phone line.

He picked up the receiver and the voice over the line asked in an abrupt, straight forward and high-pitched voice, "Well Arne, are you prepared to tie-up? We can't get Harbor Joe to sign now."

It was Junior, the call was from Bodega and they had trouble up there now.

"What happened? I just told my guys down here everything was fine up there, Junior. Hell, we're all in the hall right now and the guys are in a stir," Arne said with a combination of alarm and disgust.

"Well it's not fine up here. Dee called me and said he can't sign unless Bogota signs. It's a mess I tell ya."

"Did you have a meeting yet?" Arne asked.

"A meeting? What good does that do now? We lost our main buyer. And all the out-of-town boats sell to him to boot! Cal-Shell doesn't want to have a meeting until after the weekend." Junior's voice raised a decibel.

"Junior, you know that's no good. We got boats from out of town here too and they're restless to go, the City too. They can smell a rat and if you don't even have a meeting, what's that say? It says we're just try 'in to hold them back from fishin', that's what that says. At least have a meeting and submit a market order for unity's sake. At least that shows you're trying. The worst they can do is turn you down- but give the buyers the chance to sign. We were just about to vote on a price down here. I can't tell these guys this and still have a hope to hold it all together down here. This isn't anything but dock-talk you're telling me."

"You better well goddamn believe it isn't dock talk, Arne. These guys don't have a buyer and you better hear that even if you don't like it." Junior was a straight shooter and he was also prone to excitability. His voice raised an octave when emotions took hold, and nobody talked over Junior.

"What I like and what I don't like doesn't have a lot to do with it, Junior." Arne made a concerted effort to hold his temper and tone the conversation down an emotional notch. He continued, "All I know is I'm in a hall with fifty men that expect that their time is being well spent talking about the price of crabs and market orders. If you ever want to get cooperation from this association again you better have a meeting before the season opens. You better calm down and think about this before you start talking tie-up and go away for the weekend." Arne didn't raise his voice throughout his toned-down reply, even though his dander was up under the surface. Junior was a force to reckon with and the conversation continued.

"You telling me to calm down?" Junior began and Arne knew he was in for both barrels now, "You oughta be in my shoes up here and see how calm you are!" Junior almost shouted into the receiver. He and Arne were not gaining on the situation; losing ground was more like it.

Out in the rumbling crowd, Duster stepped forward from Wilbur in the back of the hall. He found a clear space on the hardwood floor near the door and he spoke.

"You're all crazy. This is the stupidest thing I *ever* seen! You know there's lotsa crabs out there waitin' for us. Let's go get 'em! Shit, it's not hard to figger' out!". Duster exclaimed aloud and Wilbur started laughing at his partners' gutsy stance. Only a few looked at Duster. They were familiar with him and what he was. They didn't respect his boozy opinion now or before. Voices from the crowd were buzzing.

"We waited too long as it is to get these market orders out. We can't get in a jam now or it's a strike right on through the opener for sure. I say ask for what's fair and something that's reasonable, something we can go for right now!"

"I think he's right; we don't hold all the cards in this." Grumbles of agreement rippled across the crowded floor.

Back on the phone call, Arne was getting nowhere with Junior and his meeting was getting out of control. Arne thought Bodega was flying by the seat of their pants or trying to pull a fast one up there without a meeting. Either way it was bad. Arne spoke, but Junior kept posing arguments that made sense, mostly emotional. They did agree to continue talking tonight and not just go home for a few days. Arne hung up the phone and walked out of the office to address the crowd.

"That was Junior. Harbor Joe won't sign now, wants to wait and see what Cal Shell does in the City. Our 75 cents is not looking too good," Arne finished with a reference to what had been discussed around the harbor as a fair price. The wind had gone out of his sails and nothing had ended on a good note. Arne was out of fresh ideas. Tom and Bill approached him, and Bill spoke.

"You just gotta save what you can Arne, just move ahead and do the right thing even when the other guy might not. You can't let the other ports influence us, not now. You said it yourself; you gotta get a price here first. Hold a vote, submit market orders, see where the chips fall, that's all you can do." Bill spoke reason to Arne in quiet conspiratorial tones.

"You're right Bill, make a motion and let's get this over with." Arne said.

The motion to submit for $.75 was made by Tom, Bill's son. There was plenty of discussion to follow, plenty of tempers flared and points were followed by counterpoints. In the end, the motion carried, and market orders were to be drawn up and submitted immediately. Guys were feeling good about the accomplishment and the $.75 position. Arne was in the little room ready with his little stack of blank market orders. He was just about to call Junior and tell him of the decision when the phone rang. It was Junior on the other end of the line.

"Tiny Tim just called me. The City submitted for sixty-five cents this afternoon and the orders were immediately signed by all the buyers. They're gonna set gear tomorrow at midnight. The buyers up here say they'll all sign too. It looks like the matter is settled for us Arne and they probably did us a favor, considering. They got us out of what could've been a helluva mess."

Arne resisted a temptation to get angry. "And it only cost us a dime a pound."

This was no favor the way he saw it, it was a submarine job, torpedoed, sabotage and he wouldn't soon forget it. They City could have at least *called*. He took a deep breath and focused on Junior, "Thanks for calling Junior, you're probably right, got us out of a jam. We'll get market orders out this afternoon down here. Good luck." He was reserved and with that he gently set the receiver down and contemplated the crowd still assembled in the hall. There was no easy way to tell them.

He emerged from the office and stepped up to the table and banged on it with a book until the hall got quiet. He spoke and he gave it to them straight,

"The City signed for $.65 cents, Bodega is gonna submit for the same, Junior was on the phone. It's a go for the opener at $.65. They'll be setting gear at midnight tomorrow and that's it. We gotta submit for $.65 and go with them, they set the price for us." and turning to Bill he said quietly, "at least Junior had the decency to call, more than I can say about the City."

The first shout was from Dewey's deckhand Duster, "See there, those fuckers never wait for you! They made fools outta you all! Well good; I'm glad we're goin!" He turned to his partner and said loud enough for the crowd to hear,

"C'mon Wilbur, let's get outta here, get away from all this stupidity, *stupidity* so thick you could cut through it with a knife. That guy who ramrods this outfit might be the stupidest fucker of them all." Duster spit on the floor and they both left the hall.

Duster was a drifter and what he said, his insult to Arne, had only been heard by a few around him and he was ignored by those, just as they always ignored no-counts like him. Unfortunately for Alex, he was right behind Duster and blushed red upon hearing this disrespect directed toward his father and then seeing Duster spit indoors. On the floor? That was an outrage to his thinking. Unfortunately for Duster, Leif was next to his little brother and heard every word that came out of Duster's crooked little mouth. Leif quietly followed Wilbur and Duster outside; he was right on their heels.

Now Duster and Wilbur, whether they were separate or together, didn't amount to much and seldom were they apart. They were waterfront itinerants, moving from one situation to the next, season to season. The two constant things in their life were trouble and alcohol. They seemed to find trouble where others might not, and trouble and alcohol drove the events that shaped their lives. They spent a lot of time in bars, mouthing off at every opportunity, talking big and backing each other up. They were right at home with mouthy confrontations, engaging in small arguments that smarter men shrugged off or ignored. Duster and Wilbur would take this day as a victory and proof that they were right. They were completely ignorant of what everyone else knew; they were stupid drunks. To them, the silence meant that they had prevailed at being the smarter or the tougher man. The fact was that they were troublesome fools that no one wanted anything to do with. Today was no different and they thought they had left the meeting with the last word on the subject and were once again vindicated. Within the parameters of the world they inhabited, they were the bigshots today. They were all puffed up like big fat toads as they walked outside, headed back to the bar.

"Fuck'in pissants. We showed their asses and we'll show them again any day." Duster spoke to the empty street ahead.

"You showed *them*, Duster. Showed them where the monkey put the peanut; shoved it right up their ass, damn straight!" Wilbur added.

"Hey Duster." Leif spoke quietly right behind them, coming up on the two.

"The fuck you want, little square head?" Duster turned toward Leif and he planted both feet, squared off.

Leif was right-handed so he took one step forward with his left foot and positioned his left shoulder facing Duster. Suddenly and with poise, his left hand came up quick to Dusters face in two short jabs. Duster's head rocked rapidly back twice, not unlike a speed bag in a boxing gym. With the same speed, Leif's right hand followed, and his right foot shifted forward to add weight to the blow, his torso twisted. The weight of his body went into the punch that landed below the left eye of Duster. The impact lifted Duster's wiry frame into the air and he landed in the street with a puff of powdery dirt and an audible thump. His shoulder blades hit the ground first and this knocked the wind from his chest and made his stomach jump. He started to gasp for air and dry heave all at the same time. Leif stood looking at him on the ground, waiting. One of the letters on Leif's high school jacket towered over Duster laying on his back in the dirt and in the street. Leif wasn't a street fighter and he just stood there waiting for Duster to get up before he hit him again. As he waited, Dusters' sidekick Wilbur swung a 2x4 at the back of Leif's head. Cal caught Wilbur by the wrist like he was Maury Wills snagging a line drive up the middle. He just held it there and squeezed the scrawny wrist until Wilbur made little whining noises. Leif turned and looked at this sneaky assailant like he was a mongrel dog stealing food. Wilbur was realizing the terrible mistake he had made; he should never have snuck up and tried to hit Leif from behind. He had a few seconds to contemplate the horrible punishment that would soon be inflicted. But he was saved.

Uncle Sig arrived and stepped between Cal and Wilbur and got a hold on each man's forearm, his big hands wrapping around until his thumbs overlapped his own fingers in a vise grip.

"Vhat the hell; just vhat do you think you' boys are doing out here? That's the end of it, vhatever it is." Sig's voice was exceptionally large when he raised it and he was not to be questioned in any way when he sounded like this.

Cal immediately let go of Wilbur and stepped back. He walked over to the puking and gasping figure of Duster in the dirt and spoke. "Well, Well. Now we know *why* they call you Duster, shit-bag!" Cal chuckled before continuing, "You best stay right there in the dirt, son, or I'll settle your hash, proper."

Leif walked off and left the scene in the street to collect his little brother and return to the hall where the meeting was breaking up. Alex had watched the whole thing happen from the safety of the hall stairs, frozen solid with disbelief at what he was seeing. It was just like in the movies because the good guys won; but it was scary. Leif arrived and rubbed his blond toe-headed brother as they walked back inside.

"Boy, you really hit that guy hard. That was the coolest thing I ever saw in my life! Were you scared?" Alex said.

"I was just saving those two from Cal. He would have killed 'em both." Leif replied and then looked down at his little brother and gave him a big smile and said, "What you talkin' about, scared?"

Alex had experienced a wide range of emotions during the last five minutes; shame and uncertainty, fear and excitement, pride and vindication, the butterflies in his stomach might not ever settle. He thought for a minute during the melee that *he* might be the next one to throw up. He followed his big brother inside to wait for his dad, now leaving the empty hall.

The crew of the *Valkyrie* were done for the day; it had been a long one that started well before the sun. They headed home from the harbor and they let Alex ride in the back of the pick-up. The view looking back was sweeping and the day had held much for an eleven-year-old to think about. Alex reviewed the day's events and decided the fight was the best part, followed by the rowboat in the morning. And then there was the meeting; he didn't know what was going to happen with everybody so riled up. The day had seemed to be a weeklong event and he was now ready for the warm familiarity of home, dinner, mom and bed. He'd be in for more adventure soon enough though, because he was going out to set gear on opening day, the very moment that all this preparation and anxiety had been leading up to. He was crew. The preceding weeks had been an education; his brother, Sig, Cal and he had gossiped, laughed and told stories as they endlessly spliced the ropes, repaired the traps, painted the buoys and finally today, loaded the boat. This was how his first crab season began. Above it all however, he had the chance to be with his dad and show him his worth as a worker not just as a kid. With his dad and the crew, he anticipated adventure and money. The talk was of a good season. They would soon find out.

"Deep, wide and continuous." his Uncle Sig had joked about the antici-pated crab harvest. "You put wishes in one hand, and you put poop in the other, then you see which hand weighs more!" They all laughed.

The truck drove east toward home and away from the setting sun in the west. The sky was marked by white high cirrus clouds that turned yellow and pink to the north and the sky to the south remained a cloudless blue. By the time the truck had arrived in the front yard, the high cirrus clouds were red and magenta. There was another layer of clouds appearing in the furthest north and they looked like a dark purple wall, low on the horizon. Arne spoke to Uncle Sig after the truck stopped in the driveway and they all got out.

"Stay for dinner?" Arne asked.

"Naw, I'm all in, thanks just the same. Got a list of things to do tomorrow on the boat, I thought vee might have an extra day, but no. Just as well. I'll be seeing you around tomorrow." Sig replied and turned to Alex and added, "You did good today Alex, a helluva crewman you are"

Alex nodded and smiled. "Thanks. Bye Uncle Sig."

The kitchen was warm and humid from the cooking. Olivia had all four burners going on the stove. She smiled and greeted them, "Well there you three are, I was about to call the coast guard." She gave Arne a hug and then to Alex she said, "How was it Alex?" She gave him a hug and continued. "What's that horrible smell on your shirt? It smells like rotten eggs- take it off this minute and throw it outside! Wash up and hurry, dinner's almost ready."

Alex talked all through dinner, jabbering, told her about the whole day chronologically, leaving out no details, beginning with him rowing out to the boat and ending with the fight in the street. He didn't tell her that he had a big knife of his own now, thanks to Uncle Sig. His father commented when Alex got to the part about the fight.

"There wasn't any "fight" about it from what I heard," glancing and smiling at Leif, "More like you taught him a lesson."

Olivia had all kinds of comments and cautions for her little boy Alex, but she kept them to herself. It was his day with the men in his family and not with momma. She couldn't resist a comment about the fighting though.

"Don't you think *you* can go fighting young man." She turned from Alex to Leif. " You could have gotten hurt Leif." She felt bound to chide them both, duty-bound in a motherly way.

"I don't think there was much chance of *me* getting hurt, Mom. Maybe a scrape on my knuckles is all." Leif flexed and examined his right hand, grinning.

Olivia had the floor now, "I honestly don't know what gets into you men during crab season." She stated. "All the rest of the year you are polite and respectful for the most part. Then comes the buoys hanging on the fence and suddenly, it's like war. Is it the paint fumes? You all get keyed up and on edge and act like savages."

"It is stressful at times; I grant you that." Arne replied.

"It's a God danged free for all, is what it is. The whole season comes down to the first week and God forbid a breakdown. You work on the gear for a month, go fishin' for cheap and hate your friends. That's the truth of it." Cal laughed.

"Well it's not all that bad," Arne defended.

"Thank God things settle down after a week before you kill each other." Olivia finished and got up from the table and walked to the stove. She had seen many a crab season to know what she knew, had come by her opinion honestly.

Later that night at bedtime, Olivia gave Alex a kiss and tucked in his covers, she confided in him, "Your father said you work just like a man, I'm proud of you."

This praise from his father was about the best praise he could get. It was with a feeling of approval that he laid his tired little body to bed after dinner. He drifted off into the deep sleep of the contented innocent. Alex dreamed he was flying high above a pastoral countryside on a bright summer day, arms spread like wings. Swooping down low and fast, the terrain below him changed to a brilliant blue and green swamp with crystal clear water. He could see fish beneath the surface and among the grasses. He skimmed over the water for a close look and he came face to face with a smiling bullfrog. The friendly amphibian had big frog eyes and a human grin of white teeth like the Cheshire Cat. It was a shock and he woke up. There was a sound against the window. He sat up and identified the sound as that of the swishing of the trees in the wind and rain. Half awake, he listened and heard the sharp report of the whistle buoy and then he fell back to sleep.

* * *

Sometimes it is hard to tell when summer ends and winter begins in the latitudes below thirty-eight, but there are signs that a change is nigh. Sometimes, the gradual arrival of winter is accompanied by an autumn that is warm and mild. The tides seem a bit lower and the water a little higher on the pilings at high tide. The afternoon light has a bit more gold and the shadows are longer. These clues can foretell that a change in the season will occur more sooner than later.

Then in a different year, autumn can leave with a bold statement. It briskly leaves behind those mild days in the harbor, it is dark and windy. The sound of the sea and swell is a rumble in the quiet night and a fresh breeze has piled all the leaves against a fence. This wind is different from the summer wind that blows off the top of the fog bank or breezes off the land. This new wind started many a mile away and now comes from the opposite direction of the summer winds. The fetch between it and the shore has generated a sharp and quick sea, unrelenting in its march along the coast to pound upon the rocks and beaches. Looking out upon the hazy horizon, the waves are pushed on by winds that leave foamy trails stretching behind the churning sea of corrugated energy. Boats are dwarfed between the watery valleys, rising in and out of view if they are unlucky or unwise to be out among them. Such was the weather on the opening day of the crab season that the Skarsen family had prepared for all autumn long.

The low-pressure front had passed through rapidly during the rainy night and now the high pressure behind it was driving the breeze from the opposite direction. The weather wasn't good, but it was hard to stop anyone from going out on the first day, anxious to get the gear off the boat and in the water and hopefully, filling up with crab. Everyone also hoped, of course, that the weather would moderate.

Uncle Sig and his crew were the first to depart from the harbor on the *Valkyrie*. She slowly turned the corner at the jetty entrance. She leaned a bit further with the added weight of the traps on deck and more down below the hatch, 35,000 lbs. of extra weight. She was still more than seaworthy, in fact more so under the weight. *Valkyrie* swung 'round to the course for the buoy upon exiting the harbor, plowing through the short and steep chop ebbing across the bar. The ebb-chop had little effect on the heavily laden boat, save for a thorough spraying of saltwater on the windows. Alex felt his stomach hollow with excitement and motion sickness as they made their way to the buoy.

Arriving at the buoy, she adjusted her course and the boat met the weather head on. The *Valkyrie* rose up and then descended gently down the back of the first swell, then the second. She had a four-hour trek out to the grounds on this course. The pitch of the engine rose and fell with the sea as it labored to push the heavy vessel forward. *Valkyrie* occasionally threw water back over the cabin roof and onto the deck as she met a sharp swell head-on and triumphantly. Many hours from now, the sun would rise in a grainy haze of purple and gray. The wind that came behind the front under the purple-dark sky was fresh and wet. Some called it a dirty northwester and it never brought anything good.

"It's not too danged good." Arne commented to Sig, both men standing at the wheel.

"No, that it's not." Sig replied.

Valkyrie was pushing through those seas with steady progress when she met the real weather about an hour out. The rising at the bow became abrupt and there she then began rolling in a side-to-side motion to accompany the rise and fall. It was sometimes irregular in its intensity and interval and this made it more challenging for the crew to work on deck, going about the business of chopping bait and stuffing bait jars. Alex, feeling queasy, was lodged in the open back door of the cabin just in case he wanted to puke. He was forbidden to go out on deck, let alone to the rail to puke, as Cal had made that very clear.

"One hand for the man and one hand for the boat!" Cal laughed and shouted as *Valkyrie* hit a sharp swell. He then turned to Alex and amended it. "Alex-you use *both* hands for yourself and don't you leave that cabin-even if you *have* to puke. Puke right on the deck and let it wash away".

Occasionally, an unexpected heave of the vessel would spur Cal and Leif to scramble and secure something that had become loose on deck. Watchful eyes then turned toward the stacks after the sharp roll and the *Valkyrie* would momentarily falter in her forward progress. The stacks of traps would sway slightly but that was okay. They were secured to themselves at the bottom trap and not to the boat. The lesson of the boat *Lisa* was a hard-learned lesson when she rolled over and sank with traps tied to the rail, all traps riding with her to the bottom. The *Valkyrie* now steamed ahead at a reduced throttle to improve the ride and Alex found a place in the galley and tucked himself away for a Dramamine sleep. Sig, in the pilothouse, considered the situation and watched the sea ahead. His one hand was always near the throttle just in case he had to back it off and punch through a wave that had no backside to cushion their descent into the watery valley below. Cal walked up to the bridge and Arne spoke.

"We better go to the top end and start setting going down the hill with this weather. It's not going to be getting any better the farther up we go, I can see that now. We got a way to go yet, but don't untie anything, Cal, until we get up to the top end and turn around. Keep an eye out for Alex, don't let him go out on deck." Arne was always even tempered. His calm demeanor inspired confidence.

"Oh, I will for sure. I already told him to not come out of the cabin even if he has to puke. He's asleep under the galley table on a pile of jackets. I'll be watching out for everything-that's for sure, you don't have to worry about that" Cal replied and then added after a reflective pause, "Why is it always rough on opening day? I'll never know."

Cal turned to go back to the galley where he had a chicken ready to put in the oven. It was his habit, along with all experienced crewmen, to let the skipper do the worrying about the weather and where to set the gear; he took care of the galley and the back deck. Old hands like he were more concerned with food, sleep and dry clothes. Besides, the boat was always tougher than the men on it, so why worry? He was vigilant about the back deck though; he presided over a wet and tidy kingdom that was safe and efficient and in the galley the coffee pot was always ready and food was always accounted

for. Cal now poured a half cup for the skipper and walked the inclined passageway to the pilothouse to hand it to Sig, standing in the faint red glow of
the compass light, red illumination across the features of he and the other
watchful faces, staring out the forward windows. The sound of the other
skippers chattering over the two-way radio blended with the low rumble of
the engine below. A voice crackled over the radio and filled the little
pilothouse.

"Well, it's not getting any better, that's for sure. We seen the better part
of this day already. Over." The transmission ending with the customary "over"
that signified the end of the transmission.

Sig held the microphone in one hand and took a cup of coffee from Cal
with the other. "Yeah, vell, vee get these traps off and then vee see the best
part of this day vhen vee put the stern to it. *That's* what's for sure. Vee be fine
vhen vee slide home. OK?" Sig signed off the end of his transmission with
the question spoken like a statement and then added,

"I see deck lights vaaaaay up ahead every now and then. I thought vee
vere the early birds." Sig said to the microphone.

"I think you know who that is. He got the jump, usually does." the
response replied flatly.

Arne and Sig knew it was Jack Dewey. They didn't approve of an early
start (unless they were at the head of it!). This was a widely held opinion for
the obvious reason, but Arne wouldn't ever give Dewey the satisfaction of
knowing that he got the ups on the fleet and how he felt about that. He didn't
approve of the way that Jack ran his operation: it bothered him for a few
reasons. The first reason was that Dewey was so darn one-way about everything, beholding to nothing except his own personal gain. Secondly, he didn't
know the first thing about sticking together or why that mattered. Of course,
as president of the association, Arne saw this as a significant and short-
sighted character flaw. The way Arne saw it, if we all acted this way, what
kinda place would this be?

The third reason was much simpler, and it galled him as much as anybody else: Jack was guaranteed to catch more crabs if his gear was soaking for hours with no other traps around them. The salt in the wound was, Jack was always high boat. That was okay but doing better than the next guy by always jumping the gun was a foul. Sig's voice drawled over the diesel rumble in the pilothouse.

"Vell I suppose you're right, vee all know whose lights those are. Not making any friends as usual; not over on this boat, for sure." Sig replied in his usual laconic understatement. Truth was, everybody in the fleet hated an unrepentant cheater, especially one who always came out on top. The radio started to come alive with random derogatory comments.

Up ahead and onboard the Warlord, it had already been a long day. They had left the harbor as soon as darkness fell after the meeting, hours before the rest of the boats. Jack had set a few traps as testers the week before as a sneak to see how much crab might be there. The results had exceeded expectations in some areas.

"Shee-it; look-eee there!" Wilbur howled as the first test trap hauled broke water, showing it to be stuffed with crabs up to the crossbars, easily a 60-pound trap.

"Crossbars!" Duster shouted.

Jack Dewey and the crew knew exactly what to do with this privileged information. They came out of the harbor and began to saturate the tested area that showed such great promise. They cleared the deck of the Warlord of her traps and started pumping up the rest from the hold. Duster and Wilbur were giddy with the knowledge that they were in the water hours before the rest of the fleet. Jack always found an angle to get away with setting gear before anyone else and this had paid off big for him many times before. It held great promise to do so once again. Jack wanted his gear in first and in the right spot; that's all he knew. Duster and Wilbur, wringing with sweat under the raingear after hours of continuous work, had cleared the deck and the hatch of all traps. All the gear was in the water and fishing. They were now in the process of flooding the hold before they would begin to run through the gear. The weather was sloppy, there was no denying that, but the flooded hold would not only act as a live tank for the crab, but the weight of the water would provide stability to the lightened vessel They anticipated catching a lot, all the traps were in a good spot and bad weather had little effect on their high hopes for opening day. They would begin to pull traps as soon as the hold was completely flooded. There might be as much as 20,000 lbs. of crab the first time through the gear and they figured they really had the 'ups' on everyone this time. They way Duster and Wilbur saw it; they were the smart ones and getting the most crabs was the only proof necessary of that. They stared into the watery darkness below the hatch and monitored the progress of the flooding of the hold. The *Warlord* had been on a slow course to the west as she made ready, wishing to stay a distance from the approaching and disapproving eyes who might see his deck empty of traps.

Wilbur did the only math he knew. "20,000 times .65? Shheeeee-it! We gon' get rich!'

"Don't jinx the whole thing stupid!"

The *Warlord* rolled far to port and hesitated there as her course came broad to the sea. She shipped a little green water over the port rail and across the deck. The big pumps hadn't filled the hold yet and the vessel was sluggish to come back from a roll, the shifting weight of the water below the hatch was in control of the *Warlord*. Jack and Duster recognized it as a *slack tank* and they didn't like it; nobody trusted a boat that was slack-tanked. Duster stood on deck at the hatch, watching.

"Shit." He muttered and stepped up on the hatch.

"Should have been full by now." Jack thought, looking down at the water roll from side to side in the hold.

"I hope there's enough room down there, hot damn we goin' get rich!" Wilbur was not on the same train of thought as Jack and Duster, all he could think about was crabs in the hold and money. He was gleefully stupid of any peril posed by a slack-tank.

"I told ya; don't jinx the whole operation for Christ sakes! You are a stupid fucker, ain't ya'?" Duster shook his head. "Go down in the engine room and make sure both pumps are runnin', this is takin' forever."

"How do I do that? Why don't you do it? I don't like it down there." Wilbur asked in a whine and a protest.

"Just go over to the pumps and see if they're all sweaty and cold, that'll tell ya if there's seawater runn'in through 'em. That's all you gotta do, stupid." Duster explained as if he were talking to an orphan child.

"All right, but I don't like it. I don't know why I have to do it." Wilbur said with resignation in his voice.

Wilbur walked up into the pilothouse and climbed down the ladder into the focsle, hesitantly making his way to the engine room. He just stood before the engine room door, bracing himself for the noise that was about to come when he opened it. He hated to be in this small space with the roar and the heat of the engine. He couldn't even think straight after being in there a while and his head rattled for an hour afterwards. Reluctantly, he grabbed the big steel wheel that secured the dogs to the watertight steel door. He gave it a turn and all four dogs released their grasp and the door swung open. Wilbur was assaulted by a wall of noise and heat coming from the darkness. The noise was threatening. It was as if the machinery would jump right off its mounts any minute and get him, screaming to deliver 300 horsepower of damage. The engine pulsed franticly in the center of the tiny room and the air around it vibrated against the ceiling, walls and ears-menacingly. He turned on the light and stepped into the hot and greasy atmosphere of a 40-weight sauna room. It was 178 degrees in the room, the exact setting of the engine coolant thermostat. There was a narrow passageway between the machinery and fuel tanks on either side of the engine and the space was lighted by a single 50-watt bulb in the center overhead, creating many shadows and dark areas amongst the hoses, belts and wires, all of them active in one way or the other.

Machinery and pipe added to the obstacles in the crowded space, but it was the noise and the heat to be reckoned with in this disorienting and hellish world. Wilbur was now hunched over and walking towards the back of the tiny compartment where he thought the pumps were located, all unfamiliar territory due to his avoidance of any job down here. His head touched the ceiling and his right shoulder brushed along the wing tank as he avoided getting close to the machinery in the middle of the room, just as if it were a thing that was alive, a monster waiting to rip and tear at him without reason. He knew where the pumps were, kind of, he couldn't see them clearly in the shadow of the massive engine block. He had to locate them definitively by extending his arm towards the place where he thought they should be. Then, the plan was, as instructed by Duster, he could put his hands on them to make sure that they were running hot or cold. This would be hard; it was scary, and he hesitated to do it. There were spinning belts down there on each pump just waiting to snare and maul his fingers and the hot metal engine block was waiting to burn his reaching forearm as soon as he stuck it into the darkness. He stood there waiting for his eyes to adjust to the dim light and he thought to himself aloud.

"That fuckin' Duster; sendin' *me* down *here*".

Wilbur was experiencing a new problem in this cramped and chaotic space. As he knelt beside the roaring engine, a queasy stomach was now added to his discomfort and this made for a hasty and hesitant effort to feel around for the pumps. Beads of perspiration formed across his forehead and slight waves of dizziness accompanied his motions. He reached in toward a chunk of metal emitting a whirring sound.

"This must be the pump."

His fingers found a cold and sweaty metal casing, confirming that it was pumping seawater into the fish hold. Wilbur recoiled his hand and steeled his nerve to mount the second attempt. That second pump was farther away from him and he knew he should walk around to the other side of the engine to check it, but crawling around to the other side of the engine was not what he wanted to do, especially with butterflies in his stomach. It only represented more time to be spent down in this noisy hell hole. Instead, he extended his bare forearm in an extended stretch, just wanting to get this over with and get the hell out of here. He reached and waved his hand around to touch it amidst the motion, noise and heat. For the painful few seconds that he extended his vulnerable arm, all he could think of were the stories of the guys that got limbs twisted off, lost fingers, broke arms, received burns or had their head spun around by tangled hair in the belts of the spinning machinery.

"I ain't doin' this no more!" He shouted into the chaos and heat.

His hand came to rest on the casing of the second pump and it was as hot as the engine: the pump was not working. Wilbur quickly pulled his hand back and stood up suddenly from his crouching position. The blood rushed to his head and his stomach was light, rising towards his throat and mouth. His knees were weak, his brow sweaty and his vision grew watery.

"That second pumps' quit," he mumbled to no one in the heat and the deafening roar of the engine. He bolted for the door.

He could not get out fast enough. He felt like he was going to throw up if he didn't get some cool air-and soon. He went through the engine room door and didn't even bother to close it behind him. He now was in a race to get out on deck before he puked. He scrambled up the focsle ladder and sighted the back door of the pilothouse like a runner sees the finish line. All he knew was to get out and he burst through the back door into the cold wind on deck and focused on the rail, where he would relieve his rising stomach of the bile he could now taste in his mouth.

Wilbur ran through the back door and rushed past Duster without a word. Duster was looking down into the hatch and never even saw the sprinting little man. Wilbur got to the 3-foot-high rail in time for his stomach to let go over the side, but his momentum and the pitching deck of the *Warlord* propelled him over the rail into the dark sea right into the bile and the contents of his stomach, now floating on the surface of the sea. The cold temperature of the water impacted against his chest like a stiff kick and then a restriction set upon him like a tight belt gripping his chest and he gasped for air. The first time he came up, gasping for air, he was thrashing in the water just past the stern of the moving *Warlord*. He saw the well-lighted deck and the hunched over torso of his partner Duster watching the hatch fill. His voice cried out like a small fire lost in the sun. It was soft and ineffective against the sound of the water in motion all around him, infused with a gurgling and lacking enough air to make his voice carry. That water was now penetrating the fragile warmth of his clothes and a slow chill began to take hold, a chill that would remain with him and never leave. He first felt it in his underarms, then his crotch and then his neck. When his head was dunked his cheeks and ears got cold-and fast. The coldness began to penetrate downward throughout his torso. His legs and arms began to get heavy and it was hard for them to support his head above water as they thrashed. He called and kept calling out to Duster, clearing and sputtering water between his furtive and inconsequential soundings. He watched only in short glimpses as the *Warlord* became a small and diminishing area of light in the watery and dark distance. Eventually, the darkness was all around him and it became quiet except for the sound of the water and the whistling of the wind, a whistle that held a final and dispassionate message for Wilbur; doom. Wilbur's thoughts turned longingly to the heat and the noise of the engine room he had been in just moments ago. These were his last thoughts as the tops of the wind-driven waves rolled over his struggling face.

Duster had waited long enough for Wilbur and went down below to look after him. He saw the engine room door open and something was not right. He got a little scared as he stepped into the noisy compartment to have a closer look around in the darker recesses, afraid to see Wilbur trapped in the machinery.

There was nothing: there was no Wilbur in there.

He hurried out past Jack and began yelling Wilbur's name as he ran out on deck. Just as he was concluding that Wilbur wasn't onboard, Duster was met at the back door by Jack.

"Wilbur's gone! I can't find him. He went into the engine room to check the pumps and that's the last I saw of him." Duster shouted.

"Gone? How long?" Jack asked

"I dunno, maybe ten minutes!" Duster answered, his voice cracking.

Jack went back up to the pilothouse and immediately looked at the compass and dis-engaged the auto pilot. He slowly brought the *Warlord* around in a man-overboard maneuver. As *Warlord* came around with a following sea on her quarter, 60,000 lbs. of water in the half-filled hatch shifted to the starboard side and the Warlord heaved over with the weight of the shifting water. She stayed on her starboard beam at a fifty-degree angle. The oncoming seas to windward pushed and pounded against her exposed chine and underside and the *Warlord* was now in a precarious position. Duster looked for a hand hold on the inclined deck and he clambered for the relative safety of the pilothouse. Jack needed to get a call out to alert vessels in the area of Wilbur's plight, but now he was confronted by a new and pressing danger: he also needed to right the listing *Warlord*, which was shipping water on the leeward side of the deck. Both needs were immediate, and he had to choose which to do first because the *Warlord* was on her port rail and water was now coming over and burying the deck with each successive wave. That pounded against her chine. His boat was showing no inclination to come back upright.

Jack braced against the wall with his feet. "Shit, we're going over." he muttered to himself as he reached for the microphone with his left hand to issue a man overboard call and spinning the wheel with his right. Jack was a lot of things but none of those things interfered with his instincts as a skipper, especially when the chips were down.

"This is *Warlord, Warlord.* We got a man overboard at our position in 40 fathoms-43250, 19 miles west of Half Moon. I repeat, 43250, 40 fathoms, man overboard."

Jack dropped the microphone and reached for the throttle. The goddamned boat was going over for sure if he didn't act fast and power her over to the starboard high side. The water in the hold was on the port, the water on deck was on the port and *Warlord* just laid there and continued to take a pounding from the seas. His last shot at salvaging all was to turn hard over to the port and try and shift the water in the hold, maybe force the deck water to run out the starboard scuppers. Jack cranked the wheel over and gave it full throttle, the engine raced when the propeller cavitated in the open air. Seconds passed slowly by and *Warlord* was not responding, she was just pivoting on her port rail, dug into the water. She stayed hove-to at fifty degrees and for the first time in his life, Jack Dewey sensed fear of the ocean. His chances of success were diminishing; he knew he might share a similar fate to Wilbur. Flares, rafts, survival suits, distress calls, all now crowded his thoughts along with the near certainty of dying if unprotected in the dark ocean. He pushed the throttle all the way to the pin and the big diesel responded with black smoke and a blast of prop wash, churning water flying high from the stern. The big propeller finally grabbed hold of green water, flinging it high behind the stern but then it impotently sucked air again, losing its grip. The *Warlord* propeller was getting no bite and no propulsion once more. Jack ran to the back door, saw it all in seconds before him: he was out of bullets, Duster was freaking out, tear soaked, talking to God. The *Warlord* was in irons and unable to break free from the weight of the water.

All the vessels in the area heard the initial man-overboard distress call come over the radio, yet they remained silent. The silence lasted only long enough for Sig to get to the microphone. All ears heard the voice of Uncle Sig booming over the radio.

"I think that's him just vest of us, I'm gonna have a look. Come back Jack and tell me how it is with you when you get the chance." Sig said and put down the microphone, adjusted course to the west and began his search for *Warlord's* crewman. Sig's commitment to the distress call was going to result in a costly delay, they still had all the gear on the boat, but that did not change a thing, Sig was answering a more important call than his self-interest.

The *Valkyrie* quartered into the weather on a westerly heading. She pitched and rolled slowly, the water was ankle-deep or better on deck on this new course.

"What are we doin'?" Leif asked.

"We're gonna go help search for the man overboard." Cal answered.

"Search for Warlord crew?" Leif asked with slight incredulity.

"You heard me. Get with it kid, let's get up top and look." Cal replied.

"Okay." Leif answered with a hint of resignation. He knew it was the right thing to do, to look for a man overboard, but he was conflicted, nonetheless. His first thought was to set the gear properly. After all, it was opening day.

Cal looked in the pilothouse on his way to the ladder and had a slight smile because he approved; he was hooked up with the right outfit. He shouted it out across the flybridge deck to Leif, above the din of the exhaust stack.

"Your old man and your Uncle Sig: They're the only ones out here who would sacrifice opening day for those no-counts on the *Warlord*. They're doin' you proud, Leif, do you know that?"

"Regular stand up guys." Leif said dryly, shouting back. He looked into the water and shook his head, not so sure of his father's plan. The chances of finding Wilbur were slim, he wanted to set the gear, he wanted to make some money, he pondered the consequences of setting the gear late or in the wrong place. He really hoped it wouldn't be too bad; he'd be the guy coiling the rope on his arm and stacking a deck load of traps all day.

Alex felt the boat wallow from the warmth of the cabin, the diesel stove cranked up behind him. He heard Leif shout from up above and he repeated Leif's words softly to himself, not knowing exactly what they meant.

"Regular stand up guys." Alex muttered quietly to himself.

* * *

On the *Warlord*, Jack Dewey continued to try and right the listing boat, helpless and in mounting disbelief at his fate.

"Was this it?" he wondered. "Is this how it would end?"

He knew that if he did go in the water, he had an excellent chance of dying, almost a surety on this very night. A small and insignificant death at that, in fear like any other man. He felt the fear creeping into the edges of his thoughts as he felt his boat lie there, helplessly on her side. Jack steeled his mind against fear and focused on the steps he needed to take right now, the steps necessary for hope. He never once thought this could happen to him.

"I better get a Mayday call off; she's not coming back over." he mumbled.

Just as he hurried to the pilothouse to make his Mayday plea over the radio, he felt the propeller get a solid bite of water again and the stern dug down hard for more: The *Warlord* had regained propulsion. She began to respond to the hard-over rudder and slowly she came iupright and onto the sea. Soon thereafter, the water on deck began running to the stern and then to the open scuppers on the starboard side, the water in the hold shifted. Jack got to the pilothouse and got a hold of the locked wheel and straightened her out and reduced throttle. He set the pilot and looked over at the microphone, still clipped in its holder.

"That's as close as I wanna get to see Mr. Davy Jones." He mumbled to himself, "*God-damned* close call."

He went to the back deck and saw Duster in the doorway, soaked from the chest down

"Wilbur's a gonner'. I never even saw him go over. He could be a half hour back for all I know. Last I saw he went down below to check on the pumps." Duster explained. "Shit Jack, I thought for sure we were goners too." He added.

"We'll start a search on the reverse course. We might find him, you don't know. Get that God-damned pump online before we tip over again." Jack said and went in the cabin to the helm. A small shudder came over him with the thought of Wilbur and what he might be feeling in his last moments. A fate he nearly shared. They made the first pass of the search and then came about for a second pass. The sea was still big and sharp, wind carried the spray from the port rail over to the starboard as they wallowed back out to the west at half speed, searching in the night.

"At least we got the gear set." Duster offered.

"Yeah, there is that," Jack replied flatly and without distraction from the thought of Wilbur and the slim chance he had

The *Valkyrie* arrived into the search area. She crisscrossed the area that the *Warlord* had established. She shipped deck water and it ran out the scuppers. She rolled back and forth in a slow pendulum-like motion. Into the night the two boats looked for Wilbur before other boats joined them in the morning light. There was no trace of the seaman who had been swallowed by the watery expanse. The other vessels who had joined the search late began to disappear back to port to get another load of traps. The weather was still rough, but it was moderating. It was now not a rescue, but a body search and none of the remaining boats were willing to tarry. Jack, Sig and Arne were the last to give it up. Sig set a course to begin setting his gear in the fishing grounds. After getting the gear off amid the many brightly colored buoys already there, he set a course for home as well.

Young Alex was conflicted; they spent all night looking for the same guys who tried to hit Leif with a board and disrespected his dad in public. And they had to set the gear after everybody else was done! He didn't understand what 'stand up guys' were, except Cal thought it was a good thing, something to be proud of. He sensed that there was more happening here than he knew about and he also knew that Leif wasn't too happy about it either.

"Do you think that the guy is still alive?" Alex asked his dad as the seas lifted the retreating stern of *Valkyrie*.

"No." was all Arne said. Leif walked over.

"That guy didn't have a chance after the first half-hour." Leif spoke to his little brother.

"Then why'd we stay all night looking for him?" Alex asked innocently and his father answered the question for Leif, who undoubtedly would have answered it differently.

"That is just the way we do things, son, that's all there is to it. You can't turn your back on a man in the water. If you do, you turn your back on the better part of yourself. It was a matter of life or death last night and we were there, that's why we looked, it's just that simple. It didn't matter who he was. I never once met him, but he had a family somewhere just like you have your family. His family will always remember that you tried all night to find him; that will always be what they say when they tell the story. People try and save other people and that's just the way it works." Arne paused and looked over to his older son Leif before he continued,

"Out here on the water we have to take care of each other, you have to do what you can if you ever expect to be treated the same, it's like a responsibility to look after each other. We aren't ever in this thing alone. That goes for when we are on shore too. Remember that." Arne finished, paused and thought for a moment and then softly added,

"Also, there's something to be said for feeling like you did the right thing, you have to feel good about who you are and what you do. That's a good habit to get into, Alex."

Arne patted his son on the shoulder before he went over and sat on the back hatch alone. He shook a cigarette out of a pack, lit it and stared off into the wake and the following seas. Alex turned to his big brother to see his response to all this, but Leif was gone and at the rail taking a leak. Alex turned and went into the cabin to find Cal who was at the wheel watching ahead.

"Whatcha' doin' little feller?" Cal asked when Alex entered the pilothouse bridge.

"Nothing." Alex answered, but he was thinking real hard.

*   *   *

So began the crab season of 1961 and so began the new decade. In this new decade, some of the young would feel an urgent need to restore ideals of justice and equality, which they felt were lacking in the country. The tide was turning, and the times were about to change. There would be a cultural war at home and a shooting war in Asia. The rules of conduct were about to be re-written and eleven-year old Alex would come of age during this time. The course had been set but the destination was not known. It would not be returning this way again, that much was certain- not much else was.

CHAPTER 2

Fickle Finger of Fate

Four teenage males were huddled in the living room watching television, they passed a joint around. None of them owned a television set, so they sat in the living room of an absent mother, away at work. A typical setting; couch and coffee table, wall to wall carpet, end tables with lamps, landscape print on the wall behind the couch. Brown and beige were the dominant colors in the room and the landscape print was a tiny island of blue, green and yellowish color on a wall. Middle American Conformity was a very common decorating style found in suburban homes. In fact, conformity was a common theme in everything suburban. But the sun was setting on the conformity that had served society well for a couple of decades. Now, parents, administrators, clergyman, etc., would ask today's youth, "Why do you want to be so different?" asking kids as if they had contracted some social disease. The sun was setting on these old attitudes and these dope smoking youths were in the vanguard of that. They had no possible way of knowing that they were rushing headlong into a newer version of conformity.

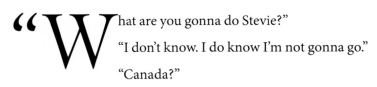"What are you gonna do Stevie?"

"I don't know. I do know I'm not gonna go."

"Canada?"

"I guess."

"Yeah, that's cool."

"Me too." another voice chimed in, sucking air in a giant inhale, "Dino's up there already, Vancooooouver." He said exhaling.

"Lotsa people up there already."

"I see Tony 's back from Nam. I think he's a junkie or something. Wow."

"He was at a party last weekend, trying to get hip to the skip. Poor Tony."

"Best athlete in school."

"Tony was a cool dude."

"At least he lived to make it back. He is different now though."

The conversation bounced around between hits off a football-shaped joint. The draft had been abolished and now there was a conscription lottery. Alex Skarsen and his pals awaited the annual drawing of the losing lottery numbers; *losing* was getting your number picked because nobody in the lottery wanted to go to Vietnam. They were kids trying to be adults but mostly, they got high at band practice and parties. If they had a job it was a minimum wage job, enough to pay for a room in a house they shared with others their age. Alex still lived at home with his mom. The teens were floating through this phase of their life without solid plans of what they wanted to do-long term, because the future was uncertain on the turn of a lottery number. But they did have strong emotions about what they did *not* want- getting drafted and sent to the jungles of Vietnam. They had seen the high school pals who joined; they shipped out and came back dead or altered for the worse.

"Whatever you do, you don't want to go to 'Nam. Fucking bugs and gooks in the jungle and they all want to kill ya." That was the gist of the tale that was told to them by those that made it back, confirming their worst suspicions.

Alex, Joaquin, Damon and Stevie had a band and the only long range plans they thought about was what they might do if they became famous rock stars. It was a common delusion among teen rock and rollers. They played loud and chaotic music with crappy lyrics and thought themselves to be artists of a sort. They weren't half bad but most of them had seen their talent peak out early, exhausting innate abilities and being lazy by nature, they declined to study music. They thought themselves touched by creative genius as did many others in this era. It was like this culture-flu going around and they had caught it. In this emerging culture, everybody was an 'individual'; an artist, musician, or a writer of some sort, or at least everybody knew one or two people who thought they were. Delusion was a practiced behavior and it figured prominently in plans for the near and distant future of these kids in front of the TV today. Not that plans were a thing that Alex and his pals dwelled on anyway, they weren't too ambitious. When the TV lottery got underway and the numbers rolled out, the excitement was subdued; they learned that they were not picked for a Vietnam jungle tour and they were relieved at their fate of course, but their cheering was more a sigh of relief, quickly replaced by the knowledge that a few close friends were destined for the jungles of Nam.

"Fuck. Frank's going, Zilm is too."

"Zilm can't hack it. He'll run."

Alex and his pals were now unencumbered by the threat of soldiering overseas. It was a bit of an anticlimax; they had gotten used to floating through their life without much ambition, suspended from the responsibility of making real plans for the future. Good times were now more frequently accompanied with pointed questions regarding the *Future,* so called. The burden of getting it together was presenting itself, more so than before. Get high, get girls, get famous was hardly a credible plan anymore. They filed out the front door toward Alex's car, a faded red Volvo sedan with a crunched in fender with a bad Bondo job. It was ugly but it started most times and it was the only car in the group. All four piled in and headed for The Spot, their favored place to get loaded. It had a view of the harbor and it was hidden by a small stand of pines.

*   *   *

Sig and Leif were out in the yard tying down a load of traps to a truck parked in the yard. Cal was bundling up shots of ropes, carefully counting out twenty to the bundle. Across the dirt yard stood a tidy one-story bungalow behind a white picket fence, the Skarsen residence, where Alex and his mother Olivia resided. Alex drove the red Volvo out into the front yard of the house then got out, ran back into the house and then quickly reemerged and got back in the car and pulled out of the yard, motoring through the gate. The sound of a busted muffler marked the car's departure down the road.

"That kid has me worried. Running around with a bad crowd." Sig broke the silence between the men.

"I wouldn't give 2 cents for any one of 'em, nor five cents for the lot." Cal said, disgusted.

"They're just kids, plenty of time yet to grow up. Alex is just on his own course since dad died." Leif said.

"I see that. Arne never figured on dying young, that's for sure." Sig said.

"We all didn't figure on that." said Leif.

"Tell you what though, tears me up to see little Alex goin' wrong. His old man would not approve if he were still around. I wanna kick his ass up around his shoulders sometimes." Cal said and spit on the ground.

"Now wait a minute Cal, Alex ain't doin' nuthin' nobody else his age ain't doin: times are changing, that's all. He's the same little kid that ran around here yesterday, just bigger and in step with the times. He's gonna turn out okay, you'll see." Leif offered.

"Yessiree, we will see." Cal replied and left it at that.

"Times are changing, that's for sure." Sig added. "I vonder if it's his own boat he needs?"

"Hell, no Uncle Sig. He's adrift with this music thing. Rock n Roll is all he thinks about right now. That and girls. He's not ready for anything that takes any gumption like a boat. But I tell you this, little Alex is gonna make his mark somewhere, someday. He's a smart little fucker and he wants to be good at something. He knows how to work; he always has a job somewhere and he likes the money. Or at least he knows that you have to have it in this world." Leif defended his little brother.

"Vellll, okay. Good to hear you say so Leif-y, you stand up for him like a good brother." said Sig. "But if the time comes, vee should stake him. That'll set him straight."

"Or sink him." said Cal, keeping his eyes cast at the dirt.

*　*　*

The four teenagers piled out of the red Volvo, walked along the worn pathway and sat down under the big pines overlooking the harbor. The afternoon sun warmed the bed of pine needles under their boney butts. They were a scraggly lot to look at; skinny, dirty Levis, long unkempt hair, various worn shirts and scuffed up shoes. Alex had a string of little colored beads around his neck and Joaquin had leather chaps on his forearms. Damon sported embroidered cuffs and Stevie wore green round sunglasses. They were hip.

"When we gonna have band practice again?" Alex spoke through clenched teeth, holding his breath after a strong inhale of cheap weed. He passed the joint to Steve.

"I don't know. Soon?" Damon asked.

"It's been a week." stated Steve, adding, "Can we borrow a PA from The Curse?" The Curse was a rival band.

"I can ask Rick. It's a no-go if they got a gig". Alex replied.

"They don't got no gig, we'd know about it if they did, Rick would see to that." Joaquin was a drummer and so was Rick, a budding teen rivalry.

"We gotta get our own PA. We can't sing through one channel and play through the other. It's all distorted." Steve put the cap onto that topic.

The sound of crunching pine needles on the path that led to them directed their collective attention to a curvy figure approaching. A woman rode up on her horse in a macramé bikini top. Her nipples, visible through the weave, were bigger than the erasers on a #2 Ticonderoga and they poked right out there, 'the high beams' as they called them. The boys were hypnotized by the sight, and they all were focusing on the fleshy nubs winking at them through the brightly colored weave of the bikini top. It may as well have just been a bikini top riding a horse, so focused they were. Their mouths were slightly agape, they were stoned and spellbound. The macramé top was working its magic, just as the curvy rider intended it to. Her long blond hair flounced around her tan shoulders and she sported Daisy Mae Levi cut-offs that rode up as tight as they could go to the camel toe. It almost wasn't fair; so overpowered by the sexuality and so ill-equipped to deal with her charms, the boys sat in stunned silence. They were very high, and they were stone-shocked in the presence of this overtly sexual creature now moseying along the pathway toward them. She was good lookin' and older, a college girl about 22 years of age and way out of their league. Somebody had to talk so Alex found his nerve and forged ahead; he was just high enough to act cute once he got started.

"I like the bikini top. You make it?" Alex asked.

She smiled. She knew she had a bite on the line, she knew men, was aware of her power over them. "Made it with my own little hands." She giggled a bit.

"You live in town?" Alex grasped for a conversational toehold, realizing he was stoned to the bone. The next words out of his mouth could prove that he was a dolt if he wasn't careful.

"Right down the street. I see you around town, you come in with the fishermen sometimes. I'm a waitress at the Crab Cottage down at the harbor."

"That's my uncle and brother you seen me with. I remember you. You look different on a horse." Alex couldn't muster the courage to tell her she looked delicious to him everywhere she was and especially half-naked.

"Maybe it's the clothes. You a fisherman too?" She smiled, conscious of what she was wearing and what she was not wearing.

She was flirting. Alex was encouraged.

"Yes. I work for them." Alex told a bold lie; it was getting easy to fib. He could do this all day.

"Maybe I'll see you around then, I'm Karen." She flipped the reins and the horse walked down the path, leaving the group of stoned teenagers silent and agape, sitting under the trees like the three monkeys who did not see, hear or speak.

"I'm Alex!" he shouted at her back and the butt of the horse.

*   *   *

"Man, she's fine." Joaquin broke the stoned silence after she was out of earshot.

"I'd walk a mile through her shit just to kiss her ass."

"That's disgusting."

"You see those nips?"

"That's all I could see."

"The high beams were on, man!"

"*You a fisherman too?*" Stevie mocked Alex in sing-song voice.

"What am I gonna say? I'm just a stoner? A high school dropout now flipping burgers at Rotten Ralph's?" Alex replied.

"It'd be the truth." Damon observed innocently.

"Fuck you."

"Stoner-Burger-Flipper, Stoner-Burger-Flipper." Damon chirped.

The group left the Spot and got back into the beat-up Volvo. They rode around smoking another joint, laughing at the folly of the world and making plans to get a gallon jug of Red Mountain for the evening. Alex opted to not be part of this plan, he didn't drink that shit and *his* mind was on *her* nipples in *that* bikini top. He knew he had to have something going on for himself to play in her league. The idea haunted him.

Was he just a Teen-Ranger after all? Fuck. Riding around in a car and getting high? Making plans to get loaded on a Friday night? They even referred to themselves as the Teen Rangers, the tacit implication that maturity was held at bay. This was *not* the impression Alex had in mind and it would *not* impress a sexy older chick. In fact, this self-image was getting a little depressing and the musician thing was also wearing thin. There was stiff competition for her time, no doubt. What was he doing anyway? Putting adulthood on hold? Was he pretending to be something he was not, a song writer for Christ sakes? Shit, he just got started living; what did he have to write about? He didn't finish high school; that was just a four-year parking place and he was too cool for school anyway. But what was he doing now, besides being a Teen Ranger and getting high, that is."

An older girl looked his way today and flirted with him, that much was a fact. He better *do* something about that if that was the way it was gonna be from here on out. It was time to get on with it, whatever or wherever. Carpe diem time kiddo.

*   *   *

"I want a job on the boats Uncle Sig." Alex walked out into the yard the next day and laid it on the line to his uncle. Cal gave him a sidelong look.

"Do you now? Vee could take you on this winter, maybe. Half share. Vee figure to go work up out of the River; vee could use another good hand. I think Leif and Cal would be happy to have you aboard. I know I would: Be doin' right by your dad." Sig said.

"I'll take it, half share or whatever share. When do I start?"

"Start right away. Vee vorkin' on gear now and vee took a truckload down already. Vee got a lot of buoys to paint, pins and jars to make up and shots to splice."

"I'll give notice at Ralph's today; they can get somebody else. Fuckin fry cook, believe that?"

"Cal says you're runnin' with a bunch of no-goods. They'll be no drinkin' or dope smokin', vee don't do that kinda thing, run a tight ship."

"Oh, I know that Uncle Sig, don't worry about that. I'm cool." Alex said defensively.

"Glad to hear it young man. *cool*, are you? Now, tomorrow you start up, painting buoys. That'll be okay?"

"What time?" Alex replied without hesitation. He was back and in tight with the family, there would be no more disapproval. This was good.

Some seeds lie dormant in the ground until some event causes them to sprout and grow. Such was the case with young Alex: Destiny walks with you and Destiny choses you when events align. Some just call it fate. The knowledge of the boats and the water that he had known as a child were under his skin and they were now awakened and revived. He knew what to do and when to do it, Uncle Sig didn't have to tell him much and didn't have to tell him any of the basics; the knots, splicing, how to tie up, safety, work habits, responsibilities and a lot more that might seem alien to a greenhorn. They were second nature to a waterman, no matter what age. Nobody on deck had to look over their shoulder to make sure Alex was doing what he was supposed to. If there was such a thing as fate or destiny, Alex was stepping into his; on the boats.

The familiarity with boats that he had enjoyed as a child only went so far now. Things in his carefree playground of yesteryear when he rowed about the harbor were not part of his workplace today. He soon found out that retraining was a thing he found himself doing every day. He kind of wished he would have payed closer attention to the work when he was a kid instead of skipping and playing through it all. He soon began to realize that the time he spent boat-riding around years ago didn't count as much as this kind of experience now. It was all kind of new in a way; and exciting too, an adventure. Another familiar thing was the warm re-acquaintance with the old gang from the harbor, the men who had watched him grow up. The group at the harbor welcomed him back into the tribe and they all knew him by name

and even though he was a lanky 6 foot 3, they still referred to him as Little
Alex. All were warm and welcoming except one: Big Bill Valentine-William
X-Ray. Big Bill Val took exception to Alex's haircut, or the lack of one.

"Get the shears!" X-Ray bellowed. "Good thing your old man isn't here
to see this! I'll cut that thing off! You look like a god damn Chinaman with
that ponytail! This ain't the Haight Ashbury!"

Every time he would see him this is how it would go. X-Ray was a big
scary guy and Alex started to avoid him, ducking around behind buildings,
cars, stacks of boxes and any available cover. X-Ray was not only *on* the
anti-hippie bandwagon; he was *driving* it. He was getting to be a pain in the
ass.

The next day came, the gear work was hard, and the day was long. In the
ensuing weeks, Alex pumped 100-pound traps to the top of an 8-foot stack,
bent stainless steel rods into hooks and pins, painted buoys and spliced rope.
It seemed like the splicing would never end. One day he showed up for work
in the morning and there were fifty coils of rope in the yard to be spliced,
mostly into ten fathom shots no less. Alex would soon find out that this
spelled out misery for his burger-flipping hands. Uncle Sig had decided to
change the ropes on 250 of his traps, a 20-fathom shot and 2 tens for each. It
started out like a fun thing: Alex stood up in the back of the pick-up with
four coils of rope, hands in leather welding gloves. Uncle Sig drove the truck
round and round stakes pounded in the ground at measured lengths until
Alex had the coils played out of their boxes and into straight runs of rope
between the stakes. Rope burns wore out two pairs of his gloves before all
the coils were done.

"Yee haa!" Alex shouted with excitement as the dust clouds swirled
around his upright body, pulling and flipping the ropes like a rodeo cowboy
with Uncle Sig at the wheel of the truck, spinning out in the dirt of an oval
track.

They cut the plastic ropes with a hot knife and stacked the rope rounds
destined for splicing. The short-lived excitement and fun stopped here on

that first day. Everyday thereafter for two weeks, Alex showed up at 8, lunch at 12, knocked off at 5; 8 solid hours of splicing rope, His hand was bent to the shape around his fid and it was just a preview of how it would be on the *Valkyrie*-long and hard days. Of course, there was camaraderie, jokes and, something new for Alex, beer drinking. Everyday Michael Henry would come down after 5PM with a couple of six packs with his crew, Skin and The Dago. Skin was a young pool hustler who worked for Mike and Dago was a grizzled, sarcastic, blue-collar version of Dean Martin with a mustache and about 45 years of hard living to his credit. They would drink and tell stories after work. Mike had the first story on this day.

"I remember one time your dad and I ran up inside the Islands, some of the Monterey guys had some salmons up there the day before. It was kind of a spooky morning and Uncle Henry turned down towards Martins Beach, he didn't like the looks of it." He was talking to Alex. "It was late May; it was my first season with the little *Gigi*. It was calm, almost flat really. A few hours after daylight this funny swell, close together like, came up on the glassy sea. We were inside the Islands in about 30 fathoms when the first cat paws whisked over the surface. We didn't think much of it; we were busy running the lines up and down. Pretty soon there was 5-10 knots of southerly breeze and when I looked around a few boats were running by me to the south. It suddenly looked kinda lonely out there! It got *my* attention. The *Gigi* was only 26 feet long, so I cut butt for the hut; home was 4 hours away or more under the best conditions. Your dad stayed and fished. After about an hour in on my way home, the wind had come up to about 25 and that swell we first saw was a sign of what was coming. By ten o'clock it was blowing 30 and gusting. I'm pretty sure it blew 60 before it backed off, at least it felt that way. It was too late for your dad, he got caught. Last I talked to him he was going to run before it. That's the last I heard from him that day." Mike told the tale.

"I was little back then" said Alex, "nobody said anything to me, but I knew something was wrong. Everyone was talking really quiet in the house and my dad was not around."

"Yeah, something was wrong all right. The Coast Guard kept putting out *overdue vessel* broadcasts every day. It's all we talked about down at the coffee shop. Everyone knew it was a lousy course from where we were; -quartering with it to the Point or in the trough to the City. And it blew hard. I felt kinda bad because I was the last one to see or talk to him." Mike said.

"That god damn boat the *Fin* was a roll-y son of a gun too." added Dago.

"Rail to rail." Uncle Sig said, "Tough old boat, so was the skipper."

Leif finished the story. "After about four days of this, we got a call at the house from the Coast Guard. My mom just froze and handed the phone to me, she was thinking the worst. But the message was my dad had been found at Pt. Reyes. Ole from Pt St George Fisheries came from the City once a week in the winter and it was him that spotted the Fin on anchor, one pole up and one pole down, the only boat in the anchorage. He put the glasses on the name on the bow and it was Dad. Ole told the guys in the City about the boat named Fin anchored up. They all jumped, knowing the story of the missing boat from Half Moon Bay."

Leif paused and smiled at Alex; Cal picked up the story from there. "Son of a bitch, it rained so hard after the wind quit that the deck on the old *Fin* leaked right on top of the batteries. The batteries discharged; they were completely dead. When we got the flares out, they were old and soggy to boot. No starter motor, no radio, no flares, no nothing. We read everything there was to read on the boat and we just sat there for four days, hoping someone would see us 'fore we died of boredom. Your dad read every magazine on the boat twice, read the soup can labels and we ate beans, canned peas and applesauce. The Coasties came up finally and gave us a battery. We were on our way home-in no time flat. One of the best sounds I ever heard was that 671 starting up."

"Mom was in tears." Leif said to Alex, "The first thing dad did after he got back was put a gen-set on the boat."

"That little old *Gigi* bucked for 6 hours against the weather to get home." Mike added.

This was a story from a different lifetime for Alex-childhood now seemed like a thing that happened to somebody else. *That was then and this is now* as they say, and *now* was the only thing that mattered to a young man. But it was always just a continuation of a theme whether he saw it or not. Fishing had always been the dominant thing in his life and his adolescent indulgences were only a brief interruption, a sidebar to the main story. Fishing was deep in his blood and the memories reemerged, clearly remembering the child who rode down to the wharf with his mom on the nights when the boats came in late with lots of fish. He remembered the box that was hoisted down onto the deck for the unloading of the fish. Alex would count the fish like a scorekeeper, hoping that his dad would be the high boat. At home, he and his little friends would climb the stacks of crab traps in the yard or would take all the crab crates and make forts and castles, stacking one on top of the other. There was always lots of rope available for tree forts, pulling carts and tying each other up. Skiffs in the yard lent themselves to pirate games. He had always been in the life and now he was back-in a different way, older and attempting to be on a par with the men as a co-worker. This beat the shit out of being a Teen Ranger. He even liked the beer better than the pot, except that in the end they both led to some form of stupidity.

The next day was just like the day before except for the rain. There was a big stack of traps and a big pile of rope and the crew chipped away at the work methodically. It was boring. On this day they broke for lunch and met up with Mike and the crew at Hazel's, a restaurant down at the harbor. Hazel knew the guys since they were children and she fed them for free. When they piled in, they didn't even order. Mary, the waitress, old enough to be their mother (and acted as such), served them hot dog sandwiches, fries and a Coke. It was free of charge and the free meal never changed. In return for this gratis meal they brought Hazel lings and Cabazone, fishes that were incidental catch from the crab traps. Occasionally the incidental catch was an octopus. They had all sorts of ideas for those creatures and it wasn't food.

Across the street from Hazels there was now the first incursion from the southern California developers who had 'discovered' a quaint little west coast fishing village, ripe for development. So of course, in their Disneyland mindset, they envisioned and thought that an *East Coast* fishing village would be nice, replete with faux lighthouse, faux mermaids (are there any other kind?), faux fishing boats, faux lobster traps (there wasn't a southern lobster in the ocean for 500 miles, an east coast lobster was easily 2500 miles away) and faux faux everywhere, all designed to make a tidy profit off the tourists who would of course be pulled in like metal to a magnet with their dependably disposable income, flung about like used tissues. They proceeded in the makeover of the little hamlet into a cash-cow: the old Ida's restaurant became the new Shorebird restaurant and it was a perfect replica of a traditional Cape Cod building. The enmity was ripe in certain quarters of the community against this makeover. Audacious pretense and the crass tourist commercialism from Southern California Arrivistas clashed with the locals' sense of *their* community, a community heretofore consisting mostly of fisherman, farmers, artists, braceros, poor whites, hippies and beatniks. The community was authentic, the developer's concept was not. The local fishermen did not balk from drinking in their new bar however, an addition to the community that they approved of, a new bar in town did have tangible value. And there were some good guys behind the bar who became their friends, Southern Cal surfers for the most part, but the manager was a corporate man straight out of Orange County, Bill McMann. Mr. McMann came from a family of 11, raised by observant Catholic parents who ran the household under strict rules. He and his siblings would often be required to line up when their father wished to address them, replying to their father with "Yes Sir" or, "No Sir". Little Bill thought this behavior to be normal (if not optimum), he modeled it and was propelled by this attitude to life in a middle management position. That being said, of course he resented the occasional takeover of his domain by the crude, unruly and intoxicated fishermen. They came to be known as

The Basic Fishermen and T shirts were made by the female wait staff, presented to them in a drunken ceremony.

The Basic Fisherman settled into their free lunch at Hazels. Outside of the blue tinted windows it was still raining, a little harder now. The wind chop in the harbor caused the anchored boats to strain against their moorings, testing the soundness of the anchor gear that they depended upon. One of those boats had already broken loose and was stranded on the beach, left high and dry by the tide. This was entertainment and the topic for a derisive discussion of the stupid boat owner. Their attention turned from the harbor to the recently built structure across the street.

"Shit: will you look at that place? I thought Ida's was bad with that paint job, but this is ridiculous. They name it after a stinkin' seagull? What are those, Old Salt statues outside now? What are they supposed to be, us?" The Dago said.

"I heard Barry from the head shop and his gang ordered dinner, ate and refused to pay-said *fuck you* and walked out" Alex joined in.

"Good for him. What's a god damned head shop?" asked Dago.

"He sells pipes, incense, posters, beads, you know, hippie stuff." Alex replied.

"Jesus. What is worse I don't know. A head shop is it now." Dago shook his head.

"Our little town is being invaded" Sig threw in and continued, turning to Alex, Leif and Cal. "Vhy don't vee knock off for the day; it's too vet and vee done enough for one day."

"Fine by me." Cal said.

"Me too." said Leif. "I'll probably go over the Hill this afternoon then. Wanna go Alex?"

"Sure." he replied.

After lunch and after Sig and the boys left, Mike, Skin, Dago and Cal lingered at the table playing pinochle. It was about 2PM and the blustery day was quietly passing them by.

"Is it too early for a cocktail?" Skin posed the pregnant question.

"It's always 5 o'clock somewhere in the world." The Dago growled positively with the old tome.

"Hell yes, I'm ready." Cal said.

"Let's go." Mike said, standing from the table, telling Hazel goodbye and thanking her.

They crossed the street and entered the Shorebird bar, the only ones in the place. The wood planking walls, and the ferns were accented by weak spotlights fanning out the shadows upon the weathered wood-a popular decor of the times. The overall atmosphere was dark, dark as bars should be when one seeks escape from the bright lights of reality. One got the feeling of being in an old barn except this had leather benches and barstools. After sitting at the bar, Dago reached for the dice cups, shook them and slammed the five dice on the bar. Mike followed suit and the Boss dice game was on, best two out of three. Mike lost and he bought the first round of drinks. This game was repeated throughout the afternoon, all got a turn to see who would buy the next round. The crash of the leather cups and the clack of the dice rose above the increasing din created by a growing gathering of types. Multiple rounds of drinks were purchased and consumed. The day progressed and turned to dusk. More locals drifted in, alerted by the sight of the familiar pick-up trucks and cars. Before long, the bar resembled a clubhouse of fishermen, carpenters, contractors and barflies. It was a lively group to say the least. Bill McMann, the manager on the sidelines, was eyeing the raucous and swelling group in his bar with suspicion. This was not his idea of a classy dinner house in which he presided.

"Ishta dopia spyovachia dbroshia! Malo minkya! I am what I am!" Pablo bellowed gibberish just before his head collapsed on the bar with a thud.

"What a fuckin beauty." Dago gave a sidelong glance and chuckled from his place on the adjacent barstool.

"Holy shit, talent in there. You see that waitress?" Skin asked no one in particular, watching the waitresses go to and fro in another room. His real name was Pete and that led to Peter, which led to Peter-skin, then that was shortened up to just Skin. It fit; chasing women and shooting pool was what Skinner was all about when he wasn't working. He was a type; glib, well groomed, fit, clean and sporting a tight silver chain around his neck. Skin was in his early twenties; he was a pool hustler and a deckhand for Mike Henry. He almost always ended his statements with a short and hearty laugh, and he was a fun guy to hang with in a bar. He was a confirmed bachelor who always took his clothes to the cleaners to be washed and folded and he only cooked when he was on the boat; on shore he ate dinner in a restaurant every night. He made a distinction between the traditional roles of work prescribed for women and men and he held a good-natured disdain for what he called *women libbers*. He was among a vanishing breed as were they all, endangered species in the coming era.

Mike asked. "The Butterfish?"

"You know her?" Skin and Mike Henry were either working or drinking together. They were in a good-natured competition, flirting with the eligible womenfolk.

"You figure that out Peter-skin, but I will tell you this; that skin of yours will get so tight you won't be able to close your eyelids." Mike laughed. Mike was also a type. He looked like a 30 year-old Elliot Gould; curly hair, heavy beard, warm smile, tall and husky. He was kind of an understated guy, relying on his achievements to speak for him. A prodigious fisherman, he started young with a little boat in a group of other little boats from Half Moon, dubbed 'the mosquito fleet' by the old-timers. Tales of hi-jinx seemed to follow this group of young guys around. Soon, they all made the step up to bigger boats and then they got serious about fish catching. They became known as the Z Squad and never abandoned the hi-jinx and fun. By the time

Mike built his steel boat he had arrived on the West Coast as a name. A fishy guy, extremely popular and he could drink like an Irishman.

Cal walked up to the bar and re-ordered his new favorite drink, a Harvey Wall Banger-Galliano, Vodka and orange juice. He could drink a lot of these orange juice drinks. This guy Bobby came up to the bar besides him. Bobby was a drunk and a regular, a southern California hanger-on with this Shorebird management team. He went to high school with McMann in Newport and menial work was always found for him, more out of pity than necessity. Work that he found for himself was as a semi-pro boxer and sparring partner. He looked like a boxer with his pug-nose, cauliflower ears, not much neck and stocky frame. After semi-pro he went total pro; a total pro-drunk that is. He was stupid too. He began a conversation as they waited for their drinks.

"So. You the muscle man of this gang?" Bobby asked, assessing the biceps below the rolled-up T-shirt sleeves of Cal, his neighbor standing at the bar.

"No, a fisherman." Cal replied, annoyed. He knew Bobby to be a stupid drunk and a bar fighter. Cal was not going to get sucked into that tonight.

"Fish smell bad, you ever notice?" Bobby pressed.

"Fishy." Cal answered. This drunken fool is asking for it.

"See you later fisherman." Bobby scooped up his drink, sniffed at the air, wrinkled his nose, made a bad face and left.

"What a piece of work that is." Cal said to Dago after Bobby stumbled off.

"A piece of shit, if ya ast'me." Dago replied in disgust.

Leif pulled up to the parking lot at Hazels at twilight, his trip over the hill done for the day. He dropped Alex off at his car and they both noticed that nobody's vehicle had moved since lunchtime.

"Uh oh, a lot of brain cells are going to die tonight." Leif was looking at the suspicious automotive collection. "You are going in there, I'm guessing?"

"Yeah, just to see what's going on." Alex replied casually but secretly chomping at the bit to have some fun.

"Be careful, I been there, and I know how this goes." Leif gave Alex the short version.

"Okay Leif. See you tomorrow" Alex waved to his big brother as he drove off. He walked right past his car and headed straight for the Shorebird. He opened the big heavy doors and the silence was broken by a wave of familiar voices coming from the bar, a bar filled with plaid shirts, animated voices, gesticulating arms, clacking dice and laughter. The gang in the bar was loud and something was *definitely going on*. Once inside he saw the faces; fishermen and the locals. A group of restaurant diners walked past him toward the exit in silence, head down and stepping over a trail of toilet paper that led from under the bathroom door and into the bar. Alex walked in and saw that the toilet paper trail leads right into the back of Robbie's pants, sitting nonchalant on the corner barstool. Cal was right next to Rob.

"Hey kiddo, where's Leif?" Cal greeted Alex with a big smile.

"He went home." Alex replied.

"Well, that's just about right, what're you drinking, I'm buying." Cal could be gregarious when he drank, a departure from his usual wise-ass self.

"You got toilet paper stuck to your butt!" Alex blurted out, pointing to Robby's ass.

"I do? What do you know 'bout that?" Rob burst out with a laugh. This old joke could go on all night.

Alex was underage by a year, but he got a drink anyway, passing off as older in the company of his older friends and the raucous crowd. He didn't know what to order so he just said something he heard the Dago order. Dago knew a lot about booze.

"VO and water" Alex replied, anticipating alcoholic adventure with this most recent drug of choice. Booze didn't make you speechless, you didn't hallucinate, and it was legal. What could go wrong? He took a seat.

Dooley walked in, smiling as usual. Sam (Samantha) walked in. Fran-que walked in. Geno walked in. Hank walked in and it just didn't let up until all were there and it was standing room only. The waitresses had to push their way through to the wait-station at the bar and the many conversations gave the room an electric charge, a kinetic energy; anything could happen. Occasionally a commotion would break out, sustain, diminish and retreat into the din, absorbed. It was nothing short of a complete takeover by the locals, making the new place their private clubhouse on this night. This was not lost on the increasingly nervous manager Bill McMann. Chuck the Bartender told Dago that McMann was getting uneasy, maybe they should think about settling down a bit.

"Fuck em' if he can't take a joke!" The Dago laughed and flopped the dice cups extra hard on the bar.

When McMann walked into the bar the second time, the jig was up: he had seen and heard enough. He gave Chuck instructions to eject noisy patrons if cause was given. Chuck suggested that it was under control, pointing out that there had not been any trouble, just a lot of noise.

"Well I'm not going to allow any trouble to even begin." McMann adamantly replied, "This is not going to be their personal clubhouse, this is not going to be a precedent for any future shenanigans. I'll 86 the lot of them if I have to myself." Bobby the punch-drunk fighter and real life drunk hovered in the background smelling trouble like a dog smells poop.

Hank walked up to McMann. Hank was one of the older guys in the group, not shy, not afraid of anything, congenial, a gentleman from another era. He had owned a bar back in Minnesota and he knew the score about a lot of things, especially when it came to bars and drinking. He was a level-headed, soft spoken guy who could summon this dead-eye serious look when needed. He was all smiles now and reached out to McMann.

"Buy you a drink? C'mon sit with us; if you can find a seat that is, business is good." Hank chuckled.

"I don't think so." McMann replied. "I have a restaurant to run and I don't like what I am seeing in this bar. It is an intrusion. I have patrons other than you trying to enjoy themselves in the other room and quite frankly? You and your friends are counter to what this establishment is all about." McMann was all business.

"Is that so." Hank replied looking around the room, "I don't see anything 'counter' or anything to worry about." Whispers were travelling about the room now and this exchange was not going unnoticed. It got a little quiet around Hank and McMann.

"That is so-and furthermore, I think it may be time for you all to drink up and go home. That or quiet down to a respectable level." McMann said.

"A respectable level you say. Look, these kids are just having some fun, they're not a mean or angry group; they haven't thrown a punch since 10th grade for Christ sakes. They get a little excited maybe, a little loud for sure, but they don't start trouble." Hank said, looking around the room and returning to engage McMann face to face.

"If they don't quiet down, I will have to ask them to leave." McMann rejoined, "This not the place to have this kind of fun." Bobby-the-Drunk's menacing presence was right behind McMann the whole time, quietly glaring at anyone who would meet his eyes.

"I'll talk to the boys. I'm sure they will all quiet down." Hank said with a straight face, giving Mike Henry the eye in a sidelong glance in the process.

McMann and his punchy sidekick left the bar room and Hank walked over to Mike and Geno. The general commotion reduced itself to a slightly subdued level following their departure and then the ruckus in the room returned to its previous level after the twosome was gone.

"This guys' got a stick up his ass. *A respectable level*, he says, *Not the place to have this kind of fun*." Hank said to Mike.

"Yeah, he's a real beauty. Let's get Sam, I got an idea. Is she still here somewhere?" Mike stood up from his stool and looked around, saw the back of her head and walked over to where she was sitting. Sam was a petite woman with an angelic face and straight auburn hair. She always had a smile, a smile like she knew a pleasing secret or that she was constantly high. Tight jeans and a T-shirt completed the sexy mother of two darling young children, raised on an old halibut schooner.

"We oughta just all go in and get a table in his *respectable place.*" Dooley said to Hank after Mike left with Sam.

"That son-of-a-bitch will call the cops, sneaky-like if he doesn't get his way. I know the type." Hank replied and added, "He's a first-class prick."

Alex had a ringside seat to this and saw the whole thing develop from his place in a booth by the entrance to the bar. To him he thought the outcome was obvious; it was time to go. The thing was that nobody paid attention to McMann nor had anyone left, nobody had quieted down for more than the two minutes after the manager had cleared out. It *was* a takeover and now he was part of it. Is this what Leif meant in his parting warning to be careful? If it was, Alex was glad he was part of the big fun. He stood up and wobbled over to the wait station to order another drink.

"You; Basic Fisherman!" a voice called to Alex from the waitress station at the bar. It was the nipple girl on the horse.

"Karen. You work here?" That wasn't a clever thing to say thought Alex after the words left his mouth.

"No: I just dress like this and give people drinks. Yeah, I work here silly." She laughed and continued, "I work here and the Crab Cottage. I got two jobs, one kid and no husband.

"Sounds like a math problem." That was better, he was getting into the swing.

"It's not really any kind of problem, especially the last part."

"Not married?" His voice dripping with hope.

"Once, that was enough. I tried it."

"What happened?"

"More like what didn't happen."

"Too bad."

"Yeah, but I fixed the problem after I figured it out."

"How so?"

"The door hit his sorry ass on the way out. That's how." She laughed and continued, "You ask a lot of questions Basic, I gotta get back to work."

"See ya around." Alex re-entered real life after she left. It felt like he had just been talking in a bubble with Karen, just the two of them and no one else. It popped when she left and now, he was back in a noisy barroom. He looked around to get his bearings straight, he was a little tipsy. Bobby stumbled up to the bar beside him as Alex waited for his drink.

Bobby started a conversation, "You know, these guys aren't so bad, you're friends with them, right?"

"Yeah, I known them all my life, we all grew up around here." Alex replied.

"Kinda like me down in Newport Beach where we're from. It used to be a small town too." Bobby was being friendly in his psycho-killer way.

"This town was so small; I'd quit hitchhiking because no cars came by." said Alex.

"Is that so? Well things sure do change, don't they? That's one thing for sure all right." Bobby said.

Alex and Bobby stood at the bar and continued to make small talk. Alex was feeling as if the temperature was rising in his shoes, a warm sensation. He looked down and realized what Bobby was up to, leaning against the bar as they stood and talked side-by-side. Alex jumped back, gasping in disbelief.

"Nice chattin' with ya' Fisherman." Bobby smiled broadly at Alex and left.

"He pissed on my shoes!" Alex exclaimed in disbelief to no one and no one paid attention to him.

*   *   *

Mike and Sam had briefly left the bar, they now returned, pulling into the parking lot of the Shorebird. They got out of the truck.

"Keep that lid on tight." Mike spoke to Sam, lifting a 5-gallon bucket out of the pickup bed.

"Fine deal, can do." She said.

"I'll go in first and then you come in, okay? Can you lift the bucket?" Mike asked.

"Oh yeah, don't worry about me, I got it, its fine. It's a *fine* deal." Sam ended with her signature expression.

Mike walked into the bar and sat. No one noticed he had been missing and at this stage of the gathering no one noticed much of anything beyond the 3-foot radius that surrounded themselves. Empty and full glasses of booze cluttered the tables and bar, rounds of drinks were forthcoming faster than they could be consumed. Hank and Dooley were arguing when Mike joined them, Dooley was getting tipsy.

"That boat of yours will be in the museum someday! The days of the salmon troller are over! I'm going to rig up for dragging, that's where the money is!" Dooley was hollering to Hank.

"You might as well, maybe you can catch one with a net; can't seem to get one with a hook." The Dago interjected and joked at Dooley's expense.

Dooley liked to laugh. He could take a joke and dish one out too. Humor was the attribute he led with and he could laugh like a leprechaun. "Alaska: They're making real money up there, that's the place to be, I'm gonna go." He finalized.

Screams interrupted their conversation; the whole bar turned their attention towards the dining area. It also got the immediate attention of McMann who came running out of the kitchen, his head swiveling from left to right to assess what was happening on his restaurant floor. A woman ran from the restroom and sat shaking and raving at her table.

"It's in there! It touched me! It's horrible!" She screamed and McMann ran to her aid and quizzed her.

"What? What happened?" he said

"There's a monster in there! A slimy monster! It's big, don't go in there, it'll get you!"

"Calm down. I'll go straighten this out. There is nothing to fear. I want you to know that your meals at this table will be comped. I want your dining experience to be favorable." McMann was falling over himself to smooth this over in typical middle-management fashion.

"I'll never set foot in this place again. You don't know, you didn't see what I saw, what I felt! She was gathering her things as were others next to her in preparation to leave.

"Please, please stay." McMann said and left toward the women's' restroom.

In the bar Sam rejoined Mike. She had her usual smile pasted on her face. She always smiled but this time it was a little bit bigger.

"We all heard the screaming." Mike was trying not to laugh out loud.

"Oh, it was a *very* fine deal indeed." Sam was giggling and looking cute.

McMann opened the door to the women's restroom and an octopus crawled out into the foyer, he jumped back 3 feet and he screamed like the woman had screamed before. Employees rushed to his aid to see what the heck was going on. Bobby, passed out in a corner of the kitchen, came to life again. Patrons in the dining room were getting up and heading for the back exits. Screaming was not the usual sound patrons heard in a dinner house and they weren't about to take any chances and stick around. No matter the reason, leaving was the only thing of interest to them at this point. And they crowded the emergency exit. Those that did remain would soon find out that the source of this screaming was coming their way and fast. The octopus was on the floor. He made his way from the toilet, to the foyer and off to the dining room. McMann had unwittingly unleashed him upon the gen-pop when he opened the door to the bathroom and after that the eight legged molesting monster was speedily off and into the dining room. Most of the patrons had never seen an octopus before and none of them knew that this twenty-pound monster wad fast, could slither through very small openings, could change its color to match the background and could squirt jet black ink when it felt endangered. There was a trail of black ink on the floor now. The soon found out first-hand that he was an intelligent and crafty animal. The long and strong tentacle arms that sucked hard when they got ahold freaked everyone out to their core. He became a force to contend with in the close quarters of the dining room and currently he had a small child in his grips, slithering across his face to safety under the table. So far, the score was Octopus 25, Shorebird 0. The real loser was the woman who first opened the lid and sat on the toilet seat without looking. The creature had blasted out against her bare bottom and nether parts. Imagine her surprise.

"GET THAT THING OUT OF HERE!" McMann shouted to the universe. Bobby dived at it and the octopus slipped out of his grasp by momentarily gripping *his* face with all 8 tentacles and boosting himself up and out of his arms. Waitresses grabbed brooms to use as weapons; cooks from the kitchen came out with knives. The busboy, Sergio, approached the octopus slowly, carrying an inverted bus tray that he flopped on top of the animal and sat on it, saving the frantic and scrambling folks.

McMann marched straight into the bar and addressed the crowd. There was general laughter. *Pranks and hi-jinx* had risen to a new level. They had exceeded McMann's Southern Cal decorum. McMann was red faced and bursting.

"OUT!" You are 86'ed for life!" He shouted at the room.

"*Who* is 86'ed for life?" Hank questioned.

"You. And you and you and you, all of you!" McMann screamed.

Hank was calm. "Why? We didn't do anything; we're just having a drink and talking. This is a bar isn't it?"

"Don't give me that. I know you're behind this, the police are notified, and they are on their way this minute for your information." McMann was rigid with rage.

"Well it's your bar. I tell you true though: you don't know your ass from a hole in the ground. I forgot more than you'll ever know about running a bar." Hank took a step toward him as he stated this. He was calm and had that deadeye look now.

"YOU ESPECIALLY ARE 86'ED FOR LIFE! Get out of my restaurant and take your rowdy friends with you, I've had enough of the lot of you!" McMann was now a deeper shade of red.

Hank hit him under the jaw; McMann collapsed against the wall and slumped to the floor, unconscious. Bobby saw the whole thing from the dining room and this was the chance he had been waiting for all night. For him it was like a dream come true, permission to unleash the only thing he knew besides drinking, which was boxing. It was Bobby's wet dream: beating the shit out of people. He came charging toward Hank, intending great menace. Ooga Don, stuck out his foot and tripped Bobby as he rushed by. Bobby fell flat on his face on the floor. He stayed there, passed out drunk with his cheek flattened against the carpet.

Ooga smiled at Bobby lying still by his feet and said, "Bobby-baby signing off; Nanu-Nanu." Ooga never missed Mork n'Mindy show on TV.

Now it *was* time to go, the party *was* over. Shit had hit the fan. Everybody in the bar was up and walking out the door, some were hurrying but most were just casually leaving.

The Dago, perhaps the calmest one of all, passed by the unconscious McMann.

"Fuck him if he can't take a joke. The stupid bastard." He gave a little chuckle, smiled and stepped over McMann as he exited.

*   *   *

On opening day up at the River, they pulled 250 traps for 286 pounds. Needless to say, they were expecting more. Alex knew something was up, his share was $20 and change.

"Vellll. Boys, vee got a situation: vee quit and go home, or vee stack the gear and move. I think I can get us a market up above if that's vhat vee vant to do. Under the circumstances there be more traps than crabs here and vee can't stay." Sig said in his slow and laid-back manner, slipping into his Scandinavian accent more so than usual.

Alex thought he already *was* up above, 200 miles away from home and sharing a damp focsle with Leif and Cal? The plan originally had been to get a motel room that they could share but that plan was out the window now-they were completely belly up. He was for quitting and going home but he would not say so.

"I'll gut it out." Alex said to Uncle Sig

"Me too." Said Cal.

"I'm in." Said Leif

"Okay then boys, vee stack 'em; try our luck somewhere else then. You're a good crew." Uncle Sig went up the ladder to get the ticket from the wholesaler. When he returned, they took the boat over and tied up in the string.

"Let's go have a drink boys, I'm buyin." Uncle Sig pulled off his boots and slipped on his brown slip-ons, *loafers* as he called them because he never worked when he wore these shoes. He never drank in bars, either, but he was making an exception.

The first hundred traps came on the boat and they went into the dock to be loaded on a northbound fish truck. The next day they went and got the rest of the traps, kept them on the boat and away they went for a 12-hour boat ride north to Eureka, an appropriate name for their destination, considering that Eureka was named for fortuitous discovery. An ancient Greek first shouted the phrase "eureka" upon the very big discovery that displaced water equaled his weight in the bathtub. He went shouting and running wet and naked through the streets of Athens like a madman. Centuries later, gold miners adopted the phrase eureka when after many an attempt, they finally hit a strike of gold. Nothing much had changed in the search for riches. Sig and the crew were in search of the same and eureka was the operative word.

In the pilothouse of the *Valkyrie* and steaming north at 7 knots, Uncle Sig watched the water go by the windows. How many men had spent countless hours with only their thoughts to keep them company as they sat staring at the water as it went by? All the men who ever pissed in saltwater; this was the answer to *that* question, quiet contemplation, thought and boredom was part of the deal.

Velll, it'll be good goin' mostly. It might get a little bumpy up around The Cape." Sig said.

"What's the weather report say?" Cal asked.

"I listened at 10 o'clock, it was southeast 10-20, increasing."

"Increasing to what?" Not that he had any choice; Cal was stuck for the duration, good, bad or indifferent.

"Increasing tonight, 20-30." Sig said as a matter of fact.

"Well shit-oh-dear." Leif said with disgust.

"Now, now. That is no problem. We'll be sliding with it. Vhen she switches to vesterly, that's vhen she gets tough." Sig explained, "Vee be in before the swell comes maybe."

"You think there'll be any trouble at the bar then?" Cal asked about the entrance to the harbor. The Eureka bar had a bad reputation. After hours of anticipation of a safe harbor and hours of travel upon the sea, waves-big ones-could crash down on the waters of the bar, closing the entrance to the safe harbor that they had been thinking of. If the bar was closed, they would be forced to run the risk of passing through a breaking bar or wait it out in the open ocean. Taking the boat through the surf was not what anyone in their right mind wanted to do unless they had to, but that was often the choice made.

"Vee be all right, don't worry." Sig said, but he didn't let on. It could go either way and he knew it; he had been through it before; bad options. Alex was listening to the conversation, but it was just another day to him, being ignorant of the possibilities that lay ahead. He was having fun playing cribbage, eating, seeing new territory on an adventure.

That night the wind did increase just as predicted and *Valkyrie* slowly rolled from side to side as she went before the wind and sea. The sea got a little confused around the Cape where the currents and tide converged. Sig was in the pilot house and Alex and Leif were asleep down below in the focsle. Cal straddled the back door, braced against the jambs, watching the stacks of traps on the back deck for movement. Sig looked ahead into the watery blackness of the night, thinking the weather not too bad. Among his many thoughts on this trip was his dead brother Arne; what would he do? He probably would have thrown in the towel after the first pull, just gone home and sit by the fireplace this winter with Olivia, just reading his darn books. What Sig was doin' was desperate and he knew it: and that's not the way to be and stay healthy. Here he was in the middle of nowhere with a full charge of gear on deck goin' around the Cape in the middle of darkness on a chance.

"Dad gummit." he muttered to himself.

At daylight, the wind began to veer to the West and that was not good for their purposes. It was a run for the entrance now, but first he had to set this gear. The ride got a little bumpier as the swell built and the *Valkyrie* was now broadside to the weather. Cal climbed the stacks at daylight and tightened the ropes under the watchful eyes of Leif.

"Let's get these traps off the deck before we go in." Sig said and continued, "I'll just throw them off in the blind somewhere on the Southside on the way up. Start makin'up jars, Alex."

Alex pulled on his raingear and stepped out on deck. It was crowded against the back of the wheelhouse due to the traps on deck. The blocks of squid were half-frozen so he could slice off layers with his machete and then hack them up. He liked this. It sure was blustery he thought, roll-y too. He completed the task in short order and hurried back inside to the warmth of the diesel stove.

"Done Uncle Sig." he said.

The *Valkyrie* came out of the Eel Canyon in 50 fathoms on their way to Eureka. They kicked off a string in the deep and turned toward shallower water, Cal and Leif had their rain gear on and were standing by to trail out the buoy of the first trap, the first of three strings of traps. Soon, she came upon gear in the water, a string of traps with blue and yellow buoys. She kept going and passed through a few more strings. Then she came upon some yellow and red ones.

"That's far enough." Sig thought, "I know that gear, it's Jack Dewey. If there's a crab around he'll find em." They were 14 fathoms off the Eel River. Sig squared up the *Valkyrie* to lay out the gear and notified the crew to get ready. Alex left the warmth of the stove reluctantly and pulled on his damp raingear again, waiting for the last possible moment to be ready. The diesel that had been droning at a constant dull roar for hours on end, now reduced its RPM to a more comfortable rumble, almost as if someone stopped hitting you over the head for ten hours, bringing relief when they stopped.

"Trail it!" yelled Sig from the back door and they were off setting the first of the three strings. They set one string in 14 fathoms and then another in 13, then they swung to the outside and began to set the last in 16 fathoms.

"One hand for the boat and one hand for the man, you be careful now!" Sig advised the crew. That instruction was not necessary as Cal and Leif hung on, a heaving deck under their rubber boots. Alex would scurry back to refill their baskets with fresh jars of bait. On the last string, the last stack of traps on the stern posed a safety challenge. The boat had been lightened and now the roll was not slow and steady but snappy and at times unpredictable. Under the watchful eyes of Sig, braced in the backdoor, Cal and Leif cleared the deck of traps down to the last four. Uncle Sig went back and held the back of the raingear suspenders of Leif while he cleared the deck. Soon, they had gear in the water and the gear was fishing once again. Or so they hoped.

"Adios and Vaya con Dios, mother fletcher!" Cal was smiling, glad for the second chance to save his season, gear in water. "All we need is a FM now!" Cal shouted with glee. After all, half the fun was the feeling of hope. The other half was a good result.

"What's an FM?" Alex asked innocently.

"A fucking miracle, dip-shit." Cal snapped.

Valkyrie was hoping to arrive at the bar during high slack water, the tide being critical to a successful crossing of the bar. The wind was hard from the West and the swell was building behind it. It was time to go in under any circumstance. Out in the open ocean was not going to be a nice place to be by the end of this day. The *Valkyrie* got to the bar and jogged in deep water, waiting. Alex didn't know what was up and he questioned Cal.

"What are we doing? Why don't we just go in? We're here, I can see the harbor right there." He pleaded for an explanation.

"Hey Pud-knocker, look toward the entrance. Waves are breaking." Cal said

"What'll we do?" Alex wondered aloud.

"Just be ready. And stay in the house. We're gonna go in between the sets, your uncle is watching for a chance to make a break for it. That's why we're jogging here." Cal explained.

"It'll be okay Alex." Leif reassured.

The *Valkyrie* was idling just south of the jetty in wait. The water was deep enough here to prevent a breaking surf, but it was a nervous situation, nonetheless. It was always a little edgy when putting a clunky 8 knot boat through the surf or standing off with waves crashing a thunderous report behind you. Even though Sig had done this successfully before, it was something you never get quite used to. Especially in foul weather, for there had been notable bad incidents that always stayed in your mind. Today was just the kind of day when things could go sideways in a hurry, literally sideways. Broaching was the thing most likely to expect when the sea breaks as you ride upon it, surfing sideways down the face of the wave at the mercy of overwhelming power, your rudder rendered impotent. Of course, the worst-case scenario was a pitch-pole which almost always resulted in loss or drowning. The boat flips over, the stern tumbling over the bow in ass-over-teakettle fashion. The stakes were high in any event, a bad outcome could have serious consequences.

"Whaddya think Sig?" Cal walked up to the pilothouse.

"Vellll, not too bad, not closed out. I don't wanna be here to see the ebb though, that might get a little tough." Sig replied.

"We're all squared away on the back. Everything's off the deck or tied down. Alex is gonna stay right at the galley table." Cal reassured Sig.

"That's good. Vee gonna shoot right around this jetty pretty darn quick, I'm just gettin the feel of it."

Sig pushed the throttle right to the pin and *Valkyrie* sprung with all that her 40 tons could muster, which wasn't much of a spring. It was agonizingly slow, dealing with a surf that pushed along at 20 knots, more than enough to overtake and engulf an 8-knot boat, like a train wreck in slow motion. Running the bar was a commitment; filled with long minutes gauging the approaching and rising waters stealthily marching toward the stern in sets of 6 or 7 waves.

"Looks good so far, Uncle Sig!" Leif shouted up to the wheelhouse from the back door.

"Okay boys, no stopping now!" Sig returned the call over the roar of the engine.

The first wave of the set slid under them harmlessly. The second wave got a bit thin at the top as she went by but never broke, same with the third wave of the set. *Valkyrie* made progress toward safer water all the while. Leif and Cal watched the fourth wave start to take shape behind them, it was humping up larger than previous waves. Cal did not like it.

"We got a big one com'in, it's not breaking though!" he shouted, though he muttered to himself. "Yet."

Valkyrie rose up at the stern on the swell and then sunk down on the back of the wave as it passed underneath, feathering a fine spray as it almost crested up ahead of the boat. But the wave did not break. They were almost home free and almost far enough inside the jetty to be out of the break zone. Watchful eyes were turned toward the stern with a laser focus now and they did not like what they saw. It was a wave, the last wave of the set. It began to break outside of them, and the churning white water buried the stern of the Valkyrie. The decks were awash with green water that hit the main hatch and deflected, saving the inside of the house from a soaking. Cal quickly closed the door. The water squatted down the stern until the scuppers relieved the *Valkyrie* of her deck weight. The next wave was the same, but they were far enough inside the jetty and out of any real danger, it had just been a wet ride in.

"Fuck. We made it." Cal said, "Way to go Cap!" He shouted up to Sig.

The boat glided along in the smooth waters of the harbor, leaving all the heaving, anxiety and turmoil behind. She passed the Coast Guard station, passed a ship loading logs and along a waterfront that appeared to have a reduced purpose in life. Eureka, once the state capitol in the 1800's, was way past its heyday and the low-lying city had gone to seed a bit. The few once classy downtown hotels were now inhabited by those who were down on their luck and there was always a chow line outside The Seamen's Mission. Alex walked out on the back deck in preparation for tying up the boat to a wharf somewhere along the watery landscape.

"What's that smell?" he asked his shipmates.

"The pulp mill." Cal answered.

"It stinks."

"No shit Sherlock."

"Is it always like that?"

"Only every fuckin day." Cal answered with a zinger.

"Geez" Alex wondered about that.

"Let's go kid, you get on the bow, stern line first." Leif instructed.

Alex grabbed a rope and stood ready on the bow, they tied up under a fish hoist. Sig went up and talked to Les, the guy he intended to sell crab to. He made the necessary arrangements for bait and checked on the fish truck with the rest of the traps for *Valkyrie*. Les was an affable guy and a fellow Scandinavian, he and Sig went way back.

"Not a lot of crab coming in so far Sig, a lot of blank spots I hear." Les said.

"Velll, it was a tough show down at the River, I tell you that. It was quit or move, not much hoice." Sig replied.

"There's a little scratch I guess-for some of the guys, too soon to say for sure." Les said.

"Vee got a truckload of traps comin." Sig stated.

"I know. Might be here tonight." Les informed.

"Vee take them with us vhen vee go out." Sig said as he stepped on the first rung of the ladder and disappeared down to *Valkyrie*. He had a lot on his mind; Les had not offered too much encouragement about their prospects. These crabs were mysterious creatures, coming and going without a known rhyme or reason. Sometimes they didn't show at all and other times you could count on a good steady supply for years, taken for granted and thought that it would never end. It was then that abundance became a problem, such as you caught more than you could sell, more than the buyers could process and sell through a flooded market which was the harbinger of a reduced price. The fishery had been a steady source of income for many years previous. This was shaping up to be a different kind of year than that. There were guys who never even realized the possibility of going bust.

The truck arrived that night and the boys got right to the loading of the boat with traps, they would go out as soon as the weather broke in a day or two. It was clearing up, but it was still hard out of the west and the bar was breaking through the ebb. There would be a little shore time available. Alex was curiously excited to be here, and he went up to Two Street the next day as soon as things were settled on the boat. On Two Street there were a couple of bars, a café, old hotels and a few antique stores. The streets were cobblestone and the buildings were red brick and a few storefronts were papered and empty. At the end of the street there stood a rather elegant Victorian that had been completely refurbished and it was surrounded by an iron grate fence around impeccable landscaping. It stood in stark contrast to all the other buildings on the street it overlooked. It was a symbol of what used to be and the home of a lumber baron back in the day. Alex wandered and gawked like a tourist down the street, finally turning into an old hotel that advertised rock music on the weekends. He took a stool at the bar.

"Beer please, Bud." He instructed.

"You got an ID?" the barkeep asked.

"No. I got money though." Now that was smart. The bartender smiled.

"Good enough here." he replied and returned with a long neck bottle. "Glass?"

"Naw. I'm okay." Alex replied and looked around the room. There were very few patrons. It was the dayshift; the maintenance drinkers, the night shift had not yet begun. The few that were there either sat and nursed a beer and a newspaper or had a brown drink in front of them. Alex thought, "What am I doing here in this dark and decrepit place with these dark and decrepit people?" He stood up and hastily left, as if ghosts were behind him, leaving his beer half-finished like a lonely brown glass statue on the bar. Nobody said a word, nobody looked up as he walked through the heavy wooden doors and back onto the street to go back to the boat. A couple blocks into the journey he passed a café and stopped to read the menu taped to the glass. It seemed to him that the prices were more than reasonable. It looked as though he could expect to pay a few dollars for a complete dinner, according to the menu. This was enough to get him inside and seated in Peggy's Café. Looking about as he waited, most patrons were single men in various states of disrepair. Some had shopping bags at their side with clothes or food or just random stuff. Grizzled and unshaved faces hunched over the plates in front of them. They sat alone.

"Wow." Alex thought aloud, "where am I?" A voice from behind answered unexpectedly.

"You're in Peggy's sonny. Be glad that you are, and we are glad to have you." An older and smiling waitress greeted him. "Know what you want or need a menu?" She reminded him of his aunt Bess.

"I am happy to be here. I'm new in town off a boat." Alex had just met the only cheerful person in town, so far as he knew. "I got to say, the chow is affordable, what's good tonight?"

"The Special, that's what's good and that's all there is for dinner tonight. It's meatloaf, potatoes, vegetables, a side-salad with two saltine crackers, a slice of white bread and butter. Drinks are extra, waters' free." She smiled down his way. "Or you could just have a sandwich."

"The Special, that's what I'll have then. It's a good deal for all that chow."

"You're at Peggy's and that's how it is here. Most of our people eat here all the time, have their Social Security checks sent right here every month, Peggy gives them meal tickets so at the least they can eat for the month. Plenty of booze and no jobs around here. The jobs that are here now don't add up to what this town used to offer when the mill was running. You off a fish boat, huh?"

"Yes maam. We just got here with crab traps from the River. We kinda went belly-up there and we hope to save the season here. We need an FM." Alex explained innocently.

"Well that FM sounds familiar; lotta people looking for an FM in this town. That sounds like fishing all right. You fellas never give up, I like that, always trying to save it. You want something to drink?"

"No maam." Alex replied.

"No, *I don't give up,* or, *no I don't want anything to drink*'? She smiled at her own joke.

"Neither one maam." He replied.

He sat there wondering, waiting, thrust into this other side of life, alone at a table in Peggy's Café among men unlike himself. These men, their past stretched back longer than their future stretched ahead, most of these men were living month to month, mostly concerned with procuring food, lodging, staying dry and getting the medicine they required, sometimes the medicine was from the corner liquor store, sometimes from the pharmacy, sometime from both. Not all the patrons were old men; there was one fellow Alex's age. He not only stood out because of his age but there was a straightforward and congenial air about him. His mannerisms and dress spoke of a young man in possession of self-confidence and some purpose. He walked over.

"Join you?" He said.

"Sure, have a seat." Alex replied.

"I don't like to sit alone here. You look about my age, what are you doing in Peggy's?" Well kept, outgoing, the young man was a contrast to the other patrons.

"Having dinner. I could ask you the same question." Alex responded.

"Same. I'm watching my bread kind of close. This place is cheap. Breakfast is $1.50."

"I'm on a crabber, we just got here. My uncle has the *Valkyrie*."

"My uncle is in Alaska, I crew with him in the summer, and we drift for sockeye in Bristol Bay. That's not until June and in the meantime I'm on a dragger here."

"Any money in dragging?" Alex asked.

"It's steady like a shore job when the weather is good, but no big shakes. I'm just biding my time until sockeye season, that's where the money is." replied his new friend.

"I heard about it. Didn't they have a strike or something last year?"

"Yeah. Our cannery wouldn't pay the price the other cannery was offering. It went on for a couple of weeks until we had to go for the price offered. It was either that or lose the season. The Washington boats went first and then we had to go. The run of fish is only there for so long and then it's over after a month. There were hard feelings." The young man said.

"That's the part I heard, the hard feeling part. My name's Alex, yours?" Alex extended his hand for a shake.

"Tim; pleased to meet ya'll." You are the only one I met so far in this town. It's pretty rough around here." Tim said.

"I'll remember that." Alex replied and the food arrived. A little iceberg lettuce salad with a Saltine cracker pack on the side, 2 slices of meat loaf with gravy over instant mashed potatoes and vegetables sliced in spheres, cubes and cylinders. There was also a slice of white bread and a pat of butter. Tim's food was identical, they ate in silence until the plates were completely clean.

"Man, you oughta come up to the Bay sometime. There's always work, always problems with crew and spots open up, you could get a job. We work out of Dillingham but there's Naknek, Egegik, Ugashik too. It's just a place to work hard and save your money. There's nowhere to even spend money, there's nothing there except the canneries." Tim said. "One restaurant, a pizza joint with a $40." he added.

"Is it a good pizza?"

"Better than the best cardboard pizza you ever munched."

Alex laughed. "When does Bristol Bay happen?"

"June. We go up in May, start fishing in June and by the 4th of July it hits the peak of the run. It gets slower and slower from there out and we are usually home by the end of July. It's nothing but fishing and we live off the tender. They take the fish and we get fuel, groceries and water from them. We never go into shore unless it's an emergency or a closure. We went 30 days straight last year without touching shore, it got weird." Tim enthusiastically explained,

"Well, so far I'm not too impressed with crabbing. I just might check it out this summer. Where is Bristol Bay anyway? How do you get there?" Alex asked.

"A plane ride to Seattle and then on to Anchorage. You gotta take a twin-engine plane from there, its way out west in the middle of nowhere above the Aleutians." Tim explained.

"I'll file it in the memory bank. Right now, I gotta go back to the boat." Alex got up from the table and shook Tim's hand, "Nice meeting ya."

"Yeah cool. See ya around." Tim said.

"Hey, what's your phone number? I wanna go up there!" Alex asked.

"I don't have a phone. Call my sister, she can get word to me." Tim replied.

Alex wrote the number down on a napkin and said good-bye to his new friend. He then made his way to the register and was greeted by the woman who looked like his aunt. "$3.25 Hon. Everything was okay?"

"Just fine."

Twilight had settled over the town and Alex walked back to the boat along the railroad tracks. The gravel of the rail bed crunched under his feet and the anise weeds sprouted tall along the seldom used railroad that had at one time been in use daily. The terrain along the walk had the look of a wasteland, weeds, unused lots, chain link fence and abandoned warehouses. At the boat after a ½ mile walk through the forgotten urban landscape, Alex climbed down the ladder onto the *Valkyrie*. The crew and Sig were playing three-handed cribbage at the galley table.

"There's food on the stove if you're hungry." Sig said without looking up from his hand.

"Thanks Uncle Sig, I ate uptown at a place called Peggy's." Alex replied.

"Fifteen two, fifteen four, fifteen six and pair is eight." said Cal, laying his cards on the table.

"Fifteen two and the rest won't do." said Leif, laying down his hand in turn.

"Sixteen is all. Peggy's is it now?" Sig said laying down his cards, "but in the crib…eight more." He pegged twenty-four holes with obvious satisfaction.

"I know Peggy's, everyone does. She run a kitchen for the down and out- doesn't make a dime there. But the people eat. She got a big heart." Sig explained.

"I felt right at home there, made a new friend too. Three bucks for dinner, buck and a half for breakfast." Alex was enthusiastic about his discovery.

"Okay, vell, vee go fishin tomorrow, the veather gonna give us a break maybe. Vee see whether it's a steak dinner in Samoa or Peggy's." Sig said in his usual matter of fact fashion.

"What's Samoa? Isn't that an Island in the Pacific?" Alex asked.

"It's an island over there." Cal said pointing across the bridge. "All you can eat family style. It used to be the cookhouse for the mill workers. The mill is gone but the cookhouse stayed open as a restaurant. It's really good chow."

"Really good." Leif added.

*   *   *

It was dark, cold, wet and the bait was frozen. Alex wielded the machete from gloved hands and the tips of his fingers stung with the cold. The old Caterpillar engine rumbled from down below in the bowels of the *Valkyrie,* occasionally providing a whiff of diesel exhaust across the back deck. Artificial light created a bubble in the darkness as they glided along. Up ahead there was nothing but blackness and water with pinpricks of shore lights in the distance. Similar bubbles of light, accompanied by little dots of red and green light, glided along behind them as the crab fleet was on the move after the storm had passed. Alex could expect to be stuffing bait jars most of the day-and more. His job was primarily to make up bait jars, but he was available should the situation require him to stack gear on the back deck, coil rope, add shots of rope, measure crab or make sandwiches and coffee, anything that came up in the long day ahead. Cal and Leif would be right there with him at the block grabbing buoys and landing the traps with crabs. They were ever hopeful to the man, hopeful that many crabs would be tossed into the tank before the long day ahead was over. The tank was brimming over with water onto the deck and out the scuppers. The *Valkyrie* gently moved from side to side as she turned past the Coast Guard station and approached the entrance and across the bar. The bar was smooth, and no way resembled the gauntlet they had to run upon their initial arrival from the River. They didn't have far to travel to the gear, and they expected to arrive just before daylight. Before too long Uncle Sig had them running down their 1st string of gear, toward the end buoy and the beginning of this first string of traps.

"Okay boys, 2 mics to the end marker, get ready." Sig shouted back from the pilot house.

Cal and Leif got the buoy-stick and measures in position and took their places before and behind the block, looking blankly over the side in expectation of the first buoy but their minds were anything but blank. Much depended upon what they saw in this first trap; the big highs and the big lows awaited them on the emotional roller coaster they were now on. Nothing was as tedious and grim as pulling an entire string of blank traps and the reverse was true; the exhilarant feeling of pulling trap after trap brim full to the top, making one wonder how so many crabs could fit in there. Watching the tank fill with *bugs,* the eight-legged creatures with pinchers that blanketed the bottom of the ocean. Sometimes. Alex was standing by as well, watching the water go by and his mind was blank. The first buoy came into their view and

Cal gaffed it, Leif grabbed the rope and Cal threw the rope into the block and started to pull the trap to the surface of the water. The power block was perfectly named: it was a fast and a massively powerful piece of machinery that commanded respect, lest it hurt a careless or casual operator. Stories of mutilated hands and fingers were legend. An auspicious 'popping' sound from the power block was heard, as the rope buried itself deep in the shives, predicting a heavy trap.

"Stack it!" Cal shouted the customary command and Leif responded with the coiling basket, passing it back to Alex as the trap broke water. Sig always stacked the first three traps, just in case the string came bad, 'bad' as in no crabs. But there were crabs and after a few traps came aboard Sig called for an end marker. It was their inside string. The inside gear consistently averaged 15 legal crabs-good enough to leave them in the shallow water. They laid another string of traps on the inside, leaving fifty traps aboard as they headed to the outside string in 50 fathoms.

"That was good?" Alex said to Leif. "Wow."

"Good enough." Leif replied, "We see how it goes on the second pull."

Sig ran down the outside string until he came to an end marker. He circled *Valkyrie* around and approached the end marker going against the current. There was a little wind threatening but overall, the weather was good; just enough wind to hold the *Valkyrie* back from arrival at the next buoy too soon. Cal gaffed the first buoy and Leif coiled it and then passed the basket back as the trap broke water in a beige explosion of watery energy.

"Snowball!" Cal shouted with some jubilation, referencing the color of a trap stuffed with Dungeness crab.

"End marker on the next one, vee got a spot boys!" Sig hollered back at them with uncharacteristic emotion.

"It's an FM." Alex said meekly. He was relieved that he would not be stacking traps and that they had landed on a spot. It was seemingly their own as he couldn't see any other traps, unlike the inside gear in a field of multi-color buoys. The per-trap average held up as they went through the gear, each pot had about 50 pounds to the trap. Sig laid the last fifty traps they had aboard on the outside after adding shots of rope, committing another 50 traps in the deep, the rest of the gear inside of 16 fathoms. They turned toward the bar and headed in with plenty of daylight left in the day.

"Vee check a few before vee go in." Sig stood at the back door, satisfied that he had located crabs and positioned traps on them. Initially, he had some reservation about prospecting out in 50 fathoms, nobody was out in 50 fathoms. *Valkyrie* trailed out a buoy and jumped into the string and they started pulling. The first trap was a blank followed by another blank.

"Fuck." Cal stated.

"Trouble." Leif said.

"What? We just set this one, yesterday, give it a chance." Alex said. They ran ten traps for 20 crabs then Sig called a halt.

"I seen enough. Vee got work to do, might as vell face the facts. Vee gonna get fifty of these and bring 'em to the outside so let's at least do that, plenty of daylight left." Sig instructed. Alex was bummed, he was the one who would be doing the stacking and he was looking forward to getting in early. Not that he had anything going on in there; he was just kind of lazy.

They got the fifty on the boat and added shots as they headed for the deep. Alex made up fresh jars, replacing near-fresh bait with frozen fresh bait. He thought it kind of a waste but that's what Uncle Sig wanted him to do. Cal and Leif waited at their places at the rail, ready to set. Cal had his gloves off and was smoking a cigarette.

"We gonna check a couple or what?" Cal asked Leif.

"I'm guessing not- *In for a penny in for a dime*, I say, we're committed. We had crabs out here, in the shallows we have a disappointment." Leif replied.

"I guess. We got one pull out of the deal anyway-and we got hope out here." Cal said.

"And we got hope. Sleep good on that." Leif concluded.

They laid them out and headed back toward the shore, a beeline for the harbor. Alex slipped out of the rain gear and made sandwiches and coffee. They had not had a thing to eat all day except some packages of bear claws and Cokes. Sig was alone at the wheel and the guys were straightening up the back deck and hosing down. They had crab aboard; this was a huge victory as far as Alex knew and he couldn't help but think about tomorrow's catch; he was filled with anticipation.

There were boats waiting to unload at the hoist, and it was getting dark. Sig was getting some dinner going in the galley as they waited. He dished out the plates of crab spaghetti and they chowed down. The weather report and forecast droned on in the background, playing in a repetitive loop out of the VHF radio. There was too much information for Alex to absorb so he ignored it completely and focused on his crab spaghetti. He had never had it before and swore he would have it again real soon. Butter, garlic, Parmesan, the best.

"Vee up for unloading! Quick now boys, don't enjoy it, just eat it down now!" Sig said, rising from the table, placing his empty plate on the sink board. *Valkyrie* was drifting out in the channel off the dock and Sig bumped the boat in gear, regaining position, watching for the boat ahead of them to pull away from the hoist, eager to get the unloading process underway.

"The quicker vee done; the quicker vee hit the rack." he spoke. When their turn arrived, they gently approached the pilings and touched the dock, the crew threw the tie-up lines up to the awaiting dock workers and they secured the boat to the bollards. Leif and Cal walked around on deck situating a few things and waited for the empty totes to come down. Alex, who had only unloaded 285 pounds of crab in his whole life, watched from the stern and waited for someone to tell him what to do.

"Just start grabbing the crabs out of the tank and put them in the totes. You work from the other side of the tank." said brother Leif.

"Do they bite?" Alex asked.

"No numb-nuts, they pinch the shit out of ya!" Cal offered sarcastically.

"Grab then by the back of the body or by the little legs, best grab both legs at once so they don't flip around and pinch. They are quick." Leif instructed.

"Okay." Alex was tentative, knowing that pain was surely coming his way. Alex was amazed how fast Cal and Leif pulled the crabs out of the tank and tossed them into the tote, sometimes two or three at a time in a fluid motion. Alex cranked up the grate every few minutes, trying to keep up with the pace of the unloading.

"Get that fucking thing up where we can reach 'em without sticking our heads up our ass, bent over double down in the tank! Keep the grate up where we can reach the goddamned things, for Christ sakes!" Cal never stopped pitching crabs as he hollered at Alex. He was like a machine, tossing crabs in a steady flow.

"Take it easy Cal, we're all right." Leif said calmly.

"Alex: when we get near the bottom of the tank, you go up and get the bait out of the freezer for tomorrow. Put the bait in an empty tote and send it down with the last." Leif explained.

"Make sure you get those shots of rope out of the lazarette, we're gonna need 'em and we don't wanna bury them under stacks of traps! Get a hundred and fifty of 'em." Cal barked without looking up from the tank. "Gimme a *roger!*"

"Okay, okay. Roger." Alex replied, sheepish. He got the idea really quick-go fast, don't screw around, say *roger*.

"Take it easy Cal, nobody died." Leif quietly said to Cal, who was clearly over-excited.

Sig was up on the dock talking to Les. "There be a few blank spots for sure, but there's opportunity."

"I see that. Some guys get 'em and some guys don't. Dewey had about the best to come across this dock." Les offered.

"Vee see. He might get a surprise tomorrow, I seen his buoys. Vee all might get a surprise." Sig said. "Vee got the weather to work, vee thankful for that anyway. The market good?"

"Solid. The crabs are still moving through the shell market, no picking and only putting up a few sections for Christmas. Don't expect a price raise though." Les smiled knowingly.

"No, I don't expect no price raise. But you know that the grumbling is gonna start if it looks like there's not much around." Sig said.

"Right. There's not much around here maybe, but Newport's got crab." Les replied.

"They always got crab up there. And plenty of boats to catch 'em too. Any talk of limits up there?" Sig asked.

"They don't go on limits up there; they go for less money before they go on limits. The market's good, like I said. No need for any of that nonsense." Les explained.

The last of the crabs went up and the bait came down. *Valkyrie* pulled away from the dock and she went down the channel and rafted up by the new city dock. It was late and the alarm would go off early-as usual. The crew got out of the gear and got ready to hit the rack. There was very little talking.

"Into the fart-sack kid, we got a long day tomorrow." said brother Leif to Alex.

"Amen to that." said Cal.

"We did good today." Alex said.

"Don't jinx it stupid!" Cal responded.

"Roger." and Alex crawled into his sleeping bag without another word.

*   *   *

There were crabs the next day. Fate had dealt Sig and the boys a wild card and Sig played it well laying those first fifty in the deep on speculation. The next day the cards went face up.

"Oh, shit look at this!" Cal shouted as the first trap broke water.

"We're in 'em here, thank God." Leif replied.

Alex could feel the excitement as he stuffed jars and pinned hanging bait. Every trap had crab and if this kept up, he figured, the tank and more would be full today. It was a welcome thought to contemplate but Alex had little time to think about it, trying to keep up with the pace that Cal and Leif set. The end buoy approached; it went in the block. The string finished up like it had begun-consistent crab production throughout.

"Alex: Get those totes, break down a few and place them on the port side of the tank. Put the checkerboards in the tank just in case the next string comes good. Move those bundles of ropes up to the side of the wheelhouse where vee can get at them. Vee gonna stack out from that inside gear, add shots and move 'em out here." Sig instructed.

"How many strings do we have out here?" Alex asked.

"Not enough." Cal answered sarcastically.

"We got two strings out here Alex, but we will have all the gear out here before we're done." Leif was patient.

Alex did as he was told by his big brother, glad for the patient instruction, unlike Cal, who barked his head off at him all the time. He did realize that Leif looked after him a little bit ever since their dad died. Alex also realized that this was a chance to prove his mettle with the older men and he better hustle and do it right as he was told. That, and to say 'roger'. Sig had the boat running down the next string now and he was looking for the end marker. Before long, the three-buoy configuration of the end marker appeared a few traps ahead.

"End marker!" Sig shouted, alerting the back deck to get ready to run gear, adding "No stack!" *Valkyrie* turned on the buoy and headed against the current. There was current and plenty of slack going against it.

"Fuckin-A-Tweedy!" Cal shouted as the first trap broke water, the beige color of the crabs preceding its arrival beneath the surface, announcing the good fortune ahead.

"Jesus. Alex get those totes where we can reach them. We're gonna fill this tank or more if this keeps up." Leif instructed. Totes held about 600 pounds and they had brought five of them, all nestled together. He pulled 2 of them out and set them in the ready position. The excitement was contagious, and they all shared in the emotional high of the moment, a fortuitous suspended moment; no past and the future only out as far as the next trap. The present was filled with activity and reward-no time for thinking. All the rest of life faded into obscurity while the good fortune of the present moment took hold and it did not let go until the string of traps ended with a full tank and two full totes.

"Shit, we got a lot." Alex said giddily.

"Don't say that, I told you! Don't jinx it" Cal interjected. "Just get those shots of rope ready; two tens together, we need a hundred of 'em. We're gonna add forty fathoms to the next string we run from the inside and stack it. If you can add the shots and stack traps as we go, you're golden kid."

"I'll try" Alex replied. "How do you know we should stack it?"

"What the fuck Alex? You got eyes?" Cal said.

"Because we tested yesterday Alex and the inside gear was weak. We got a spot on the outside with good crabs. You see that, yes?" Leif patiently explained.

"Yes"

"Uncle Sig is gonna relocate all the gear to the deep as soon as we can, starting with the next string." Leif explained in even tones to his little brother.

"Right." Alex replied.

"And fuckin hurry!" Cal shouted.

"Roger." Alex replied.

They stacked the next string and added shots to each trap as it came aboard, doing the same with the next string. They got the gear out of the shallows into the deep water below the Eel River canyon. They were getting farther from Eureka and closer to Cape Mendocino, the furthest seaward extension of the North American continent. After they laid out the string, they turned back and headed for the entrance to the harbor with great hope and a lot of crab, it was intoxicating. In the harbor and after dark, the *Valkyrie* pulled under the hoist to unload. Sig went up the ladder and was met by Les who regarded the full tank and totes on the deck below.

"Looks like there's a few around Sig?" Les smiled.

"They're not everywhere but they're around, for sure." Sig offered.

"Some guys get 'em and some guys don't." Les repeated the old chestnut.

"Vell, that may be true… but it's not too hard to figure these crabs out. They here or they there or they not. Who's there first with the most is the thing." Sig said.

"What's it looks like for tomorrow?" Les asked.

"Half? It depends. Vee going to stay in for a day after tomorrow unless vee get a surprise, vee see." That was a lie. Sig intended to go every day if the crabs held up; he just wanted to adopt an affectation of disinterest. Inwardly and to himself, he was hopeful for a very good result to this Eureka move-every single day that he could squeeze out of it.

Many pounds to the trap did not ever warrant staying in port. Alex was up in the freezer toward the end of the unloading process, putting enough bait in a tote to run the 250 traps. Leif came up on the dock.

"Let's get 6 totes on the boat for tomorrow." Leif said quietly to Alex.

"Okay. One with the bait and six empties then?" Alex asked.

"That's right, and don't make a big deal out of it." Leif instructed.

"Roger."

The next day they came in with 10,000 pounds and it did not go unnoticed. In fact, it was the talk of all who owned crab gear in town. The next day the *Valkyrie* left early and came in late. Speculation on the whereabouts of their gear was a topic being discussed in the harbor. The discussion reached a more serious tone when *Valkyrie* came in the third day with 9,000 lbs. and then on the fourth day with 10,000 again, unloading at midnight and leaving to go fishing directly after, leaving little opportunity for the locals to quiz this outside boat who was putting the whole port in the sack. To a certain element within the home guard, the *Valkyrie's* success was pissing them off and all the rest were green at the gills with envy. Cal and the crew were pissing all over themselves with delight at their good fortune. It had been hard won thanks to Sig's perseverance.

"Vhen the goin' gets tough, it's just right for us." He had told the crew as they rounded Gorda loaded with gear that lonely night, 30 knots on the stern and eight more hours ahead of them with nothing but a hope and a chance.

Sig was plenty tough, but the thing is, all mariners are up against something much tougher and bigger than them and infinitely so, the sea. Being tough is a requirement, but Sig knew the sea was tougher than any one man. It tempered his judgement. Some had made the mistake of misunderstanding or underestimating the element they worked on, they stood against it a time or two in a show of machismo. Most times they skated through unharmed, bolstering their sense of invincibility. Other times, unexpectedly and abruptly, they paid the ultimate price for their foolhardiness and bravado, their number would come up for elimination from the wet, blue planet. Sig had seen these types come and go and he had some respect for them, but more respect for the sea he worked on. At times he struggled under the lure of gain versus the knowledge of what the consequences were of exceeding limits. And above all he was aware that he was responsible for the lives of others and all aboard *Valkyrie* were family, all were under his charge. He had lost one family member at sea and that was enough.

Years ago, Sig on the *Valkyrie* and Arne on the *Fin* had shot offshore, hoping to find a few quick tons of albacore. Other boats too were taking advantage of the bounty, a brief late summer appearance of the warm water fish. And they were biting. It was in the chasing of these fish that one got the idea of just how large the ocean was and before long, Arne and Sig were easily separated by 30 miles of water in their search for tuna. The ocean was flat calm and chasing jumpers during the mid-day hours had led them apart. The whole fleet was now scattered. The morning bite had been good, and the evening bite promised to be the same. About 3 o'clock in the afternoon, the lines started to go tight and albacore skipped to the surface, hooked. Arne and Cal pulled fish aboard the *Fin* as fast as they could, and they circled the boat on the spot. The fish didn't stop, repeatedly biting and the *Fin* was in the same circle as dusk arrived. It was a frenzy as the fish convulsively flailed on the deck, bleeding profusely, red blood and regurgitated bait fish ran out the scuppers and into the water. It was primal, an intoxicating blood sport with the fish biting just as fast as the jig was thrown back in the water, the short lines were producing all the fish they could handle. And the fish were big, twenty-pound average fish that spit up volumes of little red pelagic crabs. The ocean was alive for miles and miles with the crabs and the sea life was feasting on the bounty. Arne ran up into the wheelhouse, ignoring tight lines and fish for a moment.

"Sig, you gettin' em where you're at? They're bitin' the gall darned jigs off here." He spoke into the two-way radio.

"Vee getting a few all the time headed your way. I think you got the spot located. You're breaking up, I think vee still a vays away yet." he replied.

"Okay, well keep comin' until you see me. Out." Arne replied, signed off and hurried back to the stern to help Cal who was now clearing the deck of fish, throwing them down into the slaughter alley in the fish hold and then jumping back into the pit in the stern to pull more fish and load the deck checkers again. The *Fin* circled and the fish kept coming, the boat still alone in a big ocean.

The *Fin* gently swayed from side to side in her circling and the fish on deck began to overflow the checkers and massed on the decks. Arne, hardly aware of anything this past hour beyond fish on jigs, looked around. Something was up, he sensed something was different. He told Cal to put the fish on deck down below. It seemed to him that *Fin* was sluggish with the weight of the fish and he wanted them squared away. Cal was horrified when he threw open the hatch.

"Skipper! We got water in the fish hold!"

Arne immediately went up and looked in the engine room. There was water in the shaft alley rising to the floorboards. He checked the raw water hoses, the seacocks, the discharge hoses and nothing was amiss. Most of the water was in the fish hold and bleeding into the engine room through the shaft alley, at least that was the thought. He turned the pumps on to evacuate the rising water. He had to think of something fast.

"Cal, start throwing those fish out of the slaughter alley. The water is coming in down there somewhere." Arne jumped down alongside Cal and started pitching fish on deck, all the while with a watchful eye looking for the source of the breach. He suspected a sprung plank, but he could not see it for the fish and water. He thought he had this figured right, he just had to find the spot where the water was coming in. He better, he knew he didn't have all day in this rising water. Night was upon them soon to make matters worse. There was about a ton on deck and he knew as little as he did when he first jumped down below. Fish and water were sloshing around down there obscuring his effort to ascertain the breach.

"I think it's coming in somewhere on the starboard side!" Arne said, now sweating under his raingear, soaked in bloody water as he feverishly moved fish out of the starboard bins looking for the leak. "Go get a call off to Sig, let him know we're taking on water, it's a Mayday. It's serious."

"Roger." Cal boosted himself onto the deck in one quick motion and ran for the wheelhouse and the radio.

"Mayday, Mayday, *Fin* taking on water. Position: 43205/15650. Repeat: 43250/15650." He took the boat out of gear and they drifted in this position. He dashed out of the house and ran back to help Arne. All the boats on the tuna grounds that heard the call turned toward *Fin's* position, most especially Sig.

"Roger Arne, vee comin', hold on." Sig said into his radio.

"I think it's a plank let go!" Arne shouted to Cal, "Get some nails and a hammer, I'm gonna nail some bin boards over it, If I could just find it! These god damn fish are floating all over the place in this bloody water, can't see a damn thing!"

Arne and Cal struggled against the water, now chest deep. It was becoming obvious what the next move would be, but they didn't give up the ship just yet, hoping to get lucky and find the breach. When water started lapping onto the deck through the scuppers it was time to go. All they had were life jackets and flares and now was the time to put them into use. Cal got some fish boxes and bin boards nailed together on the main hatch to create a makeshift raft for their escape. The engine died and it was the worst silence imaginable; water lapping over the transom and slowly advancing toward the pilothouse, filling the deck.

"Let's go Arne, we gotta go in, we're goin down fast." Cal said.

"You go Cal, I can't face those sharks, that's no way for me to die." Arne said.

"I got us a raft, we're no*t gonna* die! Sharks can't get us there, let's go!" Cal replied.

"You're a good man Cal and I love ya." Arne said and he turned and waded into the wheelhouse and shut the door on his biggest fear; the fear of the flesh-tearing sharks. Arne had made a choice and was resigned to his fate.

"For Christ sakes, Arne please. Let's go while we can!" Cal stood in rapidly rising deck water and shouted at the closed door.

Arne just looked through the glass and waved goodbye to Cal. Cal turned away and floated over the stern rail in his makeshift raft, wearing a lifejacket and gripping the flare gun. He watched the *Fin* gently slip below the surface, emitting bubbles and then nothing but the mast and then that was gone as well. *Fin* was gone and so was Arne.

There were sharks and they were relentless, tearing the floating tuna to shreds as it washed off the *Fin's* deck, frenzied as they were by the blood in the water. Cal watched the swirling fins and it gave him a shiver as he watched from a few feet away on his raft.

"Maybe Arne was right to go down with the ship." He mumbled at the swirling fins.

After dark, the sharks could still be heard breaking the surface with their swishing tails and frenzied feeding motions, igniting phosphorescent trails in the water. Most of the sharks were five or six-foot blues but there were lots of little blues down there too, hard to say how many. Occasionally, a big one would bump the raft and swim through the pack slowly and all the other sharks would clear a path for him. Cal on the flimsy raft, it barely floated one safely above the blue monsters and Cal was that lucky one. Or was he lucky? He was getting cold and sleepy as the horrible night wore on without end. He knew he was in dire straits, he knew what came next so he lashed himself to the middle of the raft and talked to God, rambling on about good and evil, life, love, salvation and death in a sleepy and half-conscious mumble, saying words that he would have never expected to come through his lips. Just before he lost consciousness, pinpricks of red and green lights appeared on the low horizon. He drew back the hammer on the flat-black flare gun, held it aloft and pulled the trigger. Seconds later and high aloft, a red flare slowly parachuted to the sea below. On this night, his number had not come up for elimination. Rescue came before he fell asleep and before he fell to the same fate as the tuna.

* * *

It blew for a couple of days, kinda hard out of the northwest and the whole fleet was in. Sig had the gear relocated to the deep and had some confidence that he would have a good pull when he got out. Cal and the boys spliced 5/16 top shots during the day and Alex learned a lot about cribbage by night. On the second day they finished splicing the coils of rope and Alex found out just how boring Eureka was for a teen, wandering up Two Street, looking in windows, having a burger. He was delighted to find a maritime museum just off the street by the water, browsing through the pictures of yesteryear, finding out and surprised to see just what Eureka was about back in the day of the square riggers and lumber barons He was especially surprised to learn that it had been the state capitol, imagine that, raty old Eureka. On his way back to the boat he met Cal coming up the ladder from *Valkyrie*.

"Where you "goin?" Alex asked of Cal.

"I'm going stir crazy, that's where I'm 'goin. If I play one more game of cribbage with your brother and uncle, I'll go nuts. I can't even look at a cribbage board anymore. I'm gonna have a beer and shoot some pool over here at the Vista." He said.

"Can I go with you?" Alex asked.

Cal regarded him and smiled, "Sure kid, let's go."

The boats were rafted at the dock no more than fifty paces from the bar and grill named Vista Del Mar. Located on a gritty street along the railroad tracks, three blocks down from the Seamans Mission, the Vista was a small squat building with dirty red TNG plank siding and white trim around small windows, with paint that was fading in the wind and fog, dusty from emissions created by the pulp mill and gravel parking lot. An old-fashioned sign with letters behind neon tubes spelled, "Vista del Mar Seafood." It extended outward from the building on a crude metal frame. Two martini glasses on the sign was the indication that mixed drinks were also available here. The low squat building sat alone among empty lots with broken cement foundations and railroad boxcars on sidetracks. Weeds amidst the broken cement was all that remained where waterfront warehouses once stood. One could imagine the waterfront was once hustling with commerce in the past. Now, the Vistas' only neighbors were a city redevelopment building that housed the fish plant and the empty lots that fronted an old cold storage facility a couple of blocks down the tracks.

Once inside, it could only be described as dingy. A small L shaped room with two doors and a few little windows that emitted no light; the windows long since shrouded with dirty curtains and beer signs. The only natural light came as an intrusion when one of the two doors was opened. The artificial light of the Budweiser, Hamm's and Coors beer signs and the jukebox served as the only decoration. There were fourteen barstools, three brown Formica tables and in the corner, there was a big round wooden table.

But that was only the half of it. Walking through a narrow hallway, walking by a pay phone on the wall and turning right, you entered a café. By contrast, it was a well-lighted room with windows all around viewing the Humboldt Bay. The walls of the room were crowded with photographs of fishing boats from yesteryear, photos of families crowded on the flying bridge in their Sunday clothes and onboard for the boats' maiden voyage. They were black and white photos hanging on walls that had been painted off-white 20 years previous, now yellowing at the door jambs and windowsills. A pea soup green trim color was equally aged. Filling the small room were six tables and eight counter stools, a cash register and a chalkboard with the daily specials, although nothing on the small menu was special, just standard fare was served here. You didn't eat here for the food if you ate here at all. The café had the feeling of On the Waterfront, circa 1956. One could just imagine it crowded with men in work clothes back when the waterfront was bustling, and the pulp and lumber mill was the biggest employer in town.

"Now listen," Cal said, "you let me do the talking when we go in there. I'll get you a beer. Don't shoot your mouth off in here, some of these guys don't play around. We are outsiders in their port and in their bar. Your uncle will kill me if we get into trouble." Cal said

"I'm cool." Alex answered.

"Yeah, you're cool alright- cool as penguin shit." Cal shot back.

They walked in the side door at 4PM in the afternoon. The place already had a small crowd and a couple of them were shooting a game of 8-ball at the pool table. Cal got a couple of beers and walked over to the table.

"Winners?" he asked placing his quarter under the side cushion of the table. This got a nod from the guy lining up a shot.

Alex sat at a table and regarded the big woman tending bar; she seemed to be on a first name basis with her patrons and only 'regulars' came here. The beer bottle in front of Alex sweated and he took a pull off the glassy long neck. The anticipated alcoholic sensation set in quickly, a sensation he was getting the hang of and liked. Quite suddenly, the door burst open and street-light intruded as did a very large man.

He was loud, about 6'4" 260 pounds and long blond hair. Everything about him seemed big. He swaggered in bellowing a song, wearing high top tennis shoes and a green army surplus trench coat. He came in with a surprise in mind that was soon to be revealed to all in the little barroom. He came in singing to the tune of Blow the Man Down, *she offered her honor, I honored her offer, on her and off her and on her all night.*" All heads turned toward him, won by the audacious man's song. But that was not the extent of the show. He threw open his trench coat, mounted the bar plank, got on his back and danced *the alligator* completely naked beneath the trench coat; a writhing nakedness, the hair, the jiggling genitals, it was as much ugly as it was funny. The patrons egged him on and applauded, the bartend-ress was livid and she began to beat his fat white flesh with a broom until he quit his dance and exited, out the way he came to sustained applause. Cal walked over to Alex's table.

"Did you see that?! That was outrageous! Beautiful!" said Alex, charged by the spectacle he had just witnessed.

"Yeah I saw it. And saw plenty of it before. That's *the Mojo:* he worked with us one year. This is how he is; it's always one thing or the other. This *alligator* routine is one of his standards, a real crowd pleaser too. One year he put a greased-up piglet in a guys' cabin while the skipper was asleep and then shut the door. Another time he lowered a dead sea lion into the fish hold while the skipper was away at home." Cal was matter of fact in his explanation.

"*Offered her honor, honored her offer*? That was a good one." Alex was giggling.

"Yeah, well don't get any ideas, least of all don't share this with Uncle Sig." Cal cautioned.

"*On her and off her and on her all night*?" Alex giggled some more, shaking his head.

"He's a real beauty all right." Cal said flatly, "We better get outta here, see what's up for tomorrow. It might get ugly in here."

"What about your quarter?" Alex asked.

"Leave it." Cal said.

They picked up and left the bar and walked the short distance back to the boat. They met Leif coming up the ladder.

"Where you guy's been? We're gonna go tomorrow, we gotta put bait on the boat." Leif said.

"You shoulda seen it Leif, this guy got on the bar naked." Alex gushed with enthusiasm.

"The Mojo. We were in the Vista." Cal stated flatly.

Leif shook his head silently and made his way toward the freezer and the bait, Cal and Alex followed right behind. They pulled the bait out and got it down on the *Valkyrie*. Sig had the weather report blaring from the deck speaker, droning on and on in its automated loop.

"Wind northwest 15-25 miles per hour, decreasing to 10-20 in the evening. Swell out of the west 8-10 feet, diminishing. A high tide will occur at 800 hours at a height of 6.2 feet with a low tide occurring at 1300 hours at 0.5 feet. Sunrise will be at 700 hours, sunset at 1700 hours. The following observations were taken at 2PM................." it droned on through the observations and the loop came to the beginning and repeated itself.

"Vee be all right, she's lying down. Vees cross the bar, the swells laying down too." Sig said.

"Roger." Cal answered, throwing totes into a stack nestled against the tank. He lashed them down.

The inevitable cribbage board came out after dinner. They sat at the galley table for a few hands before turning in to catch five or six hours of sleep before the long day would begin tomorrow. All anticipated a good pull, yet none would speak of it. If they possessed religious feelings, superstition would have been a prominent piece of it. Through experience they had learned that speaking of good fortune was not allowed, lest it change the outcome. It made no sense, but it seemed to prove itself true more than once. It was better to accept the gifts gratefully rather than to expect them. Hard work was not always rewarded but it was always required as part of the ante-up. Young Alex had not had the time nor had the experiences to learn this yet.

"We should have a good pull tomorrow." he said from his narrow bunk.

"We'll see." Leif answered.

"Damn Alex, don't anticipate, I told you!" Cal snapped.

"You both know it's true, what's the big deal?" Alex defended his thought.

"The deal is I been fucked by the fickle finger of fate before and I don't like it. I don't jinx it by running my mouth. That's the big deal, fool!" Cal snapped back at Alex's naiveté.

"Take it easy Cal, he doesn't know any better." Leif said.

"Geez." Alex quietly muttered to himself, settled into his pillow and drifted off to sleep with visions of a full tank and full totes, calculating what his share might be.

In the morning they drank coffee on the dark back deck as *Valkyrie* ran down the channel to the entrance. It was a morning much like every other morning; cold, dark and wet. But it did have an unspoken emotional charge of anticipation. It had to be so, even Sig had heightened expectations for the good pull they had worked so hard to achieve. He needed to expect good things from the deep; there was nowhere else to go. It was a search and he had searched the shallows already. The past result from the deep had been very encouraging and now the gear was there; *'firstis with the mostis'*, as General Sherman said. If there were no crabs in the deep, there were no crabs anywhere. They got on the end marker before the sun came over the coastal mountain range, a range that was a black silhouette backlighted by a gold and blue-black sky that promised a brilliant sun. The ocean was ruffled by a slight northwest breeze and a low groundswell gently lifted the boat. It was good weather for pulling traps.

They threw the first buoy in the block and positioned the coiling basket underneath, stacking the first trap as was customarily done. The trap broke water and it was completely blank.

"Shit." Cal said

"Uh-oh." Leif groaned.

The next one was blank as well and the traps kept coming that way. Alex had stacked ten across the stern and he was bummed. He started to get superstitious, remembering the conversation the night before about getting finger-fucked by fate. The next trap to come up also didn't have crabs but it did have a big octopus.

"Whoa, look what we got!" Cal said smiling.

"Yeah, a thief has been at work here. An eight-legged thief." Leif said pulling the beast out of the trap and passing him back to Alex. The octopus immediately stuck to his rain gear and Alex screamed like a little schoolgirl.

"He's got me!" Alex was alarmed, terrified and Cal laughed aloud. As quick as he had glommed onto Alex he let go and was crawling down his pant leg and headed for the scuppers.

"Get him!" Leif shouted, "Don't let him get away!"

"I'm not gonna grab him, he'll get me again!" Alex replied and the octopus squished his twenty pounds down into the size of a Coke can so that he now fit out the narrow scuppers, escaping. He was quickly gone overboard and back into the ocean, jetting away with a squirt of black ink.

"We'll see him again." Cal said matter of fact without turning his head back towards them, waiting at the rail to gaff the next buoy.

The next trap came up loaded with a lot of crab. They stopped stacking, put on an end marker and they ran and rebait-ed the rest of the string, throwing crabs into the tank.

"The octopus ate the crabs Alex; they go from trap to trap eating them all." Leif explained.

"Wow, that's smart." Alex mused.

"It's fucked up, that's what it is dip-shit! That's why we don't let 'em go!" said Cal, disgusted.

The next string had crabs too. The weather was getting better with the additional downhill current. The current was already tugging at the main buoys and threatening to pull them underwater. The current eventually made good on that threat halfway through the next string. The mains went down and only the trailer buoys were up. But not for long.

"I can only see every other trap; the trailers are going down, put a marker on the next trap." Sig hollered.

They were done on that string due to the current. Sig did not want to scatter the string, an almost certainty if they continued to run it. They drifted alongside the next string for a while watching the trailer buoys spin and occasionally break the surface. They gave that up, had seen enough and they ran to where the other strings were supposed to be but all they saw was water and no buoys, a lonely sight indeed. Sig knew it only got worse from here in the ebbing tide, so he called a halt and headed for the entrance. The crew squared away the deck in silence. This was an unforeseen circumstance indeed. They had found a spot with good crabs but now the future was clouded by a new obstacle; the strong current found in this deep water had rendered the gear inaccessible and underwater. They got in early this day and unloaded their catch, then tied up the boat.

"Vee go tomorrow, vee run all of the gear" Sig said stepping out of the wheelhouse onto the back deck.

They did go out the next day, but they did not run all the gear nor any part of it. When they got to where the strings were supposed to be, all they found was water, a vast expanse of empty ocean. It was an ominous portent and an obvious new force to contend with. Sig drifted alongside the place where the string was supposed to be, but no buoys popped up. When a breeze came, he put it in gear and hit the throttle, pointed *Valkyrie* toward the harbor entrance.

"Now what?" asked Alex.

"The fickle finger you little fucker. Up the butt." said Cal.

"We wait until the current lets us work, that's all we can do." Leif replied.

They waited; through storms and swell. When they did get out, they still did not see any buoys, save for one trip before Christmas. They went home for Christmas and the fishing that had been so good had turned into some-thing that felt like a rescue mission. Sig knew the score; he had seen it before. The biggest tides came at the end of the year and the tides exaggerated the already strong currents that ran down the continent and rounded the Cape. He should have known but he, like any other crabber, was blinded by the good fortune he had found. They went home for the holidays, holidays that were spent with some cheer nonetheless, the troubles of fishing put behind them. Alex went down to the Crab Cottage and hoped to see a certain waitress who worked there.

"Hi Karen." He said as she came up to his table.

"Basic! Where you been, boy?" she asked.

"Eureka, we're fishing there now. Or trying to anyway." He replied.

"Yeah? How's it going with that?" she asked.

"Well it was okay for a while. I'm learning that there are hidden problems. We were making good money until our gear disappeared under the water." He explained.

"Bummer." she responded. "What do you want to eat?" Karen took out her pad and Alex was slightly disappointed by her mock sympathy and he not having the opportunity to tell his sad tale of woe.

"I'll have a fish sandwich and chowder." he answered.

"Anything to drink?"

"A diet Coke."

"You got it sweetie." She turned and left.

Alex sat at the table and contemplated just how he could make time with this girl. Somehow, he got the feeling that the time was not right to ask her out on a first date. He was probably going to have to spend New Year's Eve in Eureka with Cal, Sig and Leif. Any way you looked at it his love life was probably in a holding pattern. The only date he might have on this New Year's was with the Palm Sisters. After a while she returned with the chowder and a Coke.

"You wanna go to Eureka for New Year's?" he asked. He was such a fool, nobody wanted to go to Eureka, least of all her.

She laughed, "No, does anybody?" she said, "But look me up when you get back."

"I'll do that." Alex responded. *God looks over children and fools;* no mystery what category he was in.

Alex went down to the Shorebird after lunch and contemplated the circumstance with Karen, over-thinking and wondering what the best way might be to play his cards with her. He also contemplated the long ride back to the boat and spending New Year's Eve in Eureka. He drank a beer with Cal as they waited for Sig and Leif to pick them up for the long ride back to the boat. He was not looking forward to this; he had a bad feeling about it too.

CHAPTER 3

The Outsiders

The long ride back to the boat after the holidays was mostly conducted mostly in silence once they passed Santa Rosa. They had another four hours to go to reach their destination and the occupants of the car stared out the windows, alone with their thoughts. They got back to Eureka in the afternoon under cloudy skies and blustery conditions. The town appeared gray and empty and stepping out of the car all noted the temperature, easily 20 degrees colder than Santa Rosa, the last place that they had stopped for a break. Grabbing their gear from the car, they walked in silence to the ladder and down to the boat. The very first thing Sig did was light the diesel stove to chase the chill and damp from the cabin. Alex went down to his bunk in the focsle and threw his duffel bag in the rack. Cal and Leif did the same.

"Home sweet home, fuck-oh-dear." Said Cal, dripping with sarcasm.

"Kinda tough to take after a nice Christmas at home, all right." Leif observed.

Alex climbed up into the cabin and got pole position next to the warming stove. He was soon joined by his crew mates. Cal thumbed through a Playboy, Leif shuffled a deck of cards and Alex sat in silence wondering what the heck he was doing here wasting time. He knew the answer; he just didn't like it. The engine rumbled to life and the weather report droned in the background. Sig walked back to the galley table after he hit the starter button.

"Velll boys, vee got a situation here. Vee got the January storms lined up and after that comes the spring and along with that, vee get the northwest current. I see it before play out that way. Having the gear in the deep comes with a risk, for sure. I think vee got caught; pants down." Sig explained.

"What happens that's so risky, Uncle Sig?" said Alex in the innocence of a greenhorn.

"The gear disappears underwater, shit-for-brains." interjected Cal.

"Take it easy Cal!" Leif snapped, defending his brother. He turned to his uncle and privately spoke, "It might be time to quit Uncle Sig."

"What I'm thinking." Sig replied.

"I want to go home too." said Alex.

"Fuckin-A-Tweedy. Let's get out of this place." Cal said and rose from the galley table. "I'm gonna walk around for a while."

"Vee are agreed then; Vee get the gear out of the vaahter and go home." Sig concluded and that ended the conversation.

Easier said than done. The weather was against them in January and if that wasn't against you, the bar was closed because of the swell. Or maybe when you did get out the current had the gear under water. All these factors had to line up in their favor or it was a no-go. In the meantime, they just had to make the best of it. At least now they had a united agreement.

"I'm gonna walk around too before it starts raining." said Alex, rising and exiting out the cabin door and onto the back deck. He took out his wallet and checked his remaining funds. He went up the ladder and headed for Peggy's café, the economical choice. There was nobody walking around on the streets, streets that were pocked with grey puddles riffled by the wind. Alex was buffeted by gusts and quickened his step against the impending rain that was sure to soon follow. Arriving at Peggy's he entered a room full of men. Some had newspapers spread upon their table, others clutching warm coffee cups, others attending to their meal with overflowing shopping bags by their side, all getting out of the weather and killing time. Time was the thing they had the most of and some didn't even have much of that. Alex found Tim sitting by himself in the corner table and he approached it.

"Join you Tim?" he asked.

"Have a sit". He replied.

"What's happening?" Alex asked casually, already knowing the answer.

"The rent, that's what. In other words, not a darn thing. We haven't been out since the holidays, holidays I spent on the boat." Tim said.

"Ooo, that's bad. We just got back, we're gonna get the gear out of the water and go home." Alex said genially.

"Good luck with that! This weather never seems to let up, I gotta quit and I know it. I'm just waiting for Bristol Bay." Tim said. "We go up and get the boat and gear ready around May, seems like a long way away but at this rate it'll be soon. We start fishing around June, depending on how the escapement goes."

"What's escapement?" Alex asked.

"They count the fish that go up the rivers, they got people in towers and they watch it real close. When they get so many fish up the river, they make the announcement that we can go fishing. They counted 40 million fish last year. They give you about 6 hours' notice to go out and set and they tell you how many hours you can fish. It's an enduro but you can knock down a lot of dough in a month."

"Sounds pretty good to me, I wanna do it, I'm gonna do it. This crabbing is like being on a garbage truck, picking up the cans and emptying them, putting them back and repeating it over and over all day long. It's kinda fun when there is lots of crab but even that wears thin after a while. It also seems to bring out the worst in people; there's only so much to go around and what you catch is what somebody else doesn't catch." Alex said.

"Up in Bristol we are in a river or a Bay most of the time, we fish every opportunity they let us which is everyday darn near." Tim said.

"Do you sleep?" Alex wondered.

"Oh yeah; eat too, they open it for a tide or two then close it for a tide or two. Plenty of time to unload, eat and sleep for a few hours." Tim explained.

"That's cool." Alex concluded as the waitress came over to the table.

"What'll you have Hon?" she asked Alex.

"Scrambled eggs and bacon, wheat toast." He replied.

"Coffee?" she asked.

"Yeah, please." He replied, and she hurried off, energetically serving the room full of men efficiently. Her name was Peggy and it was her place.

"I gotta get back to the boat; the skipper has some chores for me." Tim said as he rose from the table.

"I really want to go to Bristol Bay." Alex urged.

"Call and see if we need crew, we always seem to have a new 3rd guy each season. You got my sister's number. But you can find work if you walk the yards when the guys are getting ready. Get the word out you are looking for work. Look up Marsha in Dillingham; she hangs everybody's nets and she knows what's going on, everybody is her friend and she's really cool." Tim told Alex and they shook hands before he left.

In the days that followed the waiting game continued and they played a lot of cards and listened to the rain pelt the roof and the VHF weather report. They had a weather break in the middle of January, and they got out for a few days in a row between the storms, loading the boat and taking the gear in to the dock. They had one load to go before they made the long slide home with the last of the gear on the boat. Spirits were high once again and the hard work and hope was proving its remedial powers. The third day out threw a damper on that mood right quick; the gear was diving under water and they dare not stack it on the boat lest they leave the hidden traps behind.

"God damn." Sig said in an unusually strong display of emotion for man like him. He drifted the *Valkyrie* alongside the string, watching the trailer buoys spin before they ducked their heads below the surface. He bumped it into gear and ran down the string, seeing every other buoy and seeing traps that had been drug out by kelp islands and were now a few hundred yards to the inside.

"Yumpin Jeesus." He muttered as he observed his string of gear in disrepair.

"Now what?" Alex asked of his crewmates as they lounged around on the back deck in the warming morning sun, still in the raingear and standing by for word from Sig. They knew the score, but nobody yet had said a word. Cal broke his silence.

"I'll tell you *what* kid; you're screwed, glued and tattooed." Cal said.

"It's not good Alex." said Leif, sounding a little deflated.

Sig threw in the towel and turned the *Valkyrie* toward the harbor, there was no fighting it, it was the force of nature and he knew it. The crew squared away the deck and got out of the raingear. The silence returned, Cal was disgusted, Leif was resigned, and Alex didn't know what to say. They got in early and tied up empty.

"Vee try again tomorrow boys; all vee can do right now." Sig said.

"Roger Uncle." Leif replied.

"I'm getting a bad feeling about this." Cal let it out and gave voice to what everyone else was thinking. It was kind of bad form to not keep a positive attitude, but he could not help himself.

"Vee all know the score Cal, no use cryin' or complainin' bout it though. Vee make the best out of a bad situation, that's how vee do things here." Sig said with firmness to his tone.

"Roger." Cal replied. "I'm goin' uptown for a while, I'll see you later."

"Don't you get in no trouble now." Sig cautioned.

"I won't start it and I won't look for it." He replied as he exited, thinking to himself, "but I sure as hell will finish it if *it* finds *me*."

As it turned out, he didn't have to go far before it did find him. He walked into the Vista, sat at the bar and ordered an afternoon beer, pouring it into a

6-ounce glass and sipping slow, feeling sorry for himself. The place was near empty save for a few patrons at the bar, sitting and thinking just like him, possibly the maintenance drinkers servicing their needs, there were a ew of them in this town. It was quiet, no pool and no jukebox.

"Did you guys go out today?" The bartender was making polite conversation.

"Yeah. The current had the gear down. We got one more load to grab before we can go home." Cal replied.

"Where's home?" The bartender kept his end of the conversation going, it was a casual inquiry just to pass the time.

"Half Moon Bay. It's a little town south of San Francisco and I sure wish I was there, out of this rain and in the sunshine again." Cal said wistfully, thinking of his home.

One of the other patrons had been listening in from his barstool and was now staring at the men conversing across the bar. He was skinny, dirty, stringy locks, wispy and scraggly facial hair: the archetypal rural-white-boy-trash in for an afternoon beer at the Vista. He erupted into life and joined the conversation.

"I like the rain; I hate that queer-San Francisco-black-dick-suck'in sunshine." He said.

His vulgar ugliness turned what few heads there were. "What's a matter with you Virgil?" said the bartender, "Don't start any trouble and there won't be any." He turned to Cal and said, "Don't pay any attention to Virgil."

Cal just sat there in silence. Thinking about how Sig cautioned him about trouble. This trash kid was really asking for it.

Thinking he had the upper hand, the trash-boy kept at it. "Out-of-town boats catchin' our crabs: that's what they are and that's what they do. Well they ain't gettin outta here easy nor anytime soon and that's a fact. Them buoys ain't gonna see daylight and it's gonna rain for another month."

These oblique insults were hitting their mark and they were irritating the shit out of Cal and everyone who heard them knew it; this kid had just about exceeded Cal's limit. Mental visions of retribution took shape in Cal's mind. Punishment became the central feature.

"Down the road Virgil, that's it." The bartender had enough and could plainly see where this was going and it wasn't good. Cal kept his peace, but he could just picture himself mopping the floor with this rag doll of a human being. Anybody in the room could see Virgil was a little light in the ass for a bar fight with *anybody*, let alone with Cal.

"I'll go gladly; don't care much for the company here this afternoon." He taunted Cal, looking straight at him as he pushed off from his barstool and stood. "Chickenshits too. I knew it." He walked slowly toward the door and opened it, muttering, "San Francisco motherfucking cocksuckers."

His vile, disgusting presence and insults lingered in the silent room like slime. The patrons either watched Cal or they kept their eyes averted from his. The air in the room was charged with the potential for violence. The averted eyes did not wish violence to come their way and the eyes that were on Cal wondered if anything was going to happen next.

"That kid is no good. He fucked his own babysitter and got her pregnant, can you believe that shit? Three *hots and a cot* in County-better than he deserved. They should have kept him there. Wife-beating, pedophile-predator little bastard." said the bartender when the door closed on the kids' exit.

"The whole family is no damn good." Added a patron.

Cal got up and walked toward the door, opened it and walked outside just as his tormentor was getting in an old Chevy pick-up truck with a Confederate flag in the back window and similar bumper stickers across the front bumper.

"Hey dickweed." Cal said calmly and kicked in a headlight on the truck with his boot heel in a kung-fu pose. The glass shattered to the ground. "You got one foul mouth kid." And he kicked in the other headlight.

The kid was standing up on the running board behind the open door when he fired his .22 caliber pistol twice at Cal. The first shot hit him in the forearm and the second shot went wide as Cal spun around and went down, grabbing his wounded arm. The shot missed the bone, but it was bleeding fairly good.

"You crazy fuckin fool!" He said to his wounded arm rather than to his assailant as he observed his wound. He had to get out of here before another shot was fired., Cal knew that much. The door of the Vista wasn't that far behind him, but the trouble was the .22 pistol was a lot closer than the door. He scrambled behind the closest thing at hand, a 10-foot length of old telephone pole that had been placed close to the building as a parking stop. Cal pressed his chest hard into the gravel. The bartender and a few patrons rushed out the door at the sound of the broken glass and the shots fired. They immediately went back inside when they saw the little snub-nosed chrome handle in the kids' hand. The third shot never came and, in its place, came the engine sound and the sound of spitting gravel as the kid backed out of the lot at a high rate of speed, tires spinning. That sound was soon followed by the sound of a distant siren. Cal stayed put, prone behind the creosote log. The bartender peeked around the door then reemerged with a bar towel for Cal's wound.

"It was just a matter of time before that kid had another run-in with the law. He really did it this time, we won't be seeing his sorry ass any time soon, he's going up for good." Said the bartender, wrapping a towel around Cal's wounded forearm.

"I never expected that punk to be so fucking crazy as to shoot me! Fuck! Lucky it was just a .22." Cal said.

The ambulance arrived at about the same time as the crew from *Valkyrie*. "Vhat happened here Cal?" Sig asked as they packed Cal onto the gurney.

"Sorry Sig. Looks like trouble found me after all." Cal replied as he looked up from the white sheets.

"And you got the voorst, by the looks of it. Don't worry, we'll get you fixed up." Sig said.

"Just a flesh wound, a little pimp gun. I'll be back to the boat after I get wrapped up." Cal replied.

"Don't you worry about that, we got you covered" said Leif.

"Yeah Cal, we got you covered." Alex repeated.

The ambulance pulled out of the lot with Cal aboard and headed for the hospital. Leif turned toward Alex and said, "Alex pay attention: this is what happens in a place like this. It attracts the worst elements in a small town and if you're an outsider, that's one strike against ya'. You don't see Uncle Sig in there, me neither. Stay out of that place."

"I come by that lesson honestly years ago in my drinkin' days Alex." Sig added, "It was worse back then because everybody drank a lot. People do things they wouldn't otherwise do vhen they drink. And I'm no different-neither are you." Sig added.

"Let's go to the hospital and collect Cal." Leif said.

"I just gonna go in and ask the bartender vhat happened. Just for a second, I'll be right out." Sig said.

"I wanna hear this too." Leif said.

"Me too." Added Alex and they went into the bar and questioned the bartender.

"That kid's a no-good; a foul-mouth troublemaker." The bartender began, "I 86'ed him: he was talking shit about out-of-town crabbers. Your man followed him outside and the next thing we knew 2 shots were fired. I ran outside and saw the kid with a gun in his hand and your man down on the ground behind a log. That's when I called the cops." He recalled the sequence of events to Sig's satisfaction and Sig said, "Let's go to the hospital."

They arrived at the ER at St Joseph's Hospital. It was a dingy, small room with four plastic chairs and un-washed walls painted a pale green (apparently a popular choice of color in this town). Head-grease stained the wall above the backs of the seats, the walls had not been painted for a long time. The room was empty save for the *Valkyrie* crew and void of any sign of hospital personnel. Sig stood at a small counter waiting for somebody to show up.

"Geez, good thing you don't show up dying' here." Alex observed.

"They don't need you and they expect the same." Leif said.

"Bob Dylan said that!" Alex exclaimed.

"I knew I heard that somewhere." Leif muttered. A nurse showed up at the counter and Sig directed her toward Cal.

"He's got a gunshot wound in his forearm." Sig stated.

"I see, well let's get him in to the examination room." She ushered Cal behind a set of swinging doors. She had the bedside manner of a somewhat severe grade school principle, made the more so by her upswept cats-eye eyeglasses and beehive hairdo. It looked like the sun was setting on her 40's.

She led Cal to an examination table and handed him a folded gown, laundered to feel like 180 grit sandpaper. "Put this on, the doctor will be in in a minute."

"But I got shot in the arm, not the ass." Cal protested the instruction to wear the gown-of-shame, open at the butt.

"I don't make the rules; I just follow them. Please put the gown on." And with that she turned and left Cal to strip down bare-ass naked for an exam of his forearm. To make matters worse, the gown was a size too small and did not even wrap around to cover his rear end. So, he sat down and waited, resigned to humiliation and a chill.

"The doctor is with him now." She said as she returned to her front desk position. She went to scribble down some paperwork and Sig presented her with his United States Public Health Service card,

"He's my crewman aboard the documented vessel *Valkyrie*, he's signed on to the papers, name's Cal Harris, vee out of San Francisco and vee fishing up here." Sig said, explaining.

"Okay, let me have your card, I'll check." She stated and collected Sig's card.

"Yah sure." Sig replied and he sat down in the little plastic chair next to Alex.

"Am I signed on the papers too, Uncle Sig?" Alex inquired quietly.

"Oh yeah, Leif-y too. Medical and dental is free on a documented fishing vessel, courtesy the United States Public Health Service." Sig replied.

"That's cool." Alex said.

"Now don't you go getting yourself shot, Mr. Cool." Sig joked.

Doctor Goldthorpe emerged from his office into the exam room. He might as well have emerged from a Norman Rockwell painting, so like a country doctor with his white smock and dangling stethoscope around his neck. He was a short man of 60 years with sandy blond hair fashioned into a flattop. His polished brown shoes and creased pants added to the Rockwell costume. He affected a rather disinterested attitude, softly whistling and humming an unintelligible and wheezy tune. Cal did hear the lyric 'whispering hope" in there somewhere, it got his attention. The country doctor gently lifted Cal's forearm and unwrapped the bandage for further examination, gingerly holding it at eye level.

"Gunshot wound from a small caliber weapon, in one side and out the other, clean." He mused to himself.

"A little punk with a pimp gun." Cal stated flatly.

"I seem to see a lot of this lately." Goldthorpe replied still examining the wound closely.

"Well, I don't know about that, but I do know that there is one more punk up in jail tonight. And I hope he's really popular with the gen-pop." Cal said with sarcasm.

"Tut, tut now. None of that." Goldthorpe remarked like Clarence-The-Angel from a Capra Christmas film.

After a time, Cal emerged from a set of swinging doors with a bandage wrapped the length of his forearm. Nobody said much as they all walked through the exit and down the stairs to the pick-up truck in the empty lot. Alex climbed into the back of the bed and the other three men squished into the front bench seat under gray and cloudy skies. Tomorrow was not looking like a "go day" for the *Valkyrie* and crew, they would listen to the weather report when they got back but the skies told the tale. A somber mood was settling over the group and Sig didn't like the trend in morale, however, it was understandable under the circumstances. He was the first to speak after the truck engine came to a slow rumble.

"Let's go over to Samoa, my treat at the Cookhouse." Sig considered a big plate of food to be a remedy to most things bad.

"Sounds good Uncle Sig" Leif replied.

In Samoa, what was left of a vast lumber mill that covered half the island, there was a long squat building housing the cookhouse. At one time this was the kitchen that produced plates of food for the workers at the mill. Now it was an all-you-can-eat restaurant filled with long communal tables upon which whole roasts and pies were placed, what they called 'family-style'. It sought to re-create the atmosphere of the once bustling chow hall and the attempt was good, but it fell a little short of the mark without the people to make it bustle. Most of the tables were empty. The town population was choosing some of the trendier restaurants in town nowadays and as a tourist attraction, all-you-can-eat restaurants were not pulling them in as they did at one time. Even the giant billboard outside of town was not helping to fill the benches. An underlying theme found everywhere you looked in this town was 'empty'.

"I about had enough of this fucking town to last me a lifetime." Cal mumbled as he sat, looking around at the near empty hall.

"Now, now. Vee all had enough that's for sure. Vee make the best of it is all we can do. You got reason to complain." Sig rejoined without much enthusiasm to a brief pep talk.

"Yeah, I am the one with a hole in his arm." Cal replied.

"Why'd he shoot you?" Alex asked.

"Why? Because he's a local loser, that's why." Cal conveniently didn't mention the headlights he kicked in. "He was in the bar bad-mouthing out of town crab boats and that's us. Trailer-trash. Just what do these people do to get that way? They must all be screwing their cousins." Cal shook his head. "I ignored him, didn't say a word. The bartender 86'ed him, I just sat there."

"Yeah, but he shot you." Alex said in his ever-innocent way.

"Yes, he did Alex. I did make the mistake of going outside where he could do that to me." Cal replied to Alex in a calm manner.

"Vhat's done is done. Let's put this behind us now, no more talk of it." Sig interjected.

"Yeah, I'm hungry and those pies look good." said Leif, abruptly changing the subject and following his Uncle's lead.

After dinner they returned to the boat and played a few hands of cribbage before turning in. Sig was feeling the mood decline on his boat. This could go bad if they didn't get out to load the gear and go home, he knew this to be true and could tell the signs; they had overstayed. The reason to be here had been removed and all that was left was the view of creosote pilings, mud and an old gray town gone to seed. Upon awakening in the morning and leaning at the rail, the weather report droned from the deck speaker and the view had not changed alongside the pilings.S ig thumbed through the tide book up in the wheelhouse.

"It's no good, maybe tomorrow vhen it switches to the Northwest, maybe." Sig said to no one in particular. He walked back into the galley where a morning game of cards was underway. "Let's get off of the boat and take a car ride up to CC."

"Take a car ride home would be more like it." Cal muttered.

"Good idea Uncle Sig. let's go up to Denny's too." Leif chimed in.

"Waffle's!" Alex interjected.

"That too." Sig replied. A change of scenery had to happen; Sig was just as downhearted in the rain in a broken old town as Cal but he couldn't afford to show it. Inwardly he was getting tired of being the cheerleader and he had his limits just as any other man.

The hour ride up the coast did have its moments of distraction. They got out to look at the grazing herd of moose in a field along the way, stopped at the Klamath and watched its muddy brown water spread out over the ocean at the mouth. In Crescent City, Sig looked at some crab gear for sale. They walked the new marina and looked at the boats tied up there, went uptown and browsed in a secondhand shop. Alex bought an old brown Fender amp for ten dollars, he liked the name, it reminded him of home; it was a Princeton amp. Sig bought a cigarette case that played music when you opened the lid. He didn't smoke-just had to come away with something. After a late lunch they headed back. Mission accomplished, they had shot the day away and got off the boat. The windshield wipers started flapping and Alex squeezed into the front seat, four across on the bench. They had a view of the ocean as the road rose above the sea. It didn't look too bad here, but Sig knew where his gear was, down by the lightship in the deep, it wasn't too swell. He had really dug a hole for them when he put the gear there. It was a different ocean and different weather by the Cape. Alex gazed out at a few boats on the ocean.

"We gonna make it out tomorrow Uncle Sig?" Innocent and unaware of the emotional charge that question held.

Sig was nearing his limits of patience. He considered the question for a moment before he answered. In that moment the entire history of this crab adventure flashed through his mind; the high moments and the low, the month of preparation, the expectation, the defeat at the River, the move to Eureka, the brief jubilation of crabs, the gunshot, the hospital, the pilings and mud, all of it.

"Tomorrow vee go. Time to go home." It was the only answer possible under these circumstances.

"Amen." Cal said.

They approached town after an hour down the road. They passed more and more houses and then came by a trailer park by a stoplight. Faded plastic toys, garbage cans and a few old tires were scattered about, some of the tires were turned inside out and the edges had been scalloped to make it look as if it were a giant black tulip. Blue tarps seemed to be a popular roofing choice. The place had an unkempt look, one of the lower rent places you find in a low rent town. There was silence in the truck until Alex exclaimed,

"Isn't that him!?" He exclaimed and pointed at an old blue pickup with broken headlights as they waited at the red traffic stop.

Silence pervaded as all investigated the trailer park. All saw that it was the blue pick-up truck from which the shots were fired. Sig spoke.

"No. You forget all about that now, that's over." That was all he said in a manner that ended the subject.

At the boat it was more cards and Sig cranked up the big diesel stove, cranked it up to a level that had everyone in their T shirts. He browned a pot roast on top of the big diesel stove and then put it in the oven, turning down the oil, the carburetor adjustment at 2 on the dial. Sig turned on the weather report and Alex and Leif squared away the table for more cards. Cal announced he was going up to the store and got the keys to the truck.

"Can I go?" asked Alex.

Cal hesitated and then answered, "I don't think so kid. I got some things to think about alone, mostly a hole in my arm".

"I can dig it, it's cool." Alex replied.

Cal went up the ladder, got in the truck and drove to the edge of town and eyeballed the blue pick-up in the trashy trailer park. How the hell did he get himself in this mess? Here he was on a mission, considering revenge in a town where he didn't have a friend. He placed his free hand on the little gas can on the seat, thinking what a surprise that punk would have when he made bail. He sure wouldn't be driving that truck anytime soon. He passed the trailer park and pulled to the side of the road a couple of blocks past it. He looked around and it was deserted so he exited the truck and walked back toward the trailer park through the field. He chose a gas can: it made for a more definitive statement. He crept through the adjacent field, keeping his bandaged arm close to his chest, it was throbbing. He heard the trailer door swing open and saw the cigarette coal and orange glow in the darkness. He froze ten yards away in the weeds and he saw the glowing coal walk about the yard. Cal tried to make out the figure, but it was too dark. He watched from his hiding place in the weeds, waiting, imagining the fire, the broken glass, the explosion

"I'll burn that little bastard out-leave him nothing, not even a broken-down trailer and a rat-shit pick-up truck." Cal muttered to himself.

Whoever was in that house was in the wrong place at the wrong time and associated with the wrong punk. Cal's pulse quickened as the images of ruin, destruction and flames built in his mind, propelling him toward the brink of action.

"Fuck it, I ain't doin this." Cal muttered in a moment of reason, throwing the gas can aside.

Cal listened to the sound of a metal garbage can lid followed by the swinging screen door of the trailer and the glowing cigarette disappeared through the doorway. He crept toward the yard, wary. He waited at certain intervals of forward stealthy progress, benefiting from the shadow of the pick-up truck in the streetlamp. He crouched alongside it and reached up to try the door, it was unlocked; he opened the door and crept into the cab keeping his profile low. He pulled his trousers down and put his bare ass over the driver's seat and let slip from his bowels a little steamy present for his former assailant, the wisps of steam rising against the cold night air, stinking up the little pick up cab. He pulled down the confederate flag from the rear window and wiped a perfect Hershey skid-mark across the *Southern Cross* and threw the soiled item on the dash, skid mark up.

"Welcome home you little turd." Cal mumbled as he hitched up his pants and left unnoticed, back through the field to his truck. A little smile of satisfaction crept across his face.

"Jesus, this place gets in your head like a bad dream. I gotta get back where I belong before I turn total-hillbilly." Cal muttered the realization.

On the short drive back to the boat, Cal stopped at the drug store to stock up on what he might need to keep his dressing dry and clean and his pain level down. He walked through the isles under fluorescent lights, throwing items in his little red basket. If there was anyone else shopping, he didn't see them, only the girl at the register. She occasionally glanced up from her magazine at him as Cal meandered through the aisles, stopping at the candy aisle momentarily before moving to the register. He placed his basket on the counter and unloaded is medical supplies. The girl behind the register was kind of pretty with her long and straight sandy blonde hair. She was younger than he, tall and thin in her drugstore smock.

"That's quite a wound you got there." She observed absently.

"Yeah. A bullet hole." Cal regretted that admission almost immediately.

"You the one? I heard about that business down at the Vista." She said.

"That's me." Cal replied, adding, "Word sure gets around, don't it?"

"My husband's a policeman. A gunshot is news around here." She said.

"Yeah well, you can tell your husband he won't be seeing me again soon, I seen enough of this rotten place." Cal responded.

"Oh, it's not such a bad place, I'm born and raised here, and you just ran into the worst, Virgil Taylor: I went to school with him." She explained.

"You don't have to convince me a' that." Cal did not like the topic of this conversation, he just wanted to get out.

"It's a bad family, every town has one and you found it." She said.

"The trouble found me. I was minding my own business." Cal defended.

"Oh, I'm sure." She agreed.

"Nice 'chattin." Cal scooped up his stuff and headed for the door.

They didn't make it out the next day or the day after, the weather was against them. All stayed close to the boat as they waited out the blow, playing cards and cooking, sleeping. Cabin fever set in. On the third day the weather laid down and the *Valkyrie* showed no hesitation as she steamed out to sea. They had no bait to chop, no shots of rope to make ready, the mission was clear: get the gear and go home. If the gear was down and they came back empty again, well, it was going to be troubling. Their patience was wearing thin. Even Sig was approaching his limit, having read every Field and Stream magazine on the boat, a boat he probably had not been off 5 times since he got here. But fortune was smiling on this day, the gear was up, mains and trailers both, laying like ducks in the water. The remaining traps were pulled and stacked aboard and by noon a course was set and down the hill they went, spirits were lifted; they were done and going home. Home was 30 hours of travel away and the weather was on the stern. It was a predictably boring ride, just more water going by the windows and a distant shoreline. They were a small and solitary traveler upon the vast and watery expanse. And boring was good because any event that broke the boredom was usually unwanted. It was a fitting end to a hard-fought attempt to save a season. After all was said and done, they did have something to show for it. It could have ended early in retreat and defeat, but the nature of these men was not to quit when there was a chance to succeed. Those that quit did not last long in this business because if anything was for certain, it was not going to be easy; you better like it and you better hang tough. Sig and the crew had been born into it; real fishermen like they had settled upon the boats and fishing because this agreed with them, spoke to something in them, made sense. It was the last frontier, as far west as they could go. They were on the edge with nowhere else worth going to.

CHAPTER 4

Diver John

Valkyrie rounded the #3 green buoy after her 30-hour boat ride home. The sun was setting on the rolling hills and the eucalyptus forest of home. After a long ride, it was the smell of the land that signified they were home at last. It had been a long campaign. Uncle Sig woke up Alex and Cal and they strode about the back deck shaking off the sleep, there had been no shortage of that on the ride down. They pulled the boat alongside the dock and made her fast around the pilings. The work of unloading could wait until the next morning, they had done enough for this day and more; shower and sleep in their own beds was the first order of business.

Leif felt the smooth linen sheets and the soft pillow under his head, contrasting to the stale flannel sleeping bag of the focsle-the life he had known these past months. He was glad to be home, but moreover, he awoke recognizing that his world of obligation was nearly over. The *Valkyrie* had taken precedence over his own ideas of his future, but that was done. He had signed on and that was that, but now it was on to the next thing for him, yet unknown. He had a few ideas, but he was not going back to that focsle, only that much was for sure. His trajectory in life had been interrupted by his father's premature death. He was destined to take over the *Fin* with Alex at his side: he was to continue with the family tradition, but it was an inheritance that was to be denied. For him and who he was, it was time for him to take the wheel of some other boat. He would do what he could for Alex, but he had a feeling that Alex was feeling the need for independence too, much the same as he.

He woke up with these thoughts colliding in his head. He wanted to lay there and ponder, come to some settled position in these matters in the quiet of the morning. He could hear Alex making morning noises and Cal would certainly be over on time to start the day. He swung his bare feet to the rug on the floor and scratched his head, he was up.

"Leif, Cal's here!" Alex shouted from the kitchen, alone with his coffee.

Olivia was long gone-off to work. Her life required immediate readjustment after Arne's death. And at 54 years of age, she faced significant challenges, completely different from the boys. The boys had so many years ahead of them and she had so many years behind her. First and foremost, she needed work right now to cover the bills. She took a job she did not like but it covered the monthly nut. Hounded by bills and alone to face them, she summoned a deep courage, strength and a conviction to carry on. Arne had left her the house, but the boat was gone, leaving her with the realization that the wheels come immediately and completely off when death or poor health strikes a fishing family. They were financially comfortable before, with her part-time bookkeeping job at the cannery and Arne's income, but now as the sole household provider she was a bill collector in the city, up at 5AM and on the Greyhound and returning at 6PM by the same transport- 5 days a week. Her income now depended upon hounding indebted souls, too poor to pay overdue bills and she was working on a commission to do so, often speaking to people in the same circumstance as she. The irony was palpable to her.

She came from a generation that was born during the Great War, lived through the Depression and World War 2. She had survived the great flu epidemic of 1918, having been sent away to her cousins on an egg ranch up the country. She married during the Depression without a wedding dress, housed a widowed mother and raised Leif alone during the War. The people of this generation soldiered on bravely and knew that attitude makes the difference between successes and failures. Resiliency. Her mother was long dead and gone and now Arne was too, she carried on alone, yet glad to have the boys around to watch over and talk to in the quiet moments, her family and her faith prevailing, carrying her through the hard times.

"Yeah, yeah, I'm up" Leif shouted back.

Alex rummaged about the cupboard looking for cereal, still in his underwear. It was good to be home, good to be warm and out of that damp boat. He had returned from his fishing adventure more of an adult than when he began, he had a few dollars in his pocket and a few stories to tell. He could see how this fishing life was now, from a different set of eyes, a perspective he had now come by honestly through experience. At times it had been sobering, stark and imminent failure loomed but they had pulled it out. The memories of the successes outweighed the memories of hardships in a season that was often in doubt. He was anxious to do more of this, thoroughly convinced that this was the walk of life for him. The camaraderie, the exclusiveness, the boats and the chance to get away from the craziness; to enter a life of simplicity; black-and-white decisions, this was the sub-text below his subconscious decision and what made it all the more appealing. Decisions were uncomplicated and the outcomes predictable; all of it informed him that this was the life. He wasn't too sure about the money thing though, there didn't seem to be a lot of that on any consistent basis. But when it did come, it was a lump sum and that was alluring too. Then again, money wasn't the thing that drew him in. Hopefully, that could just take care of itself.

Alex had a pot of coffee ready. Leif came into the kitchen at the same time as Cal came clumping up the back doorsteps.

"Okay ladies, let's get this show on the road." Cal was chirpy and alert.

Leif shot him a look and spoke to Cal from hooded eyes as Alex handed his brother a cup of coffee. "Aren't you the one-hotshot."

"Burning daylight. Let's get this shit over with." Cal said as he sat down at the table with his own cup of coffee.

The tasks that awaited at the dock were simple and they would fill the day. The traps had to go to the yard and get tarped, sell a few crabs, the tank had to come out of the hold, the block and stanchion had to go to the yard and generally square away all the crabbing paraphernalia for next season. It was good to be done with this. Alex had a few ideas about what might lay ahead in his future. An intriguing fishery to his mind was the sockeye fishery in Alaska. Alaska itself sounded like the place for adventure, action and a quick shot of dough. He hadn't completely given up on the idea of playing music, but he knew that being a teen ranger musician was not gonna happen ever again. There were other music avenues to explore. But for now, fishing was the thing that held his interest for his immediate future and Bristol Bay was quick money, the kind you could set aside, maybe do something with or live off of for a while. He heard Leif talk about Alaska too, a lot of guys were going there. But for now, he was going to go up to the yard with a loaded flatbed of traps and a head full of notions.

"Well, we pulled this one out and it wasn't easy. Glad I'm done." Cal stated absently in the cab of the truck.

"Amen to that." Leif replied and continued, "That Sig has a hard head with a back made of ironwood."

"Gotta be an easier way, but this was a *save* for sure." Cal replied.

"I got my eye on Alaska, I'm hearing good things. I think I better go look around at what that place has to offer." Leif stated.

"Me too." echoed Alex. "I met a guy in Eureka who does sockeye in Bristol Bay and it sounds good. I'm thinking about checking that out."

"Tom and Bill went to Alaska, got a seiner in Southeast now, Pink salmon. Fish by the tons, not by the pound." Leif enjoined.

"Not me, I'm good right here. I'm sticking with Sig; I like being a crewman. I go home and relax after work and I don't think about a boat, I think about calling Sally for a date night and a little nooky! I haven't had a piece in two months, my dick is so hard I can't close my eyelids." Cal had his life arranged just the way he liked it; his priorities were never in question.

Cal's crude sexual image set Alex to thinking about Karen, there was some unfinished business there he hoped, maybe even lay the pipe, always the ultimate goal in his hormone-engorged mind. He was uneasy to discuss his own sex life, most especially with Cal. He hesitated to join in the guy-talk that Cal had so easily broached, but it was always the foremost topic in his mind. He forayed. "You guys ever see that Karen waitress?"

"See her? She's famous kiddo, a man-eater." Cal replied.

" I got her phone number, maybe a promise." Alex replied.

"She's not a virgin you know kid, she gets around. The odds are good, but the goods are a little odd: independent-like. You gotta deal with *that* kid." Leif said.

"I'd like to deal with it." Alex said meekly.

"She'll make short work of your crusty butt, you little hard-on!" Cal quipped.

The first load of traps went into the yard and they returned to the dock for the second load. Sig was unloading crabs out of the tank. The guys on the dock had not seen 1500 pounds in 3 months, so this was a cause to rally round and gossip. Sig had his own ideas about what lay ahead for him: it was time to go home and do stuff around the house, stuff that had been on the back burner for a while. His workshop held a charm for him and there was always something on the floor of the workshop that was ongoing. The house needed some attention too and the springtime was a good time to do it. Sig was a homebody and comfortable with his work. Women and foolishness did not concern him much. It was approaching lunchtime when the tarps were tied down over the last of the traps in the yard.

"Crab Cottage for lunch?" Alex forwarded the idea to the sweaty group wiping their hands.

"Oh yeah. Figures you'd come up with that idea you little pud-knocker!" Cal said without hesitation and a smile.

They shuffled into the Crab Cottage; Sig was having a ham sandwich on the boat, so it was just the 3 of them. Sig always packed a lunch and it hadn't changed since grammar school-a ham sandwich, bag of chips and a Coke. He switched the routine from chocolate milk to a Coke in 7th grade and since then the menu was set in stone. The restaurant wasn't crowded; hardly anything ever was crowded on the coast. Artichokes, Brussel sprouts, flowers and beaches described it. Alex looked at Karen's table and soon found out she wasn't at work today. That was just as well under the circumstances, Cal was bound to make some sort of humiliating crack at his expense in front of her. Alex needed a little room to make some time without Cal kickin' his butt. They took a seat by a local dude, Mike Conrad, a coffee house folk singer. Alex nodded recognition. He liked Conrad, he was a jovial sort, a folkie from the Midwest, akin mostly to Country Western but now here he was in California, the state that was cranking out rock stars like Fords off the assembly line. Since the Coast side was so small, all musicians knew who-was-who and who was playing what or had played with whom. Even personal gossip and details were known. For instance, it was well known that Conrad had been couch surfing these past six months, where he would arrive as a colorful and entertaining guest but leave as a good-natured no-count loafer. It was hard to get mad at Conrad because in his eyes, fate and human kindness just directed him from place to place in hapless wonder. He had a good whiskey voice, a lengthy repertoire that spanned Guthrie, Dylan, McCroury and Ramblin Jack Ellliot. He also played John Denver stuff and anything that was popular on the radio to get him work. He had been around a long time through different troubadour genres and he had a few bluegrass and Union songs. Conrad had a Tuesday-Thursday gig at the local beer-wine-coffee house, The Spouter Inn, a tip of the hat to Melville. It was a smoky little joint with well-used ash trays on every table, a generous application of barn-wood on the walls and a singing bartender, Joe. Joe and Earl were from New York and they ran the place. Earl was huge and all smiles; good vibes behind the whitest teeth on the blackest face. He served underage patrons to the delight of every teen ranger on the coast side. It was a very down-home place that often attracted a wayward rock star with his acoustic guitar, bohemians and knife fights. It had only one shooting to its credit, and that at the hands of Joaquin's stepdad Bill. Bill was a short wiry man of early middle years with a Johnny Cash/Porter Waggoner/ Merle Haggard outlook. He confessed one day to Alex that his hero had been the bank robber John Dillinger. He lived next door in a tiny house with an Airstream trailer in the backyard, occupied by "Blinky", a frightening short woman who was Bills mother and as the name suggests, was given to blinking her eyes 20-30 times a minute. Blinky was always in her ratty bathrobe with her hair in tight curlers called "spoolies" She did not have much hair, so the effect was a baldhead studded with small round plastic studs, overall a frightening sight. She chain-smoked and looked for opportunities to use her favorite sarcastic expression. Any topic that came up in conversation would do; she would say, "It's hideous!" That household of Joaquin's mother and Bill had seen a few father figures come and go. Bill was preceded by Patsy's boyfriend Slim, who was preceded by Joaquin's biological dad, an outlaw type who ran with the Coastside Cannibal Club, a motorcycle gang of misfits. Joaquin was named after the outlaw Joaquin Murrieta. Randy's mom Patsy was an infamous wild teen and a member of this motorized pack of rebels. Randy had an odd family history, a history he was proud of.

It seems that Bill, on an evening of drinking with Patsy at the Spouter, encountered an outsider from the City and Bill didn't like him. They traded insulting words, so Bill went outside to his car and returned with a handgun and shot him dead in front of God and everyone, possibly fulfilling a lifelong ambition to enjoin his ideals in the Federal penitentiary. If so, his wish came true and he did reside in Folsom Prison for the next 10 years. Randy and Alex gladly took over the trailer when Blinky moved into the house. The trailer was a great clubhouse for weekend acid trips and visits from girls. They didn't miss Bill at all.

"I heard you quit playing." Conrad said, all smiles in his good-natured greeting of Alex. There were no secrets in this town. Alex was aware of his new fisherman persona.

"Yeah, the band wasn't going anywhere good in a hurry." Said Alex, referring to his previous band.

"It's a hard thing. I can hardly handle my one-man band." Conrad laughed at himself.

"I needed to get work too, something that pays money." Alex explained.

"I'm getting thirty bucks a night at the Spouter, plus the tip-jar, a pitcher and a burger- can't forget that." Still laughing at the folly of his lot in life and the pittance he performed for.

Alex turned back to his own table and resumed his attentions to Leif and Cal. "That's one sorry-of-a-gun, that story right there." Cal said quietly to the table, not wishing to hurt the good-natured Conrad's feelings.

It was Karen's day off and subsequently the topic of conversation stayed around boats and fishing and away from chasing women. Leif was turning over a plan to go up to Southeast and look around, Cal was thinking about hunting so he might go shoot pheasant at his buddy's ranch before Sig corralled him into a month of maintenance duty on the *Valkyrie*. Alex didn't have any such plans, but he did have a few notions.

"Hey Alex- me and Nancy are putting something together, you interested in coming by and playing with us? See if it works? Guitar, bass and vocals kinda thing?" Conrad called out to the back of Alex.

Alex turned around to Conrad and spoke. "Maybe." The wheels were turning. "What happened to Goshee-gee?" Alex referred to an older dude, David Gosche. David was a lounge lizard, Nancy's paramour. A bossa nova folkie with a smooth baritone voice and the swarthy good looks to go with it. He wore clogs and turtlenecks, had a European affect and attracted beatniks. Joaquin and he had a folk-rock trio with David at one time. Alex was the dishwasher and David was the pot washer at Albert's Miramar restaurant, that's where they met. The band they had was good but the company that hung around David's house was weird. They got loaded every day at David's house.

"Drama I guess, he dumped her." Conrad replied.

This sent Alex thinking with his dick. He had a crush on Nancy back when and she wouldn't give him a tumble. She couldn't think about anyone else but David, a total no-good. He had tried to tell her that, but she saw right through his intentions. She had gone blind to anything but David. "In the grip of the Goshee-gee," was the phrase.

The wheels started turning in Alex's head "Get your skinny ass out in front of the skirts. Nancy!" A win-win he was thinking.

"So. Nancy and David-they're not together now, is that it?" He asked.

"Done and dusted, smoke and ash." Conrad replied.

"Everybody saw that one coming." Alex said and continued, "Definitely Mike, count me in, sounds like a fun thing. I wanna play. You, me and Nancy."

Conrad handed him a slip of paper with a number one it. "I'm over at Katy's for a while. Gimme a call and we'll work it out with Nancy."

"Cool." Alex took the number and returned his attentions to his lunch table. Leif and Cal were discussing the Eureka experience. Cal eyed him suspiciously when Alex returned.

"You get a lot of nooky when you play down there, hard-on?" Cal asked.

"No." Alex said defensively. Discussing his sex life was not a comfortable subject of discussion between he and Cal.

"So, you don't really get nooky *anywhere* you go?" Cal needled.

"No, that's not true either!" Alex protested, against the ropes.

"Still going steady with the Sisters then?" Cal was unrelenting and enjoying it.

"Lay off Cal, geez. Give the kid a break, will ya?" Leif interceded. "Just eat in peace for Christ sakes."

"Just having some fun!" Cal clearly was loving every minute of it.

After lunch it was straight forward stuff on *Valkyrie*; wrenching, taking stuff off, hydraulic messes to be cleaned. Sig concerned himself down in the engine room while the crew worked topside. They finished up in the late afternoon and went their ways to shower. That was pretty much a wrap of a long season effort, an overwhelming sense of freedom began to dawn on Alex. Up at the house he stripped down outside and parked his oily clothes on the back doorstep. That put a period on the end of that chapter. It was getting on to Friday night, time to get clean and go out and sniff around.

The Princeton Inn was the spot, the best place for live music and action. There were quite a few clubs to choose from on a weekend and there as a circuit of about 5 clubs with music to check out, 9 places altogether, more than enough for a night on the town. Alex got to the PI at 8PM and the place was jumpin' already, no empty barstools and all in anticipation of the band. Alex and his band had played here sporadically over the years, but their material wasn't right for the clubs, too much improvising. Only bands that played from the radio playlist got work in these clubs. Alex was greeted by the usual cast of characters from the fishing community. His band-friends didn't make the rounds except to the Spouter. After a few drinks, a prerequisite for Alex to interact with the opposite sex in any effectual way, Alex was dancing in his wife-beater T-shirt on a sweaty and crowded dance floor. His dance partner was short, cute and about a year or two older than he. Everybody was tuned up, buzz'in.

About the 3rd or fourth dance she leaned in and bit Alex in the nipple, gently-like, but a little firmer as her teeth slid off the flesh and got hold of his T-shirt, pulling it out from his chest and snapping it back like a rubber band. Even though he was awkward, Alex got that signal loud and clear.

"I'm Alex, what do you call yourself?" He said.

"Mary." She replied.

"Want to get out of here?" He asked.

"Later. Let's dance some more. You're kinda wild, I like that." She stated with an approving smile.

"Yeah? I like it when you bite. That's wild." Alex parried.

"I couldn't resist; the rhythm, the smell; it was primal." She said.

"Is primal sexy I hope?" Alex asked for clarification.

She smiled and regarded the person in front of her. "Yes, that too. What do you do around here boy, where you been?"

I'm from here, I got a fish boat." That was a lie.

"*That's* kinda sexy, let's dance." She said. This girl knew what she wanted, and Alex liked that. A sneaky little thought began to creep into his consciousness as he looked ahead into the possibilities of the night. He realized he still lived at home with his mom and Leif.

Mental note: must get own place, or boat, for having sex.

He started thinking about the situation and there was anxiety until he came upon on the solution; the *Valkyrie* was still tied to the dock-the bunk in Uncle Sig's stateroom was big enough for two. He was getting a baby-woody just thinking about it. Uncle Sig wouldn't find out. Cal would approve. Around closing time, they headed for the boat and the garden of midnight delights.

What a tight little body she had. It was all-right-all-night, but alcohol impotency set in. That poor girl was under siege for hours and the cork would not pop, in various states of rigidity, pounding out a fearsome hump. Fortunately, she took extra ordinary measures. They finally got a couple hours of sleep before the sun came up feeling spent after going the full 15 rounds.

The next morning, they went to breakfast at the Ketch and said their goodbyes. He didn't see Mary again until a few weeks later. She was in the pickup truck of some surfer guy with a house on the beach. He should have called her, it was his own fault, he didn't know how to court a girl properly. He was just doing what he thought everyone else was doing. It was kind of challenging to be a guy in the age of feminism, unsure what the members of the opposite sex expected him to do or be, so mostly he played it cool. It didn't bother him, these random things happened, but he knew he should have called. He got home in the early afternoon, stinking like a brewery. He jumped right in the shower before being discovered by Leif who said, "Hey Stud."

"What's happening?" Alex was giving nothing away.

"Not too much. Where'd you go last night?" He asked.

"PI." Alex said.

Leif dropped the subject and switched it saying, "You wanna go up to Southeast with me? I'm thinking of going soon, maybe next week. There's nothing holding me here right now, so the time is right." Leif said.

"I don't think so but thanks anyway Leif." Alex said.

"What you got goin' on here?" Leif inquired.

"Nothing, but I just got back, I wanna settle in here at home. I seen enough water and need a break. On land." Alex replied.

"I hear ya." Leif flatly nodded in recognition of the fact.

Alex had a definite idea about the future, and it was right here at home. He was gonna call Conrad and play with him and hopefully make some time with Nancy; he was gonna call on Karen and hopefully make some time there too. Simple. In fact, today was a good day to get started. In the days that followed he took up residency at the Crab Cottage. He became friends with Tom and Louise who owned the joint. Tom was a diver, and this is where all the dive crowd hung out. A colorful bunch they were; Roy Lee, Lucky, McElvie, Gary, Ronnie and a raft of new guys from Southern Cal. Alex sat in the table by the kitchen, putting in the time chatting up Karen and hoping to win favor over the competition of which there was plenty. One day a new guy walked in and Alex groaned at the thought of more competition yet.

In walked Diver John from Avila. He looked like Prince Valiant in Ray Bans, flip-flops and a T shirt. But the thing that turned heads was his car. He drove up in a top down, white interior, jet-black 65' Cadillac convertible with writing in small white letters on the door, "The Black Moriah." Apparently, he was well known because Tom greeted him like an old friend.

"Hey John, what're you doing up here?" Tom asked.

"The otters got so bad down there we couldn't pick three dozen a day." He was talking about three dozen abalone.

"I heard. The Otter peoples. Relocating up here?" Tom asked.

"I think so, give it a try anyway, got to do something." John was cheerful. "Maybe work live-boat, cover some ground, look at the Reef and Whaleman's. Can you still get a few there?"

'Oh yeah, that's the only places we go, we work dead-boat and get what we need for the restaurant, me and Frank." Tom answered.

"I need a tender, a local guy. I pay petty good but nobody from down home wanted to up-stakes and come here. I'm just sleeping in The Black Moriah for now, I figure to go home when the weather is bad. I got a nice place in Avila; you should come down sometime." Diver John said.

Alex had been listening in to this colorful fellow and he spoke up, "I'm looking for work."

"Yeah? You ever do this?" Said Diver John.

"No. Is it hard? I am a fisherman- lots of experience on the water. I just wrapped up a crab season. What's it pay?" Alex asked in reply.

"No, it's not hard. The job is this: I am down below the surface and you are driving the boat following the bubbles from my air supply, make sure my air hose doesn't get fouled. I search the bottom and pry abalone off the rocks-I send up a bag of abs-you send an empty bag back down to me, that's it." John said. "25% off the top."

"I'll take it." Alex replied. 25% was damn good money, Uncle Sig was paying him 7.5%.

"OK, we'll see if it works out, put you on probation-like. I'll put the boat in the water down at the launch ramp, it's a little 26-footer, the Peggy Jean.

Come on down tomorrow morning and I can show you around." John said. John continued chatting with Tom and Louise and then he left.

"You're moving up in the world, Basic." Karen smiled a little laugh as she tended to her customers. God she was sexy, Alex worshipped her like a goddess.

The next morning Alex moseyed on down to the launch ramp and to the Peggy Jean. The boat was a backyard boat-building project that John began with a Thunderbird Tri-hull, and ended with a plywood and glass topside, turning it into a work platform. It was not fancy, just functional. It did have a new Volvo diesel but other than that it was bare and basic. Not like the *Valkyrie*.

Alex had always heard from Uncle Sig and his lot of fishermen that they didn't consider divers as being real fishermen; not like them. Divers tended to be fringy types, a lot like the gold miners of yore, seeking quick money and some getting it. They weren't above nefarious endeavors and living by their wits had become a way of life; getting the ups on whatever was around was the thing to do. The hope of quick and easy money was their driving force because, at times, there was good money to be had, the only glitch was you had to go to the bottom of the ocean to get it and that wasn't for everybody. They were never up before the dawn like Sig and never in after the dark. And their boats were different; shallow draft and made for working the inshore waters among the rocks. They rarely were a half mile offshore and never out of sight of land. They only ventured from the harbor when the weather was flat calm for a day or two, the visibility down in the water had to be just right to pick abalone. The more Alex learned of this the more he liked it; it suited his current loosey-goosey lifestyle. The other thing was the money; these guys made good money. Every diving workday started out with breakfast in the coffee shop and after about 3 days of work a week, they got cash. This did not go unnoticed by the rank and file fishermen in the little town, making some of them a little jealous.

At the ramp, the next day, Diver John showed Alex the set-up: hose, compressor, dry suit, mask, belt, shoes, bags, irons, dive ladder and that was about it. They untied and took a little spin out to the reef. The diesel engine moved the little boat along at a top speed of about seven knots and before long they were weaving about the wash rocks, boilers and bull kelp. It was a different inshore world of passageways between the rocks and reefs. John started pointing.

"That's King Rock, that's Sail Rock, that's Whaleman's Island up there. There's a wash rock here by the breakwater and the reef runs north south in an outside finger and two others inside of that. You be careful off a rising swell because if it starts to break on the outside-game over. P off Montara is Colorado Reef but there's nothing up there anymore since the sewer treatment plant went in. Chlorine kills the kelp and the abs that were left are stunted and starved." The little boat purred along on a beautiful day, warm, calm, solitary. This job had potential; Alex liked what he saw. They headed back to the harbor after Alex did a few boat maneuvers to John's satisfaction. Tomorrow was to be the first workday

"Very good kid, we'll give it a go tomorrow. Meet me in the coffee shop at 9 AM. I'll make a few jumps out on the reef. Pack a lunch." Alex was excited at the prospect.

"Okay *Diver John*, see you tomorrow." Alex used John's moniker with emphasis. He walked up the ramp and got in his ratty red Volvo.

He swung by Katy's place to see if Conrad was there, he was of course. Katy gave me a suspicious eye at the door; at this point any friend of Conrad's was a doubtful human being. What a funky place; it had been red tagged in the middle of a remodel and tarpaper and plywood was evidenced everywhere. Weeds, stacks of 2x4's and a power pole were the prominent features in the front yard. Conrad was on the couch.

"Mike, what's happening around here?" Alex waved his arms about the yard.

"It's bad, I told Katy I'd help." He answered.

"Help what? A bulldozer and a dumpster might help." Alex stated the obvious.

"I know, it's even worse than it looks, the house is half gutted throughout." Conrad confessed.

"Well, you still wanna play?" Alex wondered.

"Definitely. Nancy's got her PA in a studio in Miramar so that's the spot." Conrad said pushing himself up from the sunken cushions of his latest flop.

"Okay. Let's go get my amp in Montara." Alex replied and they both hoped into the Volvo and headed for the Montara ranch house, the former band house where all the equipment was.

They parked among 7 or 8 cars, it looked like a party crowd but upon entering, everyone was asleep in the ruin of a living room that evidenced heavy drinking and destruction from the night before. Someone had taken a sledgehammer to the plaster and lathe wall. This was very distressing to Alex, glad he was out of this Ranger-scene, it had obviously deteriorated. Who was responsible for this mess? What might come next around here? It was chaos as he picked his way to the band room. Hieronymus Bosch would have approved. Now, all the equipment was stacked against the wall, out of the way.

What a spot the band house had been, it had its moment in time, but Alex and the occupants lacked the maturity to pull it off. An old ranch house on a hill that overlooked strawflower fields that stretched all the way to the ocean, and horse pastures viewed through huge picture windows. It was nice while it lasted. Not much good ever came from that place in the end, it was cursed.

They arrived at Nancy's little house by the Bach Dancing and Dynamite Society. She was waiting there, and they all hugged. They played a few 3 chord constructs that sounded pretty good. Alex had anxiety at first but soon realized this was not gonna take much effort, being all simple and familiar tunes.

Nancy was looking good like Brenda Lee in her short new hairdo and Conrad said that they could take this act to the Spouter on Tuesday with one more rehearsal, a sudden change for Alex, a gig. He never did score with Nancy. Now back to his other life...

*   *   *

He drove into the yard and Cal and Leif were putting the finishing touches on the gear storage. He climbed out of the Volvo to see what was going on.

"Hey Minkya, what's happening?" Cal greeted him.

"I gotta new job today, dive tending abalone." he replied.

"Abalone? Those guys will kill you in your sleep, won't they? Your dad used to say that abalone diving was as low as you can go in commercial fishing." Cal said.

"That's bullshit Alex; they make good money, don't listen to Cal." Leif said. "Who you gonna work with?"

"A guy named Diver John from Avila, new in town but from around here originally I guess." Alex replied.

"I went to school with him, they shipped him out to Serra for high school. He was cool, valedictorian in eighth grade, I think." Cal interjected.

'Yeah, he's a local boy." Said Leif.

"I start work tomorrow; I'll see how it goes." Alex stated.

The next morning, Alex parked himself at the coffee shop at eight AM and waited. He took his toast off the little plate and buttered it on the counter top, the fatty-blond owner and waitress, Betty, came over and gave him a look of disgust, picked up the half buttered toast and put the crusty bread back on the little plate without saying a word. Alex wasn't sure if it was the toast on the counter or his long hair that pissed her off more. She was a wise-ass who held court every morning from the middle of the horse-shoe shaped counter. She didn't care for hippies in *her* court. Monaghan showed up, Frank too.

The local divers started arriving, it was a dive day. John rolled in around 9AM. The divers wanted to know where he was going.

"The Reef." He responded. That seemed to satisfy all.

After they started the day, Alex saw that John was serious, spending about 2 hours under water before he came up. Alex just watched the bubbles and followed him around as he walked on the bottom, occasionally sending down an empty bag on the bubbles and then hauling up a full one. Mostly he needed to pay attention to the sea conditions and the air hose. If any swell developed, John said they were done-for. Alex found it difficult to not stare off and day-dream, the scenery was beautiful, an almost magical remove from the sho-reside world. It was peaceful and the only neighbors were seabirds. Quietude like he never heard before. Around 4PM John came up and said they were done for the day. They had about 5 dozen abs and they motored into the harbor and placed them in a live box for safe keeping and accumulation for marketing later, apparently theft was not an issue. They repeated this for 2 days on the Reef and it became routine right away. On the third day John announced that tomorrow would be different.

"Me and the Black Moriah will make market tomorrow morning, Sakei will give us $20 a dozen. You take Peggy Jean down to Bean Hollow and I'll go through the surf and climb aboard after I take the abs to market. We're gonna work Bolsa Point down there." He said.

"Sounds good. What about this hollow bean maneuver? Sounds danger-ous." Alex asked.

"Nothing to it, just stay outside the surf line in that little cove. I'll swim out to you." He said.

"Okay, if you say so." Alex replied. By now Alex was getting used to wash rocks, bull kelp paddies, breakers, boilers, surf lines and such: inshore things that he was heretofore trained to be terrified of. It seemed like a lot could go wrong with this plan.

$20 a dozen, they had accumulated 15 dozen, $3k. Alex happily did the math; his cut was $700. John made market and Alex got to Bean Hollow about 11 AM. Peggy Jean had no navigation instruments except a compass that didn't work, but Alex was okay and in sight of shore all along the way. Black Moriah gleamed in the parking lot at Bean Hollow as Alex stood off and reconnoitered the cove from a safe distance. It was tiny and it had wash rocks. Getting bearings and landmarks, Alex established a position inshore that he should not trespass, John would just have to swim a little farther out beyond the surf-line in the cove to meet him. Alex took the Peggy Jean in and stopped outside the surf line, and inside of him, the waves would hump up and break. John was a green speck on the beach who launched himself into the surf and began to swim. Alex waited patiently, bobbing while the swells slid under him. With one eye peeled for sneaker waves, Alex found John was right, it was a piece of cake. Alex put the ladder over, John climbed aboard the little boat and Alex got them out of there without delay. John was all suited up when he swam through the surf, so they started right in after a few minutes of travel out of the cove. This spot was a little dicey, it wasn't tame like the Reef at home, Alex could see this right off. There were boilers offshore and Alex marked them in his mind; this would be the place where trouble would start if it came. They were vulnerable, inshore against the cliffs and what Alex did not realize-shallow water. There were plenty of abs though, 3 dozen bags came up every time. Skittish about the position, Alex kept the boat standing off in deeper water and away from the bubbles, he only brought the boat inshore when a bag was signaled for. There would be no daydreaming here. John picked 15 dozen before coming up.

"How's it going up here?" he asked.

"Shit John, what a spot." Alex replied.

"Yeah, but only when it's absolutely flat, it breaks here at a sneeze, so you be careful." He replied.

"Flat as the harbor now." Alex replied.

"I'm gonna make one more jump." said John. When John came up for the last time that day, Alex dropped him off at Bean Hollow and for Alex, it was a long boat ride. But they had 30 dozen aboard and Alex did the math all the way back. They went back the next day and got another 20 dozen. Monaghan and Frank were anchored and diving right next them, safely offshore and in deep water.

That day it finally happened around 2 PM. The Peggy Jean was in ten feet of water, against a cliff after picking up a bag, backed in and bow facing seaward. Alex could see it humping up on the outside as the swells swept in. The first one boiled, the second one feathered, the water thin and translucent on the top of the wave. Alex knew trouble was on the way. There was no time to think about it. Alex grabbed what hose he could lift and threw it in the water in a coil, ran forward and hit the throttle-full bore ahead. The PJ went over the top of the wave standing straight up on the stern, nothing but white foamy seawater behind her and Alex clutching to the wheel for dear-life- for not to go overboard. Peggy Jean slammed hard down the backside of the wave after it passed, and Alex ran back and threw all the rest of the hose in the water. Looking seaward, Alex saw that the next wave would break farther out, and he would be in the foam. He pushed the throttle to the pin and held on. The problem he knew, was that this time there would be less hose in the water than distance to safety. The hose jerked straight as he went over the next wave and below the surface, John was dragged over the rocks and through the swirling and surging water. It had been an unavoidable decision to run the boat out to safety and drag John with him. After reaching deep water, Alex started pulling hose, looking over his shoulder for the next wave. John popped to the surface inshore and started waving his arms in alarm. Alex put the ladder over the side in safe water. John came out and came aboard.

"What the hell's going on up here!" He threw is mask off, pissed.

"The swell just came up, breakers came in." Alex's heart was pounding dents in his chest.

"I told you so! We're done!" He said. It had been just as harrowing an experience for Diver John and adrenaline was not in short supply above or below the water.

Monaghan had escaped, he pulled anchor and was headed for home, post haste, at first sight of white water. 20 dozen; they had risked all to get them, swell marking the end of a 3-day streak of flat weather. The next day they stayed in and borrowed McElvie's flat bed and made market; Dupont, Sakei, Tokyo Fish Market and the Buckhorn in Petaluma.

John returned with $6 grand cash. That afternoon before departing for Avila, John peeled off twenty-three Benjamins and placed them in Alex's hands. Quick money, the most Alex ever held. John was going home for a few days after the boat was squared away.

"There's a storm coming, so let's anchor and stern tie the PJ to the dock by the skiff hoist and hope the dock doesn't blow over." John joked. "Let's get the lee side where it's safe." He instructed, and they executed the maneuver. They used 2 heavy stern lines to attach the boat to the top of the pilings on the pier. After, Alex went up to the Crab Cottage for dinner. Karen was there, so was Monaghan.

"I saw the whole thing; you saved that boat." Monaghan said.

"That was close, I shit my pants." Alex replied.

"That second wave had you in the soup." He said.

"I know; I ran out of hose, jerked John off the bottom and pulled him through the surf. He was pissed." Alex replied. Karen came over on her break, lit a Camel and sat down.

"So Basic; I heard you got Moxie." She said.

"Close call today. This new job is going to work out fine; I can handle this." Alex said with coy modesty. As an afterthought, he spoke. "Hey, I'm playing with Conrad at the Spouter tonight. Come down and check it out."

"Play what?" She asked.

"I'm a bass player," He said.

"Well, whaddya know about that, you're just full of surprises today." She said.

"Tuesdays and Thursdays." He informed.

"Okay, I will. What about this boat-saving episode I am hearing about?" She asked.

"We almost swamped Diver John's little boat in the surf, we got out just in time. It got heavy-quick. Monaghan was there." He replied.

"He told me about it." Karen informed. "A hero." Later that night it got exciting again, not in a good way.

Around 1 AM Sven Van Sickle was ringing the doorbell with his little toady brother-in-law, Merlon, both standing on the front steps. Merlon was about ten IQ points over moron and a Crab Cottage sycophant, Sven was affable, charming, outgoing and a violent sociopath with a screw loose, most always up to no good. He had a very dark side. It was rumored that it was he who beat Billy-the-Kid to death at his roadside candy/newsstand. Billy the kid was a handicapped old guy who died for less than $7 in the till, Sven would have been about 12 or 13 at the time. The community was sickened and saddened. It was also rumored that Sven burned down Our Lady of the Lourdes, the little Catholic church in Moss Beach. At the time Alex considered this a community service after having his boney butt suffer on the hardest oak pews ever known.

Sven had reached maturity at about 13 or 14 years of age and he had the shoulders and arms of an adult male, all lending to a very believable reputation for violence. Alex and the other Rangers called him *Van Sicko,* then just shortened that to the expression *Van,* which became *flashing-Vans,* the expression for fear and a general alarm when danger was near. As I approached the front door to answer the late doorbell, I was *flashing Vans* and expecting the worst. I opened the door.

"You gotta come down to the pier right now, Diver John's boat is sinking at the dock!" He screamed against the night, which was roaring in the wind over treetops violently swinging to and fro.

"Okay." Not knowing what to think or say, Alex grabbed his shoes and ran outside to the Volvo and he drove the short distance down to the pier. At the dock there was an array of headlights played across the harbor as the fishermen anxiously watched their moored boats strain upon the chain. And there was the little PJ, swamped at the stern, engine hatch about to float off and banging the transom against the pilings. The minus tide had dropped, and the stern lines were tight and short to the pier, the transom was banging a hole against the dock. They were fucked. Alex looked down 20 feet at the boat, no way to get on the boat but jump, so he did.

The water was warm, he swam to the bow and grabbed a rope and swam back to the stern. He treaded water and rigged a bridle to the stern, the cleats in front of his nose were practically under water. Merlon was watching from the dock above; Alex swam the bridle over to the adjacent skiff hoist where Merlon stood watching.

"Lower the hoist Merlon, swing the hooks over to me!" Alex yelled against the wind while he treaded water.

Merlon was on his game, hit Alex square in the head with the hooks as he swung the hoist. The plan was for Merlon to take up the slack on the bridle with the hoist so the little boat would rise and gain freeboard. Alex intended to get on the boat and bail out the engine compartment after it was lifted by the hoist. He saw the big hole in the transom cap rail where the water came in. A hunk of Splash Zone putty would soon be the quick fix. After, he retied the boat safely away from the pilings, this time in slider-fashion so it could move up and down, unencumbered by the rise and fall of the tide. Sven and Merlon were heroes, and they were strutting about the dock, all pumped up. They had attracted a crowd of onlookers and had the spotlight. On the pier after and dripping wet, Sven shook Alex's hand, a far cry from the last time they met the last Fourth of July when Sven had kicked Alex in the side of the head as he lay sleeping on the floor of a Montara house he shared with his bandmates; an older out-of-town dude and Joaquin. One of Sven's toadies and he were clearing out all the hippie houses in Montara that night. Joaquin, Alex and a sax plyer from Berkeley were in harm's way. Anna Banana and Alex were on a mattress on the floor when Sven burst into the house with a handgun and kicked Alex in the side of the head. Anna jumped up and screamed.

"You scum-sucking redneck pig, get the fuck outta here!" Her big floppy tits were defiant and bare.

"Sven it's me, Alex! Joaquin's in the other room! Don't shoot!" Alex screamed in terror and raised his hands defensively.

"Well who's that bearded fucker who just went through the window? He's gotta go!" He was yelling and out of control, waving his pistol and all liquored up.

"Yes, he's gotta go Sven, yes, he's gone now, calm down." Alex tried to diffuse the situation. "You never have to see him in Montara again."

"Well good. That's all right then. You guys are okay, you can stay but I better not see him around here again." He and his toady left, on their way to more mayhem and jail. Joaquin looked at Alex in the now silent house.

"Ultimate." Joaquin said. "*Flashing Van's.*"

"For reals."

That night on the pier was the rapprochement for Sven and Alex; they were tight buddies from there on out. Alex called John in Avila the next morning. He had just gotten back from a morning dip in the surf. He was incredulous at the tale, yet relieved that the boat was floating.

"Okay, I'll be up in about 4 hours. Take off the starter motor and alternator, soak them in diesel. Can you do this?" Alex thought about it.

"I think so." Alex said and hung up the phone on the kitchen wall. He turned to Cal, sitting at the kitchen table.

"I saw you last night." Cal said.

"Goddamn mess." Alex replied.

"You did good. You saved it." He replied and much to Alex's delight Cal never called him Pudknocker again.

* * *

Olivia had one day a week to sleep in and this, Saturday, was the day. Sunday was church and during the week it was up before the sun and on the Greyhound bus to work. She mulled over the plan for the day and she looked forward to having *the boys* over at the house, just as they once were there when Arne was there. Over the years the fishermen in the community would come to this kitchen table to discuss an effort to form the local Fishermen's Association and get the Army Corp of Engineers to build them a breakwater. Arne had been an All-American for Santa Clara University and played football next to Lem Britishki, now a colonel in the Army Corp of Engineers. Arne made a trip or two to DC to restore the bond and get his support to build a breakwater at Half Moon Bay. The effort bore fruit and the project was put on the short list by the Corp of Engineers. In the future, and with a breakwater, it would no longer be necessary to run the boats to the City ahead of a big southerly storm in the winter months. The breakwater would not have come to be without some organized effort, so an Association was formed to help it along. Arne was a product of the 30's labor movement on the docks of San Francisco, so he became a central figure in the formation of an Association. He had participated in the big General Strike, of 1934 with 150,000 other Bay area workers, a strike that lasted over 80 days before Federal machine guns on the rooftops of the docks and the police broke it up, killing two people.

Arne was drawn to adventuresome walks of life that took him to Canada, Alaska and the sea. Olivia was a perfect match for him, a star in her own right and had been crowned Miss Santa Clara 1933. As it happened, Olivia's father owned the creamery and soda fountain across the street from the campus and Olivia had the pleasure of innocent flirtation with the boys from the college across the street who suited for her favor. She was the star of the show with her slinky silk dress and Hollywood looks. Many suitors came to chat her up at the fountain counter and Arne was one of them. Miss Santa Clara married the All-American.

Olivia started making little sandwiches at 11AM and by noon she had identical white triangles of bread stacked symmetrically on a large platter next to a large bowl of chips and a cooler of soda. The work party which had been assembled to pitch in and help restore the little Peggy Jean boat. By 1PM, 12-14 men milled about the yard doing what they did best, eat and talk. The topics never varied, fish and boats. At about 2PM The Black Moriah rolled into the yard with the Peggy Jean in tow on a trailer, being driven by a blond shaggy haired man about Cal's age. Leif leaned into Cal and quietly asked the question that was on more than a few minds.

"What's he doing here?"

"McElvie." Cal said.

"That guy's a One-Eyed-Jack." Leif replied quietly

"Don't I know it." Cal said.

Diver John was right behind the Black Moriah, driving a newish white van. Diver John jumped out of the van and helped McElvie disconnect the trailer and McElvie drove the Cadillac away, smiling, giving Cal and Leif a small wave good-bye. Diver John walked straight over to Cal and shook his hand.

"Thanks for getting the work party together Cal." He said.

"Welcome. It's how we do things around here." Cal replied and added, "We got the starter motor and alternator off and in the oven."

"Great. I picked up an injector motor and injectors just in case." John informed.

The men began to apply themselves to the small diesel. They cranked the open cylinders and drained the pan until all doubt and saltwater was removed.

"At this rate we could start putting it back together today. Try and start it up tomorrow." Cal said.

"That'd be great Cal. The sooner the better." John responded.

"Well, we appreciate the work for Alex. He's on the right track now and he likes the money." Cal said

"He's a good kid, more than a kid: he saved me and the boat down at Pigeon and now this save on top of that." John explained.

"He was born to this life; I see that now." Cal said.

"You bet." John replied.

Men were all over the little Peggy Jean in the restoration effort that day, there was hardly room to work. The next day (after a hearty lunch from Olivia) the little boat was ready for the test with new injectors, new battery, clean oil, filters and fuel. The water hose and 'mouse ears' were on the outdrive cooling intake and the moment was nigh. The Peggy Jean fired up and came to life on the first crank, a cheer went up, smiles all around. Diver John hooked up the trailer to the new van for a morning launch and Alex followed the Peggy Jean to the launch ramp in the Volvo. The next morning the little boat was back in action tooling around the harbor and just running the engine all day. They pulled their mooring and checked it, repaired a few live boxes and just generally regrouped their stuff. The next day they were back at it at, this time at Whalemen's alongside Roy Lee. Roy motored over around 3 PM to talk boat-to-boat.

"Hey John, how's it going?" he said.

"About three dozen, just pecking along. It's getting kinda picked over." John replied.

"Well maybe you should come over here and see this. I think I found something. There's a giant anchor out here." Roy said.

They immediately went over to a marker buoy attached to a fifteen-hundred-pound anchor in twenty feet of water and it was incredibly old. Roy had happened across a shipwreck of the Rydal Hall, sunk in 1862. It became evident on the first jump John made that Roy had made a discovery. John sent up a giant brass ship's bell with the identity scripted upon it. John and Roy hatched a plan: Roy had giant steel flotation balls onshore and they would use these over the coming days to get the anchor and the ship's cannon. It was fun work and Diver John sent up many brass artifacts in the process. Roy got the anchor and it went right in front of the Shorebird Restaurant. The only thing missing from the fun was money; John had a rusty old cannon and some cool brass artifacts and Alex had a story to tell. Another non-paying opportunity came along. A troller from Monterey hit the rocks and sank. More salvage work.

Pietro Genovese had bought a 32-foot Monterey, the *Santa Rosalia*. His life journey had led him to this boat at the age of 46. He had spent all his years on the back decks of sardine and squid boats, now he owned a Monterey of his own, his first. Five thousand of these stout little boats had seen local owners over the years and had been built in the yards between Monterey and Pittsburg. Their hull design was first established and tested in the Mediterranean Sea in the feluccas of Sicily. They were graceful and well built, so finely fitted that caulking was not required to make them watertight as the water swelled the planks tight.

On this morning, Pietro (nicknamed Pete the Arab) fired up the *Santa Rosalia*, lit the stove for coffee and threw off the lines. He headed for Half Moon Bay. His running partners were salmon fishing there now and were doing well. The migration was on and it was time to go north to Half Moon Bay, The City, Bodega and maybe even further to *Buffalo Country*, as the San Francisco gang referred to it. Anywhere above Point Arena was Buffalo Country, an odd name. The stories varied as to just *why* they called it Buffalo Country. One of the stories was because it was thought to be a wild untamed frontier, another was that the whitecaps there were as big as buffalo. For these stay-at-home bodies, it was akin to going to the moon even though it was only a day's journey up the coast. The summer migration was so much more than a quest for money, although that was always the unstated point of it all.

The little boats would raft up together and cook, gossip and laugh almost as much as they would spend their days on the water fishing. They refused to do this any other way. Any self-respecting fishermen with Sicilian blood or associates of the same considered their port time sacred. It was a place for eating abalone, sea urchins, music, laughter, fellowship. Friendships were renewed and new stories were born. They came in everyday to unload their catch and then tied the boats up together to engage in the social congregation, equally half as important as the fishing was. Putting ice on the boat and staying out days at a time was not for them, that was jail, that was to consign yourself to the workhouse; that was for the okies and the square-heads. Pete Genovese was a mix of ethnicities and stood apart from his swarthy paisans in appearance. He had a light brown complexion and reddish hair, some called him The Arab, but unknown to him and the others the red tint hair was of Viking influence, gained when the Nordic Sea Lords came to the Mediterranean seeking, plunder, slaves and *Danegeld.* It was the Viking way of doing business for centuries. Annually, they would sail to the Mediterranean, sail up the Seine to Paris, threaten to burn it to the ground and rape everybody or *else:* the Parisian residents had to pay them gold and silver to make the invaders go away. It was a win-win, Viking style. This is where Pete got his red hair.

So, *Santa Rosalia Pete* was on his way as the sun rose over the Salinas Valley and around three o'clock in the afternoon, he was off Pescadero in calm weather, on his way to join his paisans who were already tied up in Half Moon Bay. He began eyeing a sealed box as he crumpled up his empty pack of Chesterfield cigarettes. The box held two cases of cigarettes and two cases of scotch whiskey, duty free and without tax stamps, courtesy of the customs house official who put them there and sealed the box. He broke the seal, took out a carton of smokes and one bottle of Johnny Walker Red. He poured a neat drink and lit up thinking, "this is the life for me". That first drink tasted so good he had another one. The calm weather and drone of the 353 GM diesel began to weave a hypnotic spell and he drifted off to sleep without a hint that a rude awakening lay ahead. It happened at Whalemen's in shallow water when the sleeping Pete grounded hard on the rocks and sank; he had overshot the buoy while he was dreaming. He stepped off in a daze, patted his shirt pocket to make sure he had smokes and waded ashore.

Diver John and Alex drove to Monterey that week to buy the salvage rights. There was not much value to what was left of the soggy and splintered boat, and effort was required to get even that-it might be a waterlogged junk pile-you just did not know. The hull was in splinters for sure, only the metal had a chance of surviving intact. So, under somber summer grey skies they went to *Spaghetti Hill* in Monterey. It was a modest suburb populated with Sicilian-Americans, fishermen mostly. They turned down streets with names like, *Isola de la Mujeres* and *Palermo* street. They parked along a line of curbed cars at *Rosalia Pete's* house. They were greeted at the door and folding chairs were brought from the kitchen to a living room packed with relatives and friends. It soon felt like they were waiting for the undertaker, for it was indeed as if there had been a death; the sinking of a boat was akin to the loss of a family member for fishermen. The room had a heaviness that hung in the air, uncertainty: They knew that nothing good that lay ahead and trouble would be no stranger. The family was welcoming and congenial, nevertheless and Alex and Diver John were offered food and drink as they took a seat amongst the mourners. Diver John began the negotiation.

"I think I can float the engine, so I need to buy the salvage rights. There is a guy in town who wants the 353 for a boat he is putting together." John began.

"How much can you give us?" Pete's wife said like a shot. She was the one to deal with here, John could see that from the git-go and he explained with difficulty.

"Well, it's just a legal thing really, I have to own it to salvage it. I was not thinking of a value, just a token exchange so I can salvage it legally. It was worth a lot last week but now it's underwater and any value at all is uncertain. I might be able to raise it from the bottom, I don't know for sure. It's damaged and it's work to get it up at all." John replied.

"How much money is this *token exchange*?" she persisted in her straight-forward questioning.

"I was thinking a dollar. As a legal formality you understand-not the value you were thinking I know." said John.

The room gasped audibly and started jabbering in Sicilian. Alex squirmed in his chair. "*That* went over like a fart in church." He thought. He glanced at the door.

"Get out of my house! Grave robbers! Buzzards! Go back to *Affamoona*. The boat stays where she is- underwater! Go!! I curse you; I curse your eyes; I curse your family!" said the wife, now full of venom and not hesitating to spit it out. Alex was halfway out the door when Pete spoke.

"No, stop; forgive her, we are stricken with grief, we cannot even think straight. The boat was all we had; we have nothing now. You could get the gurdies, engine, winch, davits, floppers, whatever gear, and a little more maybe. You could come out, make profit? Give me something more than the insult of a dollar for sweet Jesus's sake, please. It is a dishonor we could not bear." Pete said in heartfelt manner.

Diver John opened his wallet and took out all the money he had in there and handed it to Pete in front of the living room crowd.

"That's all I got; you take it all." He announced.

Pete reached over and took the money. He signed it over for three hundred dollars. It was a quiet drive back to Half Moon; Alex did not say a word and neither did Diver John.

CHAPTER 5

The Caper

The salvage work did not pay, but it was fun. Being kinda broke was getting kinda normal. The money would come eventually Alex hoped. But being broke was inconvenient and at times worrisome. Alex had taken a 4-bit 8x12 room in a boarding house in a rundown area of El Granada. The residents jokingly called it Sevilla West. It was a dump; filthy and uncleanable. The walls were torn out to expose studs, and the general use area had exposed rafters. It had no shower that a person wanted to be naked in. Dorothy was the landlady and the owner was old man Johnny Cabral. Dorothy may have been a lot of things but one of them was not stupid. She had an innate ability to know when and who to marry a predatory sense. She was stealing old Johnny blind through marriage. She got Sevilla West, his ranch in Pescadero and Dan's Motel in Moss Beach. And here was Alex, Hal, Jersey George, Dave, Pitts, Suzie and the twins in the attic. The cast of characters in this comedic drama consisted of 1)Jersey George, hermitic in his room painting a wall mural and reading all day, 2)Dave, who was AWOL from the aircraft carrier Oriskany in Alameda, 3)Hal was a Tom Selleck look-a-like, 4)Pitts a Southern Cal trust baby, 5) Suzie and twins, 6) Alex. Dorothy was bopping in and out, flirting like crazy with everything in pants at 55 years old and George was honing his poker skills at our expense a few nights a week. Dave was dope-stupid 24/7. He always had a joint or two at the ready to fire up as soon as the current one burned his yellow fingernails. Alex had fun living with such an odd collection of souls; they played cards and then Hal and Alex would make the rounds of the nightclubs; Hal hustling "tunas" as he would say. Hal was batting a thousand and Alex was batting about .150

with the girls. He usually wandered home half drunk and munching an infra-red sandwich from the local Short Stop minimart. He had to listen to Suzie joke the next morning about the noise he made last night when he jacked off. There was no slack to be had in this house to save your life.

A week of bad weather followed the salvage work and they finally recon-vened at the launch ramp to prepare for the following day of diving for abs. The Peggy Jean was not there but in her place was Diver John on a 30-foot Radon, newish and outfitted.

"What's this?" Alex asked.

"I traded. I gave MclVie the Black Moriah and the Peggy Jean and I got this. Signed them over just yesterday, time for us to make some money."

"Amen to that. Wow, it looks new, I like the paint job." The paint was a bluff-sand hull with a brown cabin.

"Yeah, it's a camouflage-job when it's against the shore and it's fast, it's got a 354 gasser and it'll do about 25 knots empty. We're going to hit the Islands tomorrow."

"Sounds good to me, I'm broke."

"Me too."

They started out the next day at sunup, skipping over the flat ocean like nobody's business. This boat was fast, and they arrived at the Farallon Islands about 9AM. John suited up and they positioned into Fishermen's Cove, the flattest place imaginable for the Islands. And there were abalone all right, plenty. Alex pulled a few 3 dozen bags right away before John began to walk around and pick and measure. The boat was a stone's throw from the shore all day and Alex watched the mammals come and go and the birds were shrieking all day on bare rocks frosted with bird shit. A hoist at a boat landing for the dories and supplies was the only exception on this white and tan rock scape. A few green shoots were sprouting from the deep and layered guano, springtime green in small patches. The Islands had a history of exploitation. Seal hunters came first, then egg-takers came, then the coast Guard erected a lighthouse and then the birdwatchers. The original lighthouse burned down and now a radio beacon from a new lighthouse guided the ship traffic to and from the City. Today it was warm and sunny at noon and John came up for lunch.

"There's abs here." Alex said.

"Yeah, pretty healthy bottom and lots of shorts. Something else, there's some stuff over there under the Sugarloaf, brass stuff." He pointed to a prominent rock jutting upward toward the sky.

"There used to be a lighthouse there I think, but it burned down 100 years ago. Must have just pushed the burned rubble over the cliff. I'll make a jump over there before we go."

After lunch he was back at it, He could spend a lot of time down there walking around in his dry suit, he was known for that. But three o'clock came around and they had twenty dozen aboard, so John called a halt, satisfied by the first day at the Islands. Alex was ready to go, bored with birdwatching and the Radon skipped home at twenty knots. Well before dark they were putting the abs in the live boxes and getting ready for another go-round tomorrow-if the weather held. The Islands, like most of the good spots, required calm weather and good visibility. The next day they were on their way again.

They got to the Cove and John by-passed it and went to the exposed West side of the Island. It was deep water and the vegetation was close into the rocks and so were the abs. Alex had to get the boat right in close and he kept looking over his shoulder for a sneaker wave to wipe them out. It was possible to lose all in a hurry. No one had ever dived here before, so the bags came 3 dozen at a time and all big ones. John didn't break for lunch and when he had sent up 30 dozen they stopped for the day; Diver John was a hard-working diver with moxie.

"You ever see white sharks?" Alex asked. No one dove the Islands out of fear of white sharks, but John did. Alex had never heard the word uttered once by John; it was like bad luck.

"Oh yeah, they come around. They swim along the surface looking for little sea lions to eat. I just go lay on the bottom and watch until they go away." He said. Pretty cool cucumber he was, watching a twenty-foot monster. He said it like he was watching the bus pass by. Alex squared away the hose and deck and they bolted home on the afternoon of the second day at The Islands. They had 50 dozen in the water, and it was time for them to be on their way to a processer in Santa Barbara, Orville would buy them. That would be a happy ride and a happy paycheck.

Orville was tough, especially with his money. As a family member-employee once said in wry understatement,

"His sense of humor is not well developed, but it does surpass his generosity."

As it turns out Orville did not even like John. The fact that he had sunk an El Morro Co. lease boat years ago was never forgotten. Orville had a small fleet of boats that he leased to young divers and years ago, John was one of them. Too make it worse, John thereafter sold a load to another buyer to get a dollar extra and avoid Orville's deducts for the loss of the boat. But the story was a little more complicated than that. He offered the load to Orville's mother first, Agnes, who ran the place. Orville was just her step-and-fetch-it when she was alive. John made his case to Agnes.

"Agnes, Brebs is paying $12 a dozen and you're still paying me $11. Do you think you could pay me $12?"

"Well John, let me see. When I get my Social Security check maybe we can do something for ya."

"Agnes, you don't look anywhere near 65."

"Well John, you don't have to wait too long. I'm almost sixty in two months." That broke it, John went up the estuary and sold to Brebs. Later,

John made the mistake of tying up to Orville's dock without product to sell, having sold uptown to somebody else. This was a foul.

"You sell uptown-you tie uptown!" Orville hollered as he hustled down from the office to the apron of the dock, little bald head glistening with sweat. No mistaking that message.

"And when you gonna pay for that boat, huh? Half and half when you come back-and you damn well better come back under this hoist with abalone the next time I see you!" Orville's bald head was red with popping veins. In his boots, apron and beach-ball body he was a roly-poly pain in the ass. But that was long ago: today they arrived by truck with a load and all was forgotten or so it seemed. Orville and John had made a deal, he paid them off and check in hand, they headed back home.

"What's the deal with Orville." Sensing that he was an odd little man.

"He has a grudge. He's got reason from long ago. He's also a SOB to work for; it's always a battle to get the best price."

A few days passed and they had some time due to bad weather and dirty water. It looked like tomorrow was a go-day though, so when Alex went to the boat in preparation there was strange new gear aboard in addition to John's, most notably a 5/8 wet suit. John was a dry suit guy. John came down the launch ramp and explained.

"McElvie is going with us tomorrow."

"Why? You seem to have this covered fairly well. You don't need him, do you?"

"Look, truth is we are doing a deal, something different. I'll lay it on the line: we're gonna go hit the closed area at night, night diving with hydrophones and lights. You can say no, but I got to tell ya; we're gonna get a lot. I seen them, it's virgin country. McElvie is gonna make the jump at night, this is what he does best. He doesn't even have a license anymore, Fish and Game jerked it a long time ago. He's a criminal. Don't ever tell anybody he was even on this boat, you got that?" he said.

"No, I'm cool. And I'm in, let's do it."

"Good. I was hoping you'd say that. I'm getting used to you, you got good karma Alex."

"Thanks."

They left late the next day. They picked up McElvie off the end of the breakwater and motored at a course of 310 degrees. It was, as always when they worked, flat calm. They approached the bluffs of Pt Reyes. They skirted under the lighthouse and went around up to Elephant Rock. Alex had seen Elephant a thousand times but always from miles distant, but now he was right next to it and looking up. It was huge and covered in the customary bird shit a foot thick. John was looking beneath the water. With his years of experience, he judged it not quite right; surge, turbidity and just a creepy feeling.

"I don't like the looks of the place, shark-y." John said.

It looked like ordinary saltwater to Alex.

Alex looked around for sharks but saw nothing but saltwater and rock. McElvie had not emerged from the cabin yet, he was quietly sipping coffee under a space blanket. They headed back towards Pt Reyes and John swung in real close to the bluffs and ran down to Chimney Rock, looking intently at the shoreline and biding his time until dark. He didn't say but Alex got the feeling that the spot for the first jump was already chosen before they even left port.

"Well, whaddya think?" Alex said.

"We wait for dark, and then go back up the bluffs to that second cove down from the light where we will be in the shadow."

"Right on, this is fun."

It was a caper; they were going to pull a fast one. It was Alex's hob-goblin, 1960's, anti-establishment, criminal-guerilla fantasy come to life and he was a bad-ass. They drifted over by the Ranger Station, Mclvie started to suit up as the sun went down and they slowly motored toward the bluffs in complete darkness. As the darkness descended upon Pt Reyes and for the next 8 hours, they would not dare to even turn on a flashlight.

Getting into position was eerie. Alex could hear the proximity of the water lapping against the rocks before he could even *see* the rocks. The sweep of the lighthouse light was all there was; lonely cold light sweeping upon a distant rock, casting shadows over the cove. They were in a small cove about 50 feet wide, holding position until McElvie made his first jump. Alex thought *this* looked shark-y; mammals barking on the shore calling in the white sharks, calling out to be eaten alive, cruel world that it was. When McElvie jumped in and turned on the underwater light, it was a green eerie glow that followed him about, a shark attraction beam. If there was a shark in the area it would find him without any problem. The hydrophone came to life and we had our first communication from below. In a garbled voice he said:

"John, they are everywhere. Use the big bags."

The 5 dozen bags had to be floated to the surface with air bladders and they had to winch them aboard, 150-pound bags or better. The bags would rise to the place where he was below the surface and they would have to drive over to pick them up rather than haul them in from a safe distance. Usually it takes a bit of doing to fill a five-dozen bag but that was not to be the case tonight. The air bladders that floated the bags popped to the surface in short order-one after the other. They ended up next to a cliff almost all night, fending off. McElvie wasn't moving much from the spot he was working. Alex stacked abs in the cabin up forward as it became obvious this was a maxi-pack load coming aboard in the night ahead. Beads of perspiration formed as he attempted to keep up with the program. Around about midnight Jim McElvie came up for the first time and he was whacked out but extremely excited.

"You got the Motherlode down there Johnny Boy. Never seen nothing like that in my time, don't think I ever will again."

"What'll this thing pack?" John asked.

"50 dozen I'm guessing$ More? We're gonna find out."

"I put the first five bags up in the cabin already: the holds are empty." Alex offered.

"Okay then, let's start on the hatches back there and see how it goes." John said.

"You'll get another 25 back there at least, it's not gonna quit down there, I mean the snails are everywhere, every rock and ledge, they're lined up; lunkers waiting to die of old age. It's just a workout. I haven't measured one yet either."

McElvie poured a cup of coffee. He didn't waste a moment when the last drop ran over his blue lips, he put on his mask, jumped, turned on the light and was back at it, inspired, caffeinated and ensconced in the eerie green glow until 3 AM. I was starting to learn about this McElvie guy from bits and pieces of conversation. Alex learned that he had a rich girlfriend; Alex learned he didn't have a license; Alex learned Cal and Leif went to school with him and Alex learned they weren't too friendly. That's all he knew for sure, except McElvie had balls to be underwater at night with a light, Alex figured that out for himself.

Then in the silence and bubble of the exhaust he heard it:

"Fuck! Shark!" John yelled. Alex heard that from his hunched over position stacking abs in the holds. It got Alex's attention right fast, the word that was never uttered was now shouted as a warning, and Alex instinctively reached for the hose.

John had seen the shadow-and a big one, Alex did not see the shark, just heard the threat of him. John hollered down on the hydrophones for McElvie's attention to look up. He was in about twelve feet of water against a rock wall, crowded now by the beast. This was not a 'lay on the bottom' situation; the shark's belly was *near* the bottom and his fin was just under the surface simultaneously, the big belly crowding the shallows. Not a lot of room for a mammal-eater and a mammal.

"I don't see him, where is he?" McElvie's voice came through the hydro-phone and asked in panic.

"He's right over your light! Better get out, we're hauling you up now!" John said.

"Don't!! I can't be on the surface when he's around! Don't do it, wait!" Jim McElvie expressed his terror. Alex didn't know what to do so he asked.

"What should I do now?"

"Haul him in now!" John motored over right on top of the light as Alex pulled the hose aboard for all he was worth, frantic with the realization he had nothing but a piece of shark-bait on a string. It was getting real, real fast. McElvie was half on the ladder in no time but so was the shark and he was big and quick. All Alex saw was water splashing over the top of the boat and a little rubber man on the ladder lunging for the safety of the deck, a pointy snout and eyes black, cold and cross-eyed on McElvie, the terrible rows of white serrated teeth under the rolling eyes; nightmare. The report of the shotgun boomed in Alex's ears as it went off at close range and John emptied the old Model 12 into the ladder and blackness, pumping all 5 rounds at the cascading water, holding his fire just long enough to not hit McElvie square in the chest. It appeared that McElvie had two chances; mauled at the point-blank range of buckshot or being mauled from the gleaming white teeth. Fortunately, a third chance had presented itself. John had 5 shots off and then the shark was gone. It was over, nothing left but blood, smoke and an eerie quiet.

"Do you think you got him?"

"I don't know, not sticking around though to find out for sure."

"You got me, that's for sure." McElvie said from a prone position across the deck.

"You gonna make it?"

"Yeah, hit in the arm."

"Let's go Alex." John motored away, cleared the little cove and punched it full throttle. They were shaken and they were out of there in a flash. McElvie was on the deck and bleeding under the suit, hit by a couple of shotgun balls. Alex dressed it and stopped the bleeding, but the little rubber man was hurt.

"Cut up that suit and throw it overboard, I'm never getting in that thing again."

"Amen to that." Alex said.

The plan: Jim McElvie was to get off on the breakwater, walk off, drive to the launch ramp, haul boat, abs and all and head down the highway to Santa Barbara in the Black Moriah, towing the boat and all to make market. This wound was a problem to that plan.

Quite suddenly, McElvie piped up as we discussed it. "I can do it; I want to do it; nothing has changed except you shot me, you bastard." He said this good naturedly.

"He saved you, you mean." Alex added.

"Well, that too, I guess. I never did see a shark, but I sure felt the buckshot."

"They say you often don't see the shark until you are halfway to heaven." John said.

"Or hell."

"Or hell in your case."

It was breaking daylight as the breakwater appeared and McElvie easily made the transition to the rocks and made the long walk to shore. Before long the Black Moriah backed the trailer down the ramp, and they parked the Radon. Now securely fastened, John and Alex hoped off the boat and into the red Volvo. The abs were gone behind the Black Moriah. Down the road and just like that, what a night. Alex was having second thoughts about this criminal life. Right about now a predictable and safe career ashore was looking kinda good.

Ten hours of sleep later, Alex woke up around 6PM, ate at the Spouter, listened to Conrad, got half-drunk and stupid, went home and went to a deep alcoholic sleep. As he drifted off, he thought he saw Suzie, in the attic peeping through holes in the attic floor.

Jim McElvie called the next day from Santa Barbara, from the ER. He was okay he said but needed a day or two of rest, but he had the cash in hand and would drive it up.

"I'm wasted and wounded."

"How'd it go with Orville?"

"He loved the size and quality. The little bald-headed bastard."

"Did he give you $22.50?"

"Oh yeah, no problem."

"Good." See you in a couple of days then?"

Yeah, I'll be up after I sleep for a day."

"Okay, call me when you get here." John said and hung up the phone.

But a day or two passed and there was no call from McElvie and no answer at his house in Santa Barbara. Something was not right, John didn't want to, but he called Orville.

"Hey Orville, how you doin'? How'd you like that last load I sent? Pretty good stuff, huh? Healthy." John was cheerful and upbeat, hoping to get off on the good foot with the fat little bastard.

"Where's my abalone? Don't give me that shit. What are you talking about you criminal?" Orville was not in a good mood as usual.

"McElvie. Delivered it 2 days ago, damn near 60 dozen?" John did not like the tone or trend of this conversation.

"McElvie? Another criminal. That figures you two are together. The way I heard it he sold to Rusty Brebs for $20.00 cash. You divers are the shakiest group I ever seen; I swear." Orville never did have trouble making his negative thoughts plainly known.

John was stunned. He had been hoodwinked; he intuitively knew it. The caper began to play out in his head. John began to reconstruct the deal and his stomach got hollow, which turned into a small sweat that beaded his brow. That fuckin' McElvie had the Black Moriah, the Radon, the pink slip for the PJ and he had the cash for the abalones. He had everything and John realized he had nothing. He headed for the van and headed off down the road for Santa Barbara with murder in his eye.

John called Alex from a roadside stop and told him of his suspicions. Alex had had a bad feeling about this Jim McElvie guy, Leif told him he was shaky, but this was above and beyond that; it was grand theft, it was a double-cross, the betrayal of a friendship. The problem was that McElvie had the ups on them and got away clean with everything. They couldn't even put the word out for him. Even word that they were poachers was a black mark against themselves in a small town like this and that would not do. John arrived in Santa Barbara and went right to the nearest waterfront bar looking for Jim McElvie.

"Seen Jim McElvie?" he asked the bartender.

"I have not senior."

"Gimme a Bud and shot out of the well." John said and then swiveled on his stool at the bar, sizing up the room and its occupants. It was a Mexican bar, cowboy boots, belts, hats, turquoise and silver. Swarthy complexioned men in animated conversation. The jukebox belted out mariachi music. A man next to him moved over a stool and spoke.

"You are looking for the McElvie person?"

"Yeah, seen him?" John asked.

"Maybe so. He drives a new convertible now, a Cadillac?"

"Yeah, a black convertible caddy, that's him. Where is he?"

"Saw him yesterday, his house."

"Went there. Looked like he cleared out. Who are you amigo?" John said.

"They call me El Hombre Hormiga, I get around, nobody sees hormigas."

"I'll give you a hundred bucks if you find him."

"I can find 'em senior, that's not a question. It's *when* I can find him. Some things take longer than others. More time, more effort, more money."

John wrote down his phone number on a bar napkin and handed it to him. "When you do locate this prick, you call me. We can work out the money when you do."

"Okay senior." He turned away and disappeared into the crowd. It would be a while but John would see him again.

John slept in the front seat of his van down the street from McElvie's house that night. The next morning it was off to see Rusty Brebs and then Anita the Girlfriend. The trail was colder by the minute, he could feel the chill.

Rusty was in business with his dad down on Harbor St. They processed pinks and greens and red abalone and bought a little halibut for the restaurants they sold abs to. Rusty never got big and seemed to always be behind in the pay but he always paid, it was kind of hand-to-mouth, getting your pay when he got paid, but the price was always better because of it. Certain accounts favored a guy like he, never COD, always a dollar down and a dollar when you get it. There was a bit of something shady going on, always a payment in cash. John walked in the plant and a Hispanic crew was up-trimming and steaking the whole sixty dozen relaxing on the counters. John was sick looking at them.

"Rusty. McElvie sold these to you."

"No." A lie.

"I know he did.

"Get the fuck outta here with that bullshit John Wagner."

"I also know you paid him cash. He skipped town with my half of the cash."

"Well, I would say that you got fucked royally, didn't you?" Rusty said and John's blood began to rise in his temples.

"We'll see about that. How much did you give him?"

"I TOLD YOU HE GOT NOTHING FROM ME. NOW HIT THE DOOR AND DON'T LET IT HIT YOUR ASS ON THE WAY OUT!" Rusty was done and he turned away and walked into his office in his slimy boots and slimy apron, throwing his gloves forcefully to the floor and slammed the door.

"Fucking divers, nothing but trouble."

Well that didn't work out too well for John, who was currently running out of bullets down here in Santa Barbara. McElvie was a cheap confidence man, confining his schemes to women, family and friends, all the easy marks who bought into his cons and fabrications. That was his MO and the bad part was that John knew it but never thought he would be the one who got taken in by it. He was out about twenty grand on this little miscalculation and he was broke.

*　*　*

Anita was a special force. She had inherited money and had never worked a day. She considered herself an intellectual and worked at it but was not very convincing due to her dabbling in mystic art forms and magical thinking. She was pretty, had a sex vibe in a dark way and was always dressed in black. She started out as a bohemian, shifted to a beatnik and was now surrounded by young hippies and old beatnik friends. She thought the hippie movement was fun-anything goes with these kids. Her living room usually had 3 or 4 people hanging around, graduates from the Beat Generation mostly, smoking dope and listening to jazz records. Everybody was some sort of fringy artist, musician, writer, sculptor, etc. They talked a strong game but did little but get high, reinforcing their raison d'etre. Over this group Anita held court.

John walked up to the porch and knocked on the door of an old Victorian. He was standing on the threshold of Anita's universe. Anita came to the door in her low-cut black dress, looking like Elvira at Halloween.

"Anita, hi." John stuck a toe in the universe.

"Well, well, well. Diver John. How is it that your fine handsome-self calls on little ole me this day?" Anita crooned.

"I'm looking for McElvie, seen him?"

"The McElvie person, interesting fellow." She mused.

"That may be so but he's on my shit list today and I got to find him fast."

"Well come and sit down, he's not here-he's got a high place on that same sort of list of mine too. I presume he is on many lists."

"Figures, that rat-fuck." John said, and he walked in the door. Every door except the bathroom door was missing and replaced with black beaded curtains except one, which was a red beaded curtain. In that room there were a few large carpeted cat-trees, play structures that were human-sized. Who knows what they were for, the imagination ran into uncharted sexual territory there. Incense and dope filled the nostrils and three guys sat around a coffee table rolling joints in a rolling machine and cleaning a ½ pound of pot of their stems and seeds. One wore a beret and turtleneck, standard beatnik black. John walked past a wall sized oil painting of red, black, yellow and white streaks thrown against the muddled brown background of dots and blotches. It was hideous-John stopped in his place in the hallway and looked at it, his eyes assaulted.

"It speaks to me." Anita said.

"Oh yeah? What does it say?"

"Diseeeease of the mind. It's pure."

"I should have guessed that."

"It is rather obvious darling, isn't it?"

Anita reached over and gently squeezed his hand. "Please call me *A-needa*, John; like a craving or a wanting, a *need* is what I am, that's what I want you to think of me as." She announced to the amusement of her stoned audience on the couch. Apparently, her little performances found an appreciative audience around here. "What the fuck kind of funhouse is this?" John thought.

"Look Anita: I gotta find this guy now, no BS. He scammed me for twenty-grand. When did you see him last, that'd help a lot, that's what I *need*, *A-needa*."

"Wow, twenty-grand. What are you boys up to, my, my? McElvie is gone from here and he has not sailed his phallic ship through *my* straits listening to *my* siren song for a while. *If* that's what you're thinking. I'd look in Mexico if I were you, he likes it there, but he's very good at disappearing. I have banished him, he won't be found here, he is false." Anita pronounced with a dramatic wave of her arm to the audience in the dark room, a room draped with purple India batiks from Cost Plus.

"Okay *A-needa*, thanks." John left the A-needa universe to re-enter the real world and continue his search elsewhere.

*   *   *

On this day, Alex had a gritty hangover. He needed food and stepped into the Crab Cottage. He ducked the company of Karen and, self-conscious, he went to the corner to sit alone. He was dealing with the feeling, hurtin' for certain. All day he had been wondering how to set his circumstances right and he was not in the mood for hound dogging Karen's ass today.

"Basic, Hi." Karen said as she sat at the table. The place was empty, save for Louise, the owner. Louise was pretty and made up in her bouffant hairdo. It seemed that Louise had adopted a Macy mannequin as a role model, always looking the same, her good looks were smoothed over and made-up, sprayed hair piled on her head. She was smoking a cigarette and composing the week's menu additions and her husband Tom was also there with his mom Mary. Mary was chattering on and on, no one as really listening, especially Alex.

"Hi Karen, how you be?" Alex said quietly.

"Good; Peter has a birthday this week, got a B on my final grade, found a new place to rent for $125. You?" She returned the question.

"Oh, I'm okay, I guess. I got some things to figure out as usual. I'm considering going to Alaska for work." Alex replied.

"What happened to the Diver John gig?" she inquired. Alex was not even ready with his lie yet and needed one quick.

"Well, that ended when we blew up the engine on the new boat. He went back to Avila." Alex said his lie in a convincing tone.

"Bummer. Been to the Spouter?"

"Got half-drunk there last night playing with Conrad. Playing again tonight."

"Oh goodie, I'll come down and see you guys."

This perked him up a bit, Alex brightened at the prospect like a 25-watt bulb-that is to say dim. "Do. I'd like that." Alex replied. He dropped it; she went about her work. Alex mulled the new no-money reality that was upon him, casting about for ideas about who best to borrow money from. Maybe $500 from Uncle Sig? He was breaking broke, busted and disgusted in Half Moon Bay under a toxic cloud.

CHAPTER 6

32 Feet and 32 days

Wandering out of the Crab Cottage and trying to chase a four-alarm hangover away, clarity of mind was not cooperating. Lunch did take the edge off the hangover, but conversation was still risky. On a pleasant day in Princeton-by-the-Sea, Alex ambled across the street to Ortisi's crab stand and stood under the brightly colored awning in front of the brick crab cooker before he entered the Princeton Market next door. Dude Fagundes was behind the counter, several years older than Alex and dull as dishwater. "How do you get this way", Alex wondered?

"Hey Dude, how you be?" Alex said lamely.

"Good." he replied.

"Nice day." Alex said.

"Yeah." he replied.

"How's Rudy; haven't seen him around." Alex said, referring to his brother.

"He's good." Dude replied.

Apparently, all was well, good in fact in the Fagundes hemisphere. His mom ran a hairdresser business as a sideline in the back and she emerged. His mom was Pauline, a loud and notable figure in the small community. She had two changes of clothes: a red flower print muumuu and a green flower print muumuu. It was impossible to tell what shape her body was, but it most likely resembled a pear from all outward signs. A constant in her wardrobe was her pair of brown cloth slippers that were flattened in the back, exposing her cracked, wrinkled and calloused heels. The paramount feature that gave Pauline her notoriety was her ability to constantly gossip. Pauline knew what was going on, she worked at it and she was not shy to share what she knew. As her customers sat in her chair in hair curlers, she would rattle off about who was steppin' out with who, who had money, who was a gambler, who was a drinker, who was hiding out, who was in trouble with the law, who's kids were a mess, who was poor as dirt, who was untrustworthy, who had a checkered past, who put on airs, and et cetera. The information never ended. Half the people that patronized her shop were there to just dish the dirt. They did not leave disappointed.

"Alex. How's your mom doing?" Pauline asked.

"She's doing okay Pauline. She's working a lot, riding the bus to the City 5 days a week." Alex said.

"Everybody has to work and that's where the jobs are, I guess. Widowed like that, so sudden, so tragic, I'm so sorry for you both Alex. What's she do up there?" she asked.

"Bill collector." Alex replied.

"That's commission work, oh the poor dear, such a hard job. We need to talk. I'll do her hair for free if she likes, you tell her that." Pauline said, waving a stubby finger and then she disappeared behind the curtain into her studio.

'Okay, she'll appreciate that." Alex said to the curtain, grabbed a pack of Twinkies, paid and left, saying:

"See ya Dude, be good."

"I'm good."

Wandering down the street past the little Hancock gas station with the Frenchman, past Bud Riddell's, past the ruin of the Patroni house with the blue windows, Ida's and Hazel's, Alex began to focus on his future. He found himself at the *Valkyrie* to ask for money. Uncle Sig was eating a ham sandwich and chips at the galley table and Alex climbed down the ladder to greet him and beg for money.

"Hi Uncle Sig." he said upon entering the cabin.

"Vell, Good to see you Alex. Vhant Coke?"

"No thanks. Uncle Sig, I want to go to Alaska and fish this summer. What you think about that?"

"Lotta fish in Alaska, that's vhat I think, no real fisherman ever vent broke there, that's for sure."

"I think Bristol Bay might be good, sockeyes."

"Yah sure, lotta fish there." Sig said.

"You ever been there?" Alex asked.

"Yah, years ago, about your age. Vee vere in the sailboats back then, the donkey boat would tow us in and out, vee lived off the cannery in the bunkhouse."

"Did you like it?"

"Oh yeah, vee liked it fine, vee all liked it. Vee vent up on the Star of Alaska, a four-master and vee made up the cans on the trip. Vee leave from Oakland. Took us a few veeks to get there. Most everyone was Sicilian or from the Old Country." There was a hesitation in his conversation.

"Well I want to go and see it. I can get work if I can get there."

"Easy enough nowadays, get on the plane and go."

"Well that's the thing Uncle Sig- I'm broke." Alex came right out with it.

"I thought you vere making good money with the ahba-lonees?" Sig had a little trouble getting those vowels out. That was Alex's cue to lie again.

"Engine blew up; Diver John went back south and no more work."

"Ahh, damn shame it is, engine trouble. I'll stake ya if you vant, you pay me back vhen you get home again, you'll have money if you find vork, I know that. But it's not easy." Sig said and added, "Always pay attention to the tide, it runs like a river, 25 feet it drops and rises. Vhen its low the sand banks rise like islands-all around you and vhen it's high it's all water for miles. I know, I been on those banks-stranded."

"You have? Tell me about it."

"Me and the Lundeberg brothers, there was the four of us in the two boats and vee missed the tow back to the cannery. Vee sailed for all vee vere vorth vit the tide, but vee got caught and went dry on a sand bank. There vee sat. All of us had gone dry before and vee just had to wait for the rising tide; so, vee played cards and sat in the little boat, resting on the sand all around." More hesitation from the story and then he continued. "Jalmar, Odd and Lonnie Lundeberg; all good men."

"Do they still go up every summer?" Maybe Uncle Sig still knew someone there. His hope was quickly dashed.

"In the graveyard in Dillingham, that's vhere they be. They got caught in the tide: Jalmar was cut off-the damn fool was walking around on the bank! All of sudden, he be valking on a different sandbank than us, cut-off he was! Lonnie vaded in the vahter to help him over. I vas in the boat. In five minutes, Jalmar and Lonnie were chest deep in the vahter, trying to cross over to our bank but vee be shrinking too. Odd was running and hollering at me for rope." Sig said.

"Shit." What else could Alex say?

"Vee vahtch 'em- Odd and me on the bank. Jalmar and Lonnie, they be floating away in the tide. Odd kept throwing the line but vas too short and the current vas too fast. He yump in and swam to them with the rope around his waist, me on the other end. I vahtched him swim. The vahter reached me, got deep, I got back in the boat and the rope came to the end, vhat they call the bitter end, I lose it. I drag boat to vahter, I sail for them but too slow. Saw the three men alive for the last time, all clutched together and swimming with the currents. I hoped they could last the night, but they did not. They vahshed up at Coffee Point, still locked arm in arm, tied together with Odd's rope. That was enough for me-I seen enough of the Bay." Sig took a bite of his sandwich; Alex wandered out to the back deck, thinking about it.

"If you wanna go I'll stake ya." Sig hollered to Alex's exiting back.

"I wanna go. Soon."

"$500 do it?" Sig said

"That sounds just about right, thanks Uncle Sig."

"Your mother's not gonna be so happy with me."

Alex walked down Main street in Half Moon Bay toward the travel agent's storefront. Past the fire house, Granelli and Cook, the bakery, Cunha's, Gilcrest drug store, auto parts, Johnny's and Ernie's Cafe. The travel agent was on a side street and Alex walked into a modest office with walls covered in posters of Europe, Hawaii, India and Japan. The furniture and plants were plastic and slightly dusty. He was greeted by a matronly woman.

"How can I help you Hon?" she asked.

"I need a ticket to Alaska."

"Okay. Alaska is big, where do you want to go? We got a good deal to Ketchikan?" She said.

"No, I think I need to get to Anchorage and then to Dillingham."

"Well I can get you to Anchorage, Dillingham is a separate trip you have to arrange, not sure on that but I will check." She said and picked up the phone to an airline. Alex gazed about the room as he waited out her conversation, glancing at a stack of glossy travel magazines in the waiting area and noting how sterile the place was.

"I can get you to Dillingham." She announced after a time and a few calls. It's $80 to Seattle, $135 to Anchorage and another $65 to Dillingham. That Dillingham flight is a twin-engine prop, Anchorage is a 727 from Seattle."

"Okay, sounds like a deal to me. I'll take it."

"Well then; when do you want to leave? Is this a round trip or one way?" This caused Alex pause for consideration. He didn't know.

"June 15 to...... I don't know, can I leave the return open?" He said with a degree of thought. The woman wrote it down and proceeded to book him a flight and take his cash.

It didn't take much to get ready to leave. He packed a duffel with raingear, boots, sweats, hat, jacket, sleeping bag and a book. Karen was not around. Cal and Mom-a short adios. It was a little scary but exciting as Alex stepped to the airport curb from the taxi.

After the Seattle flight and on the flight to Anchorage, Alex had a starboard window seat and clear weather enabling him to look down below out the airplane window. A lot of water and trees, that is all he saw for hundreds of miles. This went on before the water and trees gave way to snow covered rock peaks that reached up until they almost scraped the belly of the plane in a formidable land barrier, impassible and resolute, prohibitive of any trespass. Life could not exist there for even a night. This gave way to a broad area of flat terrain as the plane descended into Anchorage to be discharged at the Ted Stevens airport. Waiting at the taxi station, Alex flagged a cab and hopped in the back.

"A hotel; any hotel." Alex told the youngish driver.

"The Chelsea. It's clean." This started Alex to thinking that unclean conditions were also available.

The Chelsea was a motel and Alex walked into the shabby lobby and approached the desk. The kid behind the desk was a younger version of the cab driver and he didn't look up from the Playboy magazine that was open in front of him. The lobby had an oversize tank of tropical fish on top of the Coke and snack machines, which bracketed the soap and bleach dispenser. A large wall map of Alaska covered a portion of the opposing wall. Dillingham was a big dot on the map, this was encouraging. The kid behind the desk eventually looked up and sold Alex a room for the night. The room was sparse and full of rectangles; rectangle beds, nightstands, TV, desk, all with hard Formica edges. Alex looked in the bathroom. It was *clean*.

In the morning, Alex showered, and it flooded the bathroom, the shower curtain was about 3 inches shy of long enough to span the tub. Also, it was several mils heavier than Saran Wrap and flapped wildly in the draft created by the shower downspout. It had this annoying habit of clinging to your body if you approached too closely, it jumped out at your wet nakedness. He did have lots of towels for the mess though, towels that were the consistency of medium grit sandpaper and bleached to an almost fluorescent white. The foam drinking cup was "hermetically sealed in plastic for your safety" and it should have said "for your annoyance." Alex destroyed the cup in the process of unwrapping it, punching holes and dents with his thumbs and fingers, it was impossible to unwrap it without damaging the flimsy Styrofoam. Alex got his water drink out of his cupped hands. The tap water was the vilest of solutions and thoroughly undrinkable, so it didn't matter in the end. Alex walked out into the street and walked past the adult video store and the Original Alaska Restaurant. This was a restaurant whose stated motto was "If you don't say WOW! When the food arrives, it's FREE!" He had made up his mind in advance to say "wow" and when it arrived it was more like a deflated, *oh wow...* 6000 calories of carbs piled on a plate. He found out his quiet *oh wow* did not qualify for a freebie. Alex walked with a gut-bomb to the Chelsea to collect his stuff, the Ted Stevens International and Dillingham International awaited. He boarded a little twin-prop for the flight, it was packed to capacity with plaid shirts and baseball capped men.

After an initial range of mountains west of Anchorage, the landscape turned flat and filled with ponds and marshland; thousands of ponds for miles exposed now that the snow and permafrost had melted, home to innumerable mosquitos. As he neared Bristol Bay, lakes and rivers appeared. Lake Iliamna began and went on for 10 minutes before the airplane cleared it, Alex thought he was over the ocean it went on so long. Finally, the Nushagak River began to wind down from the headwaters, the annual destination of 30 million sockeye, spawning in pristine river gravel and unchanged for hundreds of thousands of years. The turboprop descended into Dillingham over isolated homes, barns, collections of junk boats and junk vehicles. The plane was over the outskirts of town headed for the runway, but it was hard to say for sure because it looked to be landing in the treetops. The plane touched down and taxied to the terminal and stopped. The terminal looked like the rear entrance of small-town mechanics shop. He walked across the grainy and worn tarmac toward the single wooden door in bright sunshine and seventy-degree temperatures. Inside, it was abuzz with fishermen waiting for their baggage and shipmates. Alex went to the baggage claim area, a clean dumpster bin in front of a closed roll-up door. Soon, it rolled up to the great outdoors and two men began hurling duffels, boxes and ice chests wrapped with duct-tape. It soon turned into a problem as the baggage pile began to overflow the dumpster and pile up on the floor. The passengers threw unwanted baggage aside, digging into the pile. It was chaos. After Alex fought his way to his duffel bag, he stepped out into the parking lot and quickly understood that he was about 5 miles from Dillingham in the middle of a bushy nowhere without a hint of the amenities that an airport might be expected to have. He hooked a ride before everybody disappeared.

"Going into Dillingham? Can I get a ride?"

"Hop in the back." And Alex was on his way into Dillingham The Town.

Town was a quick study much like the airport. There was a bar, a school, a post office, an ice hockey ring, half dozen houses and 2 general stores. The fronts of these stores doubled as social spots. One store attracted a retinue of the old and the other attracted the young, all of them congregating out front in both locations. 15 or 20 residents, all native Innuits, chatting, arguing and waiting for the pay phone. The truck stopped here, and Alex got out. He went inside and it was a jumbled mess of dry goods, hardware, toys and frozen food. It dawned on him right away that he was in the wrong place to find work, far, far away from home. Not one boat in sight.

"Where's the boats?" he asked a woman in front of the general store. She raised her arm in stoic silence toward a road that led out of town.

"Thanks." Alex said feeling very Caucasian. He started to walk through town along a flat and scrubby landscape that went down to the marina. The marina was a perfectly small rectangular basin carved out of the mud with bulldozers at low tide. A few boats were in the water tied to a bulkhead with a hoist, 300 boats were high and dry in the adjacent yard. There were a lot of boats and they all were out of the same mold-32 feet long. The yard was a conglomeration of steel shipping containers, plywood huts, boats and one makeshift coffee kiosk cobbled together in the middle of it all. There was also a newish steel building that housed the Lummi gear store. He walked in and addressed the clerk.

"Hi, I'm looking for Whatsit2ya Marsha."

"She's down that way in that big barn." said the guy behind the counter. Alex thanked him and left into the warm and sunny day. It was the only wooden building and he could see the rooftop at the end of row after row of 32-foot boats, all of them waiting for word that the season would open. Alex approached the wooden barn which stood out in contrast to its surroundings. It was homey with a few planter boxes outside the windows and a door with a brightly colored sign-WHATSIT2YANETS. The door was ajar and inside was a pretty-ish woman hanging net, piles of cork lines, bales of net, couches, over-stuffed chairs, a coffee machine, a popcorn machine and high ceilings with a loft. A guy was asleep on one of the couches and a dog greeted Alex as he entered.

"Marsha?" he asked.

What's it to ya?" she replied.

"Hi, I'm Alex and I'm looking for work."

"What kinda work?"

"A deckhand job on a sockeye boat."

"Experienced or green?"

"No experience here in the Bay, I'm from the lower 48 and I know boats and fishing from there."

"Okay. You stay here and strip nets. No drugs, alcohol, or you are O-U-T, out." she said and handed him a little red handled knife. That knife never left his hand for the next 4 days, except for eating, sleeping and pissing. Over this time, it became clear that this was a bit of a social hub. Fishermen passed through here and just said hello and passed the time. It was perfect for Alex's purposes. Marsha had a lot of leads and corks to be stripped and Alex earned his keep. One day a little Swedish looking gal came in. She was about 4'11', straight blonde hair and pretty. Marsha and she gossiped awhile, and Alex perked up his ears when she said this.

"We need another guy, our third guy had to go, we fired him."

"He's looking for work. I had him striping nets for 4 days and he's been sober and no trouble." Marsha said.

And that's how Alex met Sig; they became crewmates. During the season, they talked as crewmates do between sets, working on the back deck and at the galley table, sharing enough information to not get too close, but to get a feel of who the person was you were living and working with. The vibe Signe gave was good and she was a force. Sig was older than Alex, blonde, blue eyes, 4'11' foot, a petite mother of three sons and capable in the extreme. The father of her sons was a fisherman and her sons were fishermen save for the black sheep of the family: he was a Phd. Physicist at MIT. It was impossible to outwork Sig. She set net and picked fish, reset, and stacked a stern pile, cooked dinner and did the dishes. In between she would bake an apple cobbler or make scones for breakfast in the morning. If the net had a hole or a tear, she patched it while waiting to unload at the tender. If something was going on in the engine room, Sig was down there to look around or else getting out the right tools for the skipper. As Alex watched her with increasing wonder, he was intrigued by this dynamic woman. Near as he could piece it together, the thumbnail sketch of her timeline went like this:

Signe grew up with her Swedish parents in Northern California. Her parents had a lumber mill and she crewed on charter boats out of Eureka. After high school, she left for the University of Santa Barbara. At first, her parents were proud but soon became concerned that she was becoming a hippy. They watched on TV as the Goleta Bank of America burned and the

chanting UCSB students ran about throwing rocks. They were relieved to not
see their little girl in front of the TV cameras, but they still figured no good
could come from her being at UCSB. What else could a practical Scandinavian
presume? Sig did well in school, but when she wanted to leave it, the parents
were all for it. Ready to take life head-on, she went to Southeast Alaska where
she homesteaded land, built a cabin, settled, met the father of her children,
began her fishing career trolling with a hand-cranker. She loved her life,
reveling in the beauty of it all. Apparently, her parent's fears and suspicions
were confirmed: she was a hippy and jumped on the back-to-the-land bandwagon as it rolled through the state. Signe lived it and did it all. She bought
the dream and her no-nonsense Swedish practicality made it happen. Though
practical, her stories had an element of playfulness and a fun-loving spirit
did shine through. She was also no stranger to the occasional beer after the
work was done.

Most of all, Alex was struck with how Signe looked after him with an
endless patience. She was always first to step up to handle the heavy work
when the going got tough. She taught Alex how to do everything. Alex had
to assert himself to pull his weight because she was quicker, always. She
weighed about 120 pounds and could do the work of two. She was the glue
that kept the boat together as a tight operation.

The first official announcement came on a Friday; the season would open
at 6PM Saturday. Immediately the tractor and trailer began to launch boats
day and night and the marina began to fill, boats rafted together in long
strings 20 boats deep. It was all activity through the night and twilight. Boats
went in the water in short order and there was an exodus out the marina
when opening day was nigh, Nushagak Bay was filled with an armada of boats
headed toward the line. Things were happening fast, and Alex's boat was
among the group. They anchored up in a mosquito infested slough. Sig made
dinner around midnight; Alex made sure the screens stayed on the
windows.

Nushagak Bay is big, many miles across. The southern end is lined with low sandstone bluffs that give way to scrub brush land. The northern edge is lined by high mountains in the far distance. The Bay is wide and pocked with sand banks at low tide on the north side, extensive flats at low tide on the south side. Coffee Point marks the northern point and beyond that is Dillingham, the Wood River and the headwaters of the Nushagak River. The 'line' was at the southern end of the bay and it is here that the fish first enter the Bay and the nets. The tenders anchored there, as well as the enforcement. Everything geographical was big in Alaska. There were no roads to connect the few towns, the natives had to wait until the Bay freezes over in the winter to visit family on the other side in their Sno-Cat or snow mobile. Around 5pm the boat headed down Steamboat Channel toward the line in anticipation of the opening one hour away. Just prior to opening set time, Alex held the bumper ball in his hands, ready to throw it over the stern and stand back from the net as it peeled of the drum at a high rate of speed. The 4-hour opener would come on the incoming tide and Alex's boat *Widgeon* would get their brief turn on the line before they drifted back. Another net would take the place of their net and they also would drift from the line. It was a game to get the line set in a 6-knot current. The skipper jockeyed for position until it he had a shot to get on the line without violation of the boundary. An enforcement plane flew overhead.

"Go!" Skipper Matt yelled from the bridge and the net spooled off, stern roller slinging lead line. In about 3 minutes the six-hundred-foot-long net was deployed, corks marking its place on the surface of the muddy water. Instantly fish started to splash, caught in the cork line. They drifted and Matt kept the net straight with the occasional tow of the net. Most of the action was on the line as net after net covered the boundary in the water, then drifting off toward the back of the pack. Our boat started to drum up the set after about 10 minutes of drifting and there were fish stuck in the meshes, the fish were about 5 pounds apiece. Alex had his little picking gaff and quickly got the hang of getting the mesh over the gills and backing out the fish. He was so excited at the number of fish that he accidentally flung one overboard in his excitement, marking him as greenhorn to his veteran shipmates. It was exciting; there were a lot of fish and after about an hour of picking, they had 5,000 pounds in the holds. As the opener drew nigh to closing, they were off to the tender to unload. They took their place in the line-up behind seven other boats, everyone was getting in line to unload. There were 6 tenders for the fleet. The next opener would be 8 hours later at the next incoming tide, as per announcement on the VHF radio channel. Alex guessed about 400 boats had set gear on opening day in the Nushagak as far as he could see. His focus was on the back deck mostly, either spinning the net out past the stern or coming back slowly with fish to be picked. They anchored up between openings, eating dinner and getting a few hours' sleep if time allowed. The weather was always calm compared to the open ocean and there was some rain and some hot days. On those sunny days, the visibility went for miles and the mountain range to the north looked small. It was then that one could gauge the immensity and scale of this land, the people who walked it barely a footnote. The scale of the landscape suited the annual return of 50 million fish. There was no comparison to anything Alex had heretofore experienced. Certainly, this was real fishing and the fish supported the entire ecosystem.

There was no change from this routine of set, pick, unload, eat and sleep for a couple of weeks. The brailer bags went up to the tender with a grocery list, fuel, water and groceries came down: the tender provided everything. After a few weeks the fishing dropped off.

'I think we'll transfer to Naknek.' Matt announced, and I asked Sig what that means.

"We're gonna go fish in the Naknek River, it takes 48 hours to transfer before you can start." Sig explained.

"When we goin?" I asked Matt.

"I think we'll go now; I'll throw my card today." he replied. And so, they were off to Naknek.

It was a run down the Bay and around into to the Eastside District. It was about an 8-hour trip before he saw a boat, Alex slept the whole way. The mouth of the River was where the boats were, they were fishing a *combat fishing zone* where all boats crowded together in the mouth of a narrow river at the line, 400 boats racing, setting and picking. We proceeded upriver because we had a wait before our transfer was due to expire. We tied up at the old Red Salmon cannery, against the tall pilings next to the vast wooden sheds. There was a lot of history in this river and the old cannery buildings showed it; the tall pilings, sheds, bunkhouse, chow hall and every plank screamed *history,* where Uncle Sig had slept and ate back in his day. There were even a few old wooden boats left in the storage sheds that someone saw fit to restore. The next morning, they were on the line along with 400 other boats, waiting for the set time, chomping at the bit to get a good set. The mouth of the river was about a thousand yards wide and the incoming current runs about six knots. 400 boats all wanted a turn on the line in the middle. It was all full speed and bumper boats and they were there to get their share. Alex found it rather intimidating. The fish splashed in the cork line as the net played out and today, two million pounds would come over the stern of the boats during an incoming tide.

They didn't talk much on the Widgeon. The routine set in and Alex did his job; pick fish, unload, eat and sleep. This went on for thirty days, first in Nushagak and then in Naknek. Toward the end of the 30 days the ADFG opened it on the outside of Naknek River. They were no longer playing bumper-boats in the river mouth; they were in the open bay down at Johnson Hill. It was also getting harder to get a thousand pounds and the end of the season was near. The *Widgeon* season ended abruptly when Matt slammed the boat in gear and spun the drive shaft coupling. Long and silent faces thought about the breakdown during the tow to the yard. Matt arranged the trailer to haul them out.

"Looks like we gotta pull the gearbox." He said.

"Okay." Alex was out of practice of conversing beyond the topics of set, pull, pick.

"I think this is how it ends. You might beat the rush at the airport and see if you can get a seat on stand-by." Matt said.

"I can stick around and help get us fixed up?"

"No need, Sig and I got this covered and parts are uncertain, it might be a few days and then a few days more after that. It's over by then; there'll be 200 guys at the airport on standby pretty soon."

"All right, I'll get my gear together."

No argument there, Alex sensed a rising feeling of joy-he was going home. Signe and Matt drove him to the airport in the fish truck and there were no long goodbyes or hugs, they didn't even get out of the truck. It dawned on Alex that the skipper might be glad to see him go. There were certainly no regrets on his part to be on his way. It was over. He walked into the airport terminal and tried to speak but found that he was tongue tied.

"I want, would like to get, a ticket, I have a ticket, but I want to be on standby, for a seat home that is." He said and produced his ticket. She took it and looked skeptically at it. This worried Alex because the thought of spending one more day in this wasteland of fish, boats, scrub brush and junk was not appealing.

"Okay" She said finally and handed it back, marked and stamped. "Take a seat and see if you can get one; next plane in is at 5pm and another tomorrow morning at 8AM." Guys his age were asleep on the floor. Alex plopped his gear there and waited. As it turned out, the wait lasted all night and the next day. Then he got a seat 24 hours later at 5PM the following day. 10 hours later, stunned and silent in civilization, Alex looked around in the San Francisco airport. About a week later Alex went to the post office to see if he had any mail. The postmaster handed him a letter marked Alex Skarsen, C/O General Delivery. It was a check for $6500.

"Fuckin A Tweedy, thank *yoouu* God!" He kissed the envelope.

* * *

Diver John came to the surface off the shores of San Miguel Island. He was working alone and had reluctantly struck a deal with Orville to run a lease-rig boat. Orville was reluctant as well to enter into the arrangement, but he knew it was his only opportunity to recoup his losses from a previous deal with John many years ago, losses he fully *intended* to collect. There were no statutes of limitations on debts owed to Orville and he had a long memory. For John the arrangement was one step above servitude, but he was desperate, Orville had him over a barrel and they both knew it. He had already canvassed the ports of the entire West Coast looking for his own boats or the Black Moriah and no dice. McElvie was out of reach. In a way it was fortunate that he didn't find the boats or car because it would have only led him to beat McElvie into the ground and possibly jail time for assault. He opened his brown lunch bag and took out his honey and peanut butter sandwich, his plastic bag of sunflower seeds and raisins and poured himself a cup of coffee from his thermos. It was nice scenery out here and the afternoon sun warmed his rubber suit, he should have been happy, but no: he was haunted, and this was not a viable situation, this was the rent money. The price of a dozen abalone had taken a nosedive thanks to Pierce and his Black Fleet. The company boats were all junkers and the divers were sketchy, but they landed enough abalones to set the price. They had driven the price down to $12 for Reds and $8 for Pinks and that was barely wages. Nobody was getting rich except Pierce. This slightly dimmed the sunshine at San Miguel Island. That God-darned McElvie had really put the hurt on him, set him back. John decided to take his dozens and go into Santa Barbara to where Orville was expecting him. Every abalone had to go to the little bald-headed devil in rubber boots.

* * *

Anita looked around and liked what she saw. She also liked *the vibe*: she put a lot of stock in *the vibe*. Like the wise men that followed the star to

Bethlehem, she followed a *vibe* to the town of Mendocino and an article in a glossy LA mag helped. It appeared to be fertile ground; old and new hippies read Georges Oshawa and ate organic food, they burned incense and entertained Eastern philosophy. They took drugs to further expand their consciousness or just to get high. The lay of the town was old and dotted with stately wooden buildings built at the turn of the century when the town prospered as a landing for the lumber schooners who moored in a natural harbor at the mouth of Big River. After the logging era passed, the town went dormant until decades later when the back-to-the-land concept took hold of the new generation. The young city dwellers, disenchanted with the establishment, politics, suburbs, city life and more, were searching for a do-over of their own design and this was the beautiful setting that they settled upon: rivers, trees, quaint towns and a blue collar vibe generated by the fishing and lumber industry. Anita knew right away that she would fit right in. She started to thumb through real estate magazines in the lobby of the old hotel where she sought to spend the night. The clerk behind the front desk register stepped up and greeted Anita.

"I love your little town!" She exclaimed.

"We like it too. Where you from?"

"Santa Barbara."

"Long way, course we get people from LA ever since that magazine article came out. It seems as if we have been discovered." The clerk said.

"I think I'll take a room for a couple of nights, maybe the rest of the week if I decide to look around."

"Which is it then? A couple nights, or a week?"

"Yes, a week I think."

"Just one?"

"No. A week for two people." She said, signed, paid and went out to the car.

"Jimmy, don't you just love it here!?" she gushed.

"Looks pretty good to me, I like *the vibe* Anita." Said the blond, long haired man in the passenger seat named Jimmy. Jim McElvie looked around at the wooden sidewalks, quaint buildings and the expansive view of Mendocino Bay with approval. And, with notions of how he might turn it into cash.

CHAPTER 7

The Biological Imperative and Salmonosis

A lex was getting signals. In the past he had considered himself to be rather ungainly and awkward. He was tall and thin like a bean pole, dirty long blond hair always unkempt, ruddy face with a hawk-like beak and imperfect teeth. Now he had to reconsider the issue: he just might be attractive to the opposite sex. Still, his shyness got in the way and hesitation prevented him from acting with a degree of confidence to these phero-mone-charged signals from women like the other guys did, but he was getting better at it, a little more confident. He got the signals alright but was just a little slow and often the signals had to land in his lap, literally. His gig at the Spouter had a happy result in this way and there was no denying a comely pair of eyes-on you. A split was developing in his interests; being on a stage or being on the deck of a fishing boat. Fishing was winning the tug, but music is where the girls were at lately. Nevertheless, he was back from Alaska and his intention was to go boat shopping. A salmon boat is what he had in mind.

Alex and Mike Conrad were just milling about on the little platform stage, a step away from the first row of tables. There were about ten people eating and drinking and none of them were listening to the music, just yak-king away and getting their buzz on. Alex recognized them all as locals, they all recognized Conrad and his trio. Mike Conrad had become synonymous with Tuesday night at the Spouter. Conrad did not have an enemy in the world (other than all his former girlfriends) and all the guys thought he was great and consequently he had a bit of a Tuesday-night following. They started their set with covers from the jukebox, some people sang along with *Country Roads,* and in the middle of this song Karen walked through the door, smiling and waving at Alex. She sat at the bar and struck up a conversation with Earl the bartender. Earl had a face as black as coal and teeth as white as snow and they were always on display in a constant smile. Everybody loved Earl. He could talk on any subject and he was a magnet for good times and laughter-the perfect bartender. Alex turned it on a bit with little flourishes of notes between verses and body movements, all for Karen's benefit. It didn't have the intended effect, she didn't notice, Karen continued to laugh and talk with Earl. Conrad went through his repertoire for an hour and then they took a break, it was a good set and the audience applauded. The house grew to a 20-person crowd.

"Hey Basic, how's your handsome self be? Where you been?" Karen greeted Alex as he approached the bar. He sat down on the stool next to her.

"I'm just back from Alaska as a matter of fact. Good to see you Karen."

"I missed you." Alex got that signal.

"Oh yeah? You might see a lot of me in that case, starting now." Alex leaned in and stole a kiss. Karen pulled back and looked at him face to face for ten seconds slightly shocked; then, she grabbed him by the shirt and pulled him in for another kiss. This one was long and wet.

"It's about time. What took you so long, Basic?" She whispered. Alex was floating in the air with joy, just about to cream his jeans.

"I've been waiting a long time too; from the first time I saw you riding on your horse in the pines. I'm just shy I guess."

"With that long sandy hair and blue eyes- I could've jumped your bones right then." She whispered at close range to his face.

"Well that's going to happen then."

"Maybe, if you play your cards right. Go play your second set." Karen said, playing her hand perfectly and reserving a 'yes'. She was a pro.

Alex went back to the stage and Conrad laughed and spoke, "I see you at the bar with Karen. Did you get a promise?" He thought this was great sport at Alex's expense.

"We'll see about that later."

"She's in the *Big Leagues* kid." Conrad said.

"And I'm in the *Bush League*." Alex mused.

"If she picks you, you're in the *Big League* forever more, your reputation will precede you. That's how it works." Conrad said, still chuckling.

"I hope so."

They started the second set with *Coal Tattoo, Cold Rain and Snow and Angel from Montgomery*, not the jukebox playlist, Conrad was getting real. You can't couch surf all your life and not have a little bit of soul. Alex turned up the volume knob and dug into his improvisation bag as Conrad sang with conviction, summoning the 20 years of hard living in his wayward life. This did not go unnoticed now by the 20 people present and none of them were talking during the songs. Conrad had them; the music was authentic and good. After the set Alex put his bass in the case and went back to the bar and Karen, squeezing his way between the suitors hanging around her and competing for her favor. Alex took his place.

"Hey, how'd it sound?" He asked as he walked up to her, dispersing a few losers.

"It was great, you guys nailed it!"

"I thought so too. Conrad got into it." Alex said.

"Listen" she said at close range, leaning in again, "I got a couple of joints at home. Wanna go burn 'em?"

"Let's go. I'll get my bass right now and we are out of here." Barely concealing his anticipation.

'Okay, let's take my car." They headed out the door and off to wonderland; looked like it was graduation night from the Bush Leagues for Alex.

Alex followed Karen to her car, a late model white Volkswagen hatch-back. He opened the passenger door and a few textbooks and notepads fell in the gutter. He picked them up and threw them in the backseat. Then he cleared the passenger side seat, occupied by a few mismatched socks, a jacket, undies and a wool cap of bright colors. Alex was relieved that the undies were of female design. They all got flung into the backseat. The floor of the passenger side was piled with plastic wrappers and empty paper food containers of different description. Alex kicked them aside as he climbed in the little car,

"The car has a name." Karen stated.

"And what might that be, pray, tell?"

"White Trash, kinda cute huh?"

"Charming and appropriate."

Karen lived in a 2-bedroom duplex on Isabella Street, across the street from The Mothership, a rundown, low rent 6-plex. She had her horse staked out in the field next to the Mothership. Alex got out of *White Trash* and fol-lowed Karen into her house. Karen went to the stereo and put on an album, sat on the couch and opened a little wooden box. Alex sat next to her, won-dering just how soon he should move in. To his mind's way of thinking, he judged it best to play it cool. He squirmed to hide the boner taking shape beneath his jeans, apparently that mind was made up independent of his thoughts. As it turned out he didn't have to wait too long because Karen took him and his boner into the bedroom. She put one joint between her juicy lips, Alex lit it and she inhaled then passed it to him. They smoked it down to within an inch of it's life and Alex rolled a crutch for the finish. They started necking and rolling around on the bedspread and Alex found nipples the size of foam earplugs. He lightly traced circles around her navel with his index finger and then moved his hand down to a soft and curly patch of fur over her pubic mound. It was a delightful area and he lingered twisting little curls until he could resist no more. His hand moved ever downward to the fleshy folds of her vulva. He parted the fleshy lips and probed for the little knobby area of her greatest sensations and he manipulated the little knob delicately until it rose into a semi-hard state. Karen began to moan and writhe. Alex knew he was on the right track to please her, confirmed by a juicy secretion that wet the entirety of her delicious nether parts. Karen ran her long finger nails up and down the length of his man-stick, his nuts had long ago tucked up and retreated into hiding. Alex was so hard it hurt, his head was swimming and he was very high. If he was ever going to ejaculate prematurely this might be the moment. He also could not get over his good fortune to be next to her like this; the fact that she had chosen him to be her partner was a high water-mark in *his* sex life. Their gear started to peel off like banana skins. Pants hit the floor; undies got chucked. They slipped between the sheets. Naked at last and next to Karen! Oh joy!

What happened next was a trip to heretofore unknown sexual paradise, the only words to describe the rolling and tumbling of naked flesh. Alex tried to control himself, make it last, but their hips were rocking gently in rhythm, perfectly together in time and building to a faster and faster speed. Karen was there all the way and Alex could not hold out much longer; it was her hips rocking him to a climax, they were running the show. It built to a simul-taneous and spasmodic explosion, athletic in intensity with sweaty skin slapping and flapping like a flag in a windstorm right up to the conclusion, leaving a giant wet spot on the sheets as proof of their mutual joy.

"I never had that happen before; we both had an orgasm at the same time, wow." He fell back on the pillow, chest heaving in accordance with *Big League* protocol.

"No? Then you are welcome, Basic."

"Yeah, really. I didn't know what I was missing."

"I like your body, not an ounce of fat anywhere."

"I like your body; you're sexy and that's where that's at." Karen lit the second joint and passed it to him, both not speaking until the roach was set aside on the nightstand. Alex broke the silence.

"Wow." Alex was stupefied.

Nothing needed to be said. They spoke with their hands; caressing and tracing the outline of each other's features and eventually the genitals again. It was a prelude to round number two and this time it was all athletic all the time, no problem with making it last, quite the opposite. It lasted as long as they wanted it to, ending in the same simultaneous explosion over a towel covering the *wet spot*. Alex's mind was blown

"Karen, what just happened to me?"

"I don't know Basic, what just happened?"

"I never had sex like this."

"Well then, you just haven't been loved like you should; now you have."

"Yes, I have." From that night on he was a smitten kitten.

Meanwhile back at the pier, the word was that Benji and Bubba Shake wanted to sell their salmon boat, so Alex made a trip to Monterey to look at it. He found the boat in the marina, right in front at the base of the ramp walkway. It was a clipper bow with sweeping and graceful lines and new cabin, a different cabin design but in every other way it was a classic. Alex decided to call the phone number and ask a few questions. He had some ideas regarding what was needed to get him started; a good engine and an auto pilot, his needs were basic true to his nickname. He fingered the rotary dial of the pay phone to the prescribed number.

"Yeah, who this?" A man answered the phone; he had a thick Middle Eastern accent.

"I'm calling about the boat you have for sale."

That's good boat; I paid $5000 for new engine, you never have to worry about that engine, good for twenty years." Alex learned he was talking to Nabu, the owner who had bought the boat for his sons. He was a force Alex learned, an immigrant who came to this country to settle in Monterey. He opened a successful restaurant on Fishermen's Wharf. Immigrants work hard, they have no choice to do otherwise.

"I'd like to look at the boat, maybe take a ride."

"Look? Go ahead look, right in marina."

"I mean go inside and crawl around and if I like what I see, take a ride."

"You got money?" Nabu did not become successful by being anybody's fool.

"Yeah I got money."

"I want $6000, a deal for you."

"Before I buy any boat, I have to take it out on the ocean on a test drive."

"Okay. I send boys down to boat. They take you out. This is good boat, engine is new. Stay there and they be right down."

The boys appeared about a half hour later and they were not what Alex supposed them to be. Instead of plaid shirts and dungarees they talked like ghetto corner boys. Bubba was an older version, affecting the same slang as his brother. He did the talking as they walked down the ramp.

"We got our eye on a bigger boat. This has been a good boat for us but it's too small-we want something to chase albacore." He said.

Alex listened patiently as he crawled around inside, getting ideas and seeing everything through rose colored glasses, dreaming about what his future might be with this boat; boat buyers and lovers are blind to the objects of their affection. It's true: Alex was falling in love with the *notion* of his very own boat just like lovers fall in love with the *notion* of happiness.

"Let's take it for a spin, I like what I see." In fact, he saw only what he wanted to see, not what was right in front of his face.

The boat was noisy, cold and claustrophobic. The fuel tanks showed rust and the steering was rusty cable through pulleys. But the engine, just like the old man said, was new. What he didn't say was it was a new engine because the old engine had sunk with the boat in the marina. Just the same, Alex was thrilled with the pilot, hydraulics, and the exalted new motor that cost Nabu $5000, basically all he needed to launch his salty salmonosis dream. There was no navigation gear beyond the compass at the helm but that did not blunt his enthusiasm. The little boat was seaworthy and rode the gentle waves of Monterey Bay gracefully before heading back and tying up in the marina. Alex hemmed and hawed at the dock before he made an offer.

"I can give you $5000 now and another $1000 after the season." Alex blurted.

"We'll think about that." Bubba said. "We'll call you tomorrow."

Alex drove home, hoping that he hadn't queered the deal with his offer and thinking of the life ahead with his own boat.

The call came into the payphone in the living room at Sevilla West, it was Bubba Shake. "We'll take the deal. We'll drive up today. You got a boat. You give us $5,000 tomorrow, $1,000 later. See you at the pier around 1 o'clock." And that was how it all began.

* * *

Alex and his new boat pulled under the hoist at Romeo's Pier. Tony Romeo was like family and he had known Alex since he was a toddler in tow. His pier was a creosote domain of the Romeo family with a bunkroom, showers, shop, office and a kitchen upstairs where lunch was served up communally every day. It was as old as old-school gets, from another era. As a service, he had parts and gear the next day if you wanted when he came down from the City and on Tuesday it was fresh French bread from Boudin bakery at the Wharf. Alex listened with interest to the stories told by the old timers; the storms that required the barricades to close the buying station on the end of the wharf, swells that kept Tony from walking out on the pier, waves breaking under the planks of the dock. In the days before the breakwater Tony's pier rode out the storm just as the boats did. The boats were hanging on tenaciously to their moorings and the pier stood resolute as the breakers crashed against the pilings.

On this day Alex was checking to make sure he had everything right for his first day out with his new boat; tomorrow was the day. He was too dumb to know the risks involved, the unknowns that he would learn the hard way were waiting patiently for him. He had a running partner, Frank, who was up from Santa Cruz. He was a homeboy now back in his hometown of Half Moon with his boat the Rasher. His boat was the same size and type of Alex's boat, so he was a perfect match for a running partner. They untied the next day a little after daylight. On the way to the breakwater entrance Alex smelled acrid smoke, it was coming from the engine room. Alex opened the little door to the black hole, and it was filled with the acrid smoke of burning wire. He saw glowing wires and freaked out. Without thinking and in a panic, he reached in and grabbed a handful of the wire and ripped it loose. It stopped glowing but kept burning across the palm of his hand, leaving white tracks of burnt flesh. He kicked the boat out of gear and called his partner boat.

"Hey Frank." He said into the microphone, "I had a little electrical fire; I gotta stop and fix the wiring." They discussed it as they drifted in the harbor and decided that tomorrow might be a better day to start and so they went back to Tony's and rafted up by the skiff hoist. The next day went a little better, he at least made it past the breakwater entrance. He got all six lines in the water. With pride and expectation, Alex stared at the springs on the poles. Alex walked around, looking and making sure he wasn't sinking or on fire. Things looked all right so he decided he should run a line, a fishy thing to do. Unfortunately, it was the wrong kind of fish that he found on his hooks, hake right up to the insulators, every hook to the top. There was no market for his hake and so his catch of the day went floating with white and gold bellies up to the sun. The hake were unrelenting, the process of shaking hake off was repeated every time he ran the line. He worked feverishly to keep up. This was not what Alex had in mind.

"Hey Frank." He called into the microphone." You got a lot of hake down there?"

"Get out of that brown colored water, its lousy with the bastards, they'll bite the poles off." He said and continued, "The water down here is clear green and no brown-bombers."

Alex sped up and headed down the hill, vowing to himself not to run a line until the water changed color. He made the last 2 trays of his bait in the meantime. Frank's voice came over the radio.

"You got any flashers? Put those out."

"Okay. What color hootchie?"

"White with a red eye."

"I got tons of those." Alex said and broke out his 2 boxes of brand-new Abe and Al flashers and started attaching hootchie-cootchies, little rubber skirts that resembled little rubber skirts.

"Fuck it, I'll put 'em on every spread." He said to himself after the water cleared up. He ran the gear and all the spreads had hake: bloated white bellies and bucket-like mouths. He shook them off and put out flashers where there were once baits, he was now a *junk* fisherman.

"This is more like it." He mused to himself. At the end of the day he had 176 pounds of large and 38 pounds of medium salmon to unload. At the end of the day he put his catch in the hoist box at Tony's with pride.

"You got the knack kid, just like your dad." Tony said to Alex as he lowered the fish tag down on the string, clipped to a clothespin.

And this is how it all began for him. In the following months it was Frank and Alex at Half Moon, The Point and Bodega right up until the last week of the season in late September. In that week they were on their way home, the only boats anchored up at The Point. They talked it over the night before and decided that the next day they would set the gear below Chimney Rock and troll down to C Buoy. Then pick up the lines and run home. In the morning, they had no bites on the set nor for the next hour trolling down the hill toward home. Alex got his first bite an hour above C Buoy, then another and then another. He had straight bait out. More bites and more fish hit the deck. He called Frank and then rushed back to the pit to run gear and punch bait. The fish were following the boat and the lines kept loading up with big fish for the entire tack; there were 50 or 60 of them, more fish than he dreamed

possible. He had never seen anything like this, and he turned for the back
tack after an hour, hoping for a repeat of the first tack. But that didn't mate-
rialize-not a single bite did he have going back over the same ground that
had provided such good fortune previously. Frank didn't have any bites either
coming down the same track as Alex and it was over as fast as it had start-
ed-one tack. They went back and anchored up, Alex cleaned his fish and
covered them with wet sacks as he pondered selling his fish at the Point the
next day. Rumor had it that they stole fish and cheated on the weight.

"Hey Frank; how about you come on the boat tomorrow and watch the
scales when I go over to sell the fish here." Alex said into the microphone.

"Yeah, okay." Frank replied and the next morning they were off to the
Point Reyes dock, home of Point St George Fisheries. The buyer could not
have been more congenial and before long Frank and Ole, the plant manager,
were laughing and joking as they weighed up 750 pounds of large salmon.
Ole wished them well as they pulled away from the dock and gave them a
few loaves of French bread, urged them to come back soon. Alex put Frank
on his boat and before the hour was up, they were on their way home, two
days before the end of the season. Those fish were worth more than a thousand dollars and that was the number Alex needed when Nabu called the
very first day after the season ended.

"You got money for me? No money-no boat."

"I got the money."

"I send the boys tomorrow."

Stage One Salmonosis had set in; it would take 30 years, but it would
grow to Stage Four.

CHAPTER 8

Lost and Found

The Vietnam war ended, a US president resigned, shortages at the gas pump, economic recession, inflation, unemployment and a pardon of a disgraced president. These events hardly budged the needle on the dial of Alex's world. He went skipping into his future, oblivious to anything that wasn't floating or swimming, collecting good and bad habits along the way and embracing the commercial fishing life. He associated himself with a free spirited and rowdy gang of salty friends, having fun, and the money was just a part of the deal.

"Hey Frank, you gonna go crabbing with us this winter?" Alex asked his running partner after they tied up the boats in the marina. They had relocated to Ft Bragg after spending most of the summer in Northern California, fishing salmon and making mischief ashore. It suited them; they liked the blue-collar town, the cozy shelter in the river. The location on the California coastline was perfect for a salmon fisherman. It had been tons of fun all summer and plenty of fish every time they went out, but sometimes the fun took precedence and they didn't go out at all. Alex still lived in Half Moon Bay, but Frank had rented a place in town, putting down roots in the community; Frank liked what he saw thereabouts.

"I think so, we'll see, I'm looking at a few options here in town." Frank answered, non-committal was one of his specialties.

"Geno says October 15th for gear work. I'm gonna hang here and do some things to the boat before I go back home." Alex said.

"I'll give him a call." Frank said and Alex let that slide, not too confident that that was going to happen.

*   *   *

Groceries and a bag of ice for his ice chest, Alex was on a mission to the Fort Bragg Safeway market in town. He parked in the lot and walked in, grabbing an empty shopping cart. He wandered down the aisles, finding it an oddly pleasant experience, the piped in music in the well-lit aisles, the eating possibilities on display. He turned the corner at the tortillas and went down along the small ethnic food section. He rounded the end cap into an entire aisle of chips and soda. He scooted into the next aisle and came upon McElvie pushing a cart next to Anita. He immediately turned his back to avoid identification and to think fast. They continued down the aisle and disappeared into the frozen foods. "What's he doing here?" He thought. He turned for the checkout stand and the nearest payphone.

"John: I found McElvie up here in Ft Bragg. I saw him and Anita in Safeway."

"Did he see you?"

"No. Pretty sure I got out of the store undetected."

"You see the Black Moriah?"

"No."

"What are you doing up there?"

"I got a slip for the boat in the marina for the winter."

"I'll see you around soon. McElvie is going to pay."

"Good luck, I'll keep my eye out for him too."

"Do that." John said and hung up. He didn't waste any time formulating a plan and putting it into action. The first step was to make the long drive up the coast from Santa Barbara. He hopped in his van at 4PM in the afternoon and drove all night.

"Anita and McElvie, together again, a pair to draw to: a weirdo and a con-man." John muttered to himself.

* * *

John parked in the Safeway lot the next day and got a few hours of sleep. When he woke up, he bought a local newspaper and a cup of coffee in the store. As he sipped the hot coffee and looked through the classifieds, his eyes locked onto a little ad in the bottom corner of the page. It read:

"A Bed and Breakfast in Mendocino. Anita Sorenson, proprietor. 235 Mendocino Ave, Mendocino. 937 877 3201. Reasonable rates." A simple ad, a solid lead.

"You're gonna get what's comin' to you dickweed." John said quietly to himself and the newspaper as he glanced at the ad. "That was too easy; Anita is in business, McElvie is back at it sponging."

John got a pastry and a sandwich and headed down to Mendocino, intent on a stakeout at 235 Mendocino Ave. On the drive down John could see why people were moving here-it was beautiful. The rocky coastline met the shore that rose into wooded hills and mountains. The smell of trees was pungent in the moist morning air. Stately homes built during the lumber baron heyday dotted the coastline. John turned off the highway and onto the two-lane road headed into the town of Mendocino. Anita had purchased one of these stately homes situated right on the headlands at Mendocino Ave. John parked the van a block away and staked out the house, waiting for Jim McElvie to appear. In about an hour his patience was rewarded by the shaggy blond head bobbing out of the house and getting into a van. John followed the van as it wound through the damp morning streets and headed into the backwoods along Big River. They drove about 15 or so miles and John was beginning to question what it was that he was doing here, when suddenly McElvie pulled over into a dirt turnout and stopped the van. He got out, looked around and disappeared into the lush green underbrush. John exited his van and followed him through the forest. They both walked along a footpath at a distance from each other, the path barely discernible but trampled just enough to show use from footfall. John hesitated from time to time, looking through the underbrush to make sure McElvie was still up ahead. This went on for an hour until Diver John came upon a clearing and there was Jim in the center of it, surrounded by potted plants and rows of plants in the ground, bushy, lush, green and aromatic. McElvie was administering water and fertilizer from a watering can.

"So, this is what the fucker is up to here, it figures." John thought to himself. He turned and left undetected. It was trimming and harvest season for the new cash crop in the county-marijuana.

*   *   *

Alex took out his roll of quarters and stepped into the payphone booth. He had not talked to Karen in a while and he was thinking a lot about her lately, now that it was time to go home. He had a problem: he hadn't called all summer, now it was kind late for that but he better call her before he went back next week anyway. He dialed her number and with his ear to the receiver, he waited for her to pick up. Thoughts and excuses ran through his head, but nothing was settled. He was such a fool: it wasn't right to just call out of the blue.

"Karen? Hi it's me."

"Who's *me*?"

"Alex. You know, Basic."

"Basic! Good to hear from you. Where you been?"

I was kidnapped by pirates. No; actually, I been all up and down the coast. On the boat, fishing."

"Right, Basic, sure. That's okay. Ever coming back?"

"Well, as a matter of fact in about a week. I'd sure like to see you. I've been missing you."

"Oh? That's sweet. Well I'm right here; you know where to find me. I quit the Crab Cottage and I'm full time at the Bird-Box, you know, the Shorebird."

"You like it there?"

"Yeah. It's fun, a good crew from Southern California. I'm learning how to surf."

"How nice." Alex tried to hide his skepticism, doubts and jealousies. He didn't have a lot of use for this Shorebird gang or surf culture. "Who's your teacher?" He asked, dreading the answer no matter who was teaching her. Emotional masochism: it sucked him in, he waited for the answer to administer his verbal beating.

"Barry, he's a bartender here." She replied.

Barry Cardiff, the worst possible answer, a pussy hound through and through. He was a phony fuck with a phony laugh, an older dude who was tall, glib and good looking-Alex's worst nightmare.

"That's nice, well hey, in about a week I'll be home, and I'll look you up." He said with abrupt resignation, realizing where he stood with her and the mess he had made.

"You do that Basic, and don't be a stranger." She said.

"Okay, see ya later then." Alex hung up. He looked down at his broken roll of unused quarters. "Well that didn't go the way I hoped, Barry and surf lessons, a horror show. He mumbled to the graffiti on the dirty plate glass windows of the phone booth. He had hoped to confess admissions of mutual longing, the desire to be in each other's company. Wrong, that didn't have a snowball's chance and a booty call was not such a good idea.

"Well she did say it was good to hear from me, that's something," he thought, grasping for a lifeline. He tried to console himself, but the reality was that she was learning how to surf from the worst pussy-hound in Princeton-by-the-Sea.

"Don't be a stranger." His interior conversation continued like the whips on a flagellate back. He was his own worst enemy. He reached deep into his 'love-bag' and pulled out his go-to emotion-justified jealousy. He walked back to the boat with his little bag of groceries. An awkward reunion awaited in his imagination.

*   *   *

Diver John drove into town and tossed around a few plans in his mind; "What would really hurt this guy?" He thought. "Got to be something that hits that con man where he lives, real personal; he's got to feel the pain." After some thought John settled on a plan, and a few supplies would be needed from the hardware store. The next day he was back on the trail.

McElvie looked around to make sure no one was watching before he ducked into the weeds and out of sight into the underbrush. He walked stealthily along the path and took out his little MAC 11 machine pistol from under his coat and clipped it into his shoulder harness in the ready position. This was a dangerous business he was in: sums of cash were stolen, valuable plants could come up missing, gunplay and Rambo of the Redwoods. He bought this little sub machine gun t a gun show, figuring that 1000 9m rounds per minute would be enough lead and protection from any bad guys that might come around. Every other grower was armed to the teeth, why not he as well? It weighed less than 3 pounds and it had a 30-round clip. It made him nervous; the one time he practiced with it, it sprayed bullets wildly with surprising recoil, it was a handful and it was a very dangerous gun if you were on the wrong end of it. The trail showed no signs of disturbance, the woods were quiet, and the little death machine stayed dormant slung over his shoulder. Jim McElvie walked along slowly and cautiously. Back at the head of the trail, some 1000 yards back, John followed. It was about noon and the shadows were short in the dead silence of the woods. The sounds of a crackling stick under John's foot was amplified by the solitary silence. McElvie thought he heard the sound and this put him on alert, stopping his activity and momentarily listening. McElvie slipped off the safety on the little spitfire pistol. He was always nervous as a three-legged cat in roomful of dogs around the grow-site. Harvest time was here and there were plenty of stories of marauders in the woods; drugs, guns and cash. He arrived at his grow site and began the process of tending his garden, he would be harvesting next week and the sooner the better he felt. It was his first summer at this business; nervous, unsure, but the results were now in full bloom; ten potted plants and twenty giant plants in the well-prepared soil of the State forest. The clearing he made had an intricate set of PVC pipes leading to an uphill spring box that kept the plants well supplied with water 24/7. He had help from an experienced trimmer who trimmed his plants into bushes that were now 4 feet in diameter, oozing with sticky aromatic buds. His crop might yield $30k he was told. He warmed to that happy thought.

John continued to approach the clearing, drawing near, he wished he had a gun. What if Jim had one, what then? Things could go terribly wrong for him. It was starting to feel like a very serious business he had stuck his nose into. He should have thought McElvie might be armed. Would Jim really kill someone out here over these damn plants?

"His own mother, yes, he would." John mumbled silently.

Jim McElvie watered his plants, adding some fertilizer to the watering can. "They sure use up the water," he thought. Every day he gave them attention. Initially, he thought he could come out here once a week and then go back home, but he soon found out different. He had to spend a few hours each *day* out here, trimming, fertilizing; guard duty, thinking of theft and mayhem. Well, he was ready for that-if any fool might want to try and make trouble.

McElvie sat down with a sandwich and coffee at lunch time, it was nice in the woods, just trees, birds and bugs in the warm sun. Not a bad way to make a living, this is what he had in mind when he first looked out on the Mendocino coast, big money in the back to nature movement, that's the *vibe* he got when he looked out on the sedate old town. It sure beat the shit out of diving for pinks at San Nicolas Island at $8 a dozen. He finished his daily routine around four o'clock in the afternoon, packed up and headed down the trail whistling a tune and quite content with the days' work. Walking down the path toward home, his world was suddenly up ended; literally. A wire noose had tightened around his ankle and jerked him upside down, suspended by one leg from an overhead branch and the top of his head was gently kissing the ground. He pulled out the little MAC 11 and sprayed bullets in the air, in the blind. The whole clip was spent into the quiet air and trees in seconds, cutting down small branches and chipping off bark. Whatever was going to happen next did not-he just hung there upside down, spraying bullets until he had only one clip left which he held in reserve for whatever may come later. Blood was pounding at his temples, his ankle hurt, his inverted vision was making him sick in his stomach.

"Hey you bastard! I'll kill you, you son of a bitch! Come out and get what you got comin!" But no one moved or answered. An hour passed.

"Okay, I tell you what; you want money? I got money, just cut me loose and we'll split what I got on me, okay?" Not a sound was heard in reply. For another hour he shouted to the silent woods, woods that did not reveal their secret.

"You can have it all-how's that? You happy with that?!" He hollered to the trees. "You can't deny that's more than fair, God dammit. Just cut me down!" The exertion caused him to start puking his sandwich out onto the forest floor.

John walked back through the woods, got in his van and turned the key. He left the sanctuary of the woods that held McElvie and his secret garden, leaving the gardener suspended for the night by a tight stainless-steel cable. John was on his way to a cafe in town. He headed down to it to have dinner before he checked into his motel room for the night, secure in the knowledge that McEvie was on ice. He had a six pack and his favorite TV show was on, it was like a mini holiday and he was ready to rest up for tomorrow's chore. It had been a long day today and the overnight ride up here the day before was catching up to him. He slept like a baby that night.

Jim McElvie was getting a bit crazy; upside down in the dark, listening to the night creatures walk around. Dangerous business, he thought; he was in a jam, unable to reach the wire around his ankle and even if he could, then what? He couldn't cut himself loose. He couldn't holler all night; nobody was around to hear him anyway. He could die, he was fucked and he knew it. Who did this? Robbers? Bushwhackers? Killers?

Diver John woke up refreshed the next morning after a good night's sleep. He showered and had breakfast at the same cafe as the night before with the local newspaper spread over the counter.

"I see they're laying off people at the mill." He chatted up the waitress.

"Times are changing for sure." She replied in a dis-interested manner, instantly bored with the topic. John persisted,

"You are getting tourists up here now, though, B and B, whale watchers and such?" He said.

"Well yeah, but the real action is dope, the pot-growers. Everybody is getting in on that." She confided the well-known fact.

"Is that a fact, well what do you know about that? I suppose that's good for the economy, eh?" John said.

"Sure. But it changes the vibe. These kids came up here from the city, dug in and built a simple life in the country. Now, they grow dope and invite all the problems they left behind. It's money, drugs and guns out in those woods. More coffee?" She asked.

"No, I'm good thanks, I gotta go." John replied, payed the check and left.

It was time to go check on McElvie. John was confident that all was as he left it; old Jim was on ice. That wire noose around his ankle wasn't going anywhere but tight every time he wiggled. John parked the van and walked down yesterday's trail to the grow-site. As he got near the site, there was old Jim McElvie all right, still upside-down hanging by the tree branch, red in the face, passed out and grasping the little MAC machine pistol. John walked up behind him and gently relieved him of the weapon. McElvie's hand was limp and like a frozen claw around the handle. He did not move.

"Jim? You okay?" John said.

A thick voice answered, "Ut me down, ease, ut me down. 'M dying here."

John took a big white zip-tie and cinched it around Jim's wrists. Then he cut him down with a lineman's pliers, snapping the taught 1/8-inch cable. McVie collapsed in a heap with a muffled and guttural sound. "Uhh, ank ou." He said.

"Jim? I cut you down; you got money for me now?" John asked.

McVie began to focus. His vision, his mental state, his circulation in his ankle: it was all fucked up after spending the night in the woods. But vision and acuity were now returning. "Diver John?" he said.

"Afraid so you snake. I found you." John said.

"Please, don't, don't-don't shoot me; I got money right here, in my pack. Take it all, just don't shoot me" He said eyeing the Mac pistol in John's hand.

John took a fat stack of bills from Jim's backpack. "I should shoot you," pocketing the cash. "But that's murder; that's crazy. I saved your life once. Remember that? Then you betray me? We were partners, Jim. Is that how you do a partner? Temptation got you, you weak fuck? I guess you showed your true colors. I'm not gonna shoot you, even though you deserve it. But I am gonna show you something. Come this way." John said, leading the bound-up captive back to the grow-site. McElvie could hardly walk and John helped him along before sitting him down and zip-tying him to a sapling tree in the clearing.

"What you gonna do?" Jim asked with a tremble of fear and uncertainty.

John produced a fresh bottle of Roundup from the backpack and began to spray the buds.

"NOOOOOO!!" Jim protested helplessly, as he watched his summer project get the misty death sentence. John continued to generously douse every green and growing thing in sight. He used all four bottles before he was done.

John turned and spoke. "Sit here, watch your plants turn brown. Here's some water to drink, make it last a few days. The way I see it we're even now Jim. I really liked that caddy convertible. Consequences: the bill has come due. I don't give a shit anymore: it did bother me for a while that I let a cheap confidence con like you got the 'ups' on me. Hell, I thought we were partners, friends even, like brothers. I made it easy I guess, I trusted you and you turned out to be a prick. Now you just sit there and watch the plants turn brown and go to shit. And I think I'll keep this little gun; just hope that you never see it ever again, 'cause it'll be the last thing you *ever* see." John knelt alongside McElvie with the gun over his shoulder, water bottles and the big pliers.

After a bit John walked out of the site and down the trail to his van and off to Santa Barbara. A couple days later Anita got a letter in the mailbox at the Bed and Breakfast. In it was a note, a map and few of Jim's dirty fingernails.

*   *   *

Alex rolled into Half Moon Bay late, about 2AM. He left the boat in Noyo, winterized. He thought about Karen all the way home and he now considered, against all reasonable thought, of making a booty call, a manifestation of pure egomania with no connection to reality. He turned in at the light and kept on going past his house to Karen's. When he got there his heart sank-he saw that surfer-fuck Barry's truck parked in her driveway. They were in there stoned, naked, fucked-out and spooning, he knew it. Whether true or not, it was *his* truth and there was nothing he could do about that imaginary visual. He drove on to Sevilla West and entered the dingy, run down boarding house where he lived. The landlady Dorothy, who never slept, dominated the place at all random hours and was into her usual craziness, flirting, cackling, flying about the living room like the Wicked Witch of the West, going on about *the boys*. She called her tenants *the boys*, like they were subjects in her petting zoo. Alex went to his tiny room and crashed face down on his pillow.

The next day Alex had lunch, by himself, at the Shorebird and he made sure he sat at one of Karen's tables. She walked up and gave him a kiss on the forehead.

"Basic! Good to see you, you're back." She said.

"I'm back, I was gonna come see you straight off the road last night, but it looked like you had company." Alex was dour and moody in his reply.

"Now Alex, don't be like that, don't be a grumpy old Eeyore." She said.

"Well how am I supposed to be?" He said plaintively.

"All right, you're not happy, but what am I supposed to do, sit around and wait for a phone call from *you*, knitting a scarf? A phone call that didn't come I might remind you. I got a life too you know. Whatever disappointment you have is not on me-you stalker!" She had a point, bullseye. Expectations are always the mother of disappointment and he had plenty of both. He had no right to foster these expectations and he knew it. But he just couldn't help his sorry self from being pathetic.

"You got me there. Apologies. But I never once was near a phone out on the water. But I thought about you while I was out there. I missed you, honest." Alex said. That was lie, he was a party animal all summer whenever he got the chance, payphones were everywhere, and he had hardly once thought of her. "It doesn't look like you missed me much." He said pathetically like a Grumpy Old Eeyore.

"What do you know about how I felt? I'm just having a life here! You're just having a life just like me, don't lie! You want my future too? And by what right do you claim that privilege mister?" She stood with her hands-on hips, challenging him to reply. Alex was feeling sheepish, put in his place in short order, dispatched. She had him dead to rights.

"All right, you got me, I'm sorry, I expected too much." He said, looking down at his napkin.

She leaned over and kissed his forehead. "Let's start this thing over."

An intriguing thought, but it felt as though a little air had leaked out of his love-balloon.

* * *

The phone on the kitchen wall of the Skarsen home interrupted the racket of the vacuum cleaner. Olivia turned off the noisy dirt bag and went in to answer the little yellow device hanging on the wall. A voice came through the line, "Hi mom, I'm in Alaska." It was Leif.

"Wondered when I might hear from you. Is it cold up there?" She asked.

"No, it's 70 degrees outside; it's Indian summer up here. It rains a lot though, that's about it. I bought a boat." Leif said.

"Did you? Is it a nice boat?" She asked.

"Yeah, it's nice, it needs a little work of course. It's a seiner with a power skiff and nets too." Leif explained.

"Are you gonna be a seiner now and stay up there?" She asked.

It's an option, I guess. These guys are doing okay up here. They fish for pink salmon. First though, I think I might bring the boat down to Noyo to work on it over the winter." Leif said.

"Isn't that a long boat ride?" She asked.

"About ten days I guess, never been." Leif replied to his boat-savvy mother.

"Well, it'll be good to have you where we can see you occasionally. Alaska; it's so far away." She said.

"Yeah it is. It will take a little time to get down there so I should be on my way as soon as I do a few things on the boat." Leif said.

"Well you be careful and don't take chances with a new boat. Keep me posted on your progress when you can. I'll worry about you." She said.

"Don't worry, I'll be fine, and I'll call when I can. Bye Ma." He said.

"Bye dear, all my love and prayers." She said and hung up.

Leif threw the lines off from the Ketchikan fuel dock. It would take days of travel for Leif in the new boat, which he named the *Fin II,* honoring his father. The scenery down the inside passage was beautiful and more than a little boring after long days and nights. There were trees and wilderness, Indian villages, rock and water. Leif marveled at the vast size of this part of the world, it was an evergreen rain forest that went on and on, whose rugged isolation prohibited civilization. The vegetation overhung the shoreline, dense and impenetrable for humans but perfect refuge for bear, deer and all manner of wildlife. Distant glaciers could be seen on the Canadian mainland. Idyllic and placid coves were a frequent geographic feature and Leif occasionally made use of them as a resting spot. The waters abounded with prawns, crabs and fish. It was this land and sea scape that Leif watched for days as the water went by the windows of the *Fin II,* gliding down the smooth waters of the Inside Passage. He liked what he saw, he could live up here he thought. By the time he got to Bellingham he still faced the hardest days of travel in the open waters of the West Coast before he passed under the green bridge at Noyo. He should be home before Christmas though, notwithstanding storms and allowing for fair weather. At least this was his hope.

*   *   *

A little twin-engine plane followed the flight path along the Mendocino coast, a frothy fringe of foamy brine showed the way and clung to the shoreline below, a shoreline that rose abruptly to the tree covered coastal mountain range. Rivers punctuated the brief coastal plain and piedmont as the winding waterways emanated from the woods before spilling out into the vast Pacific Ocean. The view stretched up the coastline to Shelter Cove and the mountain range of the Lost Coast. The flat blue expanse to the west stretched to a watery infinity, to the south was the tip of Point Arena. Kitty Coleman was tall and trim, breasts the size of ripe peaches, 24 years of age, sharp, high cheek bones with a subtle spread of freckles across the bridge of her nose. Kitty Coleman flew in on an afternoon flight, returning home to Fort Bragg and it wasn't because she was homesick. Her brother picked her up from the little airport outside of town and they were on their way to their father's house. Kitty would be staying there for a while; she didn't know how long that might be. Her brother greeted her and gave her a hug. He knew the story from his dad, so he didn't pry with questions or go on about it. She had a whole set of freshly busted dreams and no clear ideas what might be next. Her fiancée had ended the relationship abruptly when secrets were revealed and she found herself with few immediate options, so she had decided to come home and sort things out.

They rode in her brother's pick-up truck and she gazed out the window in silence. She watched the familiar fields and houses go by, giving way to the little downtown and more memories from her childhood. They went by her old high school, the fire station, Racine's, the bridge over the harbor and finally the truck came to a small circular driveway lined with low bushes and cement walkways set in front of a single story ranch-style home, all manicured, sterile and displaying anal-retentive attentions and design. They stopped in front of the house. Kitty was not looking forward to this homecoming, but here it was. Her father lived alone after being divorced and he was the town warden for Fish and Wildlife. Unfortunately for Kitty, he brought his authoritarian demeanor home every day because he found it hard to separate his personal life from being *the warden*. She had rehearsed a few explanations regarding her circumstance but quickly gave up the idea because she didn't have the energy or the heart. Dad and brother knew the score; her busted pride need not be trotted out on parade with them.

The front door opened, and her father came out to meet her. He was tall and fit, 55 years of age, square of jaw and haircut, blondish, tan and stoic. He took comfort in the umbrella of law enforcement and his nickname around town was *the bronze statue*. He had a distinguished look and his expression was always stern; emotional was not his way of being. He opened his arms and Kitty did the rest; immediately going to him and embracing. She cried and briefly felt like a safe little girl; she was home. His green wool shirt smelled like his pipe tobacco and she buried her head between his shoulders and stayed there sobbing quietly.

"It's Ok, you're home now. That son of a bitch never was any good. You're way better than him, sweetie. Good things are headed your way now, you'll see." Her father was comforting, exactly what she needed. Warden Coleman had never liked the guy she hooked up with. He never knew him well but knew he would have liked him even less if he had. Kitty just remained holding onto him for a little while and she spoke while still snuggled against his green uniform,

"Oh daddy, it was bad."

"You're lucky to get out and away from that phony four-flusher, I say. You stay with me as long as you want, this is your home." Mr. Coleman held Lisa away at arm's length and held her in regard, looking at how his little tomboy had grown into a beautiful young woman. He was happy that she had come home, he wished she had sooner. She wiped her eyes, picked up her bags and walked into the house. Outside in the driveway her brother Roddy and her dad remained. Roddy spoke to his dad quietly.

"We didn't talk about what happened." Roddy said.

"You didn't have to, and we don't ever have to bring it up again. What's done is done. Good-riddens to the bastard. I goddamn don't want to know a thing more about it. I'll kill that son of a bitch if he ever comes snooping around this town, I swear it on your mother's grave. We're gonna take care of her 'til she feels better, I do know that. It won't be long before she's doing something to get her mind off of this." Her father's confidence in his daughter was resolute and certain.

"I know. She'll be set right soon. I got work for her if she wants it at the shop, welding work from the county, brackets and stuff. Boring, but it pays good." Roddy spoke.

"All right. Let's go in and fix some lunch, then I gotta go back to work. You see to it that she's got what she needs. Can you come for dinner?" Warden Coleman asked.

"Sure thing." He answered and they entered the house and closed the door.

Kitty walked into the bedroom that she occupied as a child and as a teen. There were mementos scattered all over the place. Team pictures from softball league, trophies, newspaper clippings, heartthrob photos, small bottles and little boxes. There was a leaf pinned to the wall with a small picture of a young man in the center. Yearbooks, old magazines, sports programs, medals and more sat upon the bedroom furniture that looked like it belonged in an oversize dollhouse. Her room was just as she had left it at 18 years of age when she went off for college. Being here now was like visiting a museum and she, being in the museum like a wax figure, would have to exhibit a wax-like smile on her face whenever her old high school friends came over to welcome her back.

"This is depressing." Kitty spoke and plopped her suitcase on the bed.

The next day she woke up in the little bed, in her little room, in her little town. She wandered into the kitchen and plugged in the percolator after measuring a few scoops of coffee into the metal basket.

"Do they ever clean this thing?" she wondered as she looked at the brown stained scum on the sides of the coffee-basket. "I guess filtered coffee would be too much to hope for." Roddy walked in.

"Morning Sis." Roddy poked around, taking a cup from the cupboard and fishing a spoon out of the sink and rinsing it. He sat himself down at the table and watched the glass top of the coffee maker. The water was bubbling up, but it was still clear.

"If you want it, I got work for you Sis, anytime." Roddy said.

"Thanks, I might take you up on that. I'm gonna walk around the old town today, look at the harbor."

"It hasn't changed much."

"Well that's okay too. Where's Dad?"

"Gone to work, he gets up early."

"That figures." She rinsed out a cup.

* * *

Alex was twisting stainless wire with a lineman pliers, Frank was paint-ing buoys. Frank was older than Alex and a Vietnam Vet, a fact that he never discussed and it was hardly a personality feature that you would guess. He was a cool breeze, calm and deliberative in his responses. His Norwegian heritage made him fit right in with the rest of the Scandinavians scattered through the population of fishermen. Being older, Alex looked up to him. He was possessed of a cool self-confidence and he seemed to have a way with women and Alex did not. The skipper, Geno, was welding the junker pots that looked like hell, but they still fished so they stayed in the string year after year, they never went away. Alex had names for some of them by now and Geno had enough of them to make a string and name them *the suicide squad.* They invariably ended up in 6 fathoms in front of the Klamath River, just daring the universe to stick them or sweep them away to the beach, but no, they always came back full of crab. Geno was savvy, about the best skipper you could work for and a pal who would involve himself in the capers that Frank and Alex concocted. The three of them were a unit.

There was splicing too, and plenty of it.

"Oh no, punishment duty." Alex groused to Frank as he looked over boxes and boxes of rope coils Geno intended for them to splice day after day. They were bound for Crescent City with Geno. Uncle Sig was going to stay home this year and not fish, Leif was running the new boat down from Alaska and Cal was going to hunt ducks.

"What's the deal with the rope?" Frank asked.

"The ropes have to be good just in case we get stuck in the mud." Geno told Frank when he complained about all the splicing they had to do.

"When are we going up there?" Alex asked.

"We'll send pots up on the truck as we get them ready and go by boat right after Thanksgiving." Geno answered. "We set the gear on December first."

Alex continued to twist wire and go through the pots, looking for broken meshes or stuck triggers-and of course the splicing. It was a day's long, weeks long chore. But it was a cozy family affair: Terry made lunch every day, Baby Matt and John were crawling about and Socks-the-dog ran around the stacks of gear. "Work expands accordingly to the time that is available," Alex read somewhere, and it seemed as if Geno lived by it. He managed to find things to do right up until Thanksgiving. But that was okay, Alex got into the swing of things.

When Thanksgiving rolled around Alex got up from the table after eating and went down to the boat and they put out to sea on a 40-hour trip with a load of gear on the boat. The weather was good, mostly. A slight southerly came up above the Cape and by the time they got to CC it peeked at about twenty knots on the stern. Alex never slept so much since his first season with Sig. He would get up to eat, walk around, take a wheel watch, check the traps on the back of the boat and then back in the bunk, the diesel droning on and on, lulling him into a state of sleep. They hoped to get to CC before the the the opener, set the gear, get more loads out and in the water. But at the last moment, laid plans went awry due to a strike; a strike over a dime, a strike that would keep them from fishing for no one knew how long. As it turned out, it lasted a long time.

"What? They voted not to go? Again?" Frank asked calmly from the motel room they had rented in Crescent City. That was two weeks ago. He patiently stirred his vat of Pepsi on his lap, trying to extract a black speck of unknown matter. It was the paper ice bucket originally filled with ice. Now it was a vat of Pepsi.

"Can you believe it?" Alex answered as he flipped through the TV channels, settling on a bowling show and reclining on the bed. 5 channels were all they got if you counted the fuzzy ones, and in any other circumstance bowling would not be in the running, here it was a strong favorite. They had opted to split a motel room at the Town House Motel after the first night that they were double bunked in the damp focsle of the boat. There were other fishermen in the rooms for the Crescent City crab season just as they were. Another homeboy, Lips, was the next door over. He was out in the parking lot painting his truck with Z-Spar and a brush, just like a boat. One morning Alex woke up and Lips had the shell of a radar dome on the top of the cab and the look was complete. They ran out of jobs to do on the boat as the weeks wore on and idle hands were indeed the devil's playground. Lips threw a pack of firecrackers in Alex's room one night and it melted the rug; Alex retaliated, crushing a glass stink bomb capsule in Lips room. The owner, Olive, would have none of that and she sternly scolded them. The Frontier bartender was on a first name basis and all knew what went with that. It was now the middle of December.

"This is going to go until Christmas if they don't vote to go fishing soon." Frank said.

"I'm not spending Christmas in this motel room, that's for sure, nothing against you." Stated Alex.

"No, that's out." Frank replied. "Are we going down to the Frontier again for dinner or what?"

"God that place is bad. That Orange Chicken: I don't think a Chinese person ever set foot in that place and if they did, they didn't eat the food, that's for sure. That Orange Chicken is like a big clump of pancake batter over a little nugget of deep-fried rat, dripping with sweet orange goo!"

"Disgusting." Frank said.

"Let's go to Jimmy's, it's more money but at least it's good."

"We're running out of places to go around here, places for everything."

"We did find the swimming pool today. That was a find." Alex said.

"That was the hot set-up there."

"They don't even have a movie house here for Christ sakes, how do they live?"

"I heard Victor set a pot in the harbor to get some bugs to eat, got 26 jumbos overnight right in the harbor. Some jumbo fry-legs would be a good change from this restaurant chow." Frank said.

"Or some crab spaghetti; butter and fresh grated Parmesan." Alex mused.

"You're killing me. How about cioppino?"

"With fresh garlic bread!" Alex chimed in with enthusiasm.

"Crab cocktail with red sauce!"

"Okay, we gotta do this: we'll set one trap in the harbor, they can't kick about that, strike or no." Alex reasoned.

Tempers were running hot and boats leaving the marina with gear was suspicious under the circumstances, especially if you were an out-of-towner. Threats turned into actions. A group of fishermen, out of patience, leased a hoist on the old pier across the harbor and intended to wildcat, market their own crabs and do an end-run around the strike. Well that did not set well with the association members when they got wind of that bright idea. In the night, they just drove a boat over and threw a chain around the hoist and pulled it over into the water. That sent a strong message.

"Victor did it, you'd think it would be okay for us to do it too? We just want to get some crabs to eat!" Frank reasoned.

That afternoon they went to the freezer and got some bait out and went down to the boat in the marina. Heads turned from the decks of the other boats as they walked by with bait-squid in their bait box. It got worse as Alex started chopping it. When Frank started the engine a few of the onlookers came over to the boat. Quite suddenly Alex wished he would have consulted Geno about this idea because what Alex thought was an innocent and fun thing was threatening to get sticky with the local gene-pool. Frank stepped out of the cabin.

"What's the deal?" He asked the crowd on the dock.

"You boys think you're goin' fishin' or something?" Said the biggest of the troupe from the dock.

"We thought we'd set one trap to get some crabs to eat."

"That might not be such a good idea, you might want to re-think that. Maybe everybody wants to get some crab and we'll *all* set one trap, what then?" Said a plaid shirt with a fat body inside of it.

"Well, I suppose we'd all have crab for dinner then?" Frank replied the obvious.

"I don't think so. I don't think *any* traps are gonna be set *anywhere*. Not until we get a market order signed and end this strike." The fat boy said.

"Well Victor set a trap yesterday." Alex explained.

"That's true and we talked to him about that. Now look what happened; you want to do it too, so it's just like I said. This could get out of hand and before you know it somebody gets a bright idea and comes back with no traps on the back deck. You better think again son." He said. It was sticky as flypaper, no doubt about it now. Frank shut off the engine and came back out of the cabin and this seemed to please the growing group of locals on the dock.

"Okay, you win, no crabs for us." Said Frank to the assembled crowd. "I think you best chuck the bait over the side Alex; the crab police are here, they busted us."

"Fuck you long hair." Said the fat-plaid-shirt guy. Frank went back into the cabin and came back out with the shotgun.

"Fuck you back fat boy." It had escalated just when Alex thought it was ending.

"You guys knock it off Frank!" Alex pleaded. Frank fired a round into the air and pumped the old Remington Model 12, chambering another round.

He had four more shells to go and he fired off another round and remained silent. The Remington was doing all the talking.

"I'll see you around town, this isn't over." The plaid shirt didn't have much choice but to leave. He turned and walked away along with the rest of his congregation.

"Well, I guess we won't be having Orange Chicken at the Frontier anymore Alex." Frank said.

"Geno will not be happy about this Frank." Alex said.

"Size 46 T-shirt and a size 5 hat, that stupid fat-fuck. His elevator didn't go to the top floor." Frank spit in the harbor.

"All the lights on in the house and nobody home." Alex agreed and added,

*   *   *

Kitty Coleman stood in front of the Union Department Store windows, all made up for Christmas with an electric train circling a paper mache snow hill dotted with toy houses and toy people in all fashion of activity. It jogged her memory back to her own childhood-Christmases were happy times. Not so happy today however, Christmas always provided a generous helping of mixed emotions and she was dealing with that feeling. While on the one hand it was the defining moment of merriment for children, for some older individuals all was not so joyful and triumphant. Sticky existential questions and *happy-not happy* introspection lay at the heart of it all. Kitty was forced to contend with this.

"The God damn nerve of that lying bastard." Kitty said to the little train going around the snow hill. "To come out of the closet and cheat on your fiancée all at once." Kitty spoke to the toy house on the snow hill behind the glass. The woman next to her shifted uncomfortably and ushered her small daughter abruptly away. Kitty realized her rude error.

"I'm sorry, please excuse me."

Kitty Coleman had been in a foreign country after finding out the lurid truth about her fiancée. A country in which she did not even speak the language, where she never seemed completely accepted. It was then and there that she formulated a hasty plan; go home.

Now here she was and it was Christmas time too. She wandered down Main St. toward her brother's place. She really did need to get herself together, end this constant introspection and scratching at her soul. Get a job and turn her mind off. Roddy's offer was generous, and the time was right, just the thing to do. She was no hotshot welder, but she knew she could weld a hundred brackets a week for the County. Piano was Kitty's thing, classically trained since childhood. She didn't feel like playing lately and she didn't have piano at home anyway, sold off after her father's divorce. She didn't have any money either, another depressing existential thought at Christmas; Christmas and no money were a bad combination. There were a lot of things she *didn't* have, and she was blind to anything good that she *did* have. She wanted to see the harbor today and she waited at the bus stop.

When she got off down at the Marina it was crowded. She saw her dad's truck along with many others parked in disarray. Something wasn't right and there was activity all around her; everybody was scurrying to do something. It did not take too long thereafter for her to see what all the commotion was about; the once safe and placid marina had torn itself apart and boats were floating free in a swift current that swelled and drained at the narrow entrance. It boggled her imagination and she was compelled to ask a woman onlooker,

"What happened?"

"Big incoming tide and a 25-foot swell. Surge in the river and a big rain run-off too. That big dragger on B dock was the first to go, broke off the pilings and then it was *Katy bar the door*. The dragger crashed into the dock behind it and snapped off those pilings. It was like a line of dominoes as the boats crashed into the docks behind them, docks kept snapping loose." She watched the scene and held a camera.

Kitty looked for her dad. Men everywhere were throwing ropes and the Coast Guard was running around in their little lifeboat lassoing the boats adrift in the current. Instinctively, she walked toward the largest group of men trying to secure the boats on C dock. Just up the road from the marina another emergency, of a personal nature, was occurring at the Cliff House Café. Alex was starting to sober up from a late night of revelry and sitting alone at the counter.

For young Alex on this morning, the bad part of his hangover was the self-recrimination immediately descending like harpies upon the opening of his scratchy eyes the morning after. Alex was vulnerable: his head hurt; his mouth was a dry lakebed hosting a caravan of pooping camels. His rib cage mysteriously hurt. The mystery of how that happened was unsettling, among the many unanswered questions about the night before, questions he did not really want to know the answers to. Alex sat at the counter while he slowly sobered up. He made the usual oaths to never do it again, fragile oaths that were doomed to be broken. Feeling this way, he had tentatively gone out in public this morning, *hoping* to not see anybody or find out anything from the night before.

Alex was in Noyo for the Christmas holidays to check on the boat before he went home to Half Moon Bay. The crab fishing scene was still unsettled in Crescent and the Association had decided to quit for Christmas and revisit the strike negotiations after the holidays. The stopover was intended to last long enough to just check on the boat and get his truck, but it turned out to be more. He decided to have *just one*, which turned into one after another, and another one after that with a group of fishermen friends he ran into uptown. It all began innocently enough at the Club Fort Bragg with lunch on a rainy day and then they went into the bar and had an Irish Coffee, as if that didn't count as drinking during the middle of the day. A quarter was laid down on the pool table. The balls kept getting racked all afternoon. So did the Irish Coffee's. People started showing up early off the rain-soaked streets and before long, everywhere in the dingy room was jocularity and friends, much carrying on. They were propelled by the Irish Coffee's into the night, carrying on merrily and they went right to the wall, teetering right on the edge like blue collar Humpty Dumpty's, right on up to closing time at the Welcome Inn.

Alex could not even stand the smell of alcohol the next day (Alex had not shed his amateur standing when it came to drinking excessively-the only kind of drinking he cared for), *hair of the dog* was synonymous with puking in the morning. Alex had to seek other hangover cures-like breakfast. He was now sitting at the Cliffside Café lunch counter staring at a plate of hash browns, scrambled eggs, bacon and a giant Pepsi with ice. The matronly waitress was not fooled, she sized him up in a New York minute, she had seen plenty of hangovers before in her time. It was late morning; the place was mercifully empty, and he didn't have to talk to anyone. The cafe was oddly empty in fact. Usually there were a few old timers or retirees who could drag morning coffee out until lunch, but not this morning. Today it was just him. The waitress resembled his grammar school principle and she approached him at the lunch counter now.

"Don't you have a boat down at the Marina?" She asked accusingly, as if he had been caught being naughty.

"Yeah." He answered as dull as the spoon he clutched.

"You better get down there, down to the basin." She was chastising him, and alarm bells went off in his head. He was outta there; up from the counter, out the door, into the truck, down to the harbor, mind racing, stomach queasy, brow sweating. He had not even asked her why, didn't have to. It was as if he already knew that the Gods had summoned forces against him and his wicked ways.

It didn't take long to see that it was just like the waitress said. There was a cluster of trucks, all willy-nilly with the doors wide open, looking like a flock of seagulls with outstretched wings. The occupants were scurrying to and fro on the docks and Alex saw that something was terribly wrong right off the bat: The boats of B, C and D docks were tied in their berths, but the docks themselves were loose and crashing into everything in their path. The pilings had broken off and sent them adrift at the mercy of the surge. It was chaotic. The men who were trying to secure boats would soon find themselves cut off and adrift and surging on little wooden islands. The Coast Guard was on scene but darn near overwhelmed in their attempts to lasso and secure docks and vessels. Engines were firing up all over the basin as the owners arrived. Diesels roared; thick blue smoke hung over the mooring basin like a summer cloud cover. The high tide was allowing the surge from the westerly swell to travel upriver to the mooring basin and it was more than the pilings could stand once B dock broke loose. It got bad quick. The mooring basin, heretofore a snug sanctuary from the ocean violence, was now unsafe. The surge came and went through the narrow marina entrance at a speed of several knots. The water outside the seawall would at times be visibly higher than the water in the mooring basin. This ebb and flow at the entrance would cause the water to boil and swirl in an unnavigable and narrow passageway at the marina entrance. Boats that were torn loose from the docks that got sucked out into the river currents were towed back into the marina by the Coast Guard surf boat, careening off the pilings as they brought boats back in tow. The freshet from the previous days' rain added to the speed of the river current as the water rapidly sought release from the narrow river into the broad ocean. If any boat got too far downriver there would be no stopping its demise in the open ocean. The water was now alive and had taken on a malevolent and threatening character. Alex located his boat to confirm that it was where he left it the previous day and after he was satisfied that it was safe on E dock, he joined the effort to secure those boats that had broken loose on C dock. The sight of swirling open water in the marina was unsettling and the men were wobbling on broken docks, throwing rescue ropes.

Kitty Coleman was there with her father on C dock. She had her hands full with the effort taking place and Alex joined them. Her dad was right beside her and he was cleating lines, throwing rope, giving instructions, organizing the rescue effort on the float.

"Cleat that rope off." He instructed as he threw the rope. Kitty grabbed the line and handed it to Alex. The Coasties had the other end cleated to their tow bit and they throttled forward, towing the end of C dock to a firm piling. The group worked together for over 2 hours until things began to settle into safety. The situation was aided by the tide, now ebbing and knocking back the surge. It was still a no man's land out in the river current, but the marina was returning to its placid former self and the broken docks were secured to pilings.

"Wow." Alex said to Kitty, who was standing beside him.

"Looks like we got it. Way to go Kitty-Kat." Warden Coleman used his pet name for his daughter.

"That was really freaky." Said Kitty.

"Hope my boat is where I left it still, I should go check the boat." Alex turned to leave then turned back around when Kitty spoke to him.

"You need a hand?" Kitty inquired, long straight hair, green eyes, tight body. Only a fool would decline.

"No, I'm okay, but thanks." He answered like the fool he was. He walked over to E dock, still hung over. Sick, shy and sorry.

Alex looked at the back deck of his new boat purchased a year ago, it was bigger than his Monterey. In his mind he would map out projects for his boat, as if the boat spoke to him, requiring that he think about projects that he would undertake in the months and years ahead. He had some definite ideas; he could see how things might be. It was like a vision-the fashioning of his new boat. It played in his head like an old movie that he never tired of seeing, constantly entertained by the notions. He snapped out of his boat dream and lapsed back into the reality that he was a lonely bachelor who just turned down an offer from a good-looking woman. He came to his senses. What was he thinking? He better get to her before she gets away. He ran until he was out of breath.

"Hey, you wanna go get some coffee or something?" He asked the impressive backside figure of Kitty Coleman, tight Levi's stalking through the parking lot with long-legged strides and switch-y hips.

"Sure." She replied, turning back around.

They went up to the Cliff House. They sat in a booth; Alex searched for a conversation opener that wouldn't expose his stupidity right off. The search failed. "So, your dad's the game warden?"

"Afraid so. Ever give you a ticket?" She asked smiling.

"No, no. I'm not from around here anyway. I was just wondering; The two of you seemed pretty close down there on the dock." Alex explained.

"Yeah, well, that's us I guess." She replied.

"You work here in town somewhere?" Alex said.

"No, I been away. But now I'm back. I got a job with my brother; he has a fabrication shop uptown." She said.

"That's cool, where you been? You said you been gone, where?" Alex asked.

"Overseas, France. I was studying piano there." she answered. "I was engaged too." Alex picked up on *that*, operative word - "was".

"I never have been engaged." Alex said. His afterthought told him he could barely navigate a girlfriend after a night or two. "I had a girlfriend, but we broke up." That was a safe lie.

"Why'd you break up?" Alex was hoping she wouldn't ask, but of course she did.

"I caught her in bed with another guy." Alex admitted Barry's truck in Karen's driveway: not exactly a break-up, not exactly his girlfriend either. But Alex was thinking that it might elicit some sympathy, it did.

"That's an ouchie. Same thing happened to me. Except I caught my boyfriend in bed with another man." She said.

"Christ-on-the-cross! Your fiancée was *queer*?" Homophobia warning lights went off in his head. Kinky was scary; bi-sexual be-devilment! Heterosexual sex was scary enough as it is!

"You got out of there for good reason!" Alex stunned, exclaimed.

"Yeah, he was a lying shit-head as it turned out. The bi-sexual thing was confusing too." Kitty calmly and frankly explained.

"Yeah, I bet it was, for reals." Alex settled, wondered where this conversation was going to go; he knew nothing about scary homosexual lust. He knew a lot about heterosexual lust? In fact, it was a special talent of his. Kitty Coleman continued.

"Here's the thing; you look for honesty, the real deal, it feels good to be able to be real with somebody. You begin to emerge from the lonely wilderness. You trust them and that feels good too. You have a few laughs and that's sexy, they get the joke. A whole new wavelength opens up and before you know it, you're smiling at a bright future and surrounded by a golden glow. You are rushing headlong and telling yourself you're in love with the person across the table; sexy, charming, funny and the best thing since sliced bread. Does that sound about right?" Kitty Coleman finished with the question, raised her head and leaned directly into Alex's face. Her green eyes pierced. As far as Alex was concerned, she just put words to what he always imagined love to be once you got past the hard-on.

"Yeah, that's about right." Alex said. She went on,

"Then one day there is a distance between you, an emotional gap. That wavelength of communication, that closeness is not there, you haven't a clue why. Mysteries enter the relationship." Alex was not expecting this level of *real*; he had just met her for coffee. Did he have to be this *real* to keep up his end? Naked honesty was not his comfort zone! He had to play along.

"Is that why you left and came back?" Alex asked.

"Yeah. It was bound to happen I guess, sooner or later. I started having to overlook things, little things he'd say or the way he would say them, or the way he would talk down to me. His friends thought they were smarter than me and they were just a bunch of pretentious phonies anyway, always name dropping; people, books, places-that kinda stuff seemed to be the only way to score points in that crowd. Then the big surprise came, the sex thing, that broke it." She said.

"Wow. Weirdness." Alex said, it was his turn to be real now. "My fantasy is to find a girl who could share my boat dream. Fishing is what I got goin' on, it's what I want to do. Some women step on the boat, I start talkin' about fishing and they just look around and want to know where the toilet is. When I tell them it's not hooked up, that's the last I see of them."

"How do you live without a toilet?" She asked.

"It's a fair point; I'm starting to see that now. But there are ways." Alex replied.

"I don't even want to know." She replied.

They talked into the afternoon, sitting in a booth and drinking too much coffee. Alex started to get ideas. Among some of his depraved thoughts he wondered what she looked like under her clothes, but the predominant thought was that she was a classy and smart girl.

"I have to get back, it's getting late." She declared.

"Me too; Let me give you a lift. I should secure a few things on the boat before I hit the road for home." Alex stated this as they got up and left, they were the last people left in the late afternoon café. They climbed in the cab of the truck and drove uptown, moving under the red and green garlands that spanned the streets from the light poles and passing by the decorated store-front windows.

"Christmas." Alex said.

"Yeah, joyful." Kitty followed.

"And triumphant." Alex added.

She shot him a look. They were on the same page, no small connection. It did not go unnoticed by Kitty Coleman. Alex wanted to say something before he dropped her off, but he couldn't think of the right thing to say. She instructed him to take a right at the next stop sign, time was getting short for Alex to make a move.

"Well hey, it's been great talking to you this afternoon." He said.

"Yeah. Thanks for the lift." She said.

"You know, I was watching you down at the dock." Alex started, not knowing where he was going but trying to get to a compliment. He just had to let this girl know he was interested in getting to know her and then having sex. Or vice-versa.

"Oh yeah? What did you see?" She wondered.

"Well, I saw a woman who knew what to do, capable you know." He said.

"Is that all?" She left the door open.

"Okay, here it is. I want to see you again, I like you. You are attractive-in the extreme; anybody can see that from a mile away and that guy overseas is the biggest fool on the planet, not to mention the fact that he has a deep sexual confusion. He let the best thing he'll ever have get away." Alex said.

She wrote down her phone number on a scrap of paper as the truck pulled in front of her house. She leaned over and gave him a peck on the cheek and handed the scrap to him and instructed.

"Here's my number; use it. You're sweet."

That was how it began. Alex had just met the mother of his children-to-be.

CHAPTER 9

Changes

"Well that's the end of this fishery." Uncle Fred stared out into the night through the pilothouse windows as he spoke into the VHF microphone.

"Whaddya mean by that?" Came the reply over the VHF.

"There's a guy out here with a set of amber lights. That's all we need; now we get to fish around the clock." Uncle Fred replied.

"You don't have to fish day and night just because he does." Another VHF replies.

"Oh yes I do. And you will too. More traps and a bigger boat from here on out. 1977; mark it in the book." He said.

"I don't know, but lights sound like a smart idea, a way to up the production. Not a bad thing." Geno said on the VHF.

"It's a big boat fishery now. They'll come from all over with 1000 traps." Uncle Fred said. "It's gonna be a short season. A mop-up operation-mark my words on that. Flood the market and no more strikes."

"Amen to that. No more strikes are okay by me." The reply.

"We'll see about that." Fred signed off.

They went fishing when the strike ended on January 26 and they got their 65-cent asking price. They also got a 2000 lb. a day limit. Fortunately, the crabs did not go anywhere during the 7-week strike, there were beau-coo crabs from 25 fathoms in and 2000 pounds came in the first fifty traps. They would fill their tank and unload their limit plus a limit for a partner boat while he went home and so it went all week. Then, in the next week the same would be done for them while they went home. 2000 pounds a day for everybody. It would prove to be the last year of gentleman fishing and nobody got rich, but everybody did well. It was the end of the crab strikes, from here on out they would take what they were offered and go on opening day, hoping to make it up in volume.

When April was on the horizon, most fishermen's thoughts turned to salmon fishing, scheduling haul-outs and tying up gear. May 1st at the lightship was the main event and the April 15 opening day in the southern sector was an opportunity to shake out the bugs and sometimes there were even some fish around Pigeon Pt. A certain amount of boat pride was in the air and the dings and bleeders gave way to fresh paint and clean lines in the marinas

Opening day for Alex was at home in Half Moon Bay of course. He ran south southwest to forty fathoms, just as boats had done for years before him on opening day; to the Deep Reef they went, slowed the boat, set the gear and trolled down the hill toward Pigeon Point. It was good to be out again; the rafts of Murre birds called out in the distance, the mothers to chicks would call and the chicks would answer. The smooth water under foggy morning gray skies, the smell of salt in the air and the expectation that any minute the springs would pump; this was the sublime tension of the early morning in the trolling pit. Alex punched hooks into baits and occasionally glanced up at the poles as he did so. The racket of the deck speakers added to the scene. No bites....

He did get a bite eventually and it perked him up. As he trolled through a tide rip the starboard bowline started to pump. The action of the spring was an event; Alex watched the action until the spring went still once again. His peripheral vision was on high alert for more spring action on the other side and before long, the port main line spring began to pump. Renewed hope; another possible. He put the bowline gurdy in gear and rotated the hydraulic valve to begin the slow ascent of the line. The ring-stop and insulator had kelp and he cleared it without stopping the upward progress of the line. He unsnapped the limp leaders until he came to a line snap that was rigid and pointing away from the boat. The leader was tight, and he could see the dark green spotted back of a salmon trailing off to the side of the boat. He unsnapped the snap from the stainless cable and re-snapped it to a short piece of tuna cord. This was a peak moment; he played the fish slowly and carefully, not wanting to 'horse' him in and not wanting to lose the first fish of the day in his anxious anticipation. He gauged it to be legal by the pull, so he made sure his gaff was in the ready position, ready for the conk and the quick pick on the fish's head. The 18 foot of leader was carefully played in until the salmon was in range of the gaff and in a docile state as if waiting for a conk on the head. Alex made a short stroke with the 36-inch wooden gaff, squarely bopping the fish on the nose. It laid flat, momentarily stunned. Alex rotated the gaff round and sunk the pick into the head of the fish and lifted him aboard into the designated landing area. Still under the influence of the stun, the fish lent himself to de-hooking as he lay limp within the deck checkers, out cold. Alex had 1 fish for the morning, the first fish of the season and it never failed to be exhilarating, opening day or any other day. Just what was it about catching a 10-pound fish that caused elation? Who knows, but it was always a boost.

For one thing, it was primal; men had been catching fish since they walked about in search of food; hunting, gathering and trapping-their existence depended upon it and by now it might be in the DNA. Catching a fish required a focus of the mind if it was to be successful and anything less than 100% focus risked failure. The distracted angler who turned to look away or to listen elsewhere, the hunter who hesitated the shot, both risked failures. Complete focus was part of the attraction and only two things in the world mattered here: the angler and the fish. It was satisfying when the fish hit the deck. What other explanation was there for the joy to be found catching a fish?

Alex ran the next line and repeated the process. He only wanted more fish; he never did the math that quantified the catch into dollars, but poundage and the fish body-count were the signifying thing. The satisfaction of money would be delayed until he held the fish ticket receipt in hand, pounds and price spelled out in black and white, documented and on the books. The fish were not sold yet anyway, they were just captured. You would never hear him say he had $200 worth of fish, that sort of talk was reserved for the Okies.

"Alex, I got two fish, what's going on with you?" Frank's voice came over the radio. Alex grabbed the rope on the end of the boom and pulled himself out of the trolling pit, walked into the cabin and answered.

"I got two fish Frank, a small and a large." He replied.

"Let's keep going down: I hear these Moss Landing guys on channel 7 and it sounds like they are catching something down there. No scores. I do know they came out of New Year's this morning." Frank said.

"Sounds like a plan, ah-be-out." Alex said and returned to the pit. He overhauled the gear; most of his baits were untouched and he had a few spinning rock cod on the bottom spreads, that was all. For at least an hour they trolled towards Pigeon with nothing happening.

Frank broke radio silence. "Rigor mortis of the sticks, nothing doing." Reflecting his boredom and complete lack of activity beyond the cabin door. Alex could hear him eating between words.

"Same deal here, nothing. Can you still hear those guys below us?" Alex wondered.

"Clam-City, no word. Kinda suspicious." Frank answered.

The boats in question were the Moss Landing gang. These boats were primarily albacore boats, but for the first 2 weeks they could be found at Pigeon Point and after May 1 they were at the Lightship in Eureka. They were a close knit, independent lot, famous for their ten-day ice trips. They did catch a lot of fish-they were tried and true excellent fishermen, but they were scorned for fishing during a strike one year, yet simultaneously revered for the large amount of fish they unloaded. They always unloaded in Moss Landing in April, Eureka in May, unwelcome in Half Moon.

The morning fog began to lift, and Alex looked in at the lighthouse named after the famous wreck of the schooner Carrier Pigeon in 1853. It stood to reason that there would be a wreck on that point of land eventually; it swept away from the shore and extended far out to sea from the southern approach, the same approach that the Carrier Pigeon made as she tacked for San Francisco in the fog with her cargo bound for San Francisco. But instead of landing her cargo on those busy docks, the cargo that went around the Horn landed on the shore of Pescadero. It made the farmers happy; they loaded the wagons with whiskey, lamps and soggy new furniture.

Alex could now see the little fleet below him, and he adjusted course to the outside to intersect amongst the middle of the pack. Also, visible now were the thousands of Murre birds gathered in rafts, flapping, calling out with their signature cackle and diving. Cormorants and pelicans were making their descent below the water's surface as well, both in pursuit of the abundant baitfish. Alex had the feeling that this was the spot. The birds thought so.

He got a bite on the starboard bowline and then another on the port bowline: he waited. He got a bite on the starboard mainline and he punched up a few more baits before he ran through the gear. As he waited the starboard bowline started pumping again. In anxious anticipation he pushed the brass gurdy handle forward and started the line up to the surface. The second leader ran tight away from the boat and he took another off the bowline and thought this was newsworthy; he walked up to the cabin and the radio to report.

"Hey Frank? I just took two off the bowline and I got two more lines shaking." He reported.

"You're in 'em, nothing yet over here. I think I'm in too close, I see you and the Mossbacks, I'll tack that way." He replied.

"Good, yeah. I got my bites after I went through these birds out here; they're everywhere, making a racket." Alex said and added, "The fish are right on top."

"Ahgee, see ya" Frank signed off with his okay.

Alex came on the fleet below the lighthouse. He also came on a few cat-paws of breeze that soon after turned into about ten knots of northwest wind. The clouds scudded away, and the sky was blue as the wind came off the top of the cloud cover. From where he was and from what he could guess by the boats, the heart of the tack was below him yet. He was getting a few bites on the way down and the closer he got to the boats the more bites he got. He was now going from side to side, clearing the lines and putting them back out with fresh baits, adding fish to the morning score of two.

"Frank-I caught a half dozen fish out here by the boats. I think this is the spot. I'm cross-tacking these guys so I'm going to fall in line with them and go up and down." Alex reported on the radio.

"Okay, keep getting 'em, I'll keep coming your way." Frank replied.

Alex ran the dog lines in after he straightened out with the boats. A couple of salmon came spinning to the stern, dead from the wait to be boated. He added them to the pile. As he kept going down the hill towards New Years, the wind kept increasing. He turned around and started back up the hill. This place was a notorious spot for wind and today looked to be no exception. Usually by the time you got down as far as Davenport it was a horrible wind-blown mess where Alex did not want to be, so he bumped is way back up towards the lighthouse, getting the occasional bite along the way. He let them soak and cleaned his fish.

Alex had a string of pre-sharpened knives to work with and cleaning was his second nature. The gills came out with the first crescent-shaped cut on either side of the gill plates. The next two cuts inside the collar separated the entrails from the body. The guts were then gripped and pulled loose, leaving no bit of entrails inside. Next was a shallow cut down the spine, cutting the viscera over the kidney, a kidney soon to be scraped clean of blood with the special spoon on the back end of the knife. With the back of this spoon he pushed on the blood veins in the belly flaps to squeeze out as much blood as he could. Then he rinsed out the belly with the hose. It was automatic and quick. All the while during this process he would look up at the poles for bites and look ahead for boats. When he had all his fish cleaned, he ran the bows and mains at the top of the tack, turned around to go back and then ran the dog lines after the turn. As the dog floats passed the mainlines, he got another bite on the bow. He got 10 fish going down, turned around and bumped his way against the wind chop. Alex couldn't help but notice the wind increasing, but mostly he noticed the rate at which he was going through trays of bait. Around 2PM he began to think of the lengthy run home to unload because he, like many others, was a day-boat that unloaded fish every day. These Mosslanders he was among would anchor up at New Year's Island and ice their fish and unload 10 days from now.

"Frank, what's doin?" Alex asked.

"Nothing doin, they quit biting." He replied.

"Wanna stack 'em? We got a long run to get back." Alex said.

"Ready when you are."

"Okay, let's do it."

Alex began coiling the monofilament leaders carefully in their place. He had 2 fish on the haul out so that was a happy thing. The stabilizers hit the deck and Alex throttled up, adjusted course, engaged the pilot and he was on his way home. After he got above Pigeon the wind quit and he was able to relax and watch the water, looking towards the shore for landmarks and other things to break the boredom of travelling at 7 knots. He had a loran to fix his position on the chart. A loran station on Pt Arena and a station on Pt Concepcion put out radio signals and the lorans counted the microseconds between radio waves to establish a position, it was fairly accurate. The fathometer was an integral part of his navigational instrumentation as well. It looked about right, it put him just above Pescadero and the depth sounder showed that he was in 26 fathoms. He put a little push pin into the chart at his location. He had a DF also, a direction finder. It all jived; the visual, the loran, the DF and the fathometer. This was his location for sure. He arrived back inside the jetty around 6 PM, pulled up the poles and went into the dock and Tony the fish buyer threw him a line. It had been a long ride home, and now, all he could see were the faces of Alvin, Clyde and Tony looking down at him. The fish box was being lowered to transport his catch up. It was a heavy thing made of oak and iron. Alex had to bring it in for a landing on the deck without damage to the boat. After doing so he took off the wet sacks covering the fish and transferred them from deck to box. He sent it up, it held about 250 pounds and he still had a few more on deck. The box came down again and he got the last few off the deck. Wow, he had about 300 pounds on opening day.

"Way to go kiddo." Tony was the fish buyer; Alex grew up on his dock and it was a satisfying feeling to be here, as if all was right in the world and he was where he belonged. Now was the time to do the math: $1.35 for large, $1.15 for mediums and $1.05 for smalls and a buck for silvers, of which he had none, a grand total of $312.50 for the day! Big fun and big money in fishing.

After he unloaded, he had to park the boat. "I'll throw the anchor and back into the dock Frank, you can side tie to me." Alex said to the microphone. Frank was unloading a similar catch.

He threw the anchor and backed into the dock, threw a line around the piling and adjusted the tie-up line so he could reach the ladder. After looking around the engine room he shut off the engine and he could hear the pervasive silence. The tension in his shoulders relented.

It was an auspicious beginning to the season, a season that would run a full 6 months. It was an existence without the thought of an end, unconfined by the boundaries of time. There was slack time to have adventures during that 6 months and stories would be told at the end of it all. To miss getting in on a bite did not cause undo anxiety; if you didn't get them today, you could get them tomorrow; or even next week or next month for that matter. There was plenty of opportunity to make your season and have a social life at the same time. It was not unusual for fishermen to just tie up the boat before the season ended because they had caught enough fish and just had other things they wanted to do. There were lots of different ways to go about getting your share during the 6-month period and the easy life seemed to attract lots of different types of characters: fishing offered a rich life. It was entertaining and adventurous to be a fisherman, a way of life, much more than just a way to make money. Somehow the money seemed secondary, a thing that invariably just took care of itself by the end of the season and nobody expected to get rich doing it. The season always coasted to a relaxed and pleasant end in a cozy spot where *gentlemen fishing* was the rule.

For now, Alex took advantage and was grateful for the ongoing bite at the beginning of this season. In fact, he was fired up with anticipation of tomorrow as he punched up a half dozen trays of brined baits and mixed up another batch, awash with the warm sweet water of hope. A large boat was next to unload and it pulled under the hoist. Frank and Alex were curious, so they went up to watch him unload. To the surprise of them both it was Vernon Vilichek.

"Vernon; long time no see." Frank shouted down from the dock.

"Where you been?" Alex joined in.

Vernon had showed up under the hoist to unload fish from his 48-footer, a far cry from the little Monterey he was last seen on here. The last time Vernon pulled under the hoist at Half Moon Bay he approached with the trolling poles down. A small detail that did not go unnoticed from a shouting and screaming group on the dock, trying to make him aware and wave him off before disaster struck his cute little Monterey fishing boat. Every time thereafter when Vernon's name was mentioned that story was told. It became the signifying thing of Vernon, giving him the nickname *broke-stick-Vilichik*-there was no slack for anyone perceived as a fool. Among the witnesses on the dock that day were Alex and Frank. The poles notwithstanding, Vernon invited ridicule to his constant posturing, thinking himself better and smarter than the rest. Of which he was smarter in some ways but had proven not so smart in others. He was a college boy who had passed the bar exam but he chose to live among the blue collars in life. He had declined to join his father's law firm, electing instead to be a fisherman and that shoe fit a little bit tight. He wanted to fit in but was destined by fate not to. He struggled with that and he struggled with a rebel-against-father-thing as well. Everybody could just tell he was a misfit. Back in the day when he approached the dock with the poles down, he proved himself in front of God and everybody, unjustly marking him forever as an idiot. Vernon now looked up at Alex and Frank and answered.

"I moved to Washington, bought this rig." Vernon answered, pointing at his boat

"Well, you're a long way from home down here. No fish up there or what?" Alex asked

"Season is closed; the State cut it in half ever since the court decision. You'll see, it will affect the whole coast, sooner or later." He replied.

Alex thought this as just more sour grapes from Vernon. The guy was gloomy.

"What's this court decision Vernon, what's that all about?" Frank asked.

"A judge ruled in favor of the Indian tribes, giving them the rights to half the fish, honoring a treaty from 1842. Judge Boldt decided it. That means it's the law and you can expect other tribes with treaties to get in line for their share the same way-and soon." Vernon replied.

Frank looked at Alex and spoke, "You hear anything about this Alex?" Alex nodded his head no. Alex remained silent, he had nothing to say or add to this doomsday tale. He didn't believe it. He turned and walked back toward the boat.

"See ya later Vernon."

"See ya later Alex, good luck." Vernon said. And that was the last time Vernon Vilichek was seen unloading fish anywhere.

"Same old Vernon, that guy never has a good word." Alex said to Frank when they got back to the boats.

"I hope he's wrong about that bolted guy and his Indian pals." Frank seemed a little out of joint with this message Vernon brought down from Washington.

"I wouldn't worry about it Frank. It is too stupid; it is so typical of Vernon to say something like that. It's unthinkable actually, a doomsday scenario?" Alex was dismissive of such an outrageous claim.

"Yeah you're probably right. All the same, keep your powder dry. If half of what we catch is taken off the table, it doesn't leave a lot." Frank said.

"10-4 good buddy. Let's go eat." Alex replied. He was just getting into the swing of this lifestyle and he liked it, he couldn't fathom the government taking half the fish away.

"How about the Crabby Cottage before we hit the rack?" Frank suggested from the pit of his boat, tied next to Alex, his hands dripping from the brine bucket.

"Sounds good, I'm done over here, I got enough baits made up. I'm ready." Alex answered. He was still pensive, disturbed by the news from Vernon. It was a dark cloud over his otherwise joyful day.

Within two years the Klamath Management Zone was established in Oregon and California and salmon fishing was under Federal jurisdiction due to treaties signed with the Yuroks and Hoopas long ago on the Klamath River. Half the season was taken away and boats were never allowed to fish at the Lightship, Crescent City, Blanco and all points in between again. Vernon had been right.

* * *

It was a short ride through town; they parked and walked in the front door and sat down. Alex was facing the table reserved for the help and he couldn't help but think of all the days he sat at that table talking to Karen. Right now, he locked in his focus on the shaggy blond-haired fellow at the table across the room: it was McElvie. No sooner had he spotted him did McElvie get up and walk toward him, Alex looked down at the table. He didn't want anything more to do with this criminal.

"Hey kid. I thought I might see you here someday. Where's your buddy John?" McElvie stood over the table edge, questioning Alex like a cop. There was no friendly 'hello' or anything like that.

"I don't know. Last I saw him he was going to look for you and that was a long time ago." Alex thought he better get ready for this to go south.

"Well isn't that a coincidence, I'm looking for him too." McElvie said, smiling with obvious psychopathic sarcasm.

"I bet." Alex stated.

"You know anything about that, kid?" McVie was not at all friendly now, he got serious and his brow furrowed as he stared down at Alex. Frank had been quiet throughout, waiting to see how this was going to play out. He now stood and got into the conversation.

"What we know and what we don't know isn't for *you* to know." Frank said in a calm and steady voice. This was the voice he used just before a hay-maker was on the way.

"I don't know nuthin' 'bout nuthin.'" Alex said.

McElvie just stood there silent looking from one to the other, regarding the situation at hand. "Okay friend, keep it friendly, keep it friendly." He said with a big smile. "No need to get an attitude. Just wondering is all. Tell John I said *Hi*. See you around." He walked out the door.

"I seen that guy before. I don't like him." Frank confided.

"He burned me. Burned the guy I worked for bad. He's a con. A snake." Alex said.

"He's also a dope grower or a dealer; that's what I saw from the people he was with back home. He hangs out at the Mendocino Hotel bar; seen him a couple a times." Frank said.

"The guy I worked for had a scam going and McElvie was a part of it, we trusted him. It was all buddy-buddy-like until it came time to divvy up, then he vanished with everything. Took a dixie. Flat out stole it." Alex explained. "I did get my end, but it came from John's pocket."

"That was righteous of him." Frank commented.

"He was a good dude to work for until McElvie showed up." Alex finished. "Let's eat and get back to the boats. Seeing that guy was a bringdown."

"A turd in the punchbowl; I got a bad feeling you might see him again." Frank mused.

"I hope not." Alex opened the menu he had memorized long ago, and it offered no surprises.

Many chapters were put in the book in the following six months and travelling from one bite to the next, Alex ended the season at Shelter Cove, working out of Noyo. Most boats had long ago moved on to Oregon, either fishing for salmon or albacore. The freedom to choose fisheries and freedom to roam the West Coast was about to end. The era of the Boldt Decision was upon the industry and after that limited entry into thefisheries would prevent lateral movement. Treaties signed long ago with the tribes eventually closed the most productive areas for commercial salmon harvest by the trollers. Vast tracts of ocean were now set aside from non-tribe harvest by the dictates of a computer model. That model closed off the areas where the most landings occurred, so in effect the better a troller did during a certain time and place, he found that area closed off in subsequent years. It was a no-win model for trollers and it did not do a thing to address salmon abundance for the tribes, a classic case of mismanagement by a stodgy bureaucracy that focused on a computer model based upon restricted extraction rather than habitat and propagation. A simplistic mathematical approach was born in the halls of academia based on models and it was set in stone. It was now the trollers turn to be restricted to a reservation of sorts, just as the Indians were placed on reservations decades ago. And predictably, salmon were at the same time losing the water war all over California. Water went south for the cotton and almond farms, the water flow increased to the big farms and orchards and big money flowed like the water flowed, from the hedge fund investors to the farms. Agribusiness depended on billions of gallons daily and the large pumps increased these water flows to the burgeoning agriculture industry. These pumps also pumped little salmon to their doom. Despite all this, Alex progressed to a bigger boat as fishermen always do. It seemed to be the natural thing in an expansive economic model that worked just so long as all expanded with it. And the freedoms of the era before limited entry suffered after limited entry became the norm, an atmosphere of scarcity and desperation set in. No longer could you choose any fishery for the price of your personal license. That was no more the case.

"Different brackets for different rackets." Phillip told it true, wise words of the times.

As Alex matured, he saw the rise of fish politics, politics that often worked against his interests. The importance to organize the industry seemed the only logical step, so he joined the marketing association to discuss fish business and get active. He was the son of an association charter member; a sense of heritage and family went with this decision. On this day, the association gathered at the Grange Hall in a meeting. The tall curly haired man spoke.

"We got a duck stamp that we hunters fund for the ducks' habitat. We tax ourselves annually when we get our hunting license. Why couldn't we do the same for salmon restoration?" The speaker was Mike Henry, the de facto leader of the port, everybody respected his opinion.

"I think that's a good idea." Tom said, a duck hunter himself.

"It would sure make us look good, taking care of our own." Said John.

"You're darn tootin. We always cry and point fingers at everybody, but now we can put our money where our mouth is and raise the darn things." Bill weighed in, another duck hunter.

"But I like to cry and point fingers." Ron cracked wise.

"That's like a birthright in this group." Added X-Ray. Laughter erupted among the gathered men and side talk began.

"Okay, Okay, a good idea." The chairman called to order the meeting and they discussed instituting a salmon stamp.

Sometimes big things come from small beginnings and the salmon stamp idea was no exception. Fishing the wild stocks and the existing hatchery fish was an increasingly spotty proposition and when the area closures came to be, the economic future of salmon fishing began to look dim. The hatchery system was failing badly, yielding a zero to three percent return of adult fish returning to spawn. The fry, the small hatchery-released fish, were not surviving the long trip down the rivers to the sea. The pumps, predation, water quality; all these were the obvious culprits of the salmon decline in a river that was increasingly overtaxed by the growing population and industries of the Golden State, grown from 11 million to 40 million. The salmon stamp provided funding for restoration and eventually restoration settled upon off-site release which resulted in a 300% increase in ocean abundance. Hatchery returns spiked upwards to 10%. This brought 25 years of prosperity to trollers in the south and the highest landings in history, all occurring despite time and area closures as mandated by the Boldt Decision. Alex rode this rosy salmon future as it crested like a wave year after year and 200 to 300 fish days were not uncommon. Every fisherman benefitted as a troller and the good ones prospered as they never had before. Alex became one of those good ones and it went right to his head; fish poisoning as it was known in some circles, stage four salmonosis.

CHAPTER 10

Have a *Reeeeeel* Nice Day

Along Highway 101 in the Redwoods it gets noticeably quiet as winter approaches and sets in. That stretch of road between Leggett and Eureka can be dark and long and the only sound is that of a Jake-brake compressing the cylinders of a lumber truck, a rumbling sound that echoes along the canyon walls of the Eel River. The RV's and the tourists that clog the roads in the hot and dusty summer afternoons are long gone and, in the fall, an impending winter feels like a different reality. To Alex Skarsen it seemed as if winter arrived early.

There is a lot of time for thinking along that long ride to Eureka as you watch the trees go by. Alex would usually stop at the Peg House across from the State Park and take a break, stretch his legs and chat. He knew the owners through a history of summer associations; he and his children vacationed on the river every year and camped in the warm summer sun under the redwoods across the highway. Bob and Lilly were the owners of the store and they affectionately called each other *Grandma* and *Grandpa*. Bob was one of those gabby types, an ex-truck driver who was friendly and engaging. He kept a CB radio hanging under the cigarette shelf and tuned it to channel 19, the trucker channel. The squawky little box would occasionally erupt with some indefinable jargon and Bob would answer right back in some other sing-song talk, satisfying both parties and leaving Alex and all the rest of the people in the store wondering just what it was that they had just heard. His wife Lilly would occasionally surprise the regular customers with a new look. This year it was a shaved head with a pink and purple streaked Mohawk. It got attention as most took notice of the 75-year-old grandma in her new head, tie-dyed tank top and saggy chest. All were afraid to comment and as you might imagine, she had the attitude to match her head, like she had seen a lot in her time and dished out a lot more than she got. Bob and Lilly had two daughters about the same age as Alex's boys. Bob's girls would occasionally show up at the swimming hole across the street on the hot days in their bikinis, but mostly the boys would see them when they were working in the store. Bob and Lilly were going to sell the place, retire and hit the road in their RV the last time Alex talked to them a summer ago. He pulled into the empty lot and walked into the quiet store and noticed that the *for-sale* sign was missing out front. He was not surprised, figuring Bob and Lilly sold the store, retired and were long gone. A dour and unfamiliar face behind the counter greeted him without enthusiasm.

"Well it looks like Bob sold out and hit the road." Alex said.

The man paused and regarded him before replying, "Did you know him well?'

That was an odd response. Alex did not like the sound of that, so he answered him cautiously.

"Not well, but I talked to him every year when my boys and I camped across the road. He told me he was going to sell the store and retire." Alex replied, uncertain where this was going.

"Bob's dead. He had the place sold and he and Lilly were packed up and ready to go. He went down to Leggett to the trailer park where his daughter lived. They quarreled, there was drugs, she shot him dead, at least that's how the story goes. The sale fell through and I'm just running the place, it's still for sale but no longer listed." The man explained in flat tones. Alex was shocked and his face showed it. The next question was obvious.

'Why did she shoot him?"

The man said no one knew, an obvious lie, some knew. Anyone could've guessed that opinions on the subject were rife in the community that barely numbered 20 people and all of those opinions had the ring of truth to one degree or another. It could have been for several reasons. For one thing, drugs and a bad marriage had troubled the daughter in the past and any number of things comes with that, all of them bad. Everyone knew that this stretch of the county had become lousy with methamphetamine and it was the exclusive domain of cartel dope growers. Once you got a mile away from the roads and found yourself in the woods you took your life in your hands. Drugs had transformed a timeless and tranquil redwood shrine into a playing field of hard cold currency, replete with weapons and human wreckage. Quietly, Alex figured she may have suffered as a result of this transformation, but still and all, he was stunned by the news, caught flat footed in that dark hole of a store. The fact was that this beautiful Eel River Canyon had become dangerous. The warm summer canyon where children jumped screaming with delight into the swimming hole was no longer welcoming but shaded with drugs and darkness. This information about the shooting merged with the purpose of his trip just as the South Fork of the river joins with the mainstem of the Eel.

Alex looked around and walked out of the tiny little store where his boys and he had sat on the porch every summer in the heat, eating ice cream after a day at the swimming hole. They had watched the tourists come and go from the redwood picnic tables on the porch, listening to Bob and Lilly crack wise behind the swinging screen door. There would be no revisiting that porch again, not in the same way ever.

That was bad news on top of more bad news; he was on a five-hour ride to visit a friend in the hospital. His friend and fishing buddy, Griff, had suffered a stroke and now Alex had a long ride to think about everything they ever said and did together. Bad surprises were behind every rock and bush.

"I better get used to it." Alex said to the empty cab of his truck.

Grim surprises shake you wise to reality, but when Alex received the phone call from Nancy a few days ago and she told him that her husband Griff had a stroke, this was just about the last phone message he ever expected to get and reality tumbled upon him like a crumbling brick wall. He never figured that Griff would be laid low by anything; he was tough as nails, he was a role model, an icon.

In that morning Alex had left from San Francisco under blue skies. As he traveled north, he watched the skies change all day as a high ridge of an approaching weather system transformed blue sky to shades of black and gray and ultimately, Alex found himself under a pervasive dark layer. By the time he reached the small town of Ferndale, Alex turned on the windshield wipers, and by Eureka, the rain was a caution as it became heavy, persistent, and torrential. He had trouble reading the street signs; the gutters overflowed, and little streams of water spread across the asphalt. He was looking for St. Joseph's Hospital and was getting lost in the soggy suburbs of Eureka. Alex stumbled on his destination accidentally and it was a low squat building one story tall, dismal and in need of paint. The parking lot had a capacity of 100 and Alex was one of three cars there that afternoon. It was lonesome.

"Maybe this is the back of the hospital?" Alex thought aloud.

Alex sat there in the truck after he turned the key off. He listened to the rain pound on the roof and steeled himself for he-knew-not-what inside. Ghosts from his childhood walked all hospital halls in their loose white smocks, smiling congenially, quiet, all of them in on some frightening secret that only hospital ghosts know. He summoned a measure of courage to get out of the truck. He had seen death in hospitals before: it stalks, it is quiet, it is sneaky and often unexpected. Alex's grandmother and grandfather died within the mysterious and quiet walls of a hospital, places with long quiet corridors, bright lights, cold stainless-steel poking implements and gurneys; all giving young Alex pause and caution.

Eventually he left the truck and dashed, pushing through the swinging glass doors of the building and into an empty reception room. Alex didn't know where exactly he was in this quiet place, it could've been the service entrance for all he knew. He looked at the fine print on the directory, not looking forward to the outcome. *Room 122A, West Wing* it read and, he walked on in that direction. Nearly half of the overhead lights were off as he walked down a long corridor toward room 122A.

Griff Savage was a West Coast icon and a hardy character that met his fishing life head-on and did it with a sense of humor; the hallmark of all the best fishermen, differentiating them from the banal sort who merely caught fish or crab and where money was the foremost thing they chased. Griff had style; he was a fishermen's fisherman who could walk down to his boat in the marina, hit the starter button and go non-stop to Alaska without a thought. Other fishermen told stories about him. He built his own steel boat when he was 26, named it the Outlaw and paid for it in the first year. He took that same boat 2600 miles to Midway Island for tuna, went bust, got drunk and then turned around and ran 2600 miles back and laughed about the story. He was tough and resolute, confident that sooner or later he would do well and knew that if he did not do well it wasn't the first time and it probably wouldn't be the last: it was just part of the deal. The thing was, he almost always did *exceptionally well* when the opportunity was there to do so. The dominant aspect of his personality remained his authenticity. What knowledge he did possess he had come by honestly; there was not a phony bone in his body. His humor cut like a double edge knife and the joke could be on you or on himself just so long as it was pertinent to the topic at hand. He did not know that the only things that are funny are true, but he did know that the only things worth him talking about were things that he *knew* to be true. He had a lot of stories to relate, stories that were often told as parables gained from the blue-collar life that he led. Coming to Eureka to see him in a hospital bed was the last thing Alex ever imagined himself to be doing and he did not like it one bit.

Alex entered room 122A. Griff's wife Nancy was cuddled up in bed, snuggling. Alex was walking in on something intimate between them he feared, and he began a quiet and uncomfortable retreat. He was two steps out of the room when Nancy greeted him. She got up from the hospital bed and Griff rolled up and smiled with a degree of uncertainty on his whiskered face.

"Alex you come in here, come on in. Say hi to the Captain." Nancy said. She turned to her husband and smoothed the hair away from his forehead. She spoke to him.

"Honey, Alex is here to see you."

"Alex." Griff said, maintaining the same uncertain smile, he didn't know who Alex was.

Alex could tell right off that Griff was altered. Griff struggled to figure stuff out and convert thoughts to sentences. Nancy had the room decorated with boat and family pictures, trying to jog his memory. Nancy just wanted him to remember who he was for Christ sakes, to remember the life he had. Just one look and Alex knew the sad truth: his fishing days were over. That is not an easy circumstance for a man like him to be in. Fishing got to the core of his existence, and Alex's for that matter. Who were they if not fishermen? Instantly and starkly he realized that working people depend on health and at the same time take health for granted until it's gone. The wheels come off the whole operation when something like this happens; it's sudden and without warning.

Those four little words; *fishing days are over*; often said without the gravity they deserve. It's just not that easy to stop fishing and it's a big deal. The thing that is for sure is that sooner or later it is gonna be over and there is a big difference between choosing to quit and being forced to quit. Griff never had a thought about quitting. Now here he was, in a reduced life at only 54 years of age. Fishing was all he was about, and all he wanted to do, it defined him. This is how it is; fishing gets under your skin if you're any good at it.

Also, Griff was the epitome of a fisherman; self-made, hard-bit and tough. The pictures hanging on the walls in the room defined the life he had led. Alex tried to say the right thing but could not find the words. He felt stupid and clumsy and tried to make jokes, but he couldn't think of a God-damn thing to say and he didn't want to sound like a phony in front of the most authentic human being he ever knew. Alex shifted his attention to Nancy and ended up by hugging her, heartfelt and long. That hug was the only thing that felt right and good all day. He clung to her a bit long for his own sake, he needed that hug almost as much as she. After an awkward half an hour, Alex left them to their privacy, knowing what Griff would have said if he had been in Alex's shoes, looking at *him* in that bed:

"That son-of-bitch is fucked up." That's what Griff would have said.

Feeling empty and walking down that pale green vacant corridor back to his truck, Alex had hoped he would have seen something different and better for Griff, hoping for something positive to address the fear he was feeling. Was it a fear for Griff or a fear for his own self? At the first he had heard from Nancy, he had to summon courage to go visit Griff, because after all, this sort of thing could happen to anybody and it could have been him in that bed. This reality for all fishermen was stark; the thought kept him in its grip as he stared blank-faced into the plate glass doors, watching the rain pour down, remembering the times they once had, fishing together but also the times ashore. The time they knocked over the band's tip jar in a dingy Moss Landing bar, dancing with strangers off Highway 1, or the time Griff wrapped up the wire wheel in the breakaway straps and they laughed like children. Griff would crack wise and good naturedly about everything. Alex remembered the barbecues they would have after unloading a trip, always an adventure. Griff never missed a chance to wisecrack and he kept everyone laughing. Staring out at the rain, Alex realized that he really loved this guy and the times they had fishing for salmon.

He remembered a time he would never forget, he recalled the events as he stared at his reflection in the glass doors. Alex recalled a time and thought to himself, "we were in the life" ...

* * *

The ocean was smooth as glass. The sky and clouds were displayed on the watery surface as blue and gray marbled mirror images. There was not a breath of wind all day, nor had there been for the two previous days. I was trolling for salmon and the whole gang was in the area except one guy, Pablo.

He was never in the right area because he just didn't give a shit about being in the right spot where the most fish were. I just could not understand that. Later in my life it made perfect sense.

We were inside the North Islands, working the 40 fathom fingers right up to the rocks in 25 fathoms. I anchored behind the North Island on the first night in 17 fathoms on a gravel bottom ledge. There was only room for three boats in the good spot and I was one of them. The lay was not that good despite the flat weather, however, but you did get to sleep until first light while those anchored at the Point had to get up 2 hours before daylight, but at least they all slept in comfort. I did not. The anchor chain grumbled on the gravel bottom of the North Island all night. I imagined splintered ribs and planks against the rock wall of the Island if the anchor slipped. The five or six boats in our group were doing just all right on the fishing, scratching 30-40 fish a day. The fish came one at a time on the bottom spread throughout the day and you had to pull 45 fathoms of wire each time you ran a line. Occasionally the fish were 12 pounds or better, but mostly mediums and a few smalls, 300-400 pounds a day I figure. It was *gentleman fishing* and we didn't know where else we should be, so we stayed there. The weather was pleasant, the company was good, and I was always anchored at a decent hour.

No cell phones lent to the occasional surprise and on that day it came. We got and gave fish reports three times a day at 10am, 2pm and 6PM over the single sideband radio with a code sheet I kept handy on the pilothouse table, ready to decipher the report. I had almost memorized the whole code sheet by now.

"Fifty-nine, fifty-nine. Lima Green, Charlie 20, kinda like, uh, Delta 30. Over." The radio blasted with its first report. It was Uncle Fred, senior member and high liner of the group. I had been looking at him all day right next to his tack, so I already knew what he had for the day; we all had about the same. Currently, I was more interested in dinner and vacuuming the kelp flies from the windows before we sat down to eat. The reports continued and they were all from the guys in my own area. I listened with casual interest as one after another checked in for the evening. Then Pablo came on.

"Let's see, Thirty-seven, thirty-seven," I could tell he was reading with uncertainty from the code sheet. He continued, "Dogwood 10. Foxtrot green, Gulf 40?" He ended it there, a slow and halting delivery of his report.

I dropped my handheld vacuum and it discharged a small cloud of disoriented flies that walked about on the table like drunken sailors on a 3-day leave. Pablo had a thousand pounds at Fish Rocks!

The last time Pablo saw a thousand pounds for the day was.... way back when. Now, on this day, he had it; he was in tall cotton and all alone at Fish Rocks. This was big news. I did not even know he was out of the harbor and fishing; it was out of character for him. Pablo was an icon of sorts as well, mostly within the confines of the coffee shop where he would crack wise and play pinochle every day in Noyo. Back in the day he was one of the gang from my home port in Half Moon Bay and I could even remember him when he was packing Billy the Raison from his wheelchair up and down the ladder. He went to 'Nam and Pablo broke from fishing in '67 but got discharged from the Army in '68 due to severe burns from a helicopter crash. He recouped, got back in step with his friends and went fishing again. When he started back in, he was rather industrious and a pacesetter for the younger guys like me. Then, as things got paid for, he slacked off and he concentrated on lifestyle and a devotion to, 1) socializing in the coffee shop, 2) pinochle, 3) fishing, in that order. He tinkered on the boat and only went fishing when the weather was good. He just did not give a shit about all that hard-work and high-liner stuff. Everyone knew how he operated nowadays, and Pablo's report held tremendous catching potential for us all.

"Thirty-seven, thirty-seven? Twenty-five, twenty. Lima Green. Charlie twenty. You got a Gulf report again?" I called Pablo and gave him my day-score and asked him who was up there.

"Gulf 40," he came right back like he had read my mind and done this part of his code-sheet homework beforehand. He confirmed he was all by himself at the Rocks.

Our local VHF scrambler-band came alive with chatter and we were like seagulls on a dumpster. We were all talking about Pablo at Fish Rocks now, over-excited.

"Pablo's got the day. All by himself too." Griff growled in his normal speaking voice which sounded like un-oiled gears in a crash box about to go bad.

"Maybe we should go give him a hand?" Ronnie chimed right in, always ready to pick-up and run. The grass was always greener for Ron somewhere else.

"They gotta be thick up there; Ole Pablo doesn't generally work too hard, does he? Pretty darn thick." Billy observed in his usual laid-back manner, which was no doubt spoken past the customary toothpick in the side of his mouth, which may have been surgically attached.

"Just think what *you* could have had." Ajidu cracked.

After the initial discussions, silence descended over all the skippers in the area; it practically resounded over the ocean, you could hear the wheels turning in the heads. The imaginary voice sounded like this:

"Go to Fish Rocks. The weather is flat, you could be anchored up at The Rocks and you could wake up in the morning with high hopes of a big day in Pablo's spot."

Within the half hour, the dominos started to fall one by one: all boats in our group were running for Pablo. The decision to take flight was always made easier by the glassy waters to travel upon, especially toward a potential bonanza. Not a one of us could withstand the temptation, the high hope. Hope and caffeine were our collective drugs of choice and we used, or abused them, every day.

"Ole Pablo's gonna have a little company when he wakes up." Ronnie cracked dryly.

"Gonna gang-bang his ass. That's what we're gonna do." Griff said in character, "We'll center punch that cocksucker-but good." He added with a mischievous chuckle.

"What's the weather doing?" I asked. I had not thought about that for days on end; it was calm and that was the only weather report anybody needed. It was also May and any fresh breeze that may occur this time of year would be out of the Northwest and that was not going to be any sort of problem. There was lots of protection from the northwest wind where we were headed, so my question went unanswered. I prepared a chicken for the barbecue, tidied up the cabin, finished vacuuming the flies and enjoyed the 80-mile ride in greasy calm weather. Back behind us Uncle Fred was still dragging the gear and catching a few fish occasionally. He spoke.

"I'll be up behind you. I'll grind it out here 'til dark and then come up." He reported. This was classic Uncle Fred strategy; the gear was always in the water while the sun was up. It wasn't complicated and it was very effective. His patience was exceptionally long. He marked the tack, up and down all day like a machine.

We travelled as a scattered group as we rolled into the anchorage one by one around 2AM. The journey had been the easiest passage up that stretch of coast that I ever had. We went by Bodega around dark and there was not a ripple on the water. Usually in this stretch of coast the northwest wind machine turns on in April and runs until August. But not this time.

I approached the Fish Rock anchorage and counted 4 mast lights. It looked like Mitch, Jackie and the Lump had come down from somewhere up above. I set the alarm for 6 AM and stepped out on deck. The night air was warm, sweet and pleasant with the smell of redwood trees and lupines. I lingered on deck staring up at the darkest of skies and the phenomenal expanse of the Milky Way, displayed now in 3-dimensional form, its depth reaching back to infinity. I did not know that there were these many stars in the night sky until now, the star-filled sky revealed Infinity in all it's dark depth. I stayed on deck watching the rest of the gang come rolling in to drop the hook behind me. I was so excited about being here that I woke up a half hour before the alarm in the morning. I didn't have far to travel before I set the fishing gear because Pablo had been fishing in 40 fathoms right outside the anchorage the day before. It was all about as good as it gets.

In the morning, it started right in; the fish were biting hard. The first line on the set was pumping all the way down and I just kept clipping on snaps and leaders until all six lines were out and they were all banging away with what promised to be a gear-load. The fish were thick here and I had to caution my crewman, the Bad-Ass-Brad, from running the gear too soon, telling him to wait and get ready for the onslaught-just let the fish bite the jigs off like tuna. We sharpened the cleaning knives and then ran the bowlines. Brad was like a machine over on his side, gaffing and gilling as he ran the lines up and down, taking the silvery salmon aboard and giving them a little conk on the head. We were in high gear from the git-go. There was never a question of whether we had fish on the gear, it was more of a mechanical rotation of bringing the lines in, taking the fish off and gilling and gutting as the line went back out. All through the morning we had our head down and our elbows up when we were not taking leaders and fish off the lines. The decks ran red out the scuppers. It was all I could do to tack and back-tack and keep up with the work. It was primal and we were under the spell of killing fish. I broke a sweat at 7AM and worked with a sweat the whole time the gear was in the water.

The tack reports from the gang were big; 50-60 fishes a tack with the same all around for everyone. The reports became unnecessary after the first pass; we were all within sight of each other and were too busy to get out of the stern. The radio was silent and the only sounds to be heard were brass spools spinning and fish hitting the deck. The engine provided its constant background drone, sometimes raising and then falling. During this frenzy I was too busy to notice that a breeze had come with daylight and, oddly, it was from the south. I kept bumping the throttle higher with each successive back tack and nobody said a word about weather. The radio was silent until about 10 AM when Griff came on.

"We just kept tacking down. Jethro and I had to get caught up back there. We're down here by Black Pt now and we still get about 15 fish each time through the gear." His raspy voice reported with fades and pauses; I could tell he was looking out the windows at the trolling springs, turning his head from the microphone as he spoke. He continued.

"But it's windy down here, Christ. Got the throttle at 1350 going into it." He rasped.

Griff had seen some weather in his lengthy time, more saltwater go by the windows than Noah. If he told you it was windy, you probably didn't want to be there. He was waiting for somebody to come back and report, that was protocol; a report followed by the report of another. But I was too buried with work to answer, just trying to catch up with the cleaning as the springs kept banging away anxiously with bites. I didn't even have time to take a leak and my back teeth had been floating for the past hour. From the deck speaker, Griff continued with a slight edge of humor in his voice:

"Well... when *ONE* of you guys gets the time up there? I mean when it's like *convenient?* When you can climb over the top of that pile of fish in the stern and make it to the cabin door- can you *PLEEEAZE* let me know if they're still biting on that upper end? And one thing more," he added.

In the background, I could hear the RPM's of the engine on the Chief Joseph struggle against the weather as he held the mic button down and still transmitting. Griff finished with this request:

"One more thing. I want you all to do something for me. Can you all do this for me please?" he paused for effect and continued, "I want you to have a REEEEEEEEAL NICE DAY, ya'll hear?" He ended his request with that mischievous chuckle, his signature expression. Griff was imitating a car salesman with this *real nice day* bullshit, lifted from an AM radio commercial we had been forced to listen to between innings of the baseball game.

Sarcasm dripped from the deck speaker. I knew he was laughing on the other end as he headed back to the pit to overhaul his side of the gear. The juxtaposition of that clichéd wish against this wind lingered. He knew what they all were thinking about this weather; the best part of this day was hours ago, and they had a chore waiting for them after the gear was aboard. It was fucking rough and Griff called it. The weather came on us quick when we weren't looking, we were busy and in the primal-kill zone, we saw fish and that was all we saw. The more I thought about weather, the more I realized we were screwed here at The Rocks: we were out in the open for southerly weather for miles and miles, nowhere to hide. We just had to take our licks and that was the end of that story. Seeking shelter would soon be the only thing on my mind at this rate. I stood up straight and looked around at the water that was whipping itself into a frothy mess all around me, tops blown off waves and the foam streaking. I started laughing out loud,

"Have a real nice day he says? SHIT!" Laughing and looking over to my partner on the other side of the trolling pit, "Have a real nice day Brad!"

"It is a real nice fishing day. But the weather is getting bad." Brad said in flat tones. He was kind of a humorless son-of-gun sometimes. Brad looked at me quizzically and went back to work, all-business. He flopped a few recent arrivals from his side over to mine, evening out the piles of fish to be cleaned.

"Where's Pablo? I haven't seen him all morning." Ronnie broke radio silence, his voice coming over the deck speaker and he added,

"Griff, we got bites on the gear and we're damn near up to Saunders Reef. And I can tell you this; the weather does not, I repeat does not, get any better the farther up you get. I bet old Pablo made one tack up this morning, he's probably off Mendocino by now and he's gonna make late-coffee at the Tradewinds, the bugger."

I was the first to bail out of the spot; my concentration had been ruined by this talk of weather, banging up and down off Fish Rocks and a long way from nowhere in a southerly. And I was still behind in the cleaning at 2PM when the fish stopped biting. I caught up on the cleaning and stacked the gear on the boat, it was no kind of weather for scratch-fishing and I didn't want to be here for the chance of an evening bite. The wind was out of the south at forty knots and I had close to a few hundred fish-enough for one day I figured. The rest of the gang was still fishing but most all boats were on a long tack up the hill and going with the weather, cleaning fish. They were way above me and Uncle Fred, of course, was religiously tacking back and forth on the same plot lines as the ones he had established at 6AM-you couldn't get him outta that spot with dynamite now. I committed myself to take a beating going down the line where I knew there was shelter, albeit a long way away.

"Maybe below the Ft Ross buoy It'll lay down." I told the radio group. No reply to an idea I knew had no foundation in truth.

It was, as it turned out, a very bad idea. It was a slow-go and occasionally I was jarred by the heavy sound of a *whump* against the windows as a brace of green water came over the bow and splattered against the plate glass 12 inches in front of my nose. My plan to maybe anchor below the Ft Ross buoy was deteriorating like the weather around me. It would be rough in there and dangerous, I could see that now. Better to stay at sea than go in there. I decided to just keep going for Bodega and take my licks on the ride down. I never touched the wheel for hours after going by Ft Ross, and fortunately, the wind did back off a bit when it started raining and it started raining very, very hard. I got to Bodega a little before midnight; it had been a ten-hour boat ride that should have only taken 5 hours. The rest of the gang settled in comfortably behind Pt. Arena at Alder Creek before the end of the day, smart guys that they were. I suffered a long boat ride while they were anchored and sitting like little ducks in a millpond.

It was still raining the next morning when I woke up, a torrential downpour, way out of the ordinary. The Bodega guys were all up at the coffee shop smoking like chimneys and gossiping. I walked in and Stan turned to me and said.

"Coast Guard's towing Uncle Fred in." These Bodega guys always got the drop on you when you're half awake.

"Wha, wha what, what? Where is he?" I asked like a dummy.

"Weren't you with him up at the Rocks?" Stan asked and continued. "He anchored at Ft Ross buoy last night. It rained so hard that it ran down the exhaust stack and filled a cylinder with water. He hydraulic-ed a piston when he turned over the engine."

"Wow, no shit?" I, getting up to speed slowly.

"Yeah. You did the right thing." He reassured, "It smoked up there last night, the Lump's already home, he called." Stan said.

"I took a beating all the way down last night, that's what I did; it was horrible, it was a long ride. For a while I was afraid of taking out a window, I tell you true. There was no place for me to hide." I replied and then asked, "Where is Uncle Fred now?"

"Coast Guard has got him at the buoy out front." Stan replied. "My uncle's going out to get the tow and bring him in to the dock."

Junior, Stan's uncle, was taking the Sea Farmer out to get him because the Coast Guard didn't want to come in to the harbor with a tow when it was so windy; they wanted to wait for a weather break to tow him in close quarters and park him in the marina. This would never do to suit Junior Ames and he considered it a candy-ass decision by some Coast Guard captain, fresh out of Oklahoma. There would be no waiting for the wind to quit when Uncle Fred needed a tow while he was around. Junior would finish the job for the Coast Guard: he would tow the Barbara Marie into the harbor himself and do it right now. We all piled out of the coffee shop to watch the show because it was no small feat to bring two large boats, side-tied, into a small space in a gale and we might be needed to catch a line. We all knew Junior could do it, that was not the thing; we just wanted to see how it was done and be helpful. As expected, it was done flawlessly, the Sea Farmer, tied back at midships to the Barbara Marie, parked Fred in a slip in one gentle pass. The anticlimax dispersed us back into the coffee shop soaking wet.

That afternoon the wind switched, and it cleared. I unloaded my fishes and the rest of the gang ran down from Pt Arena to unload as well. I should have tacked up with them instead of beating my brains out to Bodega. Griff told me they anchored in the lee of the Point and slept well there.

"Everything was beautiful; slept like a baby." Griff just had to add that, just to break my balls.

All's well that ends well, except it didn't end so well for poor Uncle Fred, but he had a mechanic on the boat the next morning pulling the pistons while he went home. The gang geared up for another trip that day and laughed about good fortune and bad. We left that evening to anchor in the outer harbor and rest up, ready to start another trip. In the morning, Billy found us a spot right outside Bodega Head by the buoy. Before long, the gang was assembled for another day of good fishing amongst a massive Bodega fleet.

Stan's brother Stevie called it about right: "Everything that floats is out here!" He cried into the radio amidst sporties and commercials by the hundreds at the buoy. Still a lot of fish as if the school had followed us down.

"Jesus, they just keep comin': I can last if that's the way they want it." Griff chuckled his comment on the fishing.

He almost made good on that, but in the end the fish outlasted him. Nobody had any notion, no way of knowing, no clue at all that it would not go on in this way forever. We lived large and in the moment with these forces of nature, forces that the gang had overcome so many times before. Sometimes the largest force against us was ourselves. And Griff? He was a force in his own right.

*   *   *

Alex remained standing there awhile and remembering. He had some real good times with Griff; he fished, cooked, laughed, drank, danced, told a lot of stories and never thought twice about the way they lived. There was always the next trip or the next season to look forward to. It was as if they were in a loop of continuous adventure that tested wits, humor, strengths and weaknesses. Alex stood staring through the glass doors and he heard that same sound of a lumber truck rumbling through town, the Jake-brake, lonesome and distant. Sooner or later all the guys in this gang would be gone; retired or dead, but he never thought of that, nobody did. But the inevitable comes home to roost. He was certain in the knowledge now, that in the future, somewhere, they all would be thinking about the times they had when they stood on deck and watched the lines, listening to their friends crack wise through the radio speaker. He exited the hospital and very soon thereafter, it was down the road.

A lot of lonely road, a lot on his mind to think about. Out of habit and distracted with thought, he slowed the truck down as he approached the Peg House and pulled into the dirt parking area. He walked in, got a Coke from behind the sliding glass and put 2 dollars on the counter in front of the young girl at the register.

"I've seen you before, you're my son's age. We used to camp every summer over in the Redwood Campground." Alex said as he laid his money down on the counter and continued, "Is your older sister still around here?" He was fishing for info.

"Santa Rosa. Not much for her 'round here but trouble. Not much for anyone." She replied in the flat tones of a girl who has seen much and hoped for little.

"I heard. Sorry about your dad. Is there an investigation?" Alex asked.

She regarded Alex with a look of disdain before she spoke. She didn't like him right off the bat; he was a nosey outsider and this subject was none of his business. The residents of the canyon blabbed gossip and opinion to each other freely about this incident, no doubt, but he was forbidden to enter this kind of talk.

"It's under investigation, nobody knows anything except the sheriff." She flatly and tersely replied. That was a lie and they both knew it.

"Damn shame, mysterious too. You don't hear about this kinda thing too often." Alex said but the younger sister was not taking the bait and she was getting pissed off. It was obvious this conversation was over when she showed him her back. Alex walked out of the dingy little store, paused on the porch and looked around for the last time.

The frequency of his rubber tires on the road increased as Alex gained speed and he soon approached the town of Leggett, located at the intersection of the highway to the coast. Leggett consisted of a post office, a small market, a shuttered café and a gas pump. It also had a long-ago famous drive-thru redwood tree but now the freeway by-passed all of that, the famous tree and accompanying gift shop were shuttered. Leggett was a dusty turn-off along the road now, with a few shabby trailer homes under the redwoods. You had to have a reason to be in Leggett, by-passed as it was. A shaggy haired youth and his dog hitchhiked at the intersection and Alex slowed down to pick him up. Hitchhikers sometimes provided conversation, sometimes they provided complete silence: it almost always provided a seat next to fringy people.

"Where you headed?" Alex asked.

"Willits." Came the answer.

"From around here?" Alex asked the usual conversation starter.

"No, I'm from Ohio, I came out last summer."

"Out here trimming?" Alex knew from previous hitchhiker conversations that young people converged every summer, lured by the money. The youngster regarded him before he spoke.

"Yeah. There was a group of us from Ohio. I'll trim next summer too so I thought I would stick around. It's snowing back home and there's a lot of nothing." Replied the hitchhiker.

He was a holdover from the groups of young people hanging out in the warm summers; young girls, dogs, guitars, tattoos on tan torsos, dreadlocks and lots of pot plants that needed trimming. In fact, the local Home Depot catered to them, had 4x4x4 bins loaded with trimming scissors just for them. Good money, about ten grand a summer Alex was told. They came from all over the country to do it.

"You ever hear of a girl that shot her dad in Leggett?" Alex broke silence.

"Sure. Everybody around here knew about that, Baby Jane Madison. Last summer in the trailer park. Shot him dead." The hitchhiker answered.

"Why? Does anybody know why she shot him?" Alex inquired.

"I don't know, only a few know what really happened. One story goes that she and her husband were cooking meth and the dad walked into a bad situation where he did not belong, I don't know. Some say the husband shot him. Another story says that the dad abused her, and she killed him for that. It was the husband that went to jail though, I know that for sure." He replied and let it lay there; it was all bad and depressing either way. We continued in silence down the road towards Willits.

Down the road and four hours later, Alex was in a different world altogether-the city. The asphalt, the concrete, the cars and the many people of the city stood in stark contrast to the dark silence of the trees he had left behind hours back up the road. He called Nancy the next day to check on Griff and he checked in with her every month thereafter until the calls became less and less frequent. The events of his own life swept him up in their wake. Griff did quit fishing and sold the boat to Jethro; he had little alternative. He was a little less sharp than before but still the same old Griff. He continued to go down to the harbor, was still up on the current gossip and events in the fishing world, only now vicariously and on the sidelines. Fortunately, it had not been a major stroke for Griff, but it was a major stroke for an era in fishing when he quit: an era when characters and individuals like him were the backbone of the fishing culture, a culture that inevitably gave way to modernity and a different world. And like the famous Drive-Thru-Tree in Leggett, that era was by-passed and gone.

CHAPTER 11

Burnout

More changes came after 2001 and the collapse of the Twin Towers. Oligarchs, plutocrats and autocrats now prospered, and the rule of law was replaced with the rule of wealth and power. The internet washed over the world like a tidal wave and eventually no one was spared. Change for better or change for worse, one of the very few certainties in this life and there was no way to delay those changes coming every day. For Alex, freshly divorced now, things started to look a little different.

Alex was sitting in his truck with sandpaper and paint, contemplating the annual spring painting of the boat. It was April and the weather were either windy or overcast, basically unlivable as far as Alex was concerned, especially feeling the way he did this morning.

"Fuck fish!" he said aloud as he looked out the truck window.

He wondered about a word he was hearing more and more of lately-burnout; it resonated. Thirty years of charging into the watery weather, feeling under the gun through most of it, why shouldn't he feel a little burned? It was thirty years of his choosing of course and there was plenty of good times, even sublime and unforgettable. Throughout the entire thirty years he had been blessed with the ability to be out in the world of beautiful sunrises and sunsets, of clouds parading across the expansive panorama of the sky, of mountains, shoreline and civilization in proper proportion. But as of late this was discounted, taken for granted and newly minted pressures were bearing down, mid-life pressures, unanswered existential questions. It was April and he felt compelled to get with the program whether he wanted to or not. The boat screamed its seasonal mantra at him.

"Maintenance! Work on me you lazy bastard!"

There came a rapping on the window of the truck, and it snapped Alex out of his mental fog of resentment.

"Hey man, 'whatch 'ya 'doin?" said the window-rapper. It was Kevin, a harbor patrol guy and a character, they were pals.

Alex rolled down the window to speak. "I'm pondering. I do not want to go down there and start this process in the wind and cold. I'm sick of it actually Kevin, and it's not the first time that "burn-out" has flashed across my screen." Alex said as he stared about the deserted harbor. "I think I been around too long; ever notice how history whittles away bit by bit, leaves you thinking about the shavings? The things you left behind?"

"Shavings, huh? Very deep but you think too much. Come work for us at the harbor, man, it is the *gravy train*. It's 4 tens, paid days off, annual COLA, pension, government, union and you gotta crucify Christ on the cross before they can fire you!" Kevin was vibrating his stocky 5'4' frame with his enthusiasm and continued.

"Plus, we can do what we want all day, no shit, we don't do anything all day! Unless we want to-and *we don't want to*! We get paid the same whether we do good work or not. I tell you, it's a racket. I'll get you an application. In fact, I'll get you two!" Kevin hustled off, his little short legs working double time, his spirit animal was a little bandy-legged rooster for sure. Actually, Kevin was retired from the Plumbers union and he knew all the tricks of working a job to his advantage, which is to say not working and getting paid for it. His goal was a double dip pension-Plumbers pension and the Harbor pension. The most sacred state of being in Kevin's mind, the Holy Grail of existence, was being vested by a Union with a pension, the worthiest goal in life. While Alex pondered, Kevin came back waving papers at the closed window. Alex rolled it down and took them from his hand.

"You gotta do this man. You'd fit right in. You know everybody in the harbor, Willy is here already. No bullshit, this is the best job ever-its government, union, shit goes down and payday is Friday; the only two things you gotta know! What could go wrong?" Kevin was almost levitating.

"I'll think about it. I'll turn this app in Kevin. Right now, I got to get my mind right and get ready for the opener. It's a month away and I gotta bite the bullet and get to it. It's just so damn cold and windy this morning it's hard to get going." Alex said, looking out at the deserted and windswept pier. He started the truck and drove off, leaving the jobsite for a more inviting day. He went home and filled out the application. He turned it in before he started the season just because he had the application filled out and it had been staring at him from the dining room table for three weeks. He really didn't want the job; after all, fishing was who he was. Anything good he had ever done was about fishing, this is how he was measured as a person. But his life was in a state of flux now.

Fish, fish, fish: there seemed to be no end to their abundance, so much so that it was driving the price down to new lows, like $.85 a pound. You had to catch a hundred a day to put together a trip. It was a workhouse. The DFG instituted off-site release 25 years ago and it was wildly successful-in the eyes of most. There were doubts coming from a group of new fish biologists who were preservationist. In their view there was a genetic strain of wild fish that needed to be preserved and the abundance of hatchery fish thwarted their existence. They also thought hatchery fish were genetically defective-these biologists were like fish-Nazis. They believed so strongly in eugenics that they were willing to sacrifice the sport and commercial salmon fisheries to a theoretical experiment that they wished to set in motion. No matter that many told them that sacrificing the hatcheries to help the river spawners would not help a bit, no matter that after fifty years of interbreeding here were no so-called *wild fish,* they didn't listen to that talk. The future of the fishery was all changed in 2001 when the Joint Hatchery Review came out and condemned hatchery fish: the *wild fish* advocates were now in control. It would take a few years, but they would ultimately ruin California salmon abundance. Alex got a hold of a copy of the hatchery review and could not believe what it said and what it concluded. It said off-site release was responsible for a 300% increase in the ocean abundance of salmon and *that* was a bad thing: it said the rate of return of spawners to the hatcheries increased from 1% to 10% and *that* was a bad thing: They thought this to be a problem because the rate of straying was up, diluting the genetic purity of the wild stocks. In conclusion, the report recommended that the entire off-site release program be stopped and hatchery production curtailed. Alex knew where his bread was buttered and if this came to pass it would soon be hard to put a 10-fish day together! When Alex got the call from the Harbor Patrol telling him he had made the cut, he did not hesitate to show up for the interview.

Kevin was there for the physical test; he fudged the running and swimming test which almost killed the 47-year-old Alex. The General Manager and the Harbor Master then asked a series of questions about marine terminology. Alex could have been an ax murderer who knew how to tie a bowline and still make the cut. They smirked when they came to their final question: the stumper, the tough question, the question that struck fear into pretentious applicants who dared join The Patrol.

"Okay, what is a limber hole?" asked the Harbor Master.

"Those are the holes on the bottom side of the ribs in the bilge. They allow water to pass freely between them." Alex answered simply, having pulled rot and sludge from this exact location since he was a child.

The General Manager motioned a little imaginary duck coming down from the ceiling, trumpeting the correct answer like it was a big deal.

"Okay Alex, we'll be in touch, thanks for coming in." The General manager said, and they all got up to disperse, the interview was over.

Alex walked out of the office and onto the pier. He immediately ran into Cal. Uncle Sig had retired and now Cal had the *Valkyrie*. Cal had not changed much over the years, he was still a wise-ass, just an older version of a wise-ass. He looked at Alex and spoke.

"The fuck you doin' com'in out of the General Manager's office kid? Did you fuck up or something?" Cal said.

"Job interview for the Harbor Patrol."

"You're kidding right?"

"No bullshit."

"*You* fallin' in with these *these* cowboys? That'll be the day, you ain't like that, you're natural fish-blood: did you forget that? Are you in your right mind? You're the best fisherman in town, not some janitor in a monkey suit with a badge! People like you don't team up with a pussy-outfit like this!" Cal was almost angry.

"Look here Cal; this is just a job. If I don't do it now, I might never get a chance. Now that I'm divorced, I got to raise these boys, not be out on the water all the time chasing fish. I got a handful of fish tickets to show for the better part of my life and that don't set right with me either somehow. I always thought there might be more. I always pushed that thought aside 'cause you know how it is; fishin' is a commitment-110% or nothing at all. The kids have been mostly raised by their mom and now she's not around, so I guess I gotta step up. The time is right to take this job, Cal. Fishing is all I have ever known, and I love it, you know that. But my reality now is that I'm a single dad whether I like it or not. This harbor job has medical, dental and vision for me and the boys. I gotta do it, it's too perfect. I gotta sacrifice and I just might be ready for this." Alex gushed.

'Well, I guess. It just seems like a waste that's all. Can't say that I blame you though, the game has changed. They took the fun out of it; not the same. We don't even have an Association anymore for Christ sakes, no brotherhood. It is open ticket and go, go, go. It's every man for himself and you can feel it. It's all about the money." Cal said.

"It's not like the days when Uncle Sig and my dad were around that's for sure. I don't really care for the way things are now either, it's kind of a rat race, too much pressure. The thing of that is; even the winners of the rat race are still rats. That's not what I want to be." Alex explained.

"Right, right kid. But some of these harbor dicks are the joke of the town; like that guy who threatened to go postal in the coffee shop? What the fuck was that?" Cal exclaimed.

"I know, you're right, we'll see how it goes. I'm not selling the boat just yet; I'm hedging this bet." Alex explained and added, "They haven't even hired me yet, I might not get it."

"They're gonna hire you all right: they may be stupid, but they are not that stupid." Cal stated flatly. "Look; you are family, I'm with you win, lose or draw, even if you are a harbor dick." Cal took a poke at Alex's shoulder in a jokey way. "You hear from Leif lately?" Cal asked.

"Yeah, said he did well this year. He's up in Petersburg, bought a house there. He's dug in." Alex answered.

"He was the smart one. We should have gone up with him when he told us to." Cal said.

"That's 20/20 hindsight there, but we're here now." Alex replied.

"True. I gotta go, I'll see you around kid, I'm headed for home, the Giants are on TV tonight." Cal said goodbye and hopped in his truck, leaving Alex alone in the parking lot, considering what he had set in motion with this harbor-thing. It was a lot to think about. Alex went home to his apartment. He watered the plants, fed his tortoise a few grubs and did the few dishes lying about. Lisa and the boys were gone, it was lonely and there was no getting around that fact.

* * *

A short stocky man in his fifties with short salt and pepper hair and a mustache under a narrow-brimmed straw club hat, Juan Garcia, AKA Pedro

Rodriquez, AKA Cedro Galli, AKA El Hombre Hormiga, walked the dock of Mazatlán where the shrimpers tied up. The crews congregated on the back decks, cooking, playing cards, laughing and just killing time until they were to go out shrimping. The boats were all similar and of a common design found in the Gulf; 65 feet at the waterline, steel and rusted. By the look of them, it appeared as if they had all came from the same shipyard at the same time. The Federales patrolled the docks carrying automatic weapons; they were a permanent presence, and no one paid them any mind, especially from the back decks of the shrimpers. Their Federale commander sat at an open-air desk behind a wall of sandbags in the shade under a thatched awning suspended by poles. In a crisp uniform, he talked on his cell phone from his desk. His two guards laughed and joked in the midday sun, at ease and unthreatened in the routine of the dockside detail. Juan Garcia talked into his cellphone as he walked the docks. It was not a casual conversation; he was all business and deadly serious, agitated even, occasionally taking off his sunglasses and waving them in the air for emphasis as he talked in animated fashion. He clicked shut the phone after the conversation ended, slipped it in his front pocket and climbed down onto the shrimper next to the dock.

* * *

The harbor called Alex and said he had the job if he wanted it, and when could he start? Within a week Alex was in a blue uniform with a badge and within a few weeks after that he had his first steady paycheck in thirty years. It was not a lot, but they came with regularity and he got used to it. His duties were simple; log in boats, search and rescue, walk the docks, billing, traffic control, be helpful and answer questions, preside and janitorial duties. There was another part of the job that he did not anticipate-office politics. Kevin was the first to introduce him to it and it came on his first day.

"Okay Alex, come here." Kevin had Alex by the shirt collar and walked him into the office. He pointed up at the wall where the names of the deputies were displayed next to their numbers, the harbormaster was number one and the assistant harbor master was number two and so forth down to Alex who was the new-hire at number twelve. Kevin was his usual eccentric self, kinda funny but he was serious as a heart attack when he pointed to the names on the wall.

"Look here Alex; you are number twelve and I'm number four. I had to rat-fuck my way all the way up to where I am so don't cross me or get in the way." Kevin was making a joke about a thing in which he was completely serious, *kidding on the square*, as it were. It was a perfect preview of what was to come in the next five years.

"No problem Kevin. You're the man." Alex was laughing now but he soon found out why Kevin was the way he was. He was a product of thirty years in the hierarchy of employee-on-employee relations, able to hone pettiness to an art form when it suited his purposes and able to scheme against co-workers when he needed to. He had also been able to develop a sense of humor and his humor always had a little dig at someone or something. Alex, new to all this, was like an indigenous person exposed to smallpox, vulnerable to toxicity, a new way of being in this office-politic thing. But it was not a deal-breaker, just annoying and petty.

* * *

Diver John pulled in the air hose and coiled it on the back deck of his boat. He was now the oldest abalone diver in the state-license system. He was a product of an old era, but here he was, doing what he always had done for years. The five-dozen he took from the sea floor was now worth a thousand dollars, no longer worth $40, more than enough to justify his two-day effort at the Farallon's. He kept his time in the water to a minimum these days, subject to all the aches and pains of life at Camp Elderhood. He looked around at the beige-brown rock of the Island. How many times had he been here in years gone by? He liked it; alive with birds yakking and mammals barking but still peaceful and stark somehow in its rocky solitude. How many eras had the Island seen? The Russian fur traders, the egg takers, the Coast

Guard, the fishermen and now the birdwatchers. The Island remained timeless and John munched his tuna fish sandwich under the beige rocks of the cliffs in the warmth of the little cove. Deciding he had enough, he pulled anchor and put it on the pilot for Half Moon Bay. The comfort of the harbor and a hot shower called to him. He was done for the week.

After a few hours of travel, he got to the harbor and pulled into his berth. The berth next to him was now occupied by an odd-looking boat, rather unkempt and peopled by a retinue of folk that didn't look much like his idea of fishermen. They had tattoos and pierced flesh and odd hairdos, one of which was fashioned in gelled spikes that stuck high in the air. He looked like a stegosaurus. That was all fine by John, to each his own. He was getting used to the sights of the modern fishing era, but this loud metal music that was blaring from the deck speakers was too much. He wished he were somewhere else in the harbor, somewhere else to leave his neighbors to their own devices, neighbors that he did not have to see, smell or hear. It was annoying to a man of his old-fashioned sensibilities; these guys were an impropriety that did not have a place in his idea of a proper working harbor. To his way of thinking, they did not belong, they were not fishermen. But such was so; he was behind the times he supposed, but he liked it that way. Besides that, the harbor was as much like a trailer park for refugees and derelict boats now as it as a working harbor. The winter storms no longer had an opportunity to clean out the riff-raff, the boats and drag them into the beach. They now sheltered in the berths, rock walls between them and harsh reality. Alex, in his pressed blue uniform and badge, came down the dock and greeted him.

"John. Old timer. Still at it I see? Where you been hiding out all these years?" Alex greeted him as he walked down the float.

"Hey kid. It's a long story, we'll have to get together and have a drink sometime and I'll tell ya about it; lots of chapters in the big book my friend, been out of the country. But I'm back here now, it's not like the old days but neither am I. It's wages and I do like to participate." John replied.

"Well you see what I'm doing. I went for the wages too, I kinda like it. I have three days off a week to fuck around. I never had a day off in my life when I was self-employed." Alex said.

"Married or chasing skirts?" John said, an old skirt-chaser himself.

"Divorced, two kids. A job benefit: this badge pulls them skirts in like a magnet." Alex smiled at the admission. Now that he was single, the internet and his uniform had helped Alex to practically become a serial dater.

"Hey harbor-guy, I got new neighbors in the berth next to me. How about moving me to another slip? They are loud and annoying fucks. I don't even like to look at them." John said.

"Sure. F dock, it's quiet there." Alex replied.

"Okay, anywhere will do away from these characters." John said back.

For the most part these were the kinds of issues that Alex dealt with now as a patrolman; everybody had an issue, good or bad. It was interesting yet troublesome at times when he was sought to sort things out. It was his job; the concierge at the riff-raff hotel and there sure seemed to be no shortage of things to sort out. But watching the boats come and go reminded him of the freedom from the shoreside bullshit that he once had. With that came a new appreciation; he missed it. That appreciation grew to a longing when the down-and-outers, the alcoholics, the pot heads, the meth heads and all the rest of the refugees from life were on parade in the harbor. Or when his co-workers honed their pettiness, conniving and scheming for vain reasons or labor-faking. It was odd that the way of life that he grew to resent before, fishing, he now remembered fondly. When the noise and the pettiness became part of a normal day and the parade of misfits clamored for attention, when emotional turmoil was close at hand, he no longer had that relief valve he once took for granted, no longer could he escape the noise and go to sea to clear his head and sort issues out in peace. He realized that when he was out on the water where the vision of land and all that noise that went with it was reduced to a thin and distant margin, his perspective changed. The noise was filtered out, his nostrils filled with salt and his thoughts were distilled to the essence of what really mattered most. Today was turning out to be one of those days when the shoreside noise and BS level was ratcheted up. Everybody had an issue and Diver John was up with his.

John spoke plaintively to Alex. "You know the trouble nowadays? There's no respect, it's all *me-me-me* with no thought for the events or people that came before; almost as if history began with the appearance of them, this *me-me* gang. Most of 'em don't even know what happened ten days ago, let alone ten years ago. They can't weigh the past against the present." John paused before he continued. "It's probably always been that way, I know. We had it good and didn't even know it. I may be behind the times but it's where I belong and I know the difference between chicken shit and chicken salad, I tell you true. It's worse now than it ever was: take that gang over on that rat-shit boat for example, blaring that noise all over the harbor without a thought for the rest of us? Smok'in weed all day? Walk'in 'round with a mini-dinosaur on your head? What's the story over on that boat anyway?"

"I don't know yet, they just got here but they got our attention right quick too-and not in a good way. I was just going down to ask them to turn off the deck speakers or turn the god damn music down. If that's what you want to call music." Alex said.

"Well that's a start for sure." John said. "I'm on my way to the showers and the Ketch for a beer, see ya later."

Alex had received numerous complaints on the loud music, and he was responding-short and to the point. The boat in question was a big old rusty steel rig and it was hard to tell just what fishery it was rigged for, if any at all. It sure had a big enough crew; 6 or 8 young men lounged about on the back deck firing up the little Weber BBQ on the hatch cover and drinking beer. Alex walked up to the boat and spoke.

"Hey brother, how's it going. Say; I got a few complaints and maybe you can help me out with them. Can you turn down the music or turn off the deck speakers?" Alex asked.

A tall man dressed in khakis walked over to the rail and answered casual and slow. He thought himself to be a cool breeze as one could easily see.

"Sure, no problem *off-uh-sir*." His answer was smooth and condescending and he drew out the word *officer* and not in a good way. Alex instantly wanted to fuck him over. The Cool Breeze instructed one of his minions to go inside and turn the music down. Apparently, he was the leader of this group.

"What are you guys fishing for, anyway?" Alex asked. Dumb like a fox, he was trying to get a feel for this dodgy group of characters.

"We're getting rigged for albacore." Replied the leader.

That was bullshit. They were too dumb to know that was a phony answer. "Well, you certainly have plenty of time before they show up." Alex observed.

"We got a lot of work to do." Replied the leader.

"Well good luck." Alex turned and walked away, not willing to be subjected to a conversation that allowed smoke to go up his ass farther than it already had. In real life he would have just beat the livin' shit out of this punk but now, in uniform he was all politeness, a sometimes bothersome job requirement. Something was not right with this group and they just proved it. He didn't relish the prospect of looking at these characters every day for the next few months. Nothing but more trouble to sort out. He walked into the office and announced as much.

"There's something not right with that boat down on D dock."

The assistant harbor master responded with a smile. "There's something not right with *all* the boats on D dock." He laughed

"Yeah," Kevin responded, "the problem is they're all fishing boats, fishermen and whack-jobs!" Kevin had good reason for his skepticism of the fishy demographic group, considering the most recent sketchy group to arrive joining the rest of the sketchy misfits who resided in the harbor getting beer-money from their fishing attempts. Collectively they gave real fishermen a bad name. What was once an honorable profession had attracted a bad element. Alex clocked out and went home. He had a graveyard shift coming up as a favor to a co-worker and he needed to get some sleep.

* * *

Tommy Howard was lean, aggressive, single, age 30 and sure about much. He was certain that he had it all figured out, especially boats and fishing. He was a modern successful fisherman; he owned an immaculate boat in the harbor and what he cared for was boats and fishing. He was a *slammer*, a *high liner*, a *killer*, known for the pounds he could deliver, the mark of success in the fishing community. He had status and he liked it. Trolling season was nigh, and he sharpened hooks, fondled packs of hootchies and spoons, tuned up the machinery and took mental inventory of the things to do and acquire before opening day. He had thought about this day for a month. He had never missed any season opener and he wanted everything to be perfect; all machinery and gear ready to catch the maximum amount of fish on the first day out, the first to be on the main vein of fish. This was in his head more and more as opening day approached.

It was a curious word that, *high liner*. A lot went into it: some were consumed by it; some did not care a whit about it. But for Tommy, it held a special place-he wanted to be *the one*. Others shared this attitude of course but being *the one* on a consistent basis was right where he wanted to be. It brought notoriety; but the notoriety and reputation required constant ambition, dedication and guile. Tommy was more than up for the task and he liked it. From experience he found out that to fail was to suffer the consequence of a dark mood that was only alleviated by delivering a good trip. If the season was open and the weather was fishable-he was out there-trying to get that trip aboard. The most depressing sight for Tommy was to see his boat in an empty marina when everybody else was out and catching fish. A neighbor fisherman struck up a conversation with Tommy in the marina on this morning.

"Where you gonna go on opening day Tommy?"

"I don't know. I'll know more the day before." He answered in a nonchalant and noncommittally way; he knew where he was going to go, he knew
more than he would let on, in fact his head was filled with nothing but
pre-season fishing information, information that came his way every day.
His cell phone rang every ten minutes with updates on who was where and
who saw what. He had become selectively close-mouthed, a habit reinforced
once the season began. He was in a code-group in which he only shared
information within a select group of boats on voice-scrambled radios.
Judgement was passed on who was to be in the group. Gone were the old days
of a few channels of communications that everyone monitored, sharing fish
information, gossip, jokes, fish politics, tales of the antics of characters and
all the rest. No longer was there a forum where the pertinent information
was discussed amongst the fleet. Now it was like the Tower of Babel; you
could not speak to others outside your group and others could not speak to
you. You could not hear others, and all remained divided and isolated in
groups that didn't talk to each other.

It could not have come at a worse time in the commercial fishing timeline. It had taken 30 or 40 years to gain momentum, but the Environmental
Movement was now the order of the day-and rightly so, the future of the
planet was at stake. But the movement had taken on a dark side under the
influence of big money. Some of the leaders of the movement were zealots;
self-righteous saviors of the planet in the name of ecology and commercial
fishermen were expendable. Fisheries that were eliminated or curtailed were
low-hanging fruit for the multimillion-dollar organizations that came to be
known by the monolithic handle-the NGO's. Grants were even sought for
anti-fishing campaigns and celebrities clambered aboard the bandwagon as
they ate fish from third world countries, countries that still fished with dynamite and countries without regulation. They ate fish that arrived at the airport
with 5,000 carbon miles per pound. They ate seafood that polluted and
spoiled the environment wherever aquaculture was big business, all the while
railing at the local fishermen. Imports soared to 90% of the seafood consumed
by the population and the commercial fishing infrastructures in US coastal

communities collapsed, leaving only a façade for the gullible tourists to gawk at. And why not target fishermen? They were easy targets. No lobby, no friends, no organization. A rabble who knew only how to take from the sea. In the eyes of the population they had to be stopped. It became part of the message, like a religion of ecology that was preached to the children, the masses and the funders of the NGO's. There were two fisheries left for Tommy Howard in this era; he had a salmon permit and a crab permit. Crabs: the biggest show on the West Coast and every spare dime Tommy had was re-invested there. The feeling that he was in a zero-sum game, where you had to get yours before somebody else did and get as much as you can as fast as you can was always there. And tomorrow was uncertain; the only certainty a fisherman knew, writ large. The freedom he sought and loved was being encroached upon and not thinking about it was a popular coping strategy that Tommy adopted. Tommy would rather do and think about his personal fishing narrative and catch fish than think about the big picture-and nobody could blame him for that. In fact, all his peers were doing the same.

* * *

Alex woke up at 2PM, unable to sleep any longer during the day. He made coffee, sliced an orange, looked out his kitchen window at the rose bushes. A robin searched the dirt for a bug. Alex watched in silence. The little bird nervously twitched her head as she hopped along the yard, wary of others. Alex was pleasantly emerging from his afternoon nap. It was now time to get ready for work. The graveyard shift was 5PM to 3AM; it was a quiet shift, most duties done after a few hours. After dark, the all-night crew came out in their hoodies and on their bicycles, looking for scrap metal or others like themselves to get high with. They did not bother anybody, they didn't need Alex, so he didn't need them. Alex would patrol in the truck every hour or so, but mostly he was settled back in the office listening to the local jazz station. The harbor was quiet.

Tonight, the silence was broken by a voice over the VHF radio.

"Mayday, Mayday. I'm stranded on a rock; my boat is on a rock! I'm surrounded by kelp. I'm right outside the harbor!"

Alex pondered. There were a few things he needed to know; it was protocol. "Name and description of vessel? Number of persons onboard? Are there any injuries? Are you in a life-threatening situation? Your position?"

"Man, I'm right outside the harbor and my boat is stuck on a rock! I'm by myself, the boat is the Pelican from San Diego, it's white. You gotta come get me, I can't move!" Came the frantic voice over the VHF.

"Standby, put on your lifejacket." Alex reached for the telephone to call the on-call patrolman. It was the assistant harbormaster and he picked up the phone at his home.

"Hello?"

"John, I got a guy who is stuck on the reef and he wants help."

"I'm watching basketball, I can't go."

"Well… the guy is frantic; I think he's in trouble bad."

"Just kidding. Go fire up the patrol boat, I'll be right down."

"Roger."

It was about 9PM and all was quiet in the harbor, only the burble-burble sound of the patrol boat exhaust. John arrived and Alex threw the lines and away they went to find this guy. It wasn't too difficult. He was on the Reef all right, grounded and teetering on the keel right outside the harbor a ¼ mile. They got the patrol boat as close as they could, it was dicey; there were rocks and kelp all around the stranded vessel. Alex was standing by; John was at the wheel.

"Alex, take a tow line up to the bow. I'm gonna go in bow first, you throw the tow line to the guy and I back out the same way I came in. I spin around after I get in the clear of the kelp and rocks, put a strain on the line from the stern post. Then we pull him off on the swell-I hope." John said and chuckled.

"Roger." Alex took he coil of tow line up to the bow and stood there as the patrol boat crept between the kelp paddies toward the stranded vessel. He tossed the line and it landed right in front of the stranded mariner who made it fast to the bow. John backed the patrol boat out the way he came, got in the clear, spun around and the line came tight on his stern post. Then he put a strain on the thick and long towline.

"I think he moved a little." Alex said but it was hard to tell in the dark.

"Maybe on the swell." John said.

"Yeah, maybe." Alex answered and watched. Fortunately, the Pelican was a steel boat, otherwise, splinters would be all that would have come off the rock. He thought he saw more movement. "She's coming off!' Alex shouted.

"Good, I'll make the last quarter of the basketball game." John said.

When the stranded boat finally came off it required a tow due to rudder damage. They were off to the dock with their tow. They put him on the end-tie at F dock.

* * *

"Something's not right over on that boat." John spoke to Alex from the breakfast table the next morning.

"It's a piece of shit, I'll grant you that. The fuckin guy was on King Rock when we pulled him off last night." Alex replied.

"Well yeah, but besides that. This guy showed up last night and I seen him before. A long time ago." John explained.

"What?" Alex asked.

"I been gone a long time Alex. I was all over Central America. It's a long story but it started out when I was part of a diving crew on a big lobster freezer-boat off Costa Rica. One night, the skipper sent me over the side to free up a stuck anchor. I thought we were in twenty feet of water; he didn't tell me we were in 70 feet of water and I just kept following the anchor line down into the darkness. I got short of air and rose to the surface too fast, air embolism set in and I was sick, rolling on the deck in pain. I mean I felt like I was coming apart inside, every joint burned like I had instant arthritis. The skipper pulled up to a pier in the middle of the night and put me off the boat and left me for dead. The police got me, took me to this hospital that was like a dungeon. The walls were bare concrete and moldy, you had to buy your food or starve, nobody came to check if I was dead or alive. I lay there for weeks, not knowing if I would make it through the next day. But then I got lucky and a nurse took me to her home. Over the weeks we became sweet-hearts. At her house I recovered-but it took months. I had her to look after me or I wouldn't be here to tell the story, I wouldn't have lasted another week in that hospital hell-hole." John said and continued, "She saved me, I should have stayed put with her."

"What's the connection with the guy last night though?" Alex enquired

"Well, I spent 15 years in Central America after that; odd jobs, scams. I kicked around and finally I went to work for the CIA in El Salvador. Low key mercenary stuff, I was assigned to guard duty of this Salvadoran general. I drove him around, kept an eye out for un-friendlies, got him girls, helped him smuggle guns to the rebels, whatever he asked. I met some shady char-acters and I thought I recognized one last night on that boat-a Mexican looking guy in a hat." John said.

"There was only a white guy aboard last night. One guy." Alex explained.

"Did you search the boat?" John asked.

"No. That's not part of what we do." Alex said.

"Mistake; always search. I only know what I saw, he might have showed up later, I don't know. I think I sold weapons to that same guy in El Salvador years ago Alex." John said.

"Well shit oh dear." Alex wondered what the hell to do with this information.

"Keep your eye on that boat." John concluded and rose from the table.

"I will." Alex said.

*   *   *

On the graveyard shift again a night later, Alex played hearts on the computer in the office, an office whose large windows presided over a quiet harbor. It was about 2 AM and a few souls sauntered on to the dock after a night of revelry in the local bars. It was time for Alex to make his final rounds. He was reticent to go out in the cold morning but needed to get some air to slake off the sleepiness and push through his final hour on duty. He opened the office door and clambered into the patrol truck. He drove out on the pier, shining the spotlight on the boats as he went. All seemed well except the boat they had towed in the night before, the one Diver John thought suspicious, had all the cabin lights on. Alex debated, but something in his gut told him to go out and take a closer look at the boat that they had towed in. He walked down to the end of F dock. When he got to the boat, he hollered.

"Anybody aboard! Harbor Patrol here, anybody aboard!" Alex asked and waited for a response. There was no answer. "I'm coming aboard!"

Alex walked into the open wheelhouse, kicked a few empty beer bottles on the floor and fingered some bullets on the galley table. He walked past the galley and the captain's stateroom. He was in the pilothouse now and there was someone aboard, but he was passed out on the floor. He had pissed his pants and it smelled like shit too.

"Fuck, what a mess." Alex had stumbled into it. "Hey buddy, wake up!" The guy was out and did not move. Alex poked him in the back. "Hey buddy, harbor patrol, wake up!" Alex again shouted and there was no response, so he turned him over, face up and revealed a pool of dried blood underneath his face. Alex jumped back and looked around. "Fuckin-A, call the sheriffs." He said aloud and turned away for the back door. He was intercepted by a man coming out of the stateroom, blocking Alex's retreat through the companionway.

"You not going anywhere amigo, you don't need no sheriff, you need undertaker, you're dead man." A cold statement delivered with a matter of fact-ness and followed by a spray of bullets from a little death machine strapped over his shoulder, cold and black metal that spit fire through the silencer. Alex was hit with a pattern of bullets and the force spun him around and he fell face down by the dead man, adding fresh blood to the pool of dried blood.

El Hombre Hormiga was not fooling around. He was not about to take any chances with his last big score, all he wanted now was to escape, get the hell out of there. He was pushing 60 years of age and his smuggling days were at an end, especially now that the cartels had taken over. It was very risky now. There was no more honor, no place for an old man with these young kids who would rape and kill just for sport. Juan Garcia had 50 people down in the hatch, illegal immigrants at $5k to $10k a piece to be smuggled by boat. No more treks through the desert with 5 or 6 thirsty and bedraggled people dodging the border guards, this was his big score and he had plans. He was gonna buy a big RV and go to Disneyworld, he had never been there and always wanted to go. After that it was Florida and easy retirement where the weather suited his clothes, anywhere but Central America, it was too dangerous there now. And he was not to be stopped by this phony badge and he was not gonna share the proceeds with the skipper either, that part of the job was taken care of and he was laying on the pilot house floor. A share of the money was the last thing that gringo needed where he was going. Juan Garcia went out on deck and unlocked the chain over the hatch.

"You here now, come out. This is America, land of the free, run for your life." Juan Garcia barked down at 50 pairs of eyes that looked up from the darkness of the fish hold. They saw a little man with a little Uzi over his shoulder.

* * *

Diver John was on his way down to the boat after the bar closed. He was alone, all his prospects that night were too young for him to have a chance, the ladies were younger than his grandchildren. Besides, he had had enough of chasing skirts around-it was just the social life he sought at the bar, he just liked to participate; laugh, talk, swap stories, that sort of thing, just to be in the life. He didn't even drink much anymore. His good looks had afforded him luck with the ladies all his life. But luck was not with him tonight; it was just his *bad luck* that his boat was next to El Hombre Hormiga on his last big score.

John noticed the patrol truck parked on the dock at the head of his float with the door left open: maybe Alex had come to pay a visit? It was a little late for a social call. He walked down the float toward his boat. Something was going down: people with children were running past him without stopping or looking. They were coming from the boat on the end of the dock.

"Something's not right." John said to himself and he walked down to the mystery boat-the Pelican.

"Halloooo? Anybody?" John cried out while he stood on the dock next to the Pelican.

"John help; I'm shot, call the sheriffs-there's a man with a gun onboard and a dead man." Alex got his feeble call out.

The spray of bullets came immediately across the deck of the Pelican from behind the main hatch. A short man in a straw club hat stood up from his hiding place across the hatch from John, firing a burst of bullets. John instinctively lunged backwards into the water. He immediately recognized the little T-shaped weapon on a shoulder strap with the stubby barrel when it popped up over the hatch-it was an Uzi-and you did not want to be on the wrong end of it; 1200 rounds a minute and a 30-round magazine. John jumped backwards into the water at the first sight, but the spray of bullets hit him across the torso. He reached into his waistband and came back with his own little Glock 32 from his Honduran guard service days; fully automatic and a 10-round magazine. John took aim at the running man's backside from the water and held the trigger back.

"BUM! BUM! BUM! BUM!" Came the rapid report from the little weapon. El Hombre Hormiga went flat on his face with the impact of the four 9mm slugs in the center of his back.

"Hey John; I'm all shot to shit. I'm dying in here, help me." Alex called out a second time from inside the boat, crawling for the door. The stream of children, elders, babies, mothers, fathers, they all continued to come out of the boat hatch and run down the dock. John was in the water and bleeding but able to hoist himself out. He lay on the float, stripped off his shirt and put a tourniquet on his right arm. He had to just gut it out somehow.

"It's a war zone out here, I'm on the dock and I'm shot." John replied.

"I'm in the pilothouse and I'm shot."

"How bad?"

"I'm shot in the shoulder and the neck." Alex pleaded as he regained his feet with a hand over his neck. He stumbled out of the house and against the rail.

"Well I'm gut-shot. How you like them apples?" John was starting to get lightheaded and cold.

"Fuck. The fickle finger got us." Alex hobbled over the rail to John, lying on the dock in worse shape than he.

"I'm bleeding out kid, I think this is it."

"Okay, I'll get help. Hang on. I think I can make it up to the truck." Alex said.

"You do that, I'll just stay and lay down here, you get help. I'm gettin kinda tired, life has got me worn down to a nub 'bout now." Diver John lay his head down on the dock boards. "Who the hell would have ever guessed this?"

Hobbling up the dock, Alex started hollering as best he could and between the noise from the shots, the trampling feet of refugees and his cries, it was a ruckus. Lights came on in the adjacent boats. Live-a-boards were calling the cops.

Alex stumbled along on the dock, trying to get back to the truck and get off a call for help. Weakened due to his blood loss, he stumbled on the 2x6's and fell on his face, cheek flat against the boards. A smuggled child looked at him momentarily and then kept on a runnin'.

"John was right: this *is* it." He whispered. Trampling feet were all around his head and running on the dock. Shoes were the last thing he saw before things went completely black.

CHAPTER 12

Scenic Cruise

"Dad, can you hear me?"

Alex wanted to open his eyes and see his son, but he couldn't see past the bandage. Alex felt like he had been dropped from an airplane; his shoulder ached and it was wrapped in some kind of cooling blanket, he could not move his neck, his head had a constant ringing and hurt, his ear was on fire, his rib was fractured and all movement and breathing was a problem. Other than that, no problem. It was dark under the bandage around his head, but that didn't bother him, in fact, he kind of liked it in the dark about now.

The voice he was hearing was little Arne, he did not need to see to know that much. Arne was not so little anymore either, a high schooler.

"Where's your brother? Is the Chubber here too? Alex asked the question to the voice from beyond his dark world. The Chubber was the pet name for his younger son, Conrad, in middle school.

"He's here, he's down the hall at the vending machines, Mom gave him a dollar." Said Little Arne.

"Is she here too?" He asked.

"Yeah dad, you've had a lot of people come by. You're famous, the big shoot-out on the dock, you made the Review." Little Arne said.

"Oh shit." That was about the last thing he wanted.

He had been dreaming under the bandage. Dreaming of anchoring up somewhere in solitude, just like he had 100's of times before to get away from this crazy world. In his dream he saw himself at Pt Reyes, anchored up at the Ranger Station, watching Mendosa's cows walking lazily back to the barn in the evening sunset. The timeless wind swept down from the top of the bluffs, the gusts rattling in the boat rigging, perhaps just how they had rattled the rigging of The Golden Hind when Drake stumbled across the anchorage centuries ago. In the dream Alex was cozy at the galley table; Dickenson diesel stove cranked up to 3, NPR like an old friend. He would watch the clouds go by through the window, clouds that stopped and built on the mountain tops along a distant Marin County coastline. In his dream he put his skiff in the water to go ashore to walk around on the beach. He strolled casually on the solitary beach, picking objects from the high tide berm and feeling the beautiful solitude of the Point. He observed a little kid dragging his skiff: the little bastard was stealing it! Alex ran as fast as he could down the beach, but the sand became so deep he couldn't run, couldn't move. He started hollering but the little boat just gained distance out in the anchorage and the kid gave him the finger and waved good-bye. He watched from the lonely beach, stuck listening to the wind and without a way back to the boat. In dreams.

"How long was I out?" Alex asked Little Arne.

"I don't know, maybe a coupla days. Mom wouldn't let us know." Little Arne replied.

Alex heard Kitty and little Conrad walk in the door. Alex lifted his bandage for a peek. Conrad was clutching a bag of orange marshmallow peanuts.

"Dad, they shot your ear off!" Conrad was excited to break this news.

"Well that would explain a lot. C'mere you little Chubber, what you got in that bag?" he asked. It was too bright in the room and he lowered the bandage back down.

"Orange marshmallow peanuts." Conrad replied through a mouth stuffed with marshmallow. Alex fingered the bandage around his head, raising it and peeked again.

"Don't eat that shit Little Chubber." Alex said just like a dad. Kitty was standing a few steps in from the door but now she approached the bed.

"Okay, well, you're alive and who needs two ears when you can hear just the same with one. Half of what's being said is bullshit anyway." Kitty was trying to be funny in her uptight way.

"That's the spirit, always look on the bright side Kitty." Alex said sarcastically. It became clear to Alex in that moment just *why* they were not together anymore. The pressing question on his mind right now was not marital, however. "How about Diver John? Did he make it?" Alex asked.

"No. He died on the dock that night. The smuggler guy too. Diver John shot him." She explained.

"Dang; he knew he was done for. Saved my ass." Alex mused to Kitty and the room.

"Yes, he did. But he was in the wrong place at the wrong time." Kitty offered.

"He was in the right place at the right time the way I see it. That's why those boys still have a father above ground." Alex was annoyed, glad he had a head bandage to insulate him from the stern sight of her relentlessly stiff and uptight reality, a reality he did not share anymore.

"Well, it's getting late, I better go. The boys haven't had dinner yet and it's a school night." What Kitty may have lacked in humanity she made up for in efficiency. Alex wondered if she ever got tired of the chill that followed her around like a fog on the Moors.

"C'mere boys, give the Dadster a hug, Mom says it's time to go." Alex said and lifted the bandage a bit so he could see them again. The boys were headed out the door behind their mother after they gave Alex a kiss. Who knows what goes on inside their heads with parents like these? Alex wondered.

"See ya dad." Conrad said as they trooped out the door.

"Later dad." Little Arne said.

It got instantly quiet in the room, but quiet like a toothache.

"Here I am shot in a hospital. Seems like my life swallowed me alive." Alex's thoughts played like a tape loop through his head.

Alex began to realize that it just wasn't about fishing; it was about success. He had become driven by the pursuit of success, that's what *ruined* it all. It didn't start out that way, but he had changed along with the times, he bought into it and it had consumed him. He had reinvented himself in the Harbor Patrol but that didn't work out so well. Here he was in the hospital without an ear.

He might have to start over yet again. Be anonymous this time, where the story of his past and family were not stapled to his chest for all to see. Where judgements were few, where he had nothing to prove or live up to. That was a tough proposition if he stayed around here, impossible even. He needed a clean slate, just like those born gain folks. Heck, they weren't running *to* something, they were running *away* from something. He clicked the morphine drip a couple of times and settled back into the warm fog, drifting into sleep. When he awoke it was to the sound of the nurse, clanking around with a food tray.

"Okay good lookin', wake up, time for dinner." She was the most persistently cheerful person he had ever come across, sometimes annoyingly so.

"How long have I been in this bed?" Alex asked.

"Oh, I think it was only a couple of days that you were out." She answered and added, "You're our local hero."

"Why" Alex asked.

"Well, you survived the gun battle on the dock, of course. You freed the captives on the boat and the bad guy died. Just like on TV." She answered on an upbeat note.

"But I didn't shoot him. Or free any captives." Alex said.

"Doesn't matter, you were the survivor-the winner gets the glory, kiddo. Three people died of gunshots, you *did not*. Now scoot up and I'll swing the tray over." She instructed. "And remember that visiting hours are over at 8 PM."

"I had my visitors today; the family was here, and they left. More visitors won't be a problem." Alex said.

"Oh no, there was a steady stream of people yesterday when you were still out. You're the local hero and lots of people came by." Said the nurse.

"Sorry I missed them in that case." Alex said. His whole story was literally typed up and on the front page of the local newspaper.

Alex had an afterthought. "Hey. I gotta drop a deuce, how do I go about that?

She handed him the bed pan and said before she left, "Here, you figure out the rest."

"Can do." Alex said to her back meekly.

* * *

A rosy cheeked Irishman entered the hospital room the next morning, Alex sat in bed with the local newspaper. He peeked out from behind the paper and the full force of the rosy man's presence came upon him.

"Don't worry about a thing lad, we got you covered. Yes-siree, the union is here! You got the Golden Ticket son, you're gonna' get what's comin' to you. You are a goddamn hero. How you feelin' this fine morning, eh?"

"Pretty good considering." Alex replied.

"Well it only gets better from here on out. I'm James McCluskey from the Local No. 3; I'm your man. The Union to the rescue, son." His enthusiasm was a little off-putting at this early hour. Alex was only halfway through his first cup of weak hospital coffee and he was not quite sharpened up yet. It might be a three-cup morning.

"Hey, I'm not going back to the Harbor Patrol; I want you to know that right off." Alex said.

"No, you're not! We're gonna push for you to go out on 100% disability. That is full pay and benefits until 65-then the government takes over kid. You are on administrative leave until we get you squared away with the Harbor people. You're all set-start thinking about your future-a future in the bosom of the union with a steady paycheck." Said Mr. McCluskey, beaming with enthusiasm.

"And a future with a messed-up ear that doesn't work." Alex replied.

"Well, that too, I guess. A small price to pay." McCluskey replied with moderated enthusiastic tones. "Don't worry about a thing in the meantime, we'll handle all the details and paperwork, that's what we're here for."

"Thank you." Alex replied.

"Okay, well, I'll get out of your way, I'll be back. Here's my card, call with questions anytime." Mr. McCluskey was reassuring. This talk of lifetime cash made Alex wish he had lost an ear sooner, it would have made things a lot simpler.

And no sooner had McCluskey left than another visitor arrived while Alex was still digesting the news of the future according to McCluskey. The visitor broke the silence.

"Hey Basic. Look at you, the local hero." It was Karen, Alex didn't even have to look to know who it was. When he did, he was rewarded by the sight of a trim and tall good-looking woman with streaks of gray in her sandy-blond hair, glasses, and perfect white teeth. It looked like her jeans had been spray painted on the curves of her hips.

"Jesus, look at you Karen, you're beautiful as always." Alex said. "How long has it been? 25 years?"

"A lifetime. Last I heard about you, you got married. That was a long time ago." She replied.

"A lot has happened, as you might imagine. It feels like I been divorced and married a few times-at least. I'm divorced now for real though. Two boys. And now I got one ear. How about you, married?" Alex asked.

Karen laughed. "Oh, you know me and marriage, it doesn't fit right; I shacked up a time or two, had a lot of offers. But I'm just happier when I'm not dragging around anybody else's problems. I got enough of my own. I was never willing to trade sex for marriage either. The sex is better when you're single." She giggled like a girl.

Alex laughed, she got that right, she hadn't changed much. "You're a brave woman; You don't compromise do ya?"

"I suppose. Peter's love is enough for me. Of course, he's in college now, gone to make his own way." Karen informed.

'How'd you know I was here?" Alex asked.

"You made the front page, kid. I opened the paper and there you were, as cute as you could be in the uniform and badge. How long you been a patrolman? I thought you were a fisherman?" She said and asked the question.

"A few years, not long really. I fished for thirty years and then I quit and got this shore job after my divorce. How about you?" Alex inquired.

"I own a few rentals. I bought them with inherited money from my mom and fixed them up. I live simple, but comfortable." Karen replied.

"Where do you live these days?" Alex sked.

"El Granola, same place. Except I own the house now. Isabella Street, right across from the Mothership." Karen replied.

"The Mothership is still there?"

"Same as ever. Except I own it now too."

It was a miracle that the Mothership was still there and remained unchanged for 40 years. It was originally a beige and brown four-plex but through the combination of necessity and a lax landlord, more domiciles had been built within its walls. Best estimate was that eight renters now lived there. It was the first place that new arrivals and transients stayed. Nobody ever stayed for more than a few months. Left behind in the yard were their abandoned cars, trailers and broken-down large appliances. If you wanted to score drugs-somewhere in the Mothership you found what you sought. If you needed cheap rent-the Mothership accommodated. If you were a run-away from a partner, parents or the law-the Mothership was refuge. It was the closest thing to a slum that the increasingly suburban neighborhood had. Back in the day, everybody had a friend that had lived there at one time or another and the place was famous with the cops.

"The Mothership." Alex remarked.

"Still there, still funky. I like it that way." She answered.

"Amazing." Alex said and continued, "I kinda like that too, I don't know why."

"Because everything else around it has been gentrified, that's why. The Burbs, the commuters, the soccer moms, you name it. It's not the same Coast Side anymore. I like the Mothership just the way it is, it's like the middle finger to the neighborhood around it. Occasionally, a rumor goes around that there's a petition against it, but nothing ever happens. El Granola wouldn't be the same without it." Karen said.

"Geez-Louise. We used to stake out Poncho-the-horse in the empty lots around it, I remember now." Alex mused.

"And the trees; it was like living in a forest in Granola, but now they cut 'em all down and built houses. Or else they cut them down, so they didn't block the view from the rich folks in the Highlands." Karen always was on a *no-growth* bandwagon.

"From the ocean it looks like de-forestation. When I was a kid, there were so few houses, so many empty lots that the fire department cleared brush every fall by setting fire to the lot! It looked like the neighborhood had been hit with Napalm."

"And dirt streets!" Karen added

"Colin and Jimmy had a car, just the frame, engine and rims. They would tear around the streets and spin donuts. It looked like the street had been plowed into furrows when they were done with it!" Alex exclaimed.

"Remember the food co-op? That was me and my girlfriend!" Karen disclosed.

"And the breakwater? That was us and Dennis Wilson that drove that bulldozer off the rocks. We were in fifth grade, it was an accident, once it started up it just took off. We jumped. It made the Review. Bauer said it was sabotage. Alex was going deep into the memory bag now.

"The classic: *roving band of hippies was seen in the area*? Plucked from Bauer's imagination and into print in his newspaper?" Karen laughed and added, "I kinda miss the old rag. It's been replaced by a syndicated corporate thing, glossy and slick."

"The Half Moon Bay Review and the Pescadero Pebble." Alex said. Just then the doctor walked in.

"How's my patient this morning?" He said and nodded toward Karen, "Morning Mam."

"I'm okay Doc. I feel all right except for my shoulder and neck. My head hurts like the yellow-jackets have landed-and they are pissed. And I am told by my little son that the ear is not there anymore." Alex said.

Karen interrupted, "Alex, I should be going. Here's my number, call me, don't be a stranger now, Basic." Karen handed him a piece of paper and walked out the door.

"Rather striking woman." said the doctor as he glanced at Karen strutting out the door. "But about that ear, you see it's not entirely gone, just sort of shredded and hanging there in a rather unsightly way under that bandage. We hope to correct it with grafts. You took a bullet in the shoulder and the bullet in the neck passed clean through. Another bullet grazed and shredded your ear."

"Only three bullets is all? And here I thought it was something serious. There's hope." Alex said.

"Oh yes, there's always hope, that's a necessity around here." The doctor replied. Doctors and nurses are the most positive personalities. "It will take a bit of time, but we will set you right-as-rain." He said and continued,

"The neck required emergency surgery of course-the blood loss was great, the shoulder wound missed the bone, we hope the ear is not too serious and re-constructed as planned. A bloody mess you were to be sure, you almost bled out. The neck wound was a hair away from a fatal shot to the spinal cord, you got lucky there." The doctor informed.

"That's me; real lucky. Keep that morphine coming." Alex summed with no enthusiasm.

"Pain management is a specialty here, I assure you." Said the doc in his indefatigable enthusiasm.

"Then I'm your man, Doc, do your darnedest" Alex played along.

"First things first, you are to rest; complete bedrest for a week and then we re-evaluate the schedule of treatments." The doctor instructed.

"Treatments plural, you say?" Alex asked.

"Yes. The reconstruction of the ear will take a few procedures. We will take tissue from another area and use it to reconstruct the ear as close to its original appearance as we can. We will take tissue from your buttocks and use it for the new ear." The doctor explained.

"So, it will finally be true that I am a butt-head?" Alex cracked wise. That got a little smile from the doctor.

"That's one way to look at it." The doctor said and added, "Okay, I'll check in tomorrow. Rest, that is the instruction for now. Your shoulder will heal, we're keeping it cool for the swelling and pain."

"Cool is the rule, see ya Doc." Alex replied and pulled the bandage back over his eyes and settled back into the pillow, darkness and another wonderful drip.

The next day started out the same as the previous and was followed by a succession of sameness throughout the week. 7AM it was breakfast, then CNN until 9AM and then blood pressure and pills. Then more CNN and MSNBC until lunch at noon. Then more pills and a nap until 2PM. Then the dinner menu selections and a TV movie until 4PM. Then shave and a dump. At 5PM walk the halls 3 times. 7PM the dinner tray comes and more pills. TV until 9PM then audio book until sleep. Wake up at 3AM for pills and back to sleep until breakfast at 7AM. It was spa life without the massages and the mani-pedi's in sterile conditions and a reclining bed.

The next morning it was Cal who came by to check on Alex. Some things never change, and Cal was one of them. He still looked like he was stuck in time, around 1959. Levi's, T shirt, wide black belt and boots. He was still fit, pushing 60 years of age. His attitude had not changed a single bit.

"Well look at you; Mr. Harbor Guy, shot to shit."

"Yeah that's me."

"They sure got you all wrapped up."

"I guess. How's fishing?"

"Fishin' is fishin', you know. Chicken one day and feathers the next, weather, boat maintenance, crew same old shit. It's all right. It's a whole new gang though. Hungry fuckers." Cal said.

"To be expected, just getting it while the getting is good. Who knows what tomorrow will bring nowadays and only the hungry ones will survive to find out, eh?" Alex said.

"True, I guess. Modern times." Cal replied and continued, "How about you? You gonna' quit the Harbor?"

"Yeah, I'm done." Alex replied.

"What's next?" Cal asked.

"Oh, I don't know. Another boat, I guess. It's not that easy to quit fishing-I found that out. Every time I drive by a marina I stop and look at the boats. Every time I dream it's a fishing dream, fact is, I just had another. It's in my dang head." Alex said.

"It's in your blood, dipshit." Cal said.

"Or maybe I'll travel? I never been nowhere, I might go where the water is clear and warm, think things over. I had enough of this damp and windy weather for a while. I don't know what's next for me Cal, honestly. I just know what's behind me." Alex said.

"Well you gone about as far as you can go around here, I guess." Cal said with a degree of resignation.

"It sure feels that way sometimes." Alex replied. There was a silence, a pause, broken by Cal.

"Say....... we could partner up! It'll be like old times again, just like when I was with your dad!" Cal said with enthusiasm.

"Well that's flattering and mighty tempting Cal, but it might also not be like old times-cause the times have changed. We sure did have fun though. Remember when we went belly up in Eureka and that kid shot you? That was my first season crabbing." Alex said.

"Hell-we saved it in Eureka you mean! I remember Sig moved us up from the River to the Big E, that god-for-sake-n-hellhole. But we found crabs there!" Cal corrected.

"We did save it. And I learned cribbage until my eyes fell out of the sockets, we wore the spots off those pasteboards." Alex chimed in.

"Your uncle loved that God-damned card game. Well, you will figure it out, you'll land on your feet. But the offer stands." Cal said.

"I appreciate the offer. I got some things to figger' out." Alex replied.

"You do that. Look-I got to be goin'-hospitals give me the creeps. I'll be by and see you again. How long they gonna' keep you here anyway?" Cal asked.

"Long enough to put my ear back on, far as I can tell a coupla' weeks." Alex replied.

"Well, I'll be back. Hang in there kid, you'll be all right." Cal said. He headed for the door.

"Thanks Cal, I appreciate the offer too, I mean it."

"I know."

About ten o'clock every evening sleep would overtake Alex's boring day if he were lucky. There was only so much news he could absorb from the TV and books made his eyelids heavy. He watched every movie the hospital channels offered, including the animated children's movies. He became a Sponge Bob fan because Sponge Bob was an upbeat kind of dude and Alex liked that shade of yellow. He contemplated asking the doctor for sleeping pills, because he was waking up at 1AM, his mind racing from topic to topic like a butterfly on flowers or sometimes, like a fly on stink. When dreams did come, invariably they were boat dreams.

In one dream, Cal and Alex were partnered up and trolling for salmon. They were miles outside the other boats, and they were not catching, but neither were the boats in the fleet. It was calm. Cal was in the cabin and Alex was running a line. There was a fish and then there was another, soon they had 4 fish and they were feeling special until the scores from the fleet were revealed; the boats inside of them had a lot more fish than they did. Alex walked up to the cabin and pointed out a rock feature on the chart. Way outside of them was a high spot, a pinnacle. The high spot was a place that nobody ever went to because it was so far away. They debated whether that is where lots of fish were and quarreled whether or not they should go out there and look or should just join the fleet inside of them.

"I don't wanna be Christopher Columbus Alex, I just wanna catch some fish!" A fair point from the ever-practical Cal. Alex won the argument, nevertheless.

They turned the bow of their boat toward the outside, set on exploring. It got very foggy, and after a bit it lifted to reveal a beautiful shoreline, a landscape of coves, bays, islands, and passages. They began their exploration and they did not find fish. The dream shifted to them running for port in bad weather and gone was the beautiful shoreline. Alex woke up in the hospital room at 3AM, with the fading feeling of a beautiful dream gone bad. Reality came back into focus and there he was in a darkened hospital room.

The next night he dreamed he was in 50 fathoms off Bodega. Again, there were no fish, a big sea and it was foggy. He picked up the gear and ran most of the night to the Deep Reef and drifted in 40 fathoms until daylight. The seas became sharp and close together, yet still very foggy. There was wind on the outside of him somewhere and he became filled with a foreboding when the other boats began to run by him, on their way to port ahead of the deteriorating weather. Soon, the edge of blue sky approached from the West, driven by the wind. He woke up in the hospital room with a bad feeling upon awakening. He drifted back to sleep.

The next night another boat dream came. In this dream he was in some foreign port in a tropical harbor. He motored along the estuary, looking to tie up the boat. He kept passing boats he had not seen in years, rafted up, unloading, getting fuel, they were all from yesteryear and here they were. It was like old times; rafted up, barbecuing, laughing, talking. He looked at the chart to see where he gotten himself to and he didn't recognize anything. He woke up in his hospital room at 4AM waiting for it to get daylight in the dim artificial light. Alex wondered what the dream meant as he lay there, it felt good whatever it meant. He turned on the TV, watched the Weather Channel, waited for breakfast and daylight. These boat dreams were confusing and unsettling.

* * *

Leif got the news about Alex and immediately booked a flight to the lower 48. He worried about Alex ever since he quit fishing, it just was not right, he belonged on a boat, it was courting trouble to go against the grain the way Leif saw it. Leif had been gone a long time and made a good life for himself in Southeast AK. The lower 48 had gotten crazy, he had watched it and he worried that Alex was in jeopardy there when he heard he quit fishing and joined the Harbor Patrol. He would go down and try and talk sense into his little brother. The moment that he landed in San Francisco his suspicions were confirmed; craziness *was* in the air, the pace, the sound, the crowds. Everyone was hurrying from place to place; crowded with people, cars and buildings. An electric and subliminal message of *hurry, hurry, hurry,* was pervasive. Leif took a cab straight to the hospital.

"Leif!" Alex exclaimed as his brother entered the small hospital room.

"Hey cowboy, I heard you were in a shootout." Leif joked.

"I'm okay. Diver John died though." Alex said.

"I heard, good man. Jesus Alex, how bad are you?" Leif enquired.

"I got shot up pretty bad, but they patched me up. Except my ear, I got it shot off, but the doc said they can fix it with skin grafts from my butt." Alex admitted.

"Will it still work? Can you still hear?" Leif wondered.

"The doc said, from now on I can only hear farts." Alex said. "Just kidding. I can actually hear right now through this little hole in the side of my head." Alex said.

"Okay, I get it." Leif said and continued, "How long you in here for?"

"Sounds like a while. Doc says it takes a series of grafts to rebuild it." Alex said.

"Shit, that's a bummer. It'll give you plenty of time to rest-up, think things over. But I guess maybe that might be a problem, thinking I mean, you probably done enough of that already." Leif said.

"I sure have. I think too much for my own good Leif. I'm not gonna go back to that harbor job-that's for sure. I'm thinking about boats, been thinking a lot about boats. I even dream about boats. I'm thinking about all the things I used to do. This Union rep came in the other day and says he's got me covered with disability cash-*for life!*" Alex said.

"Then c'mon up to Southeast, look around."

"It crossed my mind." Alex said. "Cal wants us to partner up on a boat down here."

"Well you know best, but it's crazy here, I tell you that."

"We hardly notice that anymore, seems like we got used to it."

Every week it was something with his ear, the skin off his ass kept getting layered into a form that resembled a convoluted appendage with a hole in the center. It was troubling that hair began to appear all over his new ear, hair follicles from his ass were now sprouting on the fleshy protrusion on the side of his head. Alex kept telling himself he could wear a hat and cover it, but in the meantime, he kept busy plucking hair off with the tweezers. During week number four the doctor walked in with an announcement.

"Well Alex, I think reconstruction is near-complete for the moment. The ear looks fairly good. Let us start thinking about a release date, shall we?" The doctor was cheerful.

"The sooner the better doc. I forgot what life was like, being in here this long." Alex replied.

"Well, we can fix that, I'll talk to the right people today, we'll get you back on the street in short order." The doctor said.

"Swell, back on the street." Alex pondered.

"Maybe even this week, no sense sitting around here. How would that be?" The doctor asked.

"Swell." Alex answered, unsure and considering the ramifications of something he was completely unprepared for-real life. No longer infantilized in a place where all his needs were met, all his routines decided for him and nothing dependent on decisions by him. No more floating through space. It was time to get it together. Reality was a train rushing head-long and about to arrive at the station.

* * *

Leif and Alex walked through the big glass doors, he was now released from captivity after a four week stay at St Catherine's Hospital and with a new hairy ear.

"Let's go get something to eat." Alex said. Eating out at a restaurant seemed like an adventure after weeks of hospital food.

"Yeah sure." Leif replied. "Where?"

"I want a steak. I want to overeat. I want ice cream. I want a giant bake potato with sour cream. Everything they give you in the hospital is tiny, they weigh it or something." Alex replied. "Let's go to Black-Tie Diner, I'm ready for a gut-bomb, the nuclear option."

The BT Diner was notorious; muffins as big as your head with every meal, this place was the favorite restaurant of all people over 400 pounds. The food was served on platters the size of manhole covers. They featured whole pies just for your guilty personal consumption, 3 kinds of hash browns with gravy and Texas Toast. No dinner on the menu was under 5000 calories, perfect for arctic explorers warding off hypothermia: a dietician's worst nightmare.

"Okay. Let's go, you're the boss." Leif replied.

They were cruising down the road toward the BTD. The landscape was populated with an array of strip malls, Dollar General stores, Payday Loans, Subways, Mountain Mikes, nail salons, coffee places and fast food franchises.

It occurred to Leif that change had come in widespread fashion to his old stomping grounds, a makeover of the very identity of the place he had left years ago.

"There's a lot of nothing on the street now." Leif remarked casually.

"Tell me about it." Alex replied without turning his head from the view.

"What happened? They sucked the soul out of the place." Leif continued.

"You just notice that? It's the new normal down here in the lower 48-so get used to it." Alex replied.

"I don't know if I'll be around long enough *to get* used to it." Leif replied quietly and continued, "I kinda like it the way it was, the way I remembered it being."

"Everybody does. We don't like this; we just accept it. It's best to overlook the bad and focus on what good is left. We sometimes get nostalgic though; it's a regular Petri dish for nostalgia." Alex replied.

"No doubt." Leif replied and turned into the BT Diner parking lot.

Inside, it was all dressed up. All manner of bow-tied paraphernalia, like a little theme park.

"What's all this bullshit? It looks like Disneyland in here." Leif said.

"The kids like it." Alex replied.

Right on cue a waitress appeared, dressed in a simulated tuxedo with a black bowtie. She looked stupid and uncomfortable in a get-up that purposely fit too tight. "Are you ready, or do you need a minute?" She asked.

"I'll have the T-bone, medium rare with a baked potato, side salad with bleu cheese, Texas Toast, a side of onion rings and a vanilla milkshake." Alex replied.

"Well… all righty then big-boy, com'in right up! You?" She turned to Leif.

"How about a club sandwich with potato salad." Leif replied.

"Any coffee's here?" She asked.

"Sure, two coffees." Alex answered and she turned and left.

"I wonder how much she makes working here?" Leif mused.

"Minimum wage no doubt. Probably $7.75." Alex replied.

"After taxes that's about what? $ 220 a week for a 40-hour week?" Leif said.

"She only gets 27 hours a week, that way the employer ducks full-time employee benefits." Alex offered.

"You can't even make the rent. How does she eat?" Leif exclaimed.

"I dunno, she works 2 or 3 jobs I guess." Alex replied.

"It's not right." Leif said.

"It is what it is. What are you a socialist now?" Alex said.

"Less than $10,000 a year? Poverty-level is $20k? Doesn't compute." Leif said.

"Leif; you've been gone, and things have changed. You're shocked when you come down here and find that people work for peanuts or sleep under the freeway. Things are not the same down here as when you left in the 70's." Alex said.

The food arrived and it did not disappoint. It was piled in overlapping portions on the plate, the onion rings the size of tires and the shake arrived in a tall metal vat. To Alex, it was a gastronomic wonderland and he applied himself, making up for lost calories from his hospital stay. He cleaned his plate and left muffin crumbs all over the table. The hospital nutritionist would have been horrified.

"I was hungry." He mumbled and contemplated the pie possibilities while full to bursting. The two brothers paid and left.

"Let's stop by the marina and look at a boat." Alex said from the passenger seat.

"Already with the sickness?" Leif said.

"Yeah, I'm serious, there's a boat I want to look at." Alex said to his brother.

"You just got out of the hospital, what's the rush?" Leif said.

Alex replied in agreement. "Truth is, I don't know what else to do. Nothing appeals to me except boats, all I think about is boats. I gotta get something going on or I'll go nuts. I think it's boats again." Alex said.

"Come on up to Alaska with me then, get away from this craziness, it's a rat race down here; it's relentless and everybody is on the brink of poverty. Come to Alaska if you like boats, all we got up there is boats; boats, trees and fish." Leif explained.

"I should. I'm living in the past down here."

At the first sight of the boat Leif shouted out: "This thing? It's an old dog! And it's a sailboat!" Leif walked down the ramp at the marina. In front of him was an old sailboat rigged for salmon trolling.

"That's the idea. If you want to travel, it's wind power that'll get you there." Alex explained.

"You're no sailor." Leif said.

"If I can sail my little El Toro, I can sail this." Alex replied.

"If you say so, I guess." Leif said with a tone of resignation. "It's all wrong for a fish boat though, a fool can see that Alex!"

"The hull is sound. I can remake this deck layout." Alex defended.

Leif climbed aboard and looked around the boat. He didn't say a word for a half hour while Alex explained the history of the boat- one owner, mom and pop, elderly couple, fished as a team for 30 years, the boat had a rep as one that caught fish.

"No." Leif broke the silence.

"Whaddya mean *no*?" Alex said.

"No, not the boat for you." Leif said flatly.

"Well I don't see it that way, what's the matter with it?" Alex pleaded.

"Only everything. You're better than this." Leif said.

"I'm gonna make the old boy an offer." Alex said with a hint of defiance, unaware that he had gone temporarily blind, a common and curious disorder only suffered when boat shopping and falling in love.

Dixon accepted the offer of course, happy to get rid of it and retire. After the papers were signed Alex began to get ready with enthusiasm for the upcoming opening day which would occur in two months. Slowly his sight returned from the temporary blindness and the first thing he saw in the process was that the old boy Dixon had a hobby of going to flea markets and buying little things that he thought belonged on the boat as spare parts. The old boy had a motto.

"It's only junk until you need it!" Dixon proudly recited that as if it were a verse from the Bible.

That may be true, but it required that you *live in* a junkyard all the time. The second thing he found out was that everything had been mickey-moussed together with junk for 30 years.

Dixon's wife Betty had the same hobby, except her target items were housewares such as utensils, appliances, Tupperware, kitchen towels, doilies, etc. Over the weeks, Alex filled two dumpsters in the process of cleaning out the evidence of their hobby, the junk hidden in the various compartments. The boat raised at the waterline by six inches. However, the hull was sound, the engine was good, and everything went round and round. Alex had some good ideas to transform the boat into a platform for his reentry into salmon trolling and these visions sustained him. He never dreamed it would take years and tens of thousands of dollars to achieve these notions, just as no boat owner conceives of this possibility at the outset of an endeavor that never ends. Alex was living within the fog of *what could be* rather than *what was*, a common condition suffered by new boat owners. But all that visionary stuff would have to wait because the salmon season opener was imminent. Slowly Alex realized that there was only time to do the bare necessities to make it all work and that old familiar feeling of pressure returned. Unfortunately,

Alex had spent all available time so far undoing and re-making everything on the boat that the old man had mickey-moussed together. Alex had no idea where all the wiring went, most of it went nowhere to switches that controlled nothing. The plumbing from the hot water heater was an imaginative array of copper lines and valves and the holding tank had no plumbing at all, it just existed in an imaginary state taking up 100 gallons of air and empty space. Dixon's work was imaginative at times, such as the primary fuel line made from a flexible steel jacketed spritzer-hose from under a sink faucet. Little things like that tended to lift the fog a notch or two toward reality. Alex began to suspect that Leif was right; he had bought an old dog.

"I told you so, you wouldn't listen." Leif said on the other end of the phone line.

"It's got potential, I could make it into something special, just not right away." Alex reasoned.

"Yeah, like in about ten years' time maybe you could set things right." Leif quipped and added, "You know what the hidden meaning of *po-ten-shall* is?"

"No, what?" Alex knew the other shoe was about to drop.

"It's not worth a shit yet."

"What a ball breaker. I'm up to my ass in alligators here, I gotta go fishing in a week." Alex was distraught, Leif was not helping.

"Look: I'll come down and help you but what's that gonna do?' Leif explained.

"I know, I'm buried. I never missed an opener in my life, but I feel the first misfire comin' on." Alex said with a degree of resignation.

"I'll come help, we'll get you out there, but you may have to be wrenching all season as you go along." Leif said.

"Okay, thanks." Alex hung up the phone.

Alex threw the lines for the first time 2 days before the season. He had an 8-hour run in a southerly with heavy rain to get from Vallejo to Half Moon Bay and the start of the season. There was lightning and hail, thunder and wind, all in the Bay. Alex gritted his teeth thinking about what the ride would be like after he went through the Gate, a trial by fire no doubt. The first thing he learned was that the engine was stinky and noisy-cardinal offenses. And the front windows were at deck level and made of old scratched Plexi-glass so he could hardly see out of them, besides that, the anchor winch was smack dab in his forward field of vision. There was no pilot chair. This was all adding up to a bummer of epic dimension.

"What have I done?" Alex said aloud as he looked around at the old stinky indoor-outdoor carpet on the cabin floors and glued to the walls. It matched the tuck and rolled upholstery on the ceiling, circa 1971. "No sense getting a bad attitude about it. I can do this; I can make it work; I have to."

The season started and Alex went out. He had one fish for the day below the Islands. He felt bad until the reports came in-it was bad all over and, perversely, this made him happy. He could stay in port with a clear conscience now and continue to work on the boat. This lasted a few days until he heard that someone caught some fish outside the Islands-on the Gumdrop, 60 miles offshore! Okay, if that's what it takes, he thought, I'll go there. The next night he left at midnight and got to the Gumdrop in the morning, caught one fish, and ran back in. By the time the day was over his ears were ringing and his head hurt. He might have had a touch of carbon monoxide poisoning and he definitely had dents in his attitude. This just was not working out the way he had envisioned it.

Back in the slip he was content to be living in hope rather than trolling in reality. As he made little improvements, his mind was filled with how wonderful his boating future would be when he got the boat in good order. Then a couple of high liners walked by, old friends who looked on as he toiled on the ugly duckling boat. They remained silent. These guys were aware of his struggles, there was none of the usual congratulations that new boat owners receive, none of the praises for Alex's new boat because the boat was an obvious dog. They knew better than to blow smoke up his ass and talk falsely. It was an old sailboat, not a fishboat. Sailboats and fishboats were like cats and dogs-and never the twain should meet. Clearly Alex had crossed the line. There was no respect to be had, an odd turn of events for someone like Alex who once had recognition and respect for his boat and fishing ability. It was humbling; an emotion that does not mix well with salmon trolling. Alex experienced a new type of recognition-he was a fool.

But there was more to it than that. The boat was not fishing well, and Alex could tell. It was a potentially disastrous situation and he had to figure this out and soon, before the fish started biting. He could not bear to go for months on a boat that did not fish well when others all around were catching; he would be suicidal; his pride would not allow it. The weak link must be in the ground because the gurdy spools were plastic? Not enough metal underwater?

He went up to the gear yard and got an old stainless-steel flopper, bolted two of the biggest zincs he could find and rigged it off the bow of the boat. He wired it to a keel bolt embedded in the cast iron keel, hoping to boost his ground surface and potential.

The weeks progressed toward June and the week before the full moon in the last week of that month, there was good fishing of Pigeon in 55 fathoms. Alex was there and, with effort, things were working well. He got multiple bites on the gear and all seemed to be improved. Then they stopped biting on the afternoon of the third day. His partners took off for a bite up at Ft Ross and Alex started tacking for home, shortening up to go into 26 fathoms off of Pescadero and continue on up to Half Moon in that depth. He was more than ready to quit, worn out and dog-tired. This re-entry into fishing was more than he chose to remember it as and not in a good way. When he got off the Pescadero reef he got a few bites and then a few more. Alex took ten fish off the gear and called his running mates. Then it hit the fan off San Gregorio; shorts, legals, cleaning fish, back tacking, all the action came like a landslide in the middle of the afternoon. Alex realized this was the real deal he had been waiting for and now that it was here, he had to act on it, tired or not. His partners turned around and ran back. Back and forth they went until the sun went down, landing fish and cleaning fish, it was more than Alex could do to keep up and he was glad to have the gear on the boat at the end of the day-totally exhausted. On the way in he saw the fireworks, it dawned on him that it was the Fourth Of July already.

"We'll remember this day. When we're old and retired, sitting in our rocking chair on the porch, watching the kid's light fireworks, we'll recall the 4th of July below Half Moon and these fish." The radio voice said to Alex as they pulled into the anchorage around 10 PM.

The next morning Alex woke up late, made breakfast and then went back to bed before he pulled the anchor and went to the dock to unload. It was all too much, he was exhausted, he felt as if his age was catching up to him. He had to get these fish off today and go out again tomorrow, the game was afoot. What he had waited for and wanted was here in spades and it was only the force of habit that prompted him to make the most of it. The quick turn-around program was unloading, ice, fuel, groceries, back out the next day. He realized he was back in the life and he now had some questions about that. Mostly he felt like another nap. Getting back out there to the workhouse didn't have the same appeal somehow.

After unloading, Alex was in line at the ice dock and falling asleep in his chair. He was fourth in line, Tony on the drag boat *Western* was ahead of him. Everybody hated this ice dock with good reason and today was no exception. The kid announced that the machine was broken and out of ice for the day, it would have to replenish overnight, and he would re-open at 10AM.

"This kid doesn't give a shit." Tony said, pissed.

"This always happens. Half the time you can't get ice for one reason or another." Alex griped.

"Well, I'm gonna just do what I should have done in the first place-go up to the City." Tony said with disgust. I'll make a halibut tow this afternoon on my way up, this is bullshit."

"Well I'm just gonna tie up to this ice dock and go to sleep. I'll just go fish tomorrow without the ice, the hell with it." Alex said.

"See ya later, Alex." Tony threw the lines and put the Western in gear and motored off. Alex tied up to the ice dock and climbed into his bunk.

The alarm clock went off at 4AM and Alex ignored it, enjoying his 12th hour of sleep. He had to take a leak, and this is what finally got him up from his bunk. Half awake, he fished around for his dick in his long johns, struggling to get the member out through the many layers of undergarments, an annoying chore that always made Alex feel like he had a small dick. It was dark out; the gunwale was damp against his long johns and the air smelled of salt and diesel fumes. Alex was waking up. A procession of lights was exiting the harbor, the fishing boats were on their way out to the fishing grounds.

"This is impossible to sleep through, I'm in the workhouse now." Alex groused and a sense of urgency began to intrude. It was time to make coffee.

Coffee was consumed, the starter button was pressed, and the long day began with a rumble. Next it was the second cup. Then the knob on the radio must be turned and the squawky little box came alive with scrambled conversations from his code group. He sat down at the table with coffee and thought about it.

"I gotta go, get my share. You wanted this kid and here it is, get it while the getting is good."

Feeling the rising sense of urgency, watching the boats go by ahead of him, he reluctantly went out on deck and threw the lines from the pilings before his coffee was finished. Soon, the blinking green light of the buoy was ahead and further out, a line of white mast lights travelling seaward, all of them headed in the same direction, some of them quite distant. Alex was almost dead last to leave the harbor.

The VHF radio channel was interrupted by a channel 16 broadcast.

"Poh-pon, pon,pon. All boats are advised that the *Western* is overdue from its destination to San Francisco. Last seen departing Half Moon Bay on the afternoon of the 5th of July. Vessel is white hull and house, yellow trim, 48 foot long with one aboard. All vessels are asked to give search while in the vicinity and be on the lookout. All information is to be reported to Coast Guard Group San Francisco, channel 16. This broadcast to be repeated hourly, Coast Guard Group San Francisco-out."

"That's Tony." Alex said to himself. "Jesus Christ."

Alex reached for the button to disengage the auto pilot, change course and give search, then he hesitated. Nobody else was diverging from their course? All the mast lights continued toward yesterday's kill zone to the south. If the *Western* and Tony were to be found, it would be to the *north*. Surely many had heard the pon-pon break through on the VHF? Nobody is that far from the vicinity. None were responding to the search effort and Alex knew why because he was feeling the same thing- *must catch fish-must get my share.* This was the fleets reason to ignore the pon-pon and Alex felt it too. He was not proud of it.

In the next instant in his imagination, he was eleven years old again with his dad.

"Feeling like you did the right thing: you have to feel good about who you are and what you do. That's a good habit to get into Alex. That message, that advice from his dad, it came through in his head.

Alex clicked the button and disengaged the auto pilot, he took the wheel and put the boat on a northerly course to engage in a search for Tony.

"Don't even think about it kid, there's no decision to be made here." Alex mumbled.

Could Tony even last overnight in this water? Barely if at all, was the answer that came. Hypothermia was sneaky: it came on as sleepiness, a sleepiness from which you never wake up. Alex hoped Tony made it onto his raft. Did he have a raft? Did it pop open? That would be the thing Alex hoped to find, a bright orange canopy over a raft with Tony inside. Or maybe just Tony floating in the cold gray dawn, floating inside a bright orange rubber suit. Either way, it was the only hope for Tony to be found alive. Alex searched with binoculars for a contrasting color in the corrugated sea rising and falling outside the pilot house windows. Nothing but a vast and uncaring seascape in the cold gray dawn. Alex was as alone as the man he searched for.e was as alone asa Tony from the Wetsrn

"Tony is gonna die. What happened? Cal was right." Alex said aloud.

A realization was engulfing him just as the waves were most likely engulfing Tony. The fishery had transformed into a zero-sum pursuit of fish and he was part of it. The boats were isolated into cliques that chased those fish. The cliques did not talk with each other and gone was the camaraderie of the Association hall. Gone with it were the characters that shaped the fishery and gave it character, waxing philosophical in their gossipy and folksy way and cracking wise. The characters on the boats this morning were all rather homogenous in their vain pursuit of fish. The era of being connected had transitioned into the era of *the self,* much like all the rest of society. The fishery had evolved and perhaps Alex had been part of the catalyst; he had helped usher in the new era and it came at a cost. It was only after stepping out that he could now view it in proper perspective, but in doing so, he came to the realization that his time had passed. There would be no songs sung, no books written, no legacy that was talked about of this era. *Who caught what* was the only story to tell. Eventually there may be no memory at all of an era past, no memory of an era that Alex had once thought so special, an era where he thought himself prominent. The reality was that obscurity was the legacy; the legacy left on an indifferent ocean. The indifference of the sea was ultimately revealed as the essence of its terrible beauty and the people on it were insignificant footnotes. The events of this morning brought this into sharp focus, not flattering, not romantic, not condemning, it just was.

*   *   *

In the previous day, Tony had slowed the boat down, the weight of the *Western* glided to three knots as he hooked the chains on the doors to set the gear to make a 2-hour halibut tow towards the City. The doors clanked as they slipped into the water and the net followed as the paravanes caught water and sunk, spreading the net. The cable followed and Tony went into the cabin after he was satisfied that all was set properly and towing effectively. He turned on the TV and settled back for the ride, eyes forward in a routine he had gone through a hundred times before. This went on for an hour before he got up to check the gear in the back. As Tony made his way through the galley to the back deck, the view out the door was startling and filled with a white froth and a bulbous wall of steel approaching at twenty knots. Tony had wandered into the inbound shipping lane and this 800-foot steel monster was now bearing down on the *Western*. He grabbed the wheel and turned hard over, throttling up but the *Western* got clipped in the stern, the impact spun the dwarfed 48-footer around and quite suddenly he was scraping along the hull-side of a ship. The starboard pole snapped off and the guy wires got caught on protruding steel pipes on the side of the ship's hull, dragging the boat sideways and immediately filling the deck with water that eventually flooded into the cabin. The *Western* was more underwater than above the water within seconds, she was a mere toy in the grip of tons of steel the size of a skyscraper. Tony pissed his pants; now he was being towed backwards, he was helpless. Tony slammed the door shut, knee deep in saltwater. The sound of scraping and snapping rigging was a terrible sound and soon the sound was joined by the deep rumble of the churning props that sucked the little boat into the swirling waters of the prop wash, a cluster of whirlpools.

"Wasn't anybody aboard up there to see this?" Tony wondered, his mind racing with no solution or answer to be found.

Soon the violence was over, and the stern of a retreating ship was all there was to see, but the *Western* was foundering, stern underwater and the decks awash. The engine had died, and the main hatch was now floating somewhere. There was a life raft up top and a survival suit in the flooded focsle, but whatever he decided to do, he had to do it now because water was rushing into every compartment that held the *Western* afloat. All was lost for the *Western* and it was time to bailout. This whole terrible episode lasted less than two minutes and Tony now pushed open the back door and barely made it to the top of the cabin before the sea caught him. He grabbed the cannister that held the raft and threw it from the cabin top before the *Western* went quietly down to the seabed.

"Jesus take the wheel." Tony said as he threw the cannister into the sea.

It popped and a canopy of bright orange dominated the foreground of the now empty seascape. Tony swam toward the raft, it was about 50 feet away, but it may have well been 500 feet away. His boots were like buckets of water strapped on his feet and his legs could hardly move when he kicked. He flailed with his arms and kicked with his legs but his progress towards the raft was minimal. In fact, the wind had the raft moving down swell faster than Tony could get to it. It was leaving him alone out there. In a panic, he got rid of his boots, jacket, hat and trousers; this was it-the jig was up. He swam for it with all he could muster, disappointed to find out *now* that he had been under the illusion that he was a better swimmer than this. It was do or die. The raft was not getting closer and worse, he might be out of energy before he could grasp it. It began to dawn on him that this was how he was going to die: all he had hoped for, the fish, the women, the family, the children, the friends, the boats; all would not work out the way he had planned it. He got scared and then cold and tired. His arms and legs burned, the blood pounded in his head and he huffed for air. Semi-helpless now and waiting for fate, a scraping brushed is neck. Tony swatted at it and his hand felt a little piece of line, a painter from the raft trailed in the water. Tony grabbed it. He yarded hand over hand until the raft was right in front of his huffing face. He boosted his gut onto the raft and fell face first under the canopy, rolled over and gasped for air staring up at the orange rubber dome. Fate arrived; he was not going to die today.

Alex scanned the horizon with the binoculars and could only see the water of the corrugated sea in the breaking daylight under overcast skies. This was a somber chore. He had been on many search and rescue missions in the harbor patrol and these rescue missions often morphed into a body search. The cadavers were fished from the water, their color gone, leaving a washed-out skin and blue lips in its place. Or worse, bodies adrift for days that became fish food and were bloated with gas and missing limbs. Time was of the essence if Tony was to be found alive.

* * *

Tommy Howard set the gear with no boats ahead of him, he was the first guy out. He was filled to bursting with hope as he methodically set the gear in the morning half-light. The lines immediately began to rattle with bites; he was first on the spot of the hungry fish school. This was it-another good day. And indeed, soon fish hit the deck. He had 350 pounds on his first tack and bites were still on the gear. He was going to add to his reputation on this day.

The VHF radio interrupted his thoughts.

"Poh-pon, pon,pon. All boats are advised that the *Western* is overdue from its destination to San Francisco. Last seen departing Half Moon Bay on the afternoon of the 5th of July. Vessel is white hull and house, yellow trim, 48 foot long with one aboard. All vessels are asked to give search while in the vicinity and be on the lookout. All information is to be reported to Coast Guard Group San Francisco, channel 16. This broadcast to be repeated hourly, Coast Guard Group San Francisco-out."

"Did you hear that Tommy? That's Tony on the *Western*." Tommy's deck-hand was in the trolling pit right next to Tommy.

"Bummer. Someone will find him, we're not in that vicinity where he might be." Tommy said and continued to unsnap the line snaps, running the line and gaffing fish.

*   *   *

As the sun rose higher above the overcast Alex was resigned to the fact that he was alone in the search. No boats, no Tony, just water. The radio blared a few tack reports from the boats below the Deep Reef and they were off to a good start. They were going to have another big day indeed, just as they had anticipated on the run out to the grounds in the darkness of the morning. Thoughts ran through Alex's head and some of those thoughts he was not too proud of. He *was not* going to have a big day on the fishing grounds. He *was not* going to be among the high liners. He *was* conflicted.

"This is all fucked up." Alex mumbled, commenting on his mixed emotions and the whole predicament.

He scanned the horizon once again. He saw the little orange dot 3 or 4 miles away and turned for it. As he got closer, he saw that it indeed was the raft and a parachute flare went up, then a smoke flare trailed orange smoke. No mistaking, Tony was alive. Alex was going to save him. Mixed emotions he felt moments earlier evaporated.

*   *   *

Alex flipped open his cell phone and dialed the number. Some soul-searching had preceded this call for days. He had butterflies in his stomach, but this was the right thing to do. He pressed the green call button.

"Hey Leif, how's things in Alaska?" Alex asked into the little device.

"It's raining Alex, good to hear from you. How are you feeling? You are fishing, you are recovering?" Leif asked.

"All better Leif. Say look-I wanna come check out Alaska." Alex said.

"Great, when you comin' up?" Leif asked.

"Soon as you'll have me." Alex answered.

"Sure anytime, but isn't it salmon season down there?" Leif asked again.

"Fuck fish; I don't care about that. I think I caught all the fish that had my name on 'em years ago. That guy told it true; *you can't go home again.* Home is not there anymore; my home on boats belongs to another era. The people, the attitudes, it's all changed. I found that out honestly."

"Did something happen to you? What's a matter; not the highliner no more? Is it another mid-life crisis or what?" Leif said.

"Maybe, I dunno. I do know it's time to move on. You got a spot for me and the boys?" Alex asked.

"Always." Leif said and added, "I'm in Petersburg. It's a lot like where we grew up here; I think you'll like it."

*   *   *

Alex tenuously looked at the number on the contact list on his phone and made the next call, to Karen. On the other end of the line Karen looked at the little screen that said, *caller unknown,* she picked up anyway.

"Hey! It's me; Basic; the one-eared-wonder."

"Where you been? I thought you were told to call me."

"It's a long story. I'm calling you now though? Whatcha been doin?"

"Oh, you know; filing my nails, eating bon-bons under the hair dryer, waiting for you to call."

"Okay, Okay. I'm sorry, okay? But listen; I got two tickets to Alaska to check it out. Wanna go?"

"Just drop everything?"

"Just drop everything."

"You're not that special, Basic."

"Whaddya mean?"

"I have spent a total of two weeks with you in thirty years, fool."

"Well, that could be a good thing, couldn't it? You missed all the bad stuff in those thirty years, you were spared a lot of drama I can tell you that. Besides, two weeks with me lasts a long time and I'm an even better version of me now."

"I'm sure that's all true. All the same, I do have a life here."

"C'mon, it'll be fun."

"Are there Eskimos there?"

'Yeah, but they all live in condos now."

"I *would* like to see the glaciers."

"We'll do that too, make a vacation out of it, take one of those scenic cruises."

"You are paying for it?"

"Absolutely!"

"The whole thing?"

"Of course!"

"Did they put your ear back on?"

"Yes."

"Okay, it's a deal then. Get your skinny ass over here boy."

"I'll be over directly."

About the Author

Ernie Koepf lives in the East Bay with his wife Jan Moestue. He fished for salmon, crab and herring on the West Coast for over 35 years and is now retired. He has written articles published in Pacific Fishing magazine, run a marine haul-out, was a deputy harbormaster at Half Moon Bay, been a member of numerous co-ops and fishermen's associations and acted as a class representative in the HanJin Shipping Co. lawsuit. Author email address: nearshoreguy@hotmail.com